Ruth Hamilton

A Mersey Mile

PAN BOOKS

First published 2014 by Macmillan

This edition published 2014 by Pan Books
an imprint of Pan Macmillan, a division of Macmillan Publishers Limited
Pan Macmillan, 20 New Wharf Road, London N1 9RR
Basingstoke and Oxford
Associated companies throughout the world
www.panmacmillan.com

ISBN 978-1-4472-0948-5

1 3 5 7 9 8 6 4 2

A CIP catalogue record for this book is available from the British Library.

Typeset by Ellipsis Digital Limited, Glasgow
Printed and bound by CPI Group (UK) Ltd, Croydon, CR0 4YY

Visit **www.panmacmillan.com** to read more about all our books
and to buy them. You will also find features, author interviews and
news of any author events, and you can sign up for e-newsletters
so that you're always first to hear about our new releases.

To my mother, Frances Evelyn Nixon,
previously Girling, née Higgins. Not a day passes
without thoughts and memories of you, Mam.
You were a beacon of light and a bundle of mischief.
Missed by me and Alice.

Acknowledgements

Wayne Brookes, Louise Buckley and Camilla Elworthy of Macmillan Publishers.

Thanks to all who remember Scotland Road before its cruel destruction.

Avril Cain for research.

Geoff Allen, tech support, without whose help I'd still be dipping a quill in black ink.

Readers, I am forever grateful.

1955

One

Polly Kennedy, whose cafe resided happily at the bread and banter end of the market, could seldom resist a well-heated argument. Already pink, bothered and over-worked, she put two fingers in her mouth and gave birth to a whistle loud enough to fetch the local constabulary and the river police. Several breakfasters shivered, while one poor chap suffered a short coughing bout after swallowing his mouthful of Horniman's 'down the wrong hole'.

Others, with food poised on forks halfway to their mouths, froze. Their eardrums still felt the pain long after the shrill sound had died. Polly's whistles were near-fatal. She spoke now. 'Hey, let's be having this right, eh? Because that's a load of rubbish, Ida, sorry. My Uncle Tom grabbed top prize in the loot. A massive gas cooker, he got. He tried to fix it in the house himself, only the back kitchen blew up and the street had to be evacuated. It was like the Great War all over again, but with more damage. Mam told us all about it. She said she'd never seen Auntie Nellie in such a state.'

Ida's jaw dropped. 'Bloody hell, love. Did he get killed or hurt?'

'Very nearly.' Polly's tone remained even. 'Auntie Nellie chased after him down the back alleys with her rolling pin and a carving knife.' A roar of laughter donated by all present followed this remark. 'He shifted like the Flying Scotsman, I was told.'

'We were all better runners in the old days,' Ida said.

Polly picked up the thread of her story. 'They moved out to Litherland and he stopped smoking after the explosion,' she added. 'But he did take to drink in a big way. They were talking about giving him a bed down the Throstle's Nest, because the landlord could never get him to go home. That would be because of Auntie Nellie and her weaponry. Even when they'd moved, he came back to the Throstle's at least twice a week and slept on floors till he sobered up.'

'Not surprised,' groaned Jimmy Nuttall, who was bent double with glee. 'He'd need a rest, the mad bugger.'

'Oh, that was nothing, because he went worse. Woke up on the Isle of Man ferry, no ticket, no idea of how he got there. So it was more than just a gas cooker; he was an idiot for seventy odd years. Specialized in it, he did. I reckon he had a degree in lunacy, but he wasn't one for bragging about his qualifications.'

'Well, a sofa's bigger than a cooker,' Ida insisted. 'See, if we're talking size and awkwardness of things what got pinched in the loot—'

'Not as heavy, though,' Polly insisted. 'Gas stoves weigh a ton, believe me. A piece of furniture gets nowhere near when it comes to shifting. I mean, it took five men to see to all Cal's cooking stuff in that back kitchen. Very, very heavy.' She waved towards the door that led from the cafe to the residential area. 'One of them got a hernia, and another slipped a disc, but our Uncle Tom was six foot five in his socks and very strong. The Kaiser never troubled him, so an exploding gas cooker was a minor problem. Died of pneumonia at the finish, poor soul.'

Ida was determined not to be outdone. 'We couldn't get the sofa through the bloody door. Wedged for over

4

an hour, half in and half out, no shaking it all about. So the mad fools took the door and the frame off, didn't they? Everybody had to come and go the back way for ages after that, because the bloody front door wouldn't open when they put it back all cockeyed.' She paused for breath and allowed her audience to laugh.

'When the rent man came, Gran paid him through the letterbox and told him she'd be withholding payment if he didn't get her a new door. They got one in the end, like. Ooh, and it was a lovely sofa, too.' She sighed heavily. 'Till our Graham peed on it. Very slow to train, our Graham. Never knew whether he was coming, going, or just been, not till he was near five years old. The doctor couldn't do nothing.' She sat for a moment and thought about days gone by. 'He's still a bit slow, our Graham,' was her final statement.

'I miss something from back then, but I can't for the life of me work out what it was,' said Jimmy Nuttall. 'Odd boots, different colours, different sizes, no laces, no socks, blinking blisters on me blisters. Cane nearly every day at school, not enough to eat, Mam crying cos Dad was down the Newsham necking his wages. Us hiding from the rent man, good thumping from a copper for pinching fruit down the market. But we all look back at the good old days, eh? Are we soft or what?'

Quiet arrived at last. Those old enough to remember it nursed fond memories of the police strike of 1919. They'd had new clothes, new towels, bedding, curtains, cushions, pots and pans, all stolen from shops in town. Military tanks and ships spilled their human cargo into the city, but the loot went on regardless of the forces. Soldiers and sailors arrested several for drawing blood, but by the time they'd carted off a few vanloads of criminals they were sorely outnumbered by amateur crooks.

Amateurs fared better, since they took real pride in the

thoroughness of their work. Professionals got over-confident and landed up in the Bridewell, but the untutored invested care in their art. And one widespread opinion was that the lads in military uniform supported the civilian force's withdrawal of labour, so a good time was had by all. Over the years, the loot, enhanced and coloured in with bright verbal paints, shone like a jewel in a box of base metal.

Jack Fletcher, costermonger, said his old man brought home four parrots and a female rabbit. 'He liked animals, me dad. But we was overrun – bloody rabbit was pregnant, and we couldn't kill 'em, hadn't the heart. So we set the little buggers loose on the allotments and they ate everything. The parrots was good. Three of them's still alive, but they don't live in our house. The blooming wife's bad enough – she's a meeting on her own, always argufying and moaning.' He sighed. 'Flaming women. Who needs a bleeding parrot?'

There followed a mixed recipe whose ingredients included headboards, a box of mouth organs, antimacassars, knickers (outsize and tea-rose pink) for Auntie Gladys, a roll of lino, cases of whisky, stockings, buckets, a tin bath, feather pillows, rugs, tablecloths, and a Hoover that never got used due to the total absence of electricity.

'It done no good for the cops, though,' said Ida. 'Only ones with guts enough to strike was us and London. Some got sacked, and others didn't thrive, never given no stripes. And we shown 'em. We shown 'em how much the cops was needed by doing the loot. We done the police a favour, or so we thought.'

Polly nodded. 'And now, we pay. The sins of the fathers, eh?'

'Even my Holy Communion frock was pinched,' mused Hattie the greengrocer. 'About three sizes too big, but it was the only one left.' She'd gone to the altar to receive

6

her first wafer without the slightest stain on her innocent soul, but with her dad's dishonesty hanging loosely from her tiny frame and secured to her liberty bodice by nappy pins.

Apart from the sound of cutlery on plates, and cups clattering in saucers, the cafe was once again silent. It had long been rumoured that certain people in the Home Office wanted Scotland Road and its network of adjoining streets demolished. The reason? Slum clearance, already begun long before the Second War, was the official line, but everyone knew that the real threat to authority was the absolute solidarity of this neighbourhood. Yes, there were rows and fights, but any intruder or interloper was seen off by a suddenly united street. Did the Home Office hate Catholics, especially those whose veins ran with the blood of Ireland, Scotland and Italy?

'I still say the loot finished us,' Polly said eventually. 'We are and always have been a force to be reckoned with. They know we're capable of misbehaving to the point of riot. Will we go quietly? Will we?'

Cutlery banged rhythmically on tables. 'No, no, we won't go,' was the chant. 'They said we can come back when they've replaced our houses,' Ida screamed above the clattering. 'Do we believe them? Do we believe this bastard government? Are they going to rebuild here?'

'No, no, we won't go.' Banging and chanting increased in volume. Scotland Road was Liverpool's Vatican, a whole city within a city, and Scotland Road was angry. When this, the very heartbeat of English Catholicism, was suffering arrhythmia, the whole city felt it, and it needed to travel further afield. But could they make a stand? Could they defeat the City of Liverpool, Westminster, the big southern institutions that held all the money in their jealously guarded, well-protected vaults?

Polly, knowing she could be done for inciting riot,

delivered a second piercing whistle. 'OK, folks. You've businesses to run until our own countrymen come and finish off what Adolf started. Eat up and shut up; we've all got jobs to do.' She walked back to her counter. They wanted to ride into battle, but they had to wait for war to come to them in the form of letters telling them to pack their bags and prepare to be moved. Guy Fawkes and his shower had the right bloody idea, Polly mused as she wiped the counter's surface.

'Polly? Can you shove this lot between a few slices of bread? I just remembered, I've got to be somewhere.' The man gave her his famous wink. She'd always suspected that it was meant to be fetching, but it was just funny. There again, he considered himself to be a laugh a minute, so perhaps he was making an attempt at humour. Polly didn't know how she felt about him. Yes, she did; no, she didn't, yes she did ...

'You should be on the stage, but don't give up your day job just in case,' she advised while stacking a few dirty dishes under the counter. It was time Frank Charleson learned to wipe his own bum.

'Polly?'

She looked him up and down. 'What gives you the idea I've got time to be making butties with a full cooked brekky? Would you like both eggs on one sarnie, and where would you like me to stick your sausage? Shall I put your fried slice between two unfried slices? Any suggestions about bacon and black pudding can be written on a postcard and sent to this address. OK?'

'Pol?' another customer called.

'Hang on, Ernie. Mr Charleson here's looking for a miracle.' The proprietor of Polly's Parlour stared into the eyes of her old friend and adversary. They'd been through a lot together, but it was time for him to get his act straight. To do that, he needed to murder his mother for

8

a start. Her gaze unwavering, she slapped bread, butter and a knife on the counter. 'Do it your bloody self while I'm busy, Frank,' she snapped. Seamlessly, she carried on. 'Ernie? Get this side of the business, give us a hand, and your breakfast will be on the house.' She poured tea into cups.

Frank Charleson, determinedly unfazed, began his attempt to make sandwiches. 'If you can give away free breakfasts, you must be able to pay more rent, Polly Kennedy,' he said. 'I seem to be undercharging you.'

'Watch the egg,' she said, addressing him in the jocular tone she'd used way back when they'd all been teenagers. 'You'll have yolk all down the suit if you're not careful. Car seats, too. Egg can be a bugger to shift. Ernie, two full cooked ready in the kitchen, one with a slice, one without, table three.' With her right forearm, she pushed damp curls from her face. 'Jimmy, four teas for yous lot here, love. Come and take them to your table for me, will you?'

Polly's Parlour was bustling this morning. People who had businesses along Scotland Road often took breakfast, lunch, or both here. She was loved for her brother's cooking, her quickness of wit, her eagerness to please, and her tendency to put down anyone who got above him- or herself. Oh, and her prices were reasonable.

Jimmy Nuttall picked up the tray of teas. 'How's Cal?' he asked.

'He's all right, love. In the back frying eggs or cooking the books. He still manages to get up to mischief in spite of everything.'

'Ah. Tell him hello from Nutter, babe.'

'I will. Mary? Were you scrambled or poached?'

'Scrambled like me head, Pol. Have you seen what they done to me hair in that bloody shop? What a nightmare, eh? I feel like hiding in the sodding coal shed. I look a right banana, don't I?'

'More like a poodle,' was Polly's delivered opinion.

'Aw, Pol. What am I going to do with it?'

Polly shouted through the door. 'Cal? Jimmy Nutter says hiya. Make some scraggy eggs for Mary. Somebody in town's done her hair, and she wants breakfast to match. She looks like a flaming poodle that wants a trim.' She gave her attention to the victim of a very tight perm. 'I told you I'd see to it for you. You know I do hair every night and occasionally at weekends. What's the point of me wearing myself to the bone when my customers go to town? I happen to be a fully qualified hairdresser, you know.' The difference was that she now had to front two establishments, since her brother might never again be fit for his own work. And he was so acutely aware of that, so damned apologetic, always blaming himself for being in the wrong place when the crane had swung down.

Frank Charleson was struggling with knife, bread, butter and a full cooked breakfast. It was clear that he was unused to fending for himself, since his mother had a full-time housekeeper who did everything for both Charlesons. Polly shook her head. Some people were spoilt. One in particular was spoilt almost beyond mending. But oh, he was attractive . . .

With things slowing down, and Ernie behind the counter, she took over, her attitude more kindly. He missed Ellen; so did she. 'Look at the state of you, Frank,' she whispered. 'Does your mother do everything for you? Does she tie your laces and thread a string through your coat sleeves with gloves on the ends?'

He grinned. 'Just between us, she would if I let her. Or Mrs Lewis would. Don't forget, my mother's busy training to be bedridden. It's a full-time job in our house, becoming disabled. She's diabetic and she lives on chocolate. She's going the right way to losing her legs or her kidneys.'

Sometimes, though not often, Polly was glad that

she and her brother were orphans. 'You all right now, though?'

'Not bad, thanks. It gets easier, but I still think about Ellie a lot. She made me happy. Made me laugh. Mother hated her.'

'I know.' She decided to leave the eggs out of the picnic. 'Take a few paper napkins to save your clothes. Where are you going, anyway?'

'To increase Mother's portfolio. Another property auction.'

'Well, don't be buying any more round here, cos we're going to be flattened.' Polly finished organizing his breakfast. 'And don't forget to bring the plate back.' They had a lot in common, because she had a twin brother in a wheelchair, while he had a mother who ruled from a ground-floor bedroom. Mrs Charleson was capable of going about her business, but her son, a widower, had become her feet, eyes and ears since he'd moved back in. She was a miserable, mean old besom who needed a kick up the withers.

'There you go. No egg. You'll have a better chance at your meeting with a clean shirt and tie. Now, get on with it, and don't eat while you're driving, because it's very dangerous.'

'You sound like my mother.'

His mother, Norma Charleson, was usually referred to as That Old Cow. 'Moo,' Polly said softly.

'Stop it.' He grinned, picked up his battered breakfast and went outside. Looking at his watch, he decided to take five minutes in the car to eat in peace. Polly's was busy at the best of times, but Mondays were always crazy. Crazy? His old girl was the crazy one, buying yet more houses to be let and looked after. West Derby and Wavertree, this time.

He started to think; thinking was not a good idea. Ellen

and Polly had been friends since infant school, and Polly had helped at the end with the nursing. Polly was the closest he would ever get to Ellen, and she was as needful as he was. Only she had a lot on her plate – a lot on dozens of plates. Oh well, she was still lovely and a good laugh. The food was a bit cold, but he was starving, so he ate.

Inside, Polly was starting her first big clear-up while Ernie ate his free breakfast. The half past eight lot had begun to leave, but there'd be another, smaller influx between nine and ten. Where a business had more than one worker, they swapped breakfast shifts. Some couldn't afford breakfast, of course. They would have a bite at home or bring a pie or a pasty for lunchtime and starve till then. The world wasn't fair.

The carry-outs had been and gone. They bought break-fast in the form of bacon butties, because they were Scotty Road's lone rangers, with no help at all in their shops, and they worked long hours. Again, she thought how unbalanced the world had become. Ellen dead, poor Frank stuck with his mam, Cal working from a wheelchair, all appliances adapted to suit his lowered position in life. Frank had seen to all changes, of course, but he wouldn't have told his mother how little he'd charged in rental increase. He was a good man, worth ten of the woman who'd birthed him.

She walked through to the back of the property. Cal worked in a scullery, which had been enlarged by Frank's team of builders. There were eight gas burners on hobs, two large ovens and a massive grill. Sculleries were known as back kitchens in these parts. The living room, which usually had a range fire installed, was called the kitchen, while a front room was nominated the parlour. Polly's parlour was larger than most, and was used as a cafe. But parlours in nearby houses were tiny, hallowed, unused except for visitors, and as well furnished as possible. 'All right, love?' she asked her brother. 'Shall I push you through while I wash up?'

'OK.' Cal Kennedy had become a man of few words since his accident. The middle room was his, though it doubled as a living area for both resident siblings. It housed a sofa, a small table and four chairs, a sideboard and his bed, which was under the stairs. He had gone from lugging heavy loads on the docks to frying eggs for the cafe. Hard work helped him to ignore his problems.

Sex, the most favoured of his pastimes, had been eliminated from his life, while the girl he had loved had fled to London three months after his accident. And he was left now with Polly, who needed her own life. She'd been abandoned, too, when she'd insisted on looking after him. She slept in the back bedroom upstairs, as the front one had been turned into a hairdressing salon. She never stopped. It was his fault that his sister was working herself to a standstill. Could he ever repay her?

Every morning and night, a male attendant arrived to get Cal out of or into bed. During the day, Polly had to cope with him, and that was what he hated most. Once the cafe closed at three o'clock, she helped him on and off the commode, kept him clean, did for him things she should have been doing for the children she might never have. He had wrecked her life as well as his own.

Cal found comfort in his second hobby – drink. The lads sometimes came for him in the evening, wheeling him down to one of many pubs, but much of his drinking was done alone. He didn't hide the evidence, partly because he couldn't, but mostly because she understood. As long as he was sober while cooking, she left him to it.

'Pol?'

'What?'

'You need a baby.'

13

She laughed. 'Miracles I don't do. Breakfasts, dinners and hair, I manage, but babies are a bit beyond me. If I see a star, some shepherds and three kings, I'll let you know and we'll sing carols, eh?' Well, at least he was talking for a change.

Cal swallowed. 'I wouldn't mind – wouldn't blame you – if you got married and left me.'

'Who'd run the cafe? Who'd do hair at night or clean the house? And who'd be the boss? Don't you think life's hard enough without having a screaming baby and a snoring husband keeping us awake at night?'

'You should be married,' he said.

'I don't know anybody I want to marry, do I?' This was an outright lie, but she clung to it. Cal and Frank were close friends, and she'd no intention of becoming the subject of a plot.

'I'd be the uncle. We both need more than this, Polly.'

'What we need is to keep going, lad. I can't stop seeing to the cafe or doing hair, can I? Not yet, anyway.' Tears stung her eyes, so she walked into the scullery to tackle a mountain of washing-up. She wanted kids. They'd both wanted kids. While he was working on the docks, she was employed by a top-notch hairdresser in town, and they'd both been on good money. In fact, they'd been thinking about deposits on a couple of houses in Bootle ...

'Thanks for the breakfast, Polly,' Ernie called before leaving for work. Ernie sometimes helped with the heaving about of Cal Kennedy. They had so many good friends; what would happen when the area was wiped out? Who would care for the weak, the young and the elderly once this society had been fractured? Who would worry about the isolated and the poor? People from the Scotland Road area embraced everyone, no matter what the nationality, colour or creed. Yes, it was largely Catholic, but there was little prejudice until Walking Days, when Catholics and

14

Protestants tormented the life out of each other. It was tradition, and tradition should endure.

She closed her burning eyes. Somebody from the Docks and Harbour Board had picked her up from work and driven her to the hospital. Cal would probably never walk again. There was a chance that some abilities might return but, for a while at least, he could be incontinent and incapable of marital relations, as they so delicately termed the intimate side of life. Lois had beggared off, anyway, as had Polly's own fiancé.

Frank Charleson had sat with them in the hospital, just as they had sat with him while Ellen lost her fight. 'Four sad people,' Polly said now as she scraped debris into the pig bin. They'd had poor luck. At school, Ellen had been netball captain, leader of the rounders team, brilliant at games. And all the time, she'd had something massively wrong with her heart, and it eventually affected other major organs. Operations hadn't worked, and she'd drifted off one sunny afternoon with her husband, her parents and two friends keeping her company at the start of that final journey.

Old Mother Charleson had struggled without success to hide her delight. She got her boy back. He was useful, and he was exactly where he belonged. She took to her room, issued orders, ate everything the housekeeper put before her and drifted towards severe diabetes on a cloud of selfishness, ignorance and milk chocolate.

When most of the dishes were clean, Polly dealt with the scouse. This stew, the universal panacea round these parts, was divided up. She shoved some into pastry cases with lids, to be nominated meat and tater pies. Other dollops she placed in circles of pastry, folding them into a shape invented in Cornwall for the miners of tin. Thus one cauldron of scouse became stew, pies and pasties. So that was dinner sorted once the ovens got turned on.

When the second surge of breakfasters arrived, she served up what Cal had left in the warmer. The lad needed his rest, and no one complained if the food wasn't quite up to scratch. They knew and understood the situation in Pol and Cal Kennedy's house, and they seldom complained.

With the later breakfast over, Polly locked the cafe door and returned to the living room. Cal was asleep in his wheelchair. She wedged a pillow behind his head and against the wall. Fortunately, customers were used to this. If Cal was asleep, they made do with a smaller menu. The best thing about Scotland Road was that its residents supported one another, though there were some wonderful fights . . .

Polly sat and fanned herself with a damp tea towel. Mam had been a fighter. Back in the day, the sight of two women rolling about on the cobbles, each with hands in the other's hair, was not unusual. Mam's arch enemy had been Theresa Malone from number thirty-four. Theresa Malone's son was a thief and a liar, and he dragged young Cal into trouble on several occasions. The solution? Another fight, of course. There were plenty of seconds, but no referee.

Mam and Mrs Malone were both Dublin girls, both redheads, both married to Irishmen. If either husband happened to be around, fighting would be postponed, but it always started with the two women in their doorways, arms folded, faces fixed in solid, stone-hard frowns, mouths turned down, eyes narrowed. As if choreographed, they would take a step towards the centre of the street, their pace quickening as they neared the arena, which always had to be equidistant from the two houses. If fighters lived on the same side of the street, the rules were similar, but the match was played out in the gutter.

Mam always won. Theresa Malone lost hair, teeth, skin,

blood and dignity every time while the crowd cheered and roared. Yet when a stranger arrived from some other area of the city and trouble started, Theresa helped Mam, and Mam helped Theresa. It was a special kind of insanity, so special that Theresa nursed Mam during her final illness. 'All gone now,' Polly breathed.

'What's gone?'

'The time, Cal. The past.'

'The past is always gone,' he said.

'I was just thinking about Mrs Malone and Mam.'

'Yes.' He moved the pillow and tossed it on his bed. 'I remember. She didn't last long after Mam, did she?'

'They needed one another, Cal. Even the fighting was part of it. Like sisters, they were. It was a sort of race memory from the old country. And the Italians were just as bad, but not as much fun, because they fought in a foreign language.'

Cal almost smiled. 'The ice-cream wars. Remember when a Manny wanted to marry a Tog? Did anyone know how to say their full names, by the way? It was worse than Romeo and Juliet. I don't know how many finished up in clink, but rumour had it that some wardens had to learn Italian at night school. And the two families carried on fighting in there, always being shoved in solitary. Even solitary got crowded.'

'Manfredi and Tognarelli,' she told him. 'They're all over Lancashire. Best ice cream ever.' He remained talkative. She needed to put the pies and pasties in the oven, needed to boil water for vegetables, but Cal was finally managing a conversation. 'They were nearly as mad as the Irish,' she said.

He sighed. 'Polly?'

'That's me.'

'There's no easy way of saying this, so I'll just come out with it. I know now when I need the commode, right?'

'Yes.' She waited. 'And?'

'And I can take some of my weight on my legs, yes? I'm capable,' he said. After another pause, he continued. 'I need a clean girl to have my child if you aren't going to have a family, because I probably won't marry. But I'd get somebody in to help with the child so that you'd be free. It's just that I want to be a dad.' Did that pretty young nurse like him? She was probably the same with all patients, yet there was warmth, tenderness, a hand on his shoulder offering comfort and encouragement... No. Who wanted the non-walking wounded? Would he ever walk? Linda Higgins, her name was ...

Polly sat down suddenly at the table. 'How the bloody hell do we manage that, Cal? Do I walk about interviewing folk and filling in forms? I mean, if I got somebody from Mother Bailey's, she could be diseased. Normal girls want a wedding ring first.'

'I don't want a wife; I need a son or a daughter.'

Polly had never heard anything like this in her life, and she said so. 'But women don't part with their kids. When they've cursed the world through all that pain, they fall in love with the baby. It's nature's way; it's why we hang on to the mucky, howling little buggers.'

He disagreed. Everybody needed money. Somewhere, there was a woman who would bear a child for cash.

'Sell her son or daughter? If I had a child, I'd keep it. No matter how much money I was offered, nobody would ever get their hands on my baby. Why do you want one, anyway? To push your wheelchair when you're older?' Immediately, she wished she could bite back her words. 'Sorry. I shouldn't have said that.'

'No, it's all right. It was a good question. The answer's no.'

'Then how could you mind a small child?'

He smiled. 'Like I said, I'll get somebody in. I'm going

to walk again. Nobody will want to marry a lame man, and I'll never walk without some kind of help. Anyway, I've a late appointment Thursday, so come and see what I can do. There's a lot of pain in my legs. The new pills are painkillers.'

Polly blinked back a new river of saline. He was pleased by pain. Any sensation in his legs, good or bad, was something to be celebrated. 'Have you walked, love?'

He nodded. 'Muscles are weak, but I'll get there, Pol. No two ways about it, I'll always be crippled, but not like this. I'll need crutches – sticks at best, but something's healed. We have to go slow, cos we could mess it up all over again, but come and watch me, queen.'

And that was the moment. She ran out of strength, knelt down and hugged him. Tears intermingled until they were both exhausted. God was there, and God was good, because He'd looked down on Callum Kennedy and allowed a miracle to take place. 'You won't need to pay, Cal. Somebody will love you.'

'But what if—'

'What if nothing. Don't be in such a rush. Look at us both; we're wiped out. You are still a good bloke and a very handsome one. There's a girl for you.'

They were tired to the bone, yet they carried on regardless, carrots and peas on hobs, pasties and pies in the oven with a huge apple crumble, Cal making custard while Polly wiped tables in the cafe. Her brother wanted a normal life. Somewhere in this city, there was a girl who could love a man with bad legs. He wanted children, sons and daughters or nieces and nephews; he wanted life around him. At last, he was confiding in her. She put dishes of pickled beetroot and red cabbage in the centre of each table. Was life threatening to improve? She shouldn't get her hopes up; neither should Cal.

Customers found Polly unusually quiet when she

opened up at dinner time. Bursting to tell somebody Cal's better news, she sealed it inside herself, scarcely daring to speak in case her twin's secret spilled out. He might walk. He might be able to sit behind a counter and take money for sweets, newspapers, or whatever they chose to sell when they moved on to ... to where?

'Where will they send us?' she asked of no one in particular.

'As far away from our city as they can,' answered Dusty Den, the rag and bone man. 'Have you got Flick's carrots there, Pol? He looks forward to his snack.'

'Eat your dinner,' was her reply. 'Let me feed him.' She went outside to Den's famous steed. He was a full-size dray horse, because his owner refused to overload a pony. 'Ruined, aren't you?' Polly asked the animal. 'Better fed than some round here. Good old days?' She stroked the blaze of white on his face. 'Were they really? Do you remember anything, or are you too young?'

There were two sides to every story, she told herself. She remembered stillbirths, neonatal deaths, the terrified screams of mothers losing their lives in childbirth. Diphtheria raced through families and from one street to another; even the church closed its doors during one epidemic. Tuberculosis had been common, as had scarlet fever, while the general health of most had been poor. But this was home. People who lived on or near Scotty had always loved the place.

Parents did what they could, but they were fighting radical decay combined with poverty, and few won that battle. It was partly due to the houses. They were draughty, sometimes infested, often damp. Yes, better housing was needed, but why couldn't the powers replace dwellings here a few at a time? 'Because they want us shifted permanently, Flick. Divide and rule's the name of the game.' Scotland Road had been blamed for the 1919 loot, and had been condemned because of it. 'Uncle Tom did more damage than he realized with that bloody gas cooker,' she told the horse.

She stood for a moment and looked at the road she loved, a road that was famous all over the world. The spine of this community would be broken within years, and no physiotherapy, no crutch, would help it back to its feet. Scotty's men had fought just years ago alongside the better fed to defeat a monster, and their neighbourhood was now threatened. Yes, give them new houses, but no, don't take their history away. Was this a country fit for heroes? Possibly. Unless you were from Scotty Road, in which case you didn't count.

It was a beautiful place, vibrant, loud, busy. It might have been cleaner, but it had everything people needed, every kind of shop from wet fish to pawnbroker, from vegetables to pianos. She tried to imagine it broken, empty and unloved, but she failed. This was the centre of so many people's universe, the very pulse of life. Could there be a Liverpool without Scotty? Could there be a port without docks, fish without chips, woman without man? She still missed the rotter who had abandoned her . . .

She went in to help Cal dole out generous helpings of apple crumble and custard. All twenty-four seats were occupied, so generosity veered towards the custard on this occasion. 'I'm going to make crème caramel,' Cal announced. 'Need a bain-marie.'

'You what?'

'French for a bath – you stick your cream caramels in the water.'

'Oo-er. You been reading again, our Cal? You want to watch that, you'll be having a brainstorm.'

'What's up?' he asked. He knew her so well. 'Thinking about Greg?'

'A bit,' she admitted. 'Pass me this morning's bacon.'

She put the cold bacon between slices of bread and went out through the back door. Urchins were fewer these days, because people managed better, but a few still arrived and waited quietly for butties. 'Share them,' she said to the tallest child. Then she supervised while the food was doled out. 'Look after one another,' she ordered. 'Cos that's what it's about. We're Scotties, and that's what we do.'

There were fewer Scotland Roaders these days. Yet those whose houses had been eradicated often walked or bicycled down from the districts in which they had been planted. They bought what they could carry, drank in the pubs, ate in Polly's and visited friends whose homes remained intact. They hated their new lives. City dwellers of long standing, they disliked flats, newly built terraces and semis, the schools, the shops if there were any; and above all, they missed each other. Gran and Auntie Lil were a mile away, God alone knew where the neighbours had ended up, and several children kept running away back to the only life they'd ever known.

One old dear had summed it up in the cafe a week ago over a cup of tea and a pudding. 'We've got gardens, but nobody has a lawnmower, so the grass is up to our ear'oles; we've got hallways so floors in rooms stay cleaner. But when dirt walked in round here, it brought friends with it. Give me the bloody muck any day, love.' They were, Polly thought, like the tribes of Israel in the Old Testament, wandering hither and yon, slaves to Egypt, to Rome and to the whims and fancies of whoever walked at the front. Except that this Liverpool crowd of displaced persons had been split up by their own government.

Polly entered the living room. 'Cal?'

'What?'

'Strength in numbers, eh?'

'If you say so.'

'Well, they're knocking some of Everton down. We need to join up with the Proddies.'

'And get our own people back from Kirkby or wherever,' he said.

She agreed. 'Relatives in Ireland and Scotland, if they can afford to come. The priests will let them sleep in church halls. Italian ice-cream folk from all over the country. We fight, Cal.'

'That's right, love. We fight. Like Mam, no rules of engagement. Teeth, hair and skin – till they run over us with demolition machinery. Park me at the front. Whether or not I'm walking, stick me in the wheelchair and see what they do. Let them squash a bloody cripple.'

'Do you think they would?' There was panic in Polly's voice.

Cal laughed. 'No, but it would make a great photo for the newspapers, eh? *Man, disabled due to poor safety control on Liverpool's docks, stops the traffic.*'

'That would go down well with the Docks and Harbour Board,' she said. 'Can you imagine the faces of Liverpool councillors when it got in the *Echo*?'

'Bugger the *Echo*,' Cal muttered between gritted teeth. 'I want *The Times* and the *Manchester Guardian*. Oh, and make sure they snap my good side. I don't want to be making a show of myself, do I?'

She sat down. 'It won't be like that, though. There won't be one big day when everybody gets shifted. They've been chipping away for twenty-odd years with a bit of help from Germany: a few houses here, a street there, pull down some affected by a nearby direct hit. We'll have to do a Jarrow. If London won't come to us, we'll go to it.'

'I can't walk. I'll never walk properly.'

'Then we go on rag and bone carts, on coal lorries, in removal vans, in hearses. We go so slowly that we bung up all the roads.'

Cal pondered. 'We need a fighting fund,' he announced after a few seconds. 'I know Frank will come up trumps, but we need collecting tins in pubs. If we're going to London and bringing in foreigners, we want cash.'

There wasn't a lot of money about even now, in 1955. Ten years after winning a war, Britain fared moderately well while Germany, though divided, seemed to be improving superbly on its western side. Cal had seen bombing and had survived, as had Polly, Frank and poor Ellen, yet they'd all taken punishment since the ceasefire, what with the deaths of their parents and Ellen, Cal's accident, and Polly's resulting imprisonment.

There were gaps in terraces, used now as playgrounds, but they had been homes. So much loss. A beloved wife gone, a pair of strong legs ruined, neighbours wiped out, and now the fruits of a Siberian salt mine were about to be poured into wounds. It would be done slowly. When enough cardboard cottages and flats had been erected on the edges of Liverpool, another Scotty terrace would bite the dust. And folk would be separated for the sake of a new, clean start where they'd be disorientated and less likely to offend. 'I'll get the money,' she said. 'And we have to be clever. No physical stuff, just London packed with objectors. A peaceful demonstration's what we want.'

Cal didn't particularly want peace. Deep down, he was furious about his injured spine, his disobedient legs, Lois who had run away from him, Greg who had rejected Polly, councillors and parliamentarians who didn't give a damn about anybody at all.

Then there were the softies who went on about bloody Dresden – what about Bootle? It was all London this, London that and God help Coventry, yet Liverpool's docks, railways and roads had carried every bit of ammunition for the whole show, and Bootle had sustained the worst damage nationwide. But who gave a flying fornication? It

24

was only Liverpool; they were only northerners. 'I want to strangle somebody,' he said. 'Very, very slowly, till their eyes bulge.'

'Why, Cal?'

He shrugged. 'Everything. Lois, who loved me forever no matter what, the bloody docks and all the accidents, mates just a few years older than me buried in France and Italy – what is there to be satisfied with? Mary's perm and a scouse pasty?'

'Don't get bitter. What we need is to express our disgust and our distrust. Because it will happen. There's no stopping what's to come, Cal. We'll be in some new, jerry-built community, but we can show them one thing. We can still assemble, still congregate and let them know what we think of them in their panelled offices and gentlemen's clubs. We can sign petitions saying we aren't satisfied with Westminster, and it's not just us; we can bring in folk from Glasgow and other disappointed cities. This country's not fit for rats, let alone heroes.'

'You have to be the spokesperson,' he said.

'No danger; try stopping me. See, people have got things arse over tip, Cal. The folk in London are our servants, but everyone acts as if it's the other way round. It's time somebody from Lancashire rattled the doors of their Rolls-Royces and filled Downing Street with silent people. Silence will upset them. We communicate in writing only. Let them know through what we don't say that we can turn Liverpool into a seething mass of civil disobedience if we choose to.'

Cal blinked. Why hadn't he noticed this before? His sister was an orator, an inspiration, a little firecracker. There she stood, five foot four in her stockings, a pretty little thing with dark curls and bright blue eyes. She served breakfasts and dinners when she should be serving her community. 'I'd vote for you,' he told her.

'So would I,' she replied, laughing. 'I'm the best man in Liverpool, and don't ever forget it. See, MPs want all their privileges removing for a kick-off. Posh dining rooms and fine wines? Sod that; they can have a plate of scouse and a cuppa, and back to work pronto. There's half of them should be in jail anyway, bloody fraudsters using inside info to line their own nests. I don't trust them. I wouldn't trust me if I got offered such an easy life. And they're supposed to look after us.' She decided to stop preaching. 'I'll have to go up and get the salon ready.'

'Will you stand for parliament?' he asked.

'No, I won't.'

'Why not?'

'Because I've no party. I don't belong with any of them – I'm the Polly Kennedy Party, full stop. And I don't want to get ... to get contaminated.' She went upstairs to prepare herself for her second job. If Liverpool's politicians gave a shit, Cal wouldn't be crippled, because they would have sought to implement better safety measures. Oh, they started off eager and decent, but the corridors of power chipped away at them, dragging them into a fairy tale where everything was free or cheap – and take it, now, now, because you may not get elected next time. One of the few decent ones among them was Bessie Braddock, and she'd always been up to her eyes in everybody's problems, poor soul. Yes, they needed more women down yonder, that was a fact.

Did she have enough hydrogen peroxide for Carla Moore's roots? Did Carla realize that she was stripping her hair of all life and dignity? 'I'd best tell her it'll start breaking off and falling out if she doesn't let it rest. Where's me conditioning oil?'

After switching on the radio in her bedroom, she turned up the volume, lay in the bath and wondered how much longer her looks would last. She was twenty-five. Half her life was spent in the company of greasy food, while the rest of her time was lived here among chemicals, or with her poor brother. He would walk. He'd need assistance, but he'd walk. There was hope, and she would cling to it while he clung to his crutches.

The girl in the bathroom mirror was still pretty. She was a mouthy, opinionated little bitch, but still a good-looking young woman. During the war years, her school peers had been jealous, since Mam could work wonders with old curtains, a bed sheet, a tablecloth and a ribbon. Ellen had stood by her, so Mam had made a few dresses and skirts for her, too. As for the green-eyed ones, this little madam had taken her revenge ...

The fifties didn't suit Polly; the new look drowned her, so she shortened everything and created her own style. 'No, no, we won't go,' she whispered. Of course they'd go. They had to go. But they would make their point. If silence could be maintained, it would speak volumes; it would say, 'You'll never know where we are, but we always know where you are.' A not quite revolution, a not quite anarchy, a not quite threat.

Revenge. Hadn't she grown up at all? Those who had teased her and Ellen had 'lost' shoes, bits of physical education uniform, text books, homework, pens and pencils. Was the idea of a visit to London just another stolen satchel, another pair of gym shoes with no laces, another blot in a writing book? She and Ellen had owned such angelic features that no member of staff had ever thought them guilty.

'You'll be at the front on this one,' she warned her reflection. 'They'll know it's you, and not before time. Because you've always been a besom, and folk should be warned.'

'Good advice, Polly.'

She turned and looked at him. Determined not to panic,

she didn't grab a towel to cover her nakedness. Instead, she reached for a robe and pulled it on at normal speed. 'I've told you not to use your key,' she said. 'You may own the bricks, but this is still our home.'

'You are gorgeous.' His voice was low and rather choked.

'I know.'

'The music was loud, Polly. I didn't want Cal to know I'm here, so I crept up the stairs, thought you'd be mixing your magic spells for hair.'

'Right. What do you want?'

Frank Charleson swallowed hard. What did he want? 'Erm . . . I've got him a television set.' What he wanted was scarcely covered by a thin robe.

'Then talk to Cal. And stop staring, will you?'

'I'll never stop staring, especially now.'

'You know the score, Francis. Now, bugger off.'

He buggered off.

Two

Norma Charleson lay uneasily on a pink velvet chaise longue under the window in her living room. She was not in a good mood, and her left knee was stiffening up again, so she ate another couple of chocolates. The doctor had advised her to stay active and concentrate on the positive. For a medical man, he knew precious little about pain. Active? With arthritis like hers? Even in these warmer months, she had trouble with her poor knees. Right. She must think positive, so she thought about her house. It was a great house, and she'd worked hard to acquire it.

The wonderful thing about Brookside Cottage, apart from its detached status, was that it was divided into two internal parts at ground level. Frank had the bulk of the house and his freedom – well, he thought he had his freedom – while his mother, who considered herself to be a sensible woman, lived in her own suite on the ground floor to the right of the building's entrance. She didn't interfere openly; if she did that, her son might well go off again with some floozie, and she didn't want that. He was in full charge of the business now, and that fact should be enough to keep him at home, or so she hoped. And yet . . . 'Positive,' she reminded herself firmly. 'Look on the bright side, and stop worrying, Norma.'

Frank would remarry eventually, she believed. He and his second wife could live here, and she wouldn't meddle overtly. When he was at home, Norma seldom ventured into the main areas of the house, as she sought to show him how independent she was. He needed to feel secure and separate from his mother. Because of that, the larger part of the property was a no-go area for the person who was its true owner.

He didn't know she checked up on him almost every day. Bad knees or good, she combed the study before climbing the stairs to look through his pockets and in his waste bin. It was all in his best interests, of course, since he'd already made one unfortunate marriage and ... no, she must entertain only happy thoughts. The orange creams were good, but she didn't like the caramels.

The house had once been a small convent with a school next door, so it retained some impressive features. The front door opened into a stone-built hall with a floor of Welsh slate. The entrance was arched, and the area still owned the pegs from which the good sisters had hung their outdoor garments. There was even a small font for holy water with some words in Latin carved into its rim. *Deo gratias*, it said, then something about the water of life. Whatever, it was different and impressive, therefore very suitable for the owner of properties all over Liverpool. Oh yes, a woman of substance deserved Brookside and its delightful setting.

Norma had her own bathroom, a walk-in wardrobe, a kitchen and a sizeable living room with a bed disguised during daytime hours as a cupboard, so the chaise under the window was her resting place until darkness fell. Through the glass, she kept an eye on the road so that she could monitor the behaviour of her neighbours, and she always saw Frank's car as soon as it entered the home straight. He was her only son, and she needed him.

The one problem attached to Brookside was the nightly blackness at the rear of the cottage. It was the last house in this part of Liverpool North, and the road that fronted it meandered into Little Crosby, an ancient Viking settlement whose feudalism survived to this day. It was believed to be the last place in England where only Catholics were allowed to occupy the tied cottages.

The housekeeper, Christine Lewis, lived there with her daughter. Christine's husband had worked on the landed family's estate, so she would be allowed tenancy for the rest of her life, or until she gave it up voluntarily. They were fascinating little houses in Little Crosby, so old that most women had to bend to get through the front doors. And at least they were in rows, with neighbours at hand, whereas it was possible to feel isolated here, especially at night. It was nice to be detached, but it certainly had its downside. Thank goodness for the few houses across the road at the front.

At the back of Norma's extended cottage, there was nothing at all, just the flat fields of the Mersey plain that stretched all the way to the river and the Irish Sea. A townswoman, Norma had never experienced the special inky darkness of countryside before she came to Brookside. She took comfort from the front, as there was movement, and several street lamps had been erected, but she didn't like to be alone at night here. She'd managed it, just about, during Frank's brief marriage, but her health had deteriorated since then.

Anyway, Frank was extremely comfortable, as he occupied the greater part of the house. There was a sitting room and a dining room, both heated by a stone-built, central chimney with an open grate that could be fed logs or coal from either room. He had a ground-floor study, three upstairs bedrooms, one of which had a garden room attached, and his own bathroom. From the first floor conservatory, a spiral staircase led down into the rear garden. The boy was living in the lap of luxury. Meals

31

were made in his large kitchen by Mrs Lewis, who also did his washing, ironing and cleaning. Why would he want to leave again? He mustn't leave again, because that would be the death of his mother.

And there was just one small, annoying fly buzzing in the ointment.

He'd gone rather dewy-eyed and thoughtful all over again. The last time he'd been in such a state, he'd upped and married Ellen Lucas, a pretty enough urchin who used to work in a large florist shop in the city. They'd lived in one of Norma's houses, rent-free, of course, and the girl had died. Norma had comforted her son and persuaded him to come home. 'I'll live in the annexe,' she had promised. It was a vow she was determined to keep – up to a point. Anything that made him remain at home was worth the effort.

She ate a third orange cream. The letter remained where she'd left it, under the desk blotter in his study. Polly Kennedy this time, and Frank had written her a love letter. Polly had been a close friend of the dead wife, and Frank seemed to have turned to her. He hadn't meant to creep up on her while she'd been naked; he'd been quiet so that Cal wouldn't hear him, since he'd brought the lad a surprise. *The music was loud, so I didn't hear you rising like Venus from the water ...*

'Yes, he's gone dewy once more,' she whispered. Frank was no use when in love. He focused fully on the object of desire and did less well in exams and the like. When they'd lived near Scotland Road back in the bad old days, he'd always hung round with Ellen, Polly and ... Greg? 'You didn't die early enough, Charlie,' Norma told her deceased husband. 'If you'd gone a couple of years before you did, I could have got him away from that motley crowd.'

The life insurance money had bought the first fifteen

houses. She now owned dozens, and Frank was in charge. Well, if he'd had nothing to do, he would have moped or gone back into office work in Liverpool. Offices were full of young women. 'Polly bloody Kennedy,' Norma cursed quietly. Still, she wouldn't leave her brother, would she? The whole area was due for demolition, and— And Frank might want to rescue his damsel in distress. If he'd made up his mind, there'd be no stopping him, blind idiot that he was.

Girls were supposed to be silly in love, but Frank did a fair job of acting the fool when it came to young women. In the letter, he said he wanted her. That could mean just sex, of course. If the girl gave him what he craved, he might calm down a bit and settle for physical love. Because if Norma Charleson's memory served her right, the brother was in a wheelchair and Greg Wotsisname had deserted the sister. Well, if Polly Kennedy stayed with her brother and served up lunch and sex for Frank, things might work out very well for a while.

Yet she knew her son only too well. He was an all-or-nothing type, in at the deep end or stay out of the water. It would be easy enough for him to find somewhere for himself, the girl and her brother. Frank would allow no obstacle to barricade his route once his mind was set. Panic and heartburn combined to bubble in her throat. She shouldn't eat chocolate; the doc had warned her about chocolate. He said if she carried on like this, she'd be resorting to insulin injections, because diet alone wouldn't be enough, and she wasn't any good at dieting.

A polite knock at the door was followed by Christine Lewis's head bobbing into the room. 'Can I get you anything before I leave, Mrs Charleson? My daughter's taking me out for a meal. I did tell you last week, if you remember.'

'What are we having?' Norma asked.

The rest of Christine entered the room. She smiled nervously; Mrs Charleson's mood had been changeable of late. 'I've made you a nice chicken salad and a trifle. Elaine's treating me for my birthday.'

'Oh, I see. Have you done Frank's clothes for tomorrow?'

'Yes, Mrs Charleson.'

'And you'll be here in the morning?'

'Yes, of course.'

'The chiropodist's coming,' the supine woman announced. 'Diabetics have to mind their feet, you see.'

Christine Lewis made no reply. Diabetics shouldn't be eating chocolate or trifle, but it wasn't her place to say anything. The job was well paid and not too difficult unless this silly woman decided to have a spectacularly moody day.

'Going somewhere nice, then?'

'Oh, I don't know, Mrs Charleson. She'll have picked somewhere decent, but it's a secret, so I have to get home and change into better clothes. My husband used to treat me to a meal for my birthday, and Elaine took over when he died. She's a good girl.'

'Does she work?'

'Oh, yes. She won a place at grammar school, then university. Elaine's a lawyer. Not criminal stuff, more conveyancing, wills, that sort of thing.' Pride made her stand taller. 'Only seventeen when she went to Oxford, so at twenty-two she's well into her first job and almost fully qualified.'

Norma's eyes narrowed. Already made small by rolls of flesh, they almost disappeared whenever she was displeased or envious. 'Is she courting?'

'No. To be honest, Mrs Charleson, she seems married to her work, brings piles of papers home at night, burns the midnight oil. And she's still learning, of course. She

34

says you don't start understanding properly until you're in the job. Ambitious, I'd say. Now, are you comfortable? Cup of tea or coffee?'

Norma's mind was doing about seventy miles an hour in a built-up area. Frank should look higher up the ladder. It would all dovetail so nicely with the mother as housekeeper and the daughter as wife to Frank. In fact, it would suit everybody. The girl could do all the legal work on the properties, mother and daughter would see each other as often as they liked, and Frank would stop writing letters to a girl who ran a dilapidated cafe on Scotland Road. Oh yes, it was as clear as daylight. Frank could have a decent future if he could find the sense to change direction.

'Mrs Charleson?'

'Sorry. Daydreaming again. No, I'm all right, dear. Go and enjoy yourself.'

'Dear' withdrew from the room. Never before had she been awarded a friendly title. Was Norma Charleson teetering on the brink of premature senile dementia? Because she was seldom pleasant with anyone other than her son. He must have taken after his father, because he was a lovely man, easy on the eye, naturally kind and amusing.

Norma rooted about in a drawer, found a suitable card, scribbled in it and pushed it into the envelope with five pounds. It was a large sum to give to a servant, but she wanted to appear generous. She rang her bell, and the housekeeper returned. 'What am I like, Christine?' Norma asked. 'I had this all ready for you, and I forgot because of daydreaming. Have a lovely birthday, and enjoy your meal with Elaine.' In a strange way, the daughter's name seemed right as well, because he'd been married to an Ellen, which wasn't a mile away, was it? Even the surnames, Lucas and Lewis, began and ended with the same letter. Was all this written in the stars? Had it been

35

foretold in the grand scheme of things? Oh, she must go for another reading soon.

'Oh. Thank you, Mrs Charleson.'

Norma smiled, and her eyes disappeared again. No matter which extremity of the mood spectrum she visited, she always lost her eyes. 'I think we've known each other long enough now, Christine. My name's Norma. Right, be off with you and get changed. Make your Elaine proud of her mother.'

At the other side of the door, Christine rested her back against its solid surface, her legs suddenly weakened. What on earth had happened to Norma Charleson? Only this morning, she'd been her usual snippy-snappy self: this was the wrong cushion, open the middle window instead of the end one, is there sugar in this coffee? What was going on at all? Christine opened the envelope, looked at the card, picked out the money. Half-turning to go back and thank her employer, she changed her mind. That could wait until tomorrow; she'd pretend to have opened the card at home.

She was halfway to the village and still mulling over recent happenings when the answer fell into her head. Oh, goodness. Leaning against the perimeter wall of St Mary's churchyard, she smiled to herself. The letter. She'd seen Norma shuffling through papers on Frank's desk and, being only human herself, had taken a look at the letter once the boss had returned to prostrate herself yet again in her sitting room. A slightly hysterical laugh bubbled in Christine's throat, but she swallowed it. This was so funny.

A love letter. The lazy old bat was worried because her Frankie was writing to some woman or other. At last, the crazy conversation and the change in attitude made sense. Norma Charleson wanted to pair off her son with Elaine. This was ridiculous. Tonight's meal would be fun. The person addressed by Frank as *My dear, sweet Polly* was clearly not good enough for Madam Chocolate. Heavens above, life was about to become dangerous. Interesting, though, she mused as she opened her front door. Once Norma fixed an idea among her few brain cells, it stuck.

'Hello, Mum. Happy birthday.' Elaine dashed in from the kitchen. 'Mum? Why are you giggling?'

'Oh, don't. Wait till we get to the restaurant. Have I got a tale for you.'

'Mum?'

'Believe me – it will be worth the waiting.'

Trouble abounded. It rattled the door handle, rang the bell, banged on windows, shouted through the letterbox and disturbed customers in the makeshift first-floor salon. 'Keep your mucky hands off my clean glass,' Polly screamed as she ran downstairs. The cafe windows had been washed just a couple of hours ago, and some loony was messing them up. She had a perm almost done, an ongoing deep conditioning and one dry cut to complete. There was no time to be messing about if she was to save Carla's hair from the ravages of bleach. The treatment had to be sweated into the bundle of hay that used to be Carla's crowning glory, and— Oh, no. Yes, this was trouble, indeed.

Trouble had a name. Its name was Frank Charleson and it was with some other people. 'We're closed,' she shouted. 'Breakfasts and dinners only – you should know that by now. Go away and let me get on with what I'm trying to do upstairs.' She turned to walk away.

'Let us in, Polly, or I'll use my key.' He banged on the door yet again.

She opened it and he fell in, left hand cradling the right. 'I think I broke my hand,' he said. 'It hurts like buggery.'

'Broken it on what?' she asked as three other people tumbled in untidily behind him. Two were women, one was a man, and all three looked vaguely familiar. 'Not on my windows or door, I hope.'

'No, I was banging with my left hand, clever clogs. I cracked the right one on the face of a plug-ugly, raving mad bastard,' he snapped. 'Lock the door and close the blinds. I need time to think about what's happened.'

She folded her arms and tapped a foot.

'Polly, find some patience,' he begged. She wasn't good at patience, but she was terrific in the nude.

'I'm working, Frank. You know I have to work.' One of the women was closing the blinds. 'Look, I can't just abandon customers upstairs with their heads half-cooked. Carla could go all limp and greasy if I leave her too long.'

'So go and bloody work,' he advised. 'We only need asylum for an hour or two. It's all right, we won't break anything. We're fully house-trained. These people are my witnesses.'

Polly drew herself up. 'If you need protection, go to a church. The church gives sanctuary to anybody, even a fool like you. And isn't the priest down at St Columba's your best mate apart from our Cal?'

He sat down in a cafe chair. Slowly and painstakingly, he spoke. 'I can't start crawling into church, because I just half-killed a flaming priest. Oh, go and sharpen your scissors on somebody else, will you?' She was still lovely, but his hand hurt and Polly could be an annoying little monkey if she worked at it.

She blinked rapidly. A priest? Gentle, good-hearted Frank Charleson had battered a priest? She found herself gabbling. 'See, Carla's got this stuff being sweated into her hair cos it's breaking off. But Cal's out with his mates, so go through. I'll ... er ..' She dashed back upstairs, but paused halfway for thought.

38

The people with him were from St Columba's, she believed. St Columba's sat over towards Everton, and it had always been a nice little church and school. A Father Brennan was temporary spiritual head while the parish priest was away on retreat. Mind, knowing Father Foley, retreat might well mean golf. He loved his golf, and his parishioners loved him. She ran down again, still struggling to digest the words Frank had spoken. 'What have you done, Frank? And why?'

He tutted at her. 'I hope you've left the half-cooked on a low light up there.'

'I'm sorry,' she blustered, 'but I have to look at your hand.'

He held out the injured party.

Polly ran her fingers over his. 'Open and close, Frank. Carefully, now. Oh, what a mess.'

'You should see the other fellow.' Like a child, he did what Mother told him. 'Will I live, Mam?' he asked.

'I think so. But you should go to hospital just to be on the safe side. Take your friends through to the back while I sort myself out.'

He couldn't tell her how he felt when she touched him, didn't dare speak about his rampant emotions, since the room was full of teachers. She wouldn't want to hear, anyway, because she'd turned him down years ago, and he'd fallen for Ellen. He had no regrets about Ellen, as he'd learned to love her dearly, but this little firecracker was probably the core of his life, damn her. And damn Father bloody Brennan, too.

When Polly finally got back to the salon, the women were full of questions, but she managed to field them. Somebody had fallen and hurt his hand, and it was all being sorted out downstairs. 'Get out from under that dryer, Carla. Let's look at the damage.' She cut Mary's hair, neutralized the perm, set it and shoved it under the second dryer. Then she washed the conditioner out of Carla's brittle mop, collected money, and sorted out her lotions and curlers before returning to the ground floor. Carla, who was saving to be married, donned a scarf and dashed home to do her own set.

As the last customer left through the cafe door, Polly joined Frank and his three companions. 'I'll make some tea,' she said. In Cal's low-level kitchen, she sat down, put the kettle on a hob and reached out for a few cups and saucers. While she waited for the water to boil, she listened.

'Exactly how long's it been going on?' Frank asked. 'I'll just keep on asking till one of you tells me. We've sat here forty minutes and got nowhere, but we'll stay here till morning if we have to.'

The man answered. 'As I said earlier, he's always been ready with his cane or his whip, but I've never seen a child beaten as badly as that. We should go to the hospital to see how he is. You can get your hand looked at while we're down there.'

Frank cleared his throat. 'You might go and visit the poor lad, but I'm going to the police station to confess my sins and report Brennan's crime.'

A lengthy pause followed.

'I think you'll find very few people in these parts will speak against a priest,' the man said eventually. 'Billy Blunt stole money from the vestry. He had to be punished.'

Frank's jaw dropped. 'Punished? Beaten by a massive drunk to within an inch of his life? You were witnesses. You all stood there and did sod all—'

'Our jobs, Frank. Who'd employ us again if we stood up in court to testify against a priest? We have families to keep, you know.'

'Then work in state schools, you brainwashed idiots. And how can you possibly believe that Brennan will go to heaven just because he's a Catholic priest? He could have killed that boy, and you'd have stood there like wet nellies in a cake-shop window. You say you have families. What if your child was treated like that?'

No answer arrived.

'Why did you drag me off him? Have you no normal human decency? Oh, bugger off, all of you. And yes, I can throw you out, because I own this place, for what it's worth in the current climate. Go on, get lost.'

The three teachers left, heads bowed in shame.

Polly picked up the first-aid tin, crept in and sat beside Frank. 'What happened, babe?'

Babe didn't mean much in Liverpool, yet coming from her it cracked him wide open. But no, he must stay in control. To Polly, he was just another injured bloke, and she dealt with those all the time in the cafe when they drifted in from their workplaces. He allowed her to stroke cream on a split knuckle and dab witch hazel on developing bruises. 'It would be better in a sling,' she told him. 'It might make the throbbing ease up a bit.'

'I can't drive in a sling,' he said.

'Sleep here on the couch, then. I'll go to the phone box and tell your mother you've hurt your hand, then I'll do your sling when I get back. Frank? Frank, don't cry.' He wasn't sobbing, but water coursed down his face. She hadn't seen a man in this state since Cal had cried himself out over his injury and Lois's abandonment. 'Frank? Come on, calm down. We'll be needing Noah to build another ark if you don't stop weeping.'

He struggled with his left hand and gave her a card. 'My home number's on there. She'll answer eventually. Go and phone her.' He wanted Pol to go away for a while. She was seeing the child in him, just as he'd seen himself in the boy he'd rescued tonight. 'Please do it. Let me settle down a bit.'

Polly couldn't help herself. She had an unwritten commandment all her own: no one in her company was allowed to cry alone. With her head on his shoulder, she burst into tears. 'Look what you've done now,' she sobbed. 'You should be locked up.'

How had he managed to forget this? She used to weep whenever Ellen wept; *Brief Encounter, Gone with the Wind*, even a Charlie Chaplin film had resulted in two bereft females howling in the picture house. He dried his eyes. 'If Cal comes in and finds you upset, he'll run over me with his chair.'

'Then stop crying.'

'I've stopped.'

'You haven't.'

'I have.'

'I'm going.'

'Go.'

'I don't like your mother.'

'Nobody likes my mother. Just go. I want to keep a low profile. God alone knows what Fred Blunt will do when he hears about Brennan.'

'Fred's a big man. So is his brother.'

'He was good to your Cal.' Fred Blunt was the salt of the earth. Twice a week he'd gone out of his way to see Callum Kennedy during his long stay in hospital and the convalescent home. 'When he hears that I was there tonight while Billy took a hiding, he'll come to me for an explanation. I don't know what to say, Polly. Fred's a great family man. When he finds out I dragged that fat bastard off Billy, he'll want me to speak up. That's why I need to talk to the police first, make it right before the news spreads and gets worse. Chinese whispers? They should change that to Scotty gossip.'

'Yes. Well, I'll go and talk to your mother, then I'll do your sling.'

'Don't talk to her in Cow. Use English. Don't be mooing at her.'

'I'll try not to.'

He swallowed. 'I love you.'

'I know you do.'

'Is there any chance?'

Smiling, she ruffled his hair. 'Where there's life, there's always hope. You know the score, Frank.'

'Cal first?'

'Always.' The smile broadened. 'A rich man's bed is warmer, eh?'

'Don't mock me, Pol. But you're welcome in my bed any time.'

'What about your mother?'

'Too fat for my taste. And my name's not Oedipus. I . . . I wrote you a letter, by the way.'

'I never got it.'

He smiled ruefully. 'You wouldn't. I hadn't the guts to post it. It was a bit Renaissance for my taste, Venus rising from the waves and all that kind of rubbish. I'm more inclined towards Impressionism.' He flexed the hand and grimaced. 'I've started my own little business. She doesn't know about it, but I'm dealing in junk with the odd antique thrown in by accident. Because when Mother Moo isn't with us any more, that's what I want to do.'

'Oh. Right. I'll just go and talk to Mother Moo, then.' She went.

'Exit stage left,' he muttered when the cafe door closed. His eyelids were heavy. As he dozed, he heard the screams of that child. They mingled with screams of his own echoing down the years; he'd been beaten, too. Suspended from school for a week, he had carried the great shame resulting from the kicking of a nun. Yes, he had kicked Sister Po-Face Paul, and she had deserved it. Being

whipped at all was horrible; being whipped when innocent was completely unacceptable.

His eyes flew open. The 'good' sister had disappeared
from the school by the time he returned. No one apolo-
gized to him when the true culprit was discovered,
because he was only a child, and children weren't people
back in 1935. Billy Blunt wasn't a person either, it seemed,
so had there been no improvement in twenty years? Billy
was a punchbag. Perhaps Eugene Brennan had run out
of whiskey; perhaps he'd needed the money stolen by the
child. Thou shalt contribute to the support of thy pastors?
That one hadn't come down the mountain with Moses; it
was the law of Rome. Why should a parish, especially one
as poor as St Columba's, give money to be spent on booze?

He looked round at the Kennedys' life. Heaven alone
knew when this place had last been decorated, and it was
a bit late in its life to start now. It was very brown and
dark green, so Victorian and depressing. She deserved
better; they both deserved better. Lois Monk and Greg
Johnson had disappeared faster than sand off a shiny
shovel when it became plain that Cal and Polly were
trapped by circumstances. Life was hard, and he needed
to speak to the police.

Polly returned. 'There's a bloody riot out there,' she
said breathlessly.

'Oh, God,' he replied. 'Oh, God, God, God.'

'No, God was one of the few who didn't turn up; must
have been eating His supper. But Fred Blunt's brother's
outside the Holy House with a gang. There's a plot on for
Sunday. Young Billy's not woken up. He threw some kind
of a dizzy fit and went unconscious. Johnny Blunt's organizing a protest, I think, while Fred and Mavis are in the
ozzy with their little lad. And you know Johnny. He's not
what you might call delicate when it comes to expressing
his feelings.'

Frank lowered his head and shook it thoughtfully. 'I'm going to the police,' he said.

'You'll stop where you are, mate. I've asked Pete Furness to call round when things quieten down a bit. He's doing his best, but he's outnumbered. He was blowing his whistle and waiting for reinforcements. But stop here, and he'll take your statement. Oh, he's not a Catholic, by the way.'

'You chose well, Polly.'

'There was no choice, because the poor lad was on his own. And your mother's horrible.' She found the sling and slipped his arm into it. 'With your hand raised, it should feel a bit better.'

'What did she say?'

'Who?'

'My mother – who else?'

'That she'd send a taxi for you. So I had to tell her you wanted to talk to the police because you'd seen a child beaten up. Then she went on about you being forced to deal with the dregs of society, and she couldn't wait for this area to be demolished.'

'And?'

She shrugged. 'I put the phone down. No way was I going to listen to that. Let's face it, she used to live not far from here, so who the hell does she think she is? Princess Margaret? Oh, and our Cal was mixed up with Johnny Blunt's lot, but he wouldn't let me push him home. What the hell have you started, Frank?'

'A fight for children's dignity,' he answered. 'It's time for some lawyers to start specializing in the defence of children. Kids have the same inborn rights as everybody else. Just because they're young and foolish, they get branded as criminal, and that turns them criminal. A beaten child becomes a poor parent. It has to stop. Somebody has to stand up for children's rights.'

She went to make a pot of tea. Frank hadn't been home, so she cooked bacon and egg for him at the same time. He'd had similar food this morning, but beggars couldn't be choosers.

She had to cut up the bacon, since he had just one hand, while the egg could go into a sandwich if she cooked the yolk right through. Having seen his vulnerability, she liked him all the more. How many inches away from loving him did she stand? Oh, she'd known the answer to that one for a while. But she warned herself at the same time, as any relationship between the two of them promised to be fiery.

He reminded her of herself, because once he developed strong feelings, he preached his gospel and entered killer mode. Frank had abandoned the Catholic faith. His attitude was that anyone who lived a decent life was a good enough person; if there was a heaven, nobody had an unfair advantage on account of a particular creed. He was probably right.

Clearly ravenous, he ate his egg sandwich while Polly fed him pieces of bacon each time he paused. She wiped bits of egg from his lips, realizing that these moments were becoming more intimate with every tick of the clock. The man was flawed, adorable and very, very human. She was feeding him as she might have fed a toddler.

'It's written in the stars in your eyes,' he said, feeling foolish after delivering the statement.

'Don't talk with your mouth full. Mother Moo would be so ashamed, she'd go green and buy a different son.'

'If I had both hands, you'd be in trouble.'

'Shut up and eat, because you've had a bad shock.'

Their eyes remained locked as he ate his way through her offerings. By the end of the strange repast, Polly was in no two minds. She couldn't win this one. Much as she needed to dedicate herself to the care of her twin, Frank

Charleson was going to be a major player in her life. It was written in the stars glistening in two pairs of eyes. 'It can't happen yet,' she whispered. 'It just can't.'

'I'll wait.'

'Until you've got both hands?'

'Until forever.'

'Quite the romantic, then?'

He nodded. 'Like my dad. I still look after his other half.'

'Your mam?'

'His lover. She's a sweet woman, lives in a ground-floor flat over in Walton. I make sure she's comfortable and fed, and we talk about him. Dad ignored my mother, and that was how he managed to keep his sanity. But she still succeeded in killing him with all her complaints and fads, so he mustn't have managed to ignore her completely.'

She wondered how Frank could live with that horrible woman.

He read her thoughts. 'She's my mother, Polly. Whatever she is, she gave me life, and she's a frightened and very stupid woman. I seldom so much as eat with her. As far as business goes, I have a free hand.' He grinned. 'Just the one free hand at the moment, but I could lose even that if I walked out of the house. She hangs on like a bulldog. Or is it bullbitch?'

'A kind of blackmail, then?'

'Oh, yes. Most women are manipulative, but she's special. Diabetic and eating herself to death, so I doubt she could manage the job of landlord now.'

Exhausted, Polly sat on the floor with her head in his lap. No words were required. In that split second, she gave herself to him as completely as if they had gone to bed together. He felt like home, smelled of soap with a slight whiff of tobacco, and he stroked her hair, played with the curls as if she were his child. This would be a good husband and father; he would do right by Cal, who remained at the forefront of her thoughts even now.

'Will you learn to love me, Polly?'

'No need.' She yawned. 'I'm already there. Been there for a while, but I didn't listen to myself. Well, I never listen to anybody, come to think about it. And Cal's always my main focus.'

Joy rendered him breathless for a few seconds. 'You're a good girl,' he finally achieved.

She chuckled quietly. 'We'll fight.'

'Oh, I know that. But let me make myself plain. Cal comes with us.'

'And your mam?' she asked sleepily.

'No bloody way.'

She relaxed. He teased rogue strands of hair from her forehead, looked down and smiled because her eyelashes touched her cheeks. This was trust at its most poignant and beautiful. Polly was here with him and for him. He could take on the Pope himself as long as she stayed by his side, and he would help her tackle Westminster if the Turnpike March happened.

She worked too damned hard. He hated knowing that she did seven hours a day in the cafe, followed by two or three more upstairs in the evenings. On Saturdays, the cafe was open all day, serving drinks and snacks, but no full meals, since Cal needed his rest. Sunday was her day off. On her day off, she cleaned the house from top to bottom, including Cal's kitchen and the cafe. Frank wanted to look after her, but he needed to bide his time until he could buy a place for all three of them.

'Don't stop,' she mumbled. She loved having her hair played with.

He remembered asking her why she'd called the proposed demonstration the Turnpike March, and she'd glared at him, a tray in one hand, an empty sugar bowl

48

in the other. 'Because Scotty used to have a turnpike on it where people paid to get to northern Lancashire. Don't you know anything? Then it became part of the road from London to Scotland. They changed horses here. The road got widened in the early eighteen hundreds.'

'I'll make a princess of you, Polly,' he said now. 'Sleeping Beauty.'

'Princesses don't swear.'

'Then you'll have to stop bloody swearing, won't you?'

'Hmm.' She dozed her way towards sleep.

He wished he could stay like this forever, with her head on his knees, the cap of silky curls in his fingers, the soft sound of her breathing a blessing to his ears.

But life would break in at any moment in the form of Constable Furness, a decent enough cop with a good nature and plenty of humour. That priest should be in jail. It wouldn't happen. A bishop would have a word with a cardinal, and Eugene Brennan's disappearing act would follow. After a few months in a monastery or some such institution, the swine would be sent to a parish far away from Liverpool. No one was allowed to pick the scabs off Catholic sores.

'I could tell she'd just written the card.' Christine Lewis polished off the last of her steak. 'That was good, thank you,' she said. 'No pudding for me, Elaine. Watching Mrs Charleson scoffing is a great appetite suppressant.'

'How?' Elaine asked.

'The table manners are sadly absent. She eats like a pig at a trough.'

'No, I mean how did you know she'd just written the card?'

Christine smiled broadly. 'I heard her jump up the minute I left the room; she can move when she needs to.

And the moths were still circling when she called me back in.'

'Moths?'

'From her purse. It creaks when she opens it.'

'Oh, Mother. Stop making me laugh, or I'll choke. So she wants her son to marry me? I have seen him, and he's handsome, but probably not my type.'

Christine took a sip of wine while her daughter ordered coffee. Elaine fitted in just about anywhere. She had grown up in a steady and loving home in a beautiful little village, had been quick to learn and good at studying, and was now a woman of the world. 'Do you think you'll marry?' Christine asked.

'Possibly. But I'll choose my own victim, thanks. I'll advertise for a sugar daddy with a weak heart, then choose the one who seems nearest to death.'

'You are a terrible girl.'

'And Mrs Charleson is a terrible woman. So her attitude changed the moment you told her I'm a lawyer?'

'Oh yes. Very impressed, though a little jealous. She has absolutely no idea when it comes to hiding her feelings. But I don't know how I'll cope if she continues nice. Something will happen very soon, perhaps a little dinner party for you, me, him and her. Just mark my words, because an extra birthday celebration for me is being arranged as we speak. If you're busy, she'll postpone it. She's made up her mind that Frank will marry someone useful, and she'll fire all guns till she gets her own way.'

'Mother, just say no.'

'She doesn't accept no.'

'Neither do I, and you have to live with me.'

They sipped their coffee and indulged in a couple of after-dinner mints.

'Right,' Christine said at last. 'Is it all right if I say you've met someone?'

'Not really, Mother. Haven't you always said that liars seldom thrive?'

'So?'

'So tell her you want your relationship to continue professional.'

It was Christine's turn to almost choke. 'Then she'll treat me very badly.'

'Leave.'

'I need a job.'

'We'll find you another one. You can't let her win.'

As Elaine drove homeward, they passed Brookside Cottage. 'Frank isn't home,' Christine commented. 'He never puts his car away in the garage. It's a bit late for him to be working, so she'll be worrying about the company he's keeping.'

'Oh, forget them, Mother. Happy birthday, no more parties, get a better job. Let's talk about something else, please.'

'There'll be murder done out yonder if I'm not mistaken.' Pete Furness placed his bobby's helmet on Polly's table. 'Were you there?' he asked her.

'No. Do you want me to leave you two alone?'

'Stay,' Frank begged.

'Nay, you're not frightened of me, Frank Charleson.' Pete had brought his inner Lancashire accent with him to Liverpool, and he'd hung on to it. 'But Polly can stop if you want. A cuppa would go down well, love. It was me against the world down at the Holy House. I've a tongue like the bottom of a birdcage, and it keeps sticking to the roof of me mouth. Holy House? Nowt holy about that pub tonight.' The Holy House was a pub about halfway between Polly's Parlour and St Anthony's. Men attending eleven o'clock Mass on a Sunday piled into the pub after worshipping in the church and paid their respects to ale before repairing homeward for Sunday dinner.

Polly went into the kitchen to make a brew. She listened while Frank spoke. From time to time Pete interrupted, since he was taking notes in his little hard-backed police book, but the eavesdropper heard most of what Frank said.

There had been several witnesses, folk just passing by, only he didn't know who they were. But a Miss Hulme, a Mrs Mannix and a Mr Cross, all teachers at the school, had seen what had happened. 'They'd stayed behind for a meeting. You can catch them at school tomorrow, I suppose. I've no idea where they live, but I brought them back here.' He paused. 'They may decide not to speak up against a priest.'

Pete sighed heavily enough to be heard by the listener in the next room. 'I know. Leave them to us. We can but try, but we're talking solid Catholic in these parts, as you well know.'

'Solid stupid,' was Frank's declared opinion.

'All right, lad. But you have to understand – it's knocked into them from birth, and the heavy stuff's crammed into their heads the minute they start school.'

Frank laughed cynically. 'You don't need to tell me, because I'm the one that got away. I went through all four Cs – catechism, confession, communion and confirmation. But the fifth C – Catholic – I am not. For me, that last word has a small C and it probably describes my taste in music, nothing more. But there's no prejudice in what I'm going to say. It will be nothing but true.'

'Aye, lad. Remember, I've known thee for a few years now.'

As the tale fell from Frank's lips, Polly found that her hands were curling so tightly that she was marking her

52

palms with her nails. The priest had whipped Billy behind his knees with a thin cane, thereby causing the boy to drop to the ground. Then he'd beaten him hard across the back before kicking him twice. Brennan was a large man; Billy was seven years of age and quite slender.

'He definitely kicked him?' the policeman asked.

'Twice, possibly three times. I was running fast, so I'm not sure about a third kick, but I'd swear in court to two kicks.'

'What then?'

'The bugger saw me running towards him, so he stopped hitting Billy and raised the cane to me. Thin canes hurt more, you know. When I was sent to fetch a cane – yes, we had the privilege of carrying the instrument of torture for the good, Christ-blessed people to use on us – I always chose the thicker one. It hurt, but it didn't whip through skin like the thin one did.'

'Hang on,' Pete said as he caught up in his notebook. 'Hey, it's not just Catholics that cane kids. I've had a few wallops in my state school.'

'Yes, but were they brides of Christ or shepherds to a special flock? No. They didn't pretend to be near to God, did they? All that praying and bobbing up and down means sod all, Pete. They're frustrated, sad bastards, and they take it out on those too little to fight back. Anyway, I grabbed his cane, broke it and smashed my right fist into his jaw. The three teachers pulled me away. And I speak from experience when I say Brennan's hard-faced. Because my hand feels wrecked.'

When Polly brought the tea in, Pete was shaking his head sadly.

'And poor little Billy lay there unconscious,' Frank was saying. 'He was picked up by a bloke, but I've no idea who he was. I gave the man ordained by the Church some advice on sex and travel.'

'The F word?'

'Too bloody right. And he effed off sharpish.'

Pete drank some tea before finishing his notes. 'Well,' he said. 'He'll be gone by weekend. That lot out there plan to invade Mass on Sunday and keep him shut inside. But the bishop will spirit him away. He'll go on retreat for a month, then he'll pop up somewhere else.' He took another mouthful of tea. 'Brennan's like a locum, isn't he?'

'Yes,' Polly said. 'Father Foley's on retreat. He doesn't kick kids.'

'Brennan hasn't got a parish of his own,' Frank added. 'And I reckon that's because they know he's a drunk who can't cope with folk. At his age, he should be settled in one place, but they protect him, you see. The Church protects the worst of all its sinners. As long as the money's in the plate, none of them gives a damn about kids.'

Peter Furness stood up and grabbed his helmet. 'I'm off duty, but I'll go and see the lad and his parents. You won't be driving with that hand, will you?'

'Not tonight, no.'

'Lend us your car, Frank. If it's owt to do with me, the bugger will be cautioned, charged and sleeping in a cell tonight.'

Frank smiled. 'Not afraid of hell then, Pete?'

'After working in these parts, hell should be a doddle for me. I'll bring your car back; give me an hour.'

When Pete had gone to join the vigil at Billy's bedside, Frank and Polly cuddled up on the sofa. They discussed what had happened, and reached the same conclusion. The faith was important to most who lived in these parts, but one vital thing rose above the Nicene Creed and all the sacraments. It was family.

'I reckon they'll go for him, Frank, if they get the chance. You know what they're like, shoot first and question the corpse later.'

'I hope they will, and I hope they get to do it legally. Eugene Brennan should be kept away from all children for the rest of his life. He should be unfrocked and stuck in a cage with other villains.'

She held his good hand. 'I'm proud of you, kid.'

'Give me a down payment, then. One kiss, and I'll buy you a ring.'

So it was signed and sealed with a kiss; they were engaged. But a cloud hung over the occasion; little Billy was hurt. And where the hell was Cal?

Three

It was the weirdest dream and it kept repeating itself, as if the reel needed changing at the cinema. It didn't make sense, because it went slowly, then quickly, like a very old cowboy movie from the silent era, as there was absolutely no sound to it. He couldn't touch anything, either, couldn't walk away or stand properly, because . . . because he'd been whipped behind his knees with a very thin, sharp cane before . . . before what? Something nasty had happened, and it was probably all his fault.

He'd done a bad thing, but couldn't remember what the sin was. His sums were all marked correct, and he was doing all right with his reading except for some very big words. His catechism was up to date, as was his map of the world with the British Empire coloured in pink. He hadn't been too bad in class, but he hadn't learned the stuff about the bad, fat king who'd killed Catholics.

A big, black dog dashed towards him. It was the size of a pony and it had a long, pink tongue that rippled every time it panted. But he wasn't afraid of dogs, so why was he running? Except he wasn't moving; his legs were trying to carry him out of danger, but they were merely marking time. The dog stood tall on its hind limbs. It had human fingers carrying a chalice that was blindingly bright each time the sun hit it. Billy was terrified when the animal's head faded away, leaving nothing in its place.

Above the nothing, there was a biretta. It was the ghost of a priest. Fat, bad king who killed his wives; fat, bad priest ...

All dreams were capable of turning daft, but this one was not funny. It was nasty and frightening for a seven-year-old who couldn't work out where he was. He screamed and yelled, yet no sound emerged from him. Silent screaming hurt, and there was dull pain in his chest, his stomach, his head, his limbs – and where was he and why couldn't he hear himself crying and shouting for help?

Suddenly, bright lights hurt through the lids of his closed eyes. When he opened them slightly, he found a masked man hovering over him. Were they robbing a bank? 'Hello, Billy,' the man behind the mask repeated. 'You with us, son? Give me a sign. All right?' Though almost closed, the eyes were mobile, indicating that the child was about to regain consciousness.

Residual anaesthesia overcame the patient once more, but the man called out till young Billy dragged himself halfway back to consciousness. The dog had become normal and it had stopped chasing and leaping about. Billy stroked its head, only he couldn't feel the fur, and someone was still calling him.

'Come on, now, young man. Show me that your brain's switched on. I shall be put away for talking to myself if you don't shape up a bit.'

Billy tried to reply, but his mouth didn't work, so he blinked instead.

'Good boy. Message received. We've mended you with a bit of glue and some drawing pins, a couple of paper clips and Auntie Dora's rusty old Singer sewing machine. That's a good little flicker of a smile. But we're going to keep you asleep for a while until you're feeling better.' There seemed to be no brain damage, and the surgeon expressed his satisfaction by releasing the boy into recovery. 'He's a fine specimen,' he told a nearby nurse. 'A tough breed, thank goodness.'

As he stripped off his scrubs and swilled specks of the boy's blood from his arms where gloves had failed to reach, the medic wished he could put these same hands round the throat of the person who'd hurt Billy Blunt, a slightly built child, seven years of age. There was no excuse for what had been done to the boy. A punctured lung plus haematomas created by blows from the foot of a grown man? It defied reason. Who the hell would inflict this sort of damage on a small boy? An ordained priest?

Billy, sedated, hovered in a place halfway between slumber and wakefulness. It wasn't a dream. Well, it was, but it wasn't. Where was Dusty Den Davenport? Dusty Den, the local rag and bone man, had rescued Billy from ... from what? Dusty was a favourite with children, because he gave away pennies, toy windmills and goldfish in exchange for rags. 'Rag-a-bone, donkey rubbing stone, a goldfish, a windmill to carry back home.' Soft, stupid song. Where was Mam? Where was Dad?

Billy dozed again. Columba's playground. The school behind him. He faced the playing field with the old air-raid shelter built for the war, a few trees near the railings. Someone behind him breathing heavily, too fat to run properly. Cane. A kick. The sound of his own bone breaking. Pain, so much pain. The priest, that ugly, nasty one, was trying to murder him. He couldn't breathe properly.

When he opened his eyes again, the bright lights had gone, and Mam and Dad were there. Money. He'd taken money to buy flowers for Mam's birthday, but he would have put it back by adding a bit of his spends to the collection plate at St Anthony's until the half-crown had been repaid. Yet he couldn't say any of it. Mam was crying. Dad was thumping the wall with a closed fist. Dad never did things like that. Dusty Den wasn't here. Sleep claimed Billy completely.

Fred stopped knocking hell out of walls; he was managing only to injure his hand, anyway. Pete Furness arrived with Johnny, who grabbed his big brother and hugged him before moving on to hold Mavis, his sister-in-law. 'He'll be all right, girl. We're a tough lot. What have they done for him?' Little Billy had blood going into one arm, clear fluid dripping into the other. It wasn't right, and his Uncle Johnny was hopping mad.

Mavis explained in fits and starts about a compound fracture of an arm, the bruising of a kidney, a rib piercing a lung, internal bleeding. 'And a priest did that,' she concluded. 'Put there to look after us, and he nearly killed my son. I don't understand it. What did Billy do that was so terrible? He's not a bad kid. I know he can be a bit cheeky, but this?'

The constable joined Fred. 'I understand that you weren't there. But I know some people who were present, so I'm taking statements. Any road, I think Father Eugene Brennan should spend the night in custody, if only for his own safety while we get to the bottom of things. Poor Billy.' He walked to the bed. 'Get well for your mam and dad, but mostly for yourself, me laddo.' He sniffed back some emotion. Policemen did not cry. Not for the first time, he wondered why the hell he was in the job. This was definitely the sharp, pointed edge of life, one child with life being dripped back into him, one priest with the biggest sin imaginable on his conscience, if he had a conscience.

'Den will speak up,' Fred promised. 'And have you talked to Frank Charleson? He's frightened of nobody.'

'I have spoken to him, yes.'

'Teachers? Dusty said there were three of them standing there.'

'Not yet, Fred. I'll have to see the sergeant first, but Brennan will be shifted to the cop shop, I'm sure, because they want his guts for garters out there. Even the kids are out of bed and looking for catapults and pea-shooters. Everton's moved in as well. I'm off duty, but I'll be called in again when I've taken Frank's car back. We've a job to keep folk rational when this kind of thing happens.'

Johnny stood next to his brother. 'Even the Proddies are after his hide, Fred. Everybody loves our Billy. There's no harm in the boy. People are baying for blood all over the neighbourhood.'

The policeman shook his head thoughtfully. 'You'd best not encourage folk to take the law into their own hands.'

Hot-blooded Johnny folded his arms. 'What are we supposed to do? Leave him where he is till the bishop shifts him a few hundred miles away to keep him safe? They don't want the bad publicity, you see. But he'll not get far tonight, because we've forty men surrounding the presbytery and a dozen inside keeping him trapped. So you go and arrest him. He'll be there. Brennan's going nowhere but the police station tonight, Pete.'

Pete Furness scratched his head. 'They won't attack him, will they?'

Johnny answered for everyone. 'Much as we'd like to kick seven shades of muck out of him, the answer's no. A prison sentence is what's needed. Let's see how he goes on living among his own kind. They'll sort him for us, cos actually most of them serving time aren't really his kind. Big difference between thieves and kiddy killers.'

'Nobody's going to die,' Mavis managed through quieter sobs.

'That's right, love.' Fred held her close. 'But it won't be for want of Brennan trying, the drunken old bugger.'

Constable Peter Furness left them to their vigil. He stood for a few minutes outside the hospital gates and pondered. Scotty was a largely Catholic area, but it was ready now to turn on one of its pastors. Roaders were a tough breed, stoic, humorous and usually kind, but if one vulnerable member of their society was injured, all were hurt. He stirred himself and climbed into the borrowed car. They had better not clout the bloody priest. In court, righteous anger would count for next to nothing.

Polly was forced to open the cafe. This had happened before in times of crisis, when what she termed the Mothers' Union turned up for a meeting. Kids got under everyone's feet as usual, yet the gathering of females was a necessity. Wives and mothers made most household decisions, and when husbands and older sons were out of reach, the activities of those missing menfolk merited as much concern as children's.

Polly produced a huge pot of tea and left it on the counter where the women could help themselves. Frank's contribution was to be put in charge of half a dozen youngsters in the middle room. He switched on Cal's television, and his charges were immediately riveted to the news. Television remained a novelty to most, so they were fascinated.

Meanwhile, Hattie Benson, greengrocer and spokeswoman separated from a brutal husband, was in full flood and off-topic, as ever. 'That dog's never chewed its food proper. Breathes it in, more like, which is what it did with me dad's teeth. I've been stuck down Maddox Street listening to folk planning on giving a dog an enema. Well, let's hope me dad's set does its job down there, cos the bloody hound never chews with its gob. Me dad's waiting on his choppers coming out the other end. Can you imagine using teeth what have come out of a dog's arse? Oh, I left them to it and came home.'

Polly called the impromptu meeting to order. 'Right, girls. Let Hattie's dog deal with her dad's falsies, because there's worse trouble on. Ida? I believe you know the score.'

Ida Pilkington, who was newspapers, sweets, tobacco and local gossip, stood up. 'There's about a dozen of our men in the priest's house with him, and the rest are outside singing – definitely not hymns. Anybody with kids out loose, go and find them, because the language down St Columba's is shocking.'

'Why singing?' Polly asked.

'To cover the noise of Father Brennan pleading for his life. Now it's a case of who gets there first. There's four police waiting for help, only there's been a big robbery down the builders' yard; the watchman got beat up. We've Evertonians lined up looking for the bishop, because a Catholic won't tell him to bugger off, but they will.'

'The bishop?' several whispered in near awe.

Ida nodded vigorously. 'The housekeeper phoned him before locking herself in the bathroom. She keeps screaming through the door, telling our lads the bishop's on his way. It's a great big stand-off. We can only wait and see what happens.'

Hattie, who appeared to have given up on her dad's dentures, spoke some words of warning. 'If the bishop gets there first, the men in the house will cripple Brennan. Because the bishop will make sure there's no case, no prison, so they'll batter him. I mean the queer feller, not the bishop. What can we do?'

'Nowt.' Pete Furness stood in the doorway. 'Stay out of it. Polly, tell Frank I still need his car. I'd best get round there and see what's what.' He left as suddenly as he had arrived.

Hattie carried on regardless. 'See, they're like kids. If you keep them in, they read their comics or their newspapers, eat their dinners, cut their toenails, behave themselves, cos they know we're watching. But when they go out to play, it's a different story. They're either fighting or drinking, sometimes both. Well, I'm not going down there, girls. I don't want nothing to do with police or bishops.'

There was little to be done, but at least they were together. These were the core of the Scotty Road mamas' mafia, and each drew comfort from company with the rest. The women in the cafe and others like them had carried generations through war, diphtheria, TB, and many births and deaths. Their wealth sat in no bank; it was here in toughened faces and gentle hearts. Mavis Blunt's lad had been attacked, so they fretted with and for her. 'This is what they'll take away,' Polly said. 'Us sitting here because we know the Blunts are sitting watching over Billy in a hospital bed. When they destroy our houses, we lose this strength.'

Mary Bartlett, the butcher's wife, came in. 'I've fetched your bacon, Pol. We've only just cleared up. Harry's gone down Columba's. I hope he stays out of trouble.' She placed a parcel on the counter. 'I hear Frank clobbered the bugger.'

'He did,' Polly replied. 'He's in the back with the rest of the kids.'

'I heard that,' he shouted.

Polly grinned. He was meant to have heard it. 'Hurt his hand, poor lad.'

Carla Moore, resplendent in blue, pink and yellow plastic curlers, fell in at the door. 'The Proddies have stopped the Bishop of Liverpool,' she gasped, fighting for breath. 'Shut in his car, he is. One of them ... I can't breathe ... I think he has a chip shop near St Columba's

... ooh, I'm winded. He said respect and all that, but a common criminal was under citizen's arrest ... Give us a cuppa, Pol.'

After a few noisy slurps, Carla carried on. 'So the bishop's in his car, and he can't do nothing. There must be fifty men down there outside the wotsname – presbytery. They're hanging on for the cops, but there's been a robbery somewhere, so Pete Furness is going to phone town for reinforcements. I just seen him. He said we've to stop here safe, like.' She sat down. 'And I've laddered me stocking.' This final incident clearly meant more than anything else to Carla. She would shop happily in the city centre in colourful curlers under a scarf of transparent nylon chiffon, but laddered stockings were a source of great shame.

'Hush.' Ida put a finger to her lips. 'Bells.'

'If they're for Brennan, they're hell's bells,' Hattie whispered.

Mary Bartlett, bringer of bacon, opened the cafe door and listened. 'Yes, the cavalry's on its way. If our lads and Everton's can hold the bishop back, Brennan will be spending his first night where he belongs.'

Knitting needles, crochet hooks and wool appeared while Polly went to make more tea. Communal gatherings like this one took place in times of trouble, and the cafe was chosen by all whose businesses were contained in what Frank termed the mile. With the exception of pubs, Polly's Parlour had the most chairs, so she had no competition, but she was only too delighted to be their place of safety. For how long would this cafe continue to be their refuge?

She found Frank and his companions playing dominoes at the table. He would make a lovely dad.

'They cheat,' he said as she passed through to the kitchen.

'Course they do,' was her answer. 'It's all part of their culture.'

Pete Furness followed her. 'We got him, Polly. Hi, Frank, and hello, kids.' He placed the keys to Frank's car on the sideboard. 'Thanks for the car, pal. Little Billy Blunt has internal bleeding, a punctured lung and compound fractures to one arm. They're keeping him asleep for a while, but he'll have to sit up soon for his chest's sake.'

'How was Brennan?' Frank wanted to know.

'Crying like a baby.' Pete struggled not to laugh. 'They gave him a guard of honour, all standing to attention and saluting as he passed. Now, they've gone down Everton way with their new Orange mates. I'll never fathom folk round here.'

'Foreign parts for you,' Polly told him. 'Took you three years to understand the language. Are you having a cup of tea?'

'No, I'm going to run and be there when he's charged.'

Frank told him to keep the car till morning.

'Thanks.' The good constable retrieved the keys and rushed off to watch while the wheels of justice began to turn. As he passed once more through the knitting circle, he was bombarded with questions, though nothing was going to stop him, because he'd visited Billy. For Billy's sake and for the Blunt family's peace of mind, Pete wanted to see Brennan in front of the magistrates tomorrow morning. Sometimes, being a copper was OK.

Cal was drunk and snoring, the resulting noise reminiscent of the trumpeting of a rogue elephant. His attendant had been and put him to bed, which had proved a difficult task, since Cal had made very little sense after an unusual amount of alcohol. The poor lad still needed nappies during the night, as he couldn't always manage to reach the commode by himself during the hours of darkness, though he had regained some daytime control. Frank was failing to settle on the sofa. There was too much noise from the man in the bed, and Polly was just above their heads in the rear bedroom.

He wanted her. But he was determined to be patient, so he urged himself repeatedly to remain strong. After dragging sheet and blanket round his ears, he reminded himself to be thankful. Mavis and Fred Blunt were the ones in real trouble, with their youngest child in hospital.

His hand hurt. Again, he concentrated on the little lad with his broken arm and rib, because an injured hand was nothing in comparison. She was so near. He longed to feel her breath on his cheek, her hair under his good hand. But it was going to be a difficult night, and he must grin and bear it. He might manage to bear it, though grinning might well prove to be impossible.

Cal's snoring had started to deliver a different sound; he was making as much noise as a ship moored in dock on New Year's Eve. Sleep promised to be impossible to achieve, so Frank counted his blessings. Polly came top; his mother was not on the list.

There was no peace to be had down at the local police station, either. Father Brennan screamed constantly for whiskey, brandy – anything to combat the pain in his face. He was given tea and aspirin, which he threw at the wall while using language seldom heard from a man whose life was supposedly dedicated to the betterment of mankind through belief in Christ.

Pete Furness hung on, though there was no overtime to be had. He found himself fascinated by the concept of an evil priest who went through life drunk, disorderly and dangerous. The visiting bishop had managed to quieten Brennan in his cell, but the old drunkard had kicked off again once the primate had left the building. 'I want a decent drink,' he yelled repeatedly. 'Get me some whiskey.'

The desk sergeant, a burly Scouser called Mike Stoneway, found himself longing for retirement, a nice bungalow in Fleetwood, a bit of sea-fishing and little picnics with the wife and Toby, their Jack Russell. 'If he doesn't pipe down in there, I'll kill him. I've a nice big pair of scissors in my desk.'

Pete finished yet another mug of tea; if he drank much more, he'd drown in it. 'He's not worth hanging for, Sarge.'

'He should swing. He only got away with it on a technicality. If Den hadn't rescued him, that little lad would have bled to death. And as for Frank Charleson, the man deserves a medal.'

Pete made no reply. He nursed the suspicion that Frank had his reward in Polly, because he'd noticed little glances, a flush along her cheekbones, hope in his eyes. God, the cleric was making a hell of a din. Another man on remand until morning was clearly being driven mad by the noisy priest. He was threatening to sue the police force and the Vatican, because he'd paid his taxes and put money in the Sunday plate for years.

'Shut up, Paddy,' the sergeant yelled. 'Whatever you paid, you'd stolen it. Father, be quiet or I'll get a doctor to sedate you, then we can all enjoy a bit of hush.'

A few minutes of total silence ensued. 'Go home, Pete. You've been on duty for about ten hours. We'll manage. Your wife'll be thinking you've left home, lad. But thanks for hanging on. You're a born copper, believe me.'

Brennan kicked off yet again, this time murdering the *Tantum Ergo* and the *O Salutaris Hostia*. He was clearly performing Benediction, though he had no bread to bless and was definitely without wine. He needed a bloody good hiding and yes, Pete had endured enough. 'Good luck, Sarge.'

The constable left his bike at the station and prepared to drive home in Frank's car. He remained uneasy; it wasn't over yet. As far as he knew, no Liverpool priest had ever stood in the dock at the Crown Court. Because of the severity of the attack on young Billy, Brennan had been charged with inflicting grievous bodily harm on a child, so tomorrow's magistrates would have no choice: the case would have to be passed on for judge and jury.

It wasn't going to happen. This near-knowledge sat in his stomach like lead settling in a pit already filled by tea. Lead didn't float; neither would the case against Brennan. Pete's much-loved territory, Scotland Road, would be up in arms. And he could only agree with them. 'Life's a bugger, then you die,' he informed Frank's dashboard. He started the car and drove home.

Norma Charleson gave up trying to read. Surrounded by magazines and snacking on sweets and chocolates, she lay in her bed and pondered her situation. Having relinquished most of her house for her son's sake, as she saw it, she was reaping no reward, because he was currently in the bed of his dead wife's friend, Polly Kennedy.

She remembered Polly. Polly was a pretty little thing; Ellen had been Frank's second choice. Norma had not known that before she saw the letter, a letter she was not supposed to have read. Underneath the elaborate apology for happening upon the girl when she was naked, Frank had written his truth: he had loved Ellen, but Polly was and always had been the fulcrum of his existence. What was a fulcrum? The trouble with sending a son to a fee-paying school for a couple of years was that he knew too many words.

He wouldn't be satisfied just by sexual favours. The stupid boy was head over heels yet again with a woman who was wrong for him. Older now, he should know better, yet he still followed his heart. Why did the male of the species have so little sense? A woman weighed things up better, mixed a bit of thought into the ingredients.

She longed for sleep. 'Charlie, if you'd gone two or three years earlier, I wouldn't be in this mess.' She spat out a Turkish delight and wrapped it in paper. Turkish delight and caramels were the only chocolates she disliked. To cover the unpleasant taste, she turned to strawberry creams.

The girl lived with a disabled brother behind a very primitive cafe on the mile. Along that stretch, the Charlesons owned most of the commercial properties, many of which had residential facilities behind and above the shops. The buildings had been cheap, and there would be some compensation due to owners from Liverpool Corporation when demolition became due.

Polly's Parlour was the name of the establishment. The eating parlour was at ground level, while the hairdressing salon was above in the front bedroom. The girl had a good business head and was willing to work hard. 'But I don't want you managing my affairs or my son, Miss Kennedy. You should have married Greg. If you'd married Greg ...' If, if, if. That was a huge word. If Charlie had died earlier, if the girl had wed her intended ...

Norma's heart started leaping about again. That bloody stupid doctor had probably over-prescribed on the thyroid medication. It was a delicate balance, and she was her own worst enemy. With chocolate, cake and biscuits as her only pleasures, she knew she was digging her own grave with her teeth. Should she go on a diet, shed a few stone and take back the reins? Better still, she and Frank could share the business, as long as she managed the Scotland Road side of things.

The decision seemed to make itself. She found herself outside in the rear garden, a brand new security light flooding the area where the dustbins lived. To prevent herself from returning, she emptied remaining confectionery into the rubbish unwrapped and unboxed; this way, she would not be tempted to retrieve the objects of her desire. Norma intended to save her life and Frank's. He would be introduced to Elaine Lewis, and there would be a lawyer in the family. A maker of breakfasts and lunches – the latter termed dinners along the mile – would not hold a candle to such a well-educated and high-earning young woman with prospects.

Surely Frank would see the sense in her plan? Elaine could well save the firm thousands over the years. And Frank was a man of substance, since he would inherit the business and the house when his mother died. But she needed to live for a while yet. Fifty-two was no age these days. All she needed to do was lose weight, take a bit of exercise and remove some of Frank's freedom. She could and would manage it. Lying around here all day was a waste of life.

Yes, it was time for the captain to steer the good ship Charleson once more. She refused to allow Frank to enter a second Scotland Road marriage. Her sweet tooth would ache, but that was the least of her problems. Wasn't it? If she had the courage ... Why couldn't she harbour that thought? If she had the courage, Polly Kennedy might suffer a fatal accident, and then ... 'Shut up, Norma,' she ordered. She was not a killer. But she knew people who might just step up to the mark. 'Stop it,' she snapped. 'Out of the question.'

*

Polly crept downstairs. The aged treads creaked a lot, and she was afraid of waking poor Frank, though she harboured little concern for her brother. After a particularly heavy night of drinking, he would sleep like a log until morning, at which point he would wake with a headache the whole world might well hear about. When drunk, Cal was a noisy sleeper; sometimes, she wondered how the house managed to remain standing with her twin rattling its old, fragile walls and windows.

Frank was, of course, wide awake. Cal's snores bounced round the room like dried peas in a tin can. 'Hello, babe,' Frank whispered during a quieter moment. 'Your brother's a noisy bugger.'

'You can talk in a normal voice,' she told him, 'because our Cal won't wake till the booze is out of him.' She thanked goodness for the rubber sheet on the mattress, because there'd be enough washing in the morning without having to worry about the bed itself. She knelt on the floor next to the sofa.

'Are we engaged?' he asked, touching her hair with his good hand.

'I suppose so. But I've come to tell you a secret.'

'Oh, yes?'

'He's on painkillers. He can feel pain in his legs, Frank. I'm going to hospital with him on Thursday afternoon.'

'Does it mean he's going to walk again?' Frank asked.

'There's a chance. I've never seen anyone grateful for pain till now. Pain means his nerves have found a way to his brain. It's unusual, but not unheard of. Any progress has to be slow, because damage could be done, so I want to be there, then they can tell me what to do and what to expect. He'll win no races, but we may be able to wave goodbye to bedsores.'

'That's great, love. Give us a kiss to celebrate.'

She kissed him. He was lovely. 'How's your hand?'

'Sore. But not as sore as poor Billy.'

'I know, love. Cup of cocoa?'

'Yes, please.'

He lay there listening to the normality of domestic sounds, a pan being set on the hob, cups and spoons clattering, Cal snoring like a tranquillized dinosaur, a cocoa tin opening. Mother would go mad, though that would be a short journey for her. She hadn't approved of Ellen, and she would hate Polly, because Polly was cheeky. If only Mother could remarry, he might be free. But who would want her? He thought about advertising her in the *Echo*. No. He wouldn't have the slightest idea when it came to description. *Free to good home, one almost house-trained female, buyer to collect*? Hardly.

Polly carried in two mugs of cocoa. 'Might help you sleep, though I doubt it. He's a noisy swine when he's drunk. And by the way, remember what I told you is a secret. If he doesn't walk again, he'll feel like a failure.'

'I won't forget. Are we engaged, by the way?' he asked again.

'I believe we are, though we can't set a date. My brother will give me away, and not from a wheelchair, I hope.'

'So I have to buy you a ring.'

She stirred her cocoa. 'Depends.'

'On what?'

It was a delicate subject, but she pursued it. 'Ellen,' she said. 'When she died, did you bury the ring with her?'

'She still has her wedding ring, but not the engagement one.'

'You have that?'

'Yes.' His mother had tried to acquire it, though it wouldn't fit even the smallest of her podgy fingers. He swallowed some cocoa and, in spite of Cal's snoring, wished he could stay here forever. Here was normal. In spite of the wheelchair and noise, this was the place for Frank.

Polly swallowed. 'Ellie was my best friend all her life, Frank. It would make her part of us. She'll always be part of us, whatever happens, but I'd love to wear her ring. But if it makes you sad, we'll get a new one.'

He pondered. 'She'd want you to have it, I'm sure.'

'Yes, she would.'

'I can afford something a bit better now, Polly.'

'There is nothing better. Ellie was like a sister to me.' She lit a night light on the mantelpiece.

'Take me upstairs and have your wicked way with me,' he begged.

'What about your hand?'

He thought about that. 'We can leave it down here and I'll pick it up in the morning.'

'OK. But I won't have my wicked way, and neither will you. I'm only rescuing you from my noisy brother. Also, I don't want a baby just yet, so behave yourself or I'll come downstairs and squeeze your hand.' She glanced at her brother. 'In fact, I'll use it to strangle him if he doesn't shut up.'

They spent a giddy hour in the bed that had once belonged to Polly and Cal's parents. There was giggling and kissing and sighing, and his hand hurt every time he moved it. He accused her of taking advantage of his injury, of being a torment and a witch, then he fell asleep like a dropped stone.

'Charming,' she whispered. 'You go out of your way to help the afflicted, and they sleep. I don't know why I bother.' She was lying. She knew full well why she bothered. Frank was handsome, generous, genuine and daft. The daft part was vital. He mumbled in his sleep. Even when unconscious, he could find something to almost say.

'Moo,' she whispered.

'Shut up.' Well, that had been clear enough.

She found herself praying for Cal's recovery, and not just for his sake. Yes, she needed her freedom, wanted Frank, wanted his babies. But Frank had promised to take care of Cal, and Frank always stood by his word. So she fell asleep in the one good arm of the man she cherished.

'Don't cry, love. Eat your butty – our Johnny's Kathleen made them special.'

But Mavis couldn't take her eyes off Billy. He was her youngest, therefore her smallest, but he looked tinier than ever in the hospital bed. The tubes frightened her, too. It wasn't easy sitting here watching while blood and other stuff dripped into his little arms. He'd been playing out, for God's sake. And he wasn't a bad lad, wasn't a fighter. There was mischief in him, yes, but nothing really bad, nothing that made him deserving of such a beating. 'Fred?'

'Yes, love?'

'That priest's committed a mortal sin.'

'He has.'

'So if he died tonight, he'd go to hell.'

'He would, damn him.'

'So there are bad priests?'

Fred nodded. 'There's bad everything, Mavis. There's nuns in Ireland that have locked up young girls who had babies out of wedlock. They got the babies adopted and labelled the young women insane so they could keep them in there for life. They grow old, them poor girls, with next to no skin on their hands, cos they run a laundry service six days a week. If they don't shape, they get whipped. And the bloody nuns keep what people pay for their laundry to be boiled and ironed.'

Mavis turned in her chair. 'Are you sure?'

'As sure as I can be without crossing the water and seeing for myself.'

She looked down at the rosary in her hands. Nothing made sense.

'Eat something,' Fred urged.

'Our Billy doesn't even go to that school. He's at St Anthony's.'

'I know, but he has mates at Columba's, Mave.'

'What have you been up to, lad?' She leaned over the child.

'Eat,' Fred ordered yet again.

She obeyed, though swallowing wasn't easy. The decision she made took little effort, though. At two o'clock in the morning, Mavis Blunt ceased to be a Catholic. She didn't announce or discuss it, didn't even turn it over in her mind. There was no perfect faith, and there were no perfect people. And the potted meat sandwiches were stale.

Many people suffered a sleepless night for a variety of reasons.

In Little Crosby, where the houses were small and steeped in history, Christine Lewis stared through her window at a moonlit scene where roses grew round doors and ivy clung to walls, and buildings of thick stone protected inhabitants from all weathers. So deep was the recess containing her bedroom window, she had made a window seat, and there she lingered, looking at the sun's light reflected in silver tones on Earth's single satellite, which, in its turn, bounced white light onto the planet.

It wasn't that she liked Norma Charleson, it was just ... it was just that she knew the job well and it was near home. Also, she had to allow that Frank was a lovely, gentle man who would make a wonderful husband for someone. Elaine found lawyers very dull and self-obsessed. They fought cases not for the clients, but in order to chalk up their scores and compare wins and losses with those of their fellows.

Elaine didn't really want a lawyer. Mrs Charleson's unspoken idea made a great deal of sense. Frank was a businessman with a decent level of education. He was a good conversationalist and a thoroughly admirable human being. If Elaine came to know him, if she could just be persuaded to spend some time with him, she might arrive at her senses. Yes, it was a reasonable plan. She shouldn't have mentioned her suspicions to Elaine ...

She closed her curtains and returned to bed, her brain still alert. The way Norma Charleson ate meant that her life might well be shortened. Christine imagined herself in the annexe with Elaine and Frank occupying the main part of the cottage. Oh, this was a terrible way to think. Really, all she wanted was Elaine's happiness. She needed little for herself ... well, not much, anyway.

Meanwhile, in the next bedroom, Elaine was dreaming. A man was making love to her. When she looked up into his face, he was Frank Charleson. Her eyes opened suddenly. Not her type? Who was she trying to kid? Bugger it, she had to go to work in a few hours. She fell asleep within minutes, but the dream resumed ...

Billy woke. Mam and Dad were dozing in two chairs. The backs and seats were padded, but they had wooden arms. His own arms weren't comfortable, and one was worse than the other. Clear fluid dripped into one tube, bright blood into a second. Breathing hurt a bit. The bank robber in the mask had gone. Except he wasn't a bank robber, he was a doctor, one of those who cut people open and stitched them up again with somebody's old sewing machine. That had been a joke, of course.

The light was poor, but he wouldn't complain about

that, because illumination in the bank robber's lair had been cruel and painful. His mouth was dry. He didn't want to wake his parents. There was no way of working out how long they'd been here; Billy and time had parted company. It was 1955, though the month, the date and the day remained a mystery. He was seven years old, it was summer, and a priest had kicked him.

Half a crown. All this for half a crown. He should have saved his spends, but hadn't been able to resist that Dinky fire engine. The money would have been returned to the church, although to St Anthony's rather than St Columba's. A lot of Columba's people went to a different parish whenever Father Brennan filled in for Father Foley. No one liked Father Brennan.

Mam's arm slipped off her chair and she woke with a start. She shook Dad. 'He's awake, love.'

They arrived at the bedside. 'Hello, Billy,' Fred whispered.

'Drink,' the child begged.

Mavis dashed off to get the night sister, who brought ice. 'Just suck on that while your mother holds it,' the blue-clad woman ordered. 'You can have a proper drink soon, when we know you're not going to vomit. We don't want you undoing all our good work.' She turned to the parents. 'He's got through with no new bleeds. Keep him as still as you can. Go home when it gets light and send somebody else to visit while you get a few hours in a proper bed.' She took Billy's temperature and pulse, declaring herself satisfied with both.

Mavis and Fred tried asking Billy what had happened. He couldn't answer, as his throat was as dry as sandpaper. But he fell asleep with a smile on his face, because Mam and Dad were here. He loved his mam and dad. Inside the dream, which was now clear of black dogs and ghosts, he grew to manhood. It was still a bit cowboyish, though,

77

because he held a gun. The gun had a purpose. The purpose was born of anger. The anger was directed at evil, and evil had a name. Brennan.

Sergeant Mike Stoneway was filling in the night sheets. These were notes listing all that had happened so far during this endless shift. Just two rooms in the hotel housed visitors tonight. Paddy Lundy was in number four, while Father Eugene Brennan was in number one. It wasn't exactly the Ritz, and they weren't exactly paying guests unless loss of freedom might be considered payment.

He wrote, *4 a.m. Lundy is sleeping it off after a long period of disturbance from Brennan in Cell One. Both checked every twenty minutes by myself or Constable Jones. Lundy is on his bunk. Brennan is on the floor in a pool of urine, but I am not inclined to disturb him, because he has been loud and verbally abusive on and off since his arrival.*

He chewed the end of his pen before continuing. 'I'll need three days' sleep after this lot,' he said aloud.

I believe he has the DTs, since he has been screaming at things crawling on walls. These things are purple with twelve legs, though in my opinion he is in no state to be counting as far as twelve. At the moment, he is quiet, but I'm worried about alcohol poisoning and have sent for Dr Warmisham, our duty medic for this shift.

He threw down his pen. Like most other people in the area, he nursed a strong dislike for the priest. Anyone who kicked a child was at the bottom of the list when it came to grading folk. However, this all had to be done correctly, because if the man died through inhaling his own puke, questions would be asked.

But when the main door to the station opened, Dr Warmisham was not to be seen. Instead, two men in pinstripe suits entered the reception area. They introduced themselves as Drs Thornton and Moorcroft before the former placed a piece of paper on the counter. 'Father Brennan is to be released into our care,' he explained. 'He needs to be supervised and medicated. If he has too swift a withdrawal from alcohol, he might die.'

Sergeant Stoneway stood his ground. 'He almost killed a child by whipping and kicking. I don't care if he's suffering from terminal cancer, he should still face court.'

'And that,' said Thornton, pointing at the paper, 'is a court order releasing him into our care at Prestwich Mental Hospital. The drinking is merely a symptom of a psychiatric disorder.'

Mike Stoneway remained unimpressed. 'So you clowns will diagnose him insane, then let him loose in society so that he could put a child on an operating table? What sort of bloody doctors are you? I'll tell you what you are – no need to answer. You're bought and paid for by the diocese.' He beat a closed fist on the counter. 'Now, you just listen to me, Dr Psycho and Dr Crackers, if it wasn't for this uniform I'd lay you both out on the floor and give you some of what Brennan gave young Billy Blunt.'

'A threat,' said Thornton smoothly.

'Noted,' was the reply from Moorcroft.

'And you can tell whichever of the bishop's minions sent you here that I don't believe a word. Why would you allow a nutcase loose on children? Eh?'

'He has deteriorated. We thought his condition was under control, but drinking has probably interfered with his medication.'

'Drinking is his bloody medication.' Mike didn't care any more. He was retiring in six months, and was quite prepared to go earlier if necessary. 'I know who and what you are. I'm telling you now that if you take that creepy priest away, Scotland Road and some of Everton will rise up tomorrow. There'll be a crowd at court in the morning, because they want to see him ordered to face a judge and jury. Have him when we've finished with him.'

Thornton folded his arms. 'Read the order,' he snapped.

'I don't need to. It's from a corrupt see, and you are part of that see, as is the judge that signed your Mickey Mouse so-called order.'

The two intruders glanced at each other. 'We are from Manchester, actually,' Thornton said. 'So you're saying that bishops are corrupt?'

The sergeant grinned. 'Think higher.'

'Cardinals?'

'And the rest. Things are coming to light here, in Ireland and even as far away as Australia. Children who were abused are growing up and speaking out. Their words will dig the graves of many crooks, and you are two of their number. Have you any idea of what you're doing? Do you know Liverpool? This is a Catholic area, but they want to see him jailed.'

Moorcroft waded in. 'I'm sure you and your fellows will manage the populace.'

Dr Warmisham entered. He looked dishevelled and heated to somewhere in the region of gas mark nine. 'Sorry, Mike. I've been delivering a baby.' He stopped in his tracks. 'Ah, excuse me, I didn't mean to interrupt. Just lead me to the patient.'

'He's in the first cell lying in his own piss,' Mike told him. 'Leave him. These ... gentlemen have come to take him away. I'm sure they're handy with a mop.'

Thornton muttered under his breath. Mops were not his province.

Mark Warmisham sank onto a bench. 'Blood and sand, he's getting away, isn't he? This is what we dreaded. I think I'll emigrate.'

'And I'll retire,' Mike said. 'We've got the bungalow, just

a lick of paint needed. Jones?' he called. 'Why can I never find him when I need him?'

Jones came in through the front door.

'Where've you–?' Mike didn't get any further; for a few terrible seconds, Sergeant Mike Stoneway felt like kissing his second-in-command. Jonesy, a nice, quiet, Welsh copper, wasn't alone. Behind him stumbled residents from the mile, women in curlers, hairnets, nightdresses with coats dragged over the top to save a little dignity, eyes screwed up against the light. The men were tousle-headed, half-dressed and still drunk with sleep or from an evening spent on the ale. Several were barefoot, while a few had left teeth soaking at home in jam jars.

'The people have spoken, and they don't need words,' Mike advised the psychiatrists. He picked up the court order. 'Show that to the magistrates in the morning, then try getting Brennan past this lot. This is Scotland Road. Take that name to the grave with you as soon as you like. Jonesy, man the desk. I'm going to phone Prestwich, see if they've heard of these two so-called doctors.'

'Our attachment to Prestwich is temporary,' gabbled Moorcroft.

Billy's Uncle Johnny stepped forward. 'Your attachment to your breath will be the same if you don't bugger off smartish.'

The two unwanted visitors fled.

Mike Stoneway shook his head. 'Right. Get home, you lot, because you look as if you need beauty sleep. Thanks for coming, I think. I say I think, because I might just have lost my job, and I'm trying hard to care. Jonesy, we're going to lock down. I know we're not supposed to, but we must. He'll be remanded tomorrow or I'll eat every helmet in the force.'

A round of applause followed his statement.

'Get out,' he laughed. 'Go on, bugger off home. You look like you fell off a moonlight flitting.'

When all had left, the two men locked all exterior doors. Mike, knowing he had probably broken the law by refusing to accept a court order, concentrated on his Fleetwood bungalow. The wife wanted a buttercup yellow front door. He hated yellow.

Four

The night seemed to last about a year, though it ended eventually. Mike Stoneway signed out for himself and Constable Jones, who had risen considerably in Mike's estimation. 'Thanks for mopping up the pee, lad. Shame about his clothes. The poor gentleman will have to appear in court stinking of dried urine. Still, your brainwave worked well. Thank goodness you had the sense to wake the troops. Tell you what, I'll treat you to breakfast in Polly's, eh? And make sure you get the sergeants' exam done. You're a natural.'

'Thanks, Sarge. A bit of toast and some strong coffee would be appreciated before court.'

Scotland Road looked different this morning. Notices in shop windows announced their owners' intention to close for an hour at ten o'clock, because everyone would be going to the magistrates' court. Men who normally wore overalls were suited and booted; some had grabbed the morning off with permission, others were taking a chance. They wanted to see the man who had whipped and kicked little Billy Blunt.

Women were working the early shift. Several with prams piled high with washing were already on their way back from the public washhouse. As the two policemen walked down the main road, they glanced down side streets and saw many female heads bobbing about in doorways; steps were being scrubbed and stoned early today, because this was a special occasion, though not for a good reason. It was no holiday. If poor Billy didn't make it, the whole area would be bereaved and Brennan should hang.

Jonesy spoke up. 'They're good people, aren't they, Sarge?'

Mike nodded. 'The best. In fifteen years or so, this place will be derelict, and that's as good a reason as any for me to retire. Man and boy, I've worked here. It's been special, but not for much longer.' They entered the cafe to a round of applause and a free breakfast. 'See?' Mike whispered to his companion. 'See what I mean?'

'I do, Sarge. Decent people.' They sat and ate with the rest. Mike gazed round at the good, the bad and those who fell somewhere between the two categories. By God, he would miss every one of them.

She stood over him. 'Oi. You with the hand and the inter-esting attitude. Open your eyes and face the world before I tip this lot over you. I've fetched your breakfast up the stairs, and you'll have to leave this place the back way, or people will think I'm working part time for Mother Bailey. I don't want my reputation getting any worse than it already is.' She placed the plate on a bedside table. 'Come on, wakey-wakey.'

He turned over and dragged a sheet over his head. 'Go away. Cruelty to a dumb animal, this is. Go and mither some other poor soul.'

'It'll be tomorrow if you don't shift. There's stuff to be done, Frank.'

'Oh, God.'

'He's not in. It's only me, the woman you spent the night with. Sit up immediately, if not sooner.'

Frank, whose hair was doing a fair imitation of a burst cushion, dragged himself up. He glanced at his breakfast and did a quick double-take at the monumental pile. 'What on earth is that supposed to be? I've heard of these high-rise flats, but—'

'It's a full English on butties.' She pointed to the large server plate heaped high with sandwiches. 'This was what you asked for when you had a meeting, and you've got a meeting this morning, so I used common sense and a butter knife.'

'Where's the meeting?'

'Magistrates' court. Sergeant Stoneway had a load of people down the cop shop in the night, got them dragged out of their beds cos two blokes came to take Brennan away. They said they were from Prestwich Mental Hospital, but they weren't. They are psychiatrists, though, but from Jersey, so he can prove they were lying. It means he can work a bit longer towards his pension. They had a court order, and he disobeyed it, but he's OK, cos they were telling lies, see.'

See? See? He could scarcely see at all. Frank was not a morning person. He was one of those annoying types who come to life at midnight and keep you awake by spouting politics and religion, plus his speciality: the rights of children and the elderly in society. 'Do I know you?' he asked. 'Have we been introduced?'

'I should bloody well hope so. That left hand of yours can shift, I'm telling you. My name's Dorothy. I'm Dorothy Kennedy, spinster of the parish of St Anthony, Scotland Road, Liverpool.'

'Eh?'

'I was baptized Dorothy Joan, shortened to Dolly. I didn't like Dolly, so I kept the olly, dropped the D and put a P on it when I was five.'

'You peed on it when you were five?'

She smiled sweetly.

'You peed on your name?'

'I did. Speaking of which, there's a bucket of tea for you on the windowsill, the biggest mug I could find – it holds just over a pint, but I think I spilled some. Now shape. I've cancelled the second breakfast sitting downstairs, but I need to be back for dinners, and so does Cal. See you in court.'

Alone, he opened the first sandwich. Two plump pork sausages placed in a V sign were the sitting tenants. On the other side of the gigantic plate, a single open slice was covered by a fried egg with eyes, nose and mouth in brown sauce turning the yolk into a face. She was a little devil. I LOVE YOU in small strips of streaky bacon travelled round the edge of the platter. The letters were square-ish, but their meaning was clear. She was a little angel.

He didn't want to go home; he wanted to stay here. Daft breakfasts, lack of space, poor Cal, loud neighbours – all these served to make him feel alive. As for Polly . . . He grinned. Polly was perfect. She was playful, quick-witted, hardworking and a sight for sore eyes.

His right hand was a lot better. But if he pretended it wasn't, he might stay again tonight, get Cal drunk and snoring, come back to this very bed and show her who was boss. He stopped chewing for a moment. There was absolutely no question about who was boss. She was, and always would be. Ellen had been in charge just occasionally, God bless her.

He ate a bit of bacon. There could be no doubt about Scotland Road women; they knew how to teach a man his place and keep him there. Exceptions existed, of course, but the general rule was *Don't tell the wife how much I've had to drink, she'll kill me. Don't tell her I put that quid on a horse* and *Remember, I was with you playing cards for matchsticks.* Frank liked strong women. The concept of getting past a strong woman was exciting. Would he get past her or would he die trying? She had a wisdom that went far beyond the reach of academia; soaked into her bones were at least two generations of Scotland Road life preceded by centuries of old Ireland.

He was in love. He'd been in love for a while, but now that the feeling was reciprocated, he hovered on the brink of delirium. Mother would throw a fit, but that couldn't be allowed to matter. If she disowned him, he had plans of his own. And yes, he was going to court. It would be a short session, just the accused's name and address, the charge, and the magistrates' decision that the case needed to go up to the Crown Court. Although this was all a formality, dozens would squeeze in just to hear the words when the charge was read out.

The chances of a case against a priest reaching the Crown Court were minimal. But Frank had contacted local presses, who would pass the information on to nationals. Brennan's character would be mud by tomorrow, and his employers would come under close scrutiny. And it was all deserved. The Church needed to sing for its supper, in Latin if necessary.

In the bathroom he found some of Cal's old shaving equipment, and he did his best, though the process left him looking rather swarthy and interesting. Wearing yesterday's shirt didn't bother him, though he drew the line at underpants. None of Cal's clothes were up here; they were currently housed in built-in cupboards at each side of the fireplace downstairs. Right. What to do now?

He raided his fiancée's drawers and went through her drawers. She had some nice ones, lacy and silky (several with matching bras), but he opted for white cotton with a double gusset. Discovering that women were a shape completely different from males caused little surprise. The waist pinched, as did the top of the legs parts, but at hip level he had material to spare. 'Oh well, *vive la différence*,' he muttered.

'What the hell are you doing, Frank?'

He turned round. 'Borrowing knickers. Is it a crime? One question. Where's the gap at the front? How am I supposed to ... What's the matter with you now? Are you drunk at the crack of dawn? I'm marrying no alcoholic. A chocoholic mother's enough, believe me. She should be awarded shares in Cadbury's, Fry's and ...' His voice died, though he refused to allow himself to laugh.

Polly, in the doorway, was sinking helplessly to the floor. 'There is no gap. Girls don't need a gap.'

He shook his head sadly. 'See? I learn something new every day. Have you any scissors up here? You must have some with all your hairdressing equipment. I need a gap.'

'No, you don't.'

'Show me what I have to do to manage this lot, then. It's definitely not suitable for a man of my calibre.'

'Oh, bugger off. I'm not fiddling with your credentials. Get dressed. Cal's ready in his chair, and you're the pusher. You can go out the front way, cos I've just been and told people in the cafe you were in the middle room with Cal. Your car's outside.'

'I can't push with this hand,' he told her.

'Then I'll push.' She left him and walked down the stairs. If he so much as glanced at her in court, she'd burst out laughing and get done for contempt or some such thing. She imagined introducing him to people. 'This is my intended, and he has no gap.'

They followed the crowd down the road in the direction of town. Polly's inclination to laugh deserted her, because this was serious business. At the front marched the exhausted parents of the child in hospital, with Johnny and Kathleen, his uncle and aunt. A strange silence accompanied the throng as it moved towards the courthouse. This was indeed serious business; even Ida Pilkington and Hattie Benson were quiet for a change.

They were ten deep outside the small civic building. When a car eventually pulled up, Brennan was helped out with a blanket over his head. 'Traitor,' the crowd called. 'Child killer,' shouted a woman near the front. Then they all stepped aside for the cameras. They wanted the cameras. They wanted his malice spread all over newspapers, spoken about on every radio station, included in news programmes on TV and in cinemas.

Polly stayed outside with Cal. There wasn't much room inside, and there was no wheelchair access, though her real reason was probably knickers. Yes, it was a solemn occasion, but she often laughed involuntarily when nervous. For a few minutes, she nursed the suspicion that Frank might have played to the gallery if she had been there to be the gallery – oh, he was a case. She pictured him pulling at the waist elastic and grimacing at her, wriggling a bit and simulating pain. But no. His interest in the encouragement and care of children was intense. Even the pain in his hand was evidence of sorts, since he'd been the man who'd stopped Brennan with a vicious and triumphant upper cut to the jaw. She was proud of him.

At the opposite side of the building's entrance, the other hero was being interviewed by a reporter. Dusty Den Davenport was sparkling clean for once. He wore a smart suit and shiny shoes, a plain navy blue tie, and a rather handsome trilby. For a ragman, he certainly scrubbed up well.

Mike Stoneway emerged. Behind him in court, the natives were revolting. 'Billy Blunt,' they chanted repeatedly. 'He's gone,' Mike told Polly. 'Whisked out at the back to be assessed by last night's visitors. But he's still down for Crown Court. I reckon they'll find him unfit to stand.'

'He will be unfit to stand,' Cal said. 'He drinks enough to keep himself unfit to stand.' With a weighty hangover of his own, he realized that his statement was rather hypocritical, though he'd belted no kids, had he?

Polly swore under her breath; Brennan might not serve time in prison. The reason for his escape weighed heavily on many shoulders. A man of God walked with the devil, his escape aided by higher-ranking members of the one, true, apostolic Faith. It made no sense.

The Blunts came out. Mavis, white-faced but calm, descended the steps on her husband's arm.

'Sorry,' the sergeant said.

Mavis awarded him a grim smile. 'Not your fault. But I'll tell you this much here and now. I'll get him. If it takes me all my life and a gun, that's a dead man.' Her tone was devoid of emotion.

'There'll be a queue,' Johnny warned her. 'There'll be half of Scotty looking for him.'

Mavis nodded thoughtfully. 'It should be me. I'm his mother, and I'm the one with no religion. If a man like him can be an ordained priest, there's a fault somewhere. The Church is built in an earthquake zone and I want nothing more to do with it.'

'How's Billy?' Polly asked in a bid to divert the conversation.

'Fine,' Fred replied. 'Sitting up and smiling, but it hurts when he coughs or laughs. It was all over a Dinky toy he couldn't resist. Saved a month's spends and bought it, then had no money left for his mam's birthday. So he took half a crown to buy flowers, and was going to put his spends in the plate until he'd paid it all back. My lad is no thief.'

'Instead of paying back in the Sunday plate, he nearly paid with his life. Thanks again, Den,' Mavis called.

The reporter, realizing that this was the child's family, left Den and came over. He explained that he might need permission from the paper's lawyers to name the priest, since the case was pending, but he wanted the full story and he'd got most of it. He would emphasize the initial severity of the lad's condition. 'Liverpool will soon fill in any missing names,' he said.

'I want the Catholics out on strike.' This statement came from Frank. 'I know a lot won't stay away, because missing Mass is a mortal sin unless they're nearly dead; even then, they have to give notice. But let those who had him declared insane know that collection plates in this end of Liverpool will be lighter for the foreseeable future. If you hit them in the Achilles pocket, they squeal.'

Polly tapped the journalist's arm. 'This is Frank Charleson. He stopped Brennan kicking Billy by knocking him down, and hurt his hand in the process. Frank, that's the man who carried Billy away. Hiya, Den.'

'Oh, yes,' Frank said. 'I think I've seen him in the cafe, but I got just a glimpse when he lifted Billy. Well done, Den.'

'Hiya, Pol,' Den called back. 'Sun's shining, but this is a dark day.'

It could easily have been darker. As Polly pushed her twin homeward, she wondered what might have happened had young Billy died. The mood was already heavy, and plans were afoot, but everything could have been so much worse. He was out of the deliberately arranged coma and was talking, thank goodness.

The cafe was packed. Polly ran herself ragged serving Lancashire hotpot, steak and kidney pies, or sandwiches and salad for the overheated. Cal sweated in the kitchen while Frank sauntered towards town in pursuit of under-pants and a shirt. He felt a bit mean, because he could have helped, but his 'bad' hand might well buy him another night at Polly's place. All was fair in love and war, he reminded himself, and she was a mixture of the two. *War and Peace*? She could have written it, though the peace bit might have been brief.

Polly caught snatches of conversation as she moved among the tables. Churches were to be picketed on Sunday. Father Foley of St Columba's was on his way back from retreat with his golf clubs. Rumour had it that Brennan had gone to a drunks' refuge in Harley Street, London, that he'd been banished to Ireland, that he'd been sent as a missionary to a remote part of the world where human flesh was sometimes on the menu, that he was in a monastery outside Coventry. This was Scotty's version of Chinese whispers, and it was imaginative.

Altar boys would be kept at home, and parents were prepared to carry the weight of children's sins. To obey the commandment *Honour thy father and thy mother*, the young would stay away from Mass. Confirmation classes and Legion of Mary meetings were going to be small. It was a shame that other priests would suffer, but a stand needed to be made. For a few moments, Polly sat at the bottom of the stairs. All this would stop. Kirkby, Knowsley and other outreaches of Liverpool were almost set to house more Roaders.

She sighed. There were even rumours of a new move further into Lancashire, an enormous estate to be built somewhere between St Helens and Ormskirk. More neighbours to be separated from neighbours, families split; and public transport to and from the new settlements was far from regular.

Frank had come up with a plan of sorts. It involved moving people round and getting them to continue paying rent on the house provided for them, but it threw up so many complications that he had been forced to abandon the idea. Children changing schools attracted too much attention, chaos threatened, and poor Frank had to throw in the towel. It was grim.

'Polly?' Cal called. 'Two sausage and chips ready here, love.'

She went to get the dinners. Soon, she wouldn't hear Cal calling for her to pick up meals, because it was all coming to an end. The promised rebirth of Scotland Road was not going to happen for decades – if ever. Yet perhaps there was a good side to this. The churches in these parts held a lot of sway, and if there were fewer of them in the new areas the priests who remained in the district while their congregations disappeared would campaign for new housing here.

In truth, everybody felt sorry for the Scotty priests. They were decent, ordinary blokes with a calling and, for the most part, they worked towards the improvement of their parishioners' lives. But beyond them lay a level of corruption that had eaten its way into the ranks on Scotland Road.

Everyone had heard of abuse within the Church. Yes, there were whispers and embellishments, but as surely as seeds sat in the core of an apple, truth nestled deep inside the stories.

Elaine Lewis, on her way back from delivering a brief to chambers on behalf of a colleague, stopped and bought an early evening newspaper from a vendor. And on the front page sat a photograph of the person who was occupying her dreams. He stood with another man, one Mr Denis Davenport, who was described as a rag and bone man, while Mr Frank Charleson was announced as a property owner and, according to a Mrs Harriet Benson, the best and kindest landlord ever.

Frank and Denis had, between them, put a stop to the

criminal behaviour of a terrible priest. There was a lecture from Frank appended.

It is time for some lawyers to dedicate themselves to advocacy for children. Children make only one mistake, that of being too small to defend themselves. In this case, I was witness to a brutal attack on a small boy by a huge, drunken man. I hit the creature so hard that I hurt my right hand, then Denis grabbed the lad and took him to hospital. Without intervention, Billy might well have bled to death internally.

We need solicitors and barristers to specialize in the prosecution of such people as this thoroughly evil man who put Billy Blunt in an operating theatre. We need lawyers to reach children and to encourage them to speak up against abusers, even if those abusers are family members. We want to stop figures of authority acting as if they can do as they like. The Catholic Church and all churches must weed out the bad immediately, instead of hiding them for a few months then letting them loose again on society's innocents. The cane of every teacher should go on a bonfire come November.

Yes, we all have anecdotes about people whose fathers and teachers beat them, who say such beatings and canings did no harm. How can they be sure? Do they occasionally lash out at kids? Because such behaviour is a learned pattern, and it must be stopped. Are they sure that they would not have been better adults without the beatings?

The newspaper reporter then questioned Mr Charleson about standing for Parliament, and his reply was interesting. He chose his words and his company carefully. *I could not enjoy working under whips in a place where partisanship overrides morals. We should be slave to no party. Perhaps an independent MP has freedom, but he is one voice among a babble of nonsense.* And thus Frank Charleson dismissed Westminster and a whole system of government, a template of democracy that had been copied, adapted and shaped to form the political back-cloth of many civilizations.

Elaine folded her newspaper. There was more to Frank Charleson than met the eye, and what met the eye was pleasing. Perhaps an extra little celebration for Norma Charleson's birthday might be a good idea after all. The man was clever, outspoken and filled with enthusiasm. Elaine leaned on the wall outside the office and lifted her face to the sun. She wanted to know him better. She wanted him. And Elaine Lewis always got what she wanted.

They lay rigid side by side in Polly's bed. She wasn't speaking to him, because she'd caught him combing his hair with his supposedly wrecked right hand. He managed to persuade her that while some movements gave little pain, he wouldn't have been capable of steering a car. He'd got Cal drunk, and she knew he'd done it on purpose. Yet these misbehaviours made him all the more desirable, since the last thing she wanted in her life was a yes man.

As Polly wasn't speaking to him, Frank decided not to talk to her. But Frank in non-speaking mode was unlike any other person Polly had ever come across. He turned his back on her and, with his left arm, inflicted grievous bodily harm on an innocent pillow before throwing his head into the hollow he had created. He muttered. Most of his words were incomprehensible, though she caught the odd one or two. If she filled in the missing letters like a crossword, he was moaning about her, his mother and the price of underwear.

'Bloody sizes all wrong,' he mumbled.

Polly coughed.

'Can I rub some Vicks on your chest?' This request was delivered fully formed.

She turned to face the window. There was a moon. Perhaps he was a lunatic, one who responded badly to phases of Earth's companion. She loved him. No matter how naughty he was, she adored him. The curtains weren't quite closed and she thought he probably looked gorgeous on the end of a moonbeam. But she was the moonstruck one, wasn't she?

'Polly?'

'We're not speaking.'

'OK.' He attacked the pillow all over again.

'Stop doing that.'

'You spoke?'

'Yes. I told you to stop attacking the pillow. I don't want feathers everywhere.'

He groaned.

'Behave,' she snapped, though she was dangerously close to laughter.

He sat up. 'Feathers tickle,' he said gravely. 'And you're ticklish. I remember Cal sitting on you whenever you got out of hand, which was almost every day. He used to tickle you.'

'Don't even think about it, or you'll need slings on both arms. Now, let me get some sleep. We've early breakfast tomorrow, two sittings.'

She was in charge. It was her bed for a start. She knew she was in charge, and she knew that he knew she was in charge. Hmm. What would Admiral Lord Nelson have done? Load the cannon, hoist the mainsail, shiver his timbers? Horatio certainly knew how to kick the frogs' legs from under the French, while Polly was a Scouser. She was tough.

He altered his position and put an arm round her waist. It was his left arm, because he didn't want further injuries. 'Polly?'

'What now?'

'Love me?'

'You know I do.' Mercurial as ever, she moved into his embrace. And this time, she allowed nature to take its powerful course. It was a warm night, so bedding was tossed to the floor while the pair of them made love in moonlight. There was joy, passion, laughter and tears, and, above all, there was gentleness and a very real love.

Afterwards, she lay stark naked next to him, also stark naked, and stroked his face till he slept. Then she picked up all the covers and spread them over him. Early mornings could be chilly, even in summer. He would be gone tomorrow back to his extended cottage with his mother in the annexe. Mrs Old Cow would question him closely, though most of the answers were in this evening's newspaper.

Polly would miss him. 'I'll miss you,' she whispered. Physically, he was quite a specimen, just over six feet in height, brown hair, green eyes, a slight bump on his nose rescuing him from perfection. Ellen had adored him. She had dashed straight to Polly's house to show off her ring. The only secret that Polly had kept from her close friend was the fact that Frank had been turned down by her. She'd met Greg, who was exciting. Oh yes, he'd been exciting and immeasurably shallow, as had Cal's fiancée. One whiff of a damaged spine, and they'd both disappeared, no real goodbyes, no excuses.

Frank was not shallow. He was a decided man, determined to the point of stubbornness, but he was gentle, affectionate and amusing. She grinned; she might have been describing a pet dog, and he was no pet. 'Don't go home,' she mouthed. 'Find somewhere for the three of us.' Oh, if only he would. Although she dreaded the loss of her cafe and the hairdressing business, a part of her wanted the pain over with. As things were, the streets would disappear first, leaving the road a blank, deserted page with all marks erased.

The barrel organ man with his monkey no longer visited. Roundabouts used to be towed along and parked so that children could take a penny ride. Polly remembered Mam telling her about kids leaping about in front of trams while passengers threw pennies onto the pavements to save the children's lives. It was quieter now, though only a small percentage of the populace had been moved. Soon, the uprooting would begin again; soon, Scotland Road would be a memory for a few decades until everyone was dead. There would never be a finer place.

It was time to start preparing to invade London where, in silence, the people from this precious part of Liverpool would rage against the dying of the light. But first, a priest must be brought to book. How the hell would he be tracked down? Polly had no idea.

Eugene Brennan was in prison. He had a tiny cell with a hard bunk, an upright chair and a desk, a crucifix on the wall above his bed and a missal as his only reading material. There were no police; his jailers were grey shapes who wore hooded grey garments that matched the grey walls and the grey floor.

Disorientated and seriously close to complete sobriety, he teetered on the brink of knowing exactly what he had done. He could easily kill for a drink. He had almost killed a child because of drink. Was he contrite? No answer to this unspoken question sprang to mind. Self-pity consumed him almost completely. Where was he? What was this dreadful place where no one spoke? They sang. Every bloody six hours, they sang the Angelus. They sang Mass twice a day. They sang Benediction. They probably sang for their supper, and the food was rubbish. Or perhaps their diet was better than the swill they served up for prisoners.

One of the grey men unlocked the door and placed a tray on the desk.

'Where am I?' the prisoner asked.

The grey man left. The cell was three paces long, two paces wide. Brennan heard another door being unlocked, then another. Each time, the door was locked when the almost invisible left a cell. The prisoner was sober enough to realize that he was incarcerated in a drying-out monastery. Next to a bowl of porridge on the tray stood a glass of water with four pills on a small saucer.

With an inhuman roar escaping from his throat, Father Eugene Brennan hurled the tray and its contents at the wall. Glutinous white slop travelled slowly over unplastered brickwork. A hooded head peered through the grille in the door. While the monk watched, the priest picked up his slop bucket, removed the lid, and threw his own effluent at the same wall. The space was so tiny that he was soaked in urine.

'I am not a priest,' he shouted. 'I resign and I am a free man.'

After this rather strenuous outburst, he placed himself on the hard bunk and slept. When he woke, his cell was clean. On the desk sat a plate of plain biscuits, a glass of water and four pills. Starving, he gobbled up the food, drank the water and hid the pills under his mattress. The holy brothers were trying to sedate him. Oh, God, he had to get out of this place. The window was barred, the door was heavy, and the monks each carried just one key. It was a skeleton, he felt sure. He had to get his hands on a key, and his hands were trembling uncontrollably.

The corridor was silent. He pushed his fingers through the grille and yes, he felt the air move. Somewhere near, a window was open. Turning, he sought a weapon. All he had was a wooden cross with the figure of Christ nailed to it.

His insides quivered. Resigning from the priesthood was one thing; battering a monk with a crucifix was on a different level altogether. His mind worked well enough to inform him that here was the safest place, that the Church might save him from facing a judge, yet the price was high. Plainchant, plain food, plain environment – this was not living, and it might go on for years. He needed his real medicine, a pint of ale and a double whiskey to follow.

The details ceased to be important. An open road beckoned. He could change his appearance, get a job, find a room, stay in or go out as and when he chose. There was money in his private bank account, but the police might keep an eye on that once he'd escaped.

Hell, must he lie back and accept his punishment? Must he be incarcerated here until the story about the boy had run its course in the newspapers?

As for escape, he'd have had as good a chance in Alcatraz, since he had no idea where he was, and there were no clues, no accents, no sounds from outside. He guessed he was in the back of beyond, but at least this wasn't Australia. England was relatively small; sooner or later, there would be a road.

But first, he had to batter a dedicated Catholic with a crucifix. This was a grim institution, and he intended leaving it behind, no matter what the cost.

*

Wednesday was to be Polly's evening off. There would be no haircuts, no perms, no colour rinses tonight. Carla needed another soaking, but she could wait. Tomorrow, Polly would be going with Cal to the hospital. But tonight, she belonged to Frank.

After Cal's card school had settled in the living room, she checked her makeup, made sure her hair looked good and her stockings weren't laddered. It was exciting. Since the accident, she had never been out on a date. She was a teenager again.

She sat in the passenger seat of Frank's humble Austin. He didn't believe in smart cars. In his oft-expressed opinion, men who needed posh cars were lacking somewhere in the testosterone department. 'Big under the bonnet, small in the trousers,' he said.

'Frank?'

'Yes?'

'Where are we going?'

'Oh, I thought I'd told you.'

She growled. 'Liar.'

'I wondered when you'd do that,' he said, 'because in bed, you purr like a contented kitten. And I thought, well, cats purr, but they also growl.'

'You know you haven't told me where we're going. You're the cat, anyway, grinning like that Cheshire thing out of Alice in Wonderland. Where are we going?' she asked again.

'To my house.'

She opened the car door. 'If you think I'm going anywhere near Old Pasteurized, you can make your own bloody cheese.'

'What?'

'You heard me.'

'But I didn't get your meaning.' He did, but he wasn't telling her that.

'Pasteurized milk, cheese, Old Cow Charleson – work it out, lad. I can't stand your flaming mother. She looked down on Ellen, and couldn't bear to be near me. When she collected our rent, I used to put it in a silver dish for her.'

'You didn't. You haven't got a silver dish. Close the door.'

She closed the door. Sometimes, she did as she was told. 'I'm not good enough for your mam.'

'You're not marrying her.'

'No, I'm marrying her little boy.'

'I'm not little.'

'I know that and you know that, but does she?'

Polly had this all wrong. Mother didn't treat him like a child: she expected him to be a replacement for his father. As soon as poor Charlie Charleson had shuffled off the coil, his boots had been passed to Frank, and he'd been forced to make them fit. 'I loved my dad,' he said now. 'He even made sure that I didn't get named Charles. All firstborn sons are supposed to be baptized Charles Charleson, but Dad put his foot down. She doesn't see me as a child, Polly. Oh, no. She views me as her next servant. I was my father's replacement. I got dragged away from accountancy and became a purchaser of houses and a collector of rent.'

'She saw Ellen as a threat, Frank. I'll be the same. And where we come from doesn't help.'

'We lived nearby.'

'And got out.'

He sighed heavily. 'She was born in a two up, two down with gas lighting and the bath hanging on a nail next to the outside lav. Her mother took in washing and her dad had a window round. The airs and graces came later when she married Dad. Dad was ambitious and hardworking, so she grabbed him.'

'And now?' Polly asked.

'And now, I'm going for your ring – Ellen's ring – and I shall find somewhere for us and Cal as soon as possible. The business will still be yours, and we'll get round the details, but she has to know that you exist.'

Polly wasn't convinced. 'You could go on your own and get the ring. She doesn't need to know yet, does she? Cal doesn't know, and he's my family.' She paused for thought. 'Are you using me to punish her?'

'No. I'm surprised if you think me capable of sinking so low. I'm not doing anything behind her back, that's all. She takes a while to get used to change. The point I need to make is that I love you, we've decided to be engaged to marry, and none of it's negotiable. She needs to get out of bed and run her business again, because my new life's in a storage place on the Dock Road.'

'And Cal? Are you absolutely sure about where you'll store him, Frank?'

'He's not negotiable, either. Your brother's also my friend.'

Polly was still slightly disappointed. On her first date in years, she'd hoped they would be going somewhere nice, a country pub on the road to Formby, or a trip to Southport. But no. Frank wanted to grab the cow by the horns right from the start. 'I thought you were taking me out.'

'I am. We're getting engaged at the Shepherd's Crook later on. With the ring. And you're coming with me while I get it.'

He was right, Polly supposed. He needed to put the old besom in the picture as soon as possible. Mrs C would probably hate anyone who threatened to interfere with the business, her prime consideration. 'All right,' she said eventually. 'But on your head be it. Because if she kicks out at me, she'll get as good as she gives.'

Frank laughed. 'Have you any idea of how proud I am of you? Feel free to start as you mean to go on.' He pondered for a moment. 'Ellen just took it from Mother, then moaned at me about her. I was the piggy in the middle, the referee, and it was hard work. My mother is my mother. She's a selfish, calculating and frightened woman. She copes by trying to make everyone else suffer as badly as she does. You, my love, are her Waterloo. And no, I didn't choose you because you'll put her in her place. I didn't choose you at all. Love allows no room for choice.'

She shivered. He was so romantic, yet so damned honest. 'All right, then. But I hope she's wearing armour, because I'm in no mood for being nice.'

Frank started the car. 'Hmm. There goes my sex life.'

'Oh, sex isn't about being nice,' she advised him. 'It's just another way of fighting.'

He burst out laughing and was incapable of driving until he calmed down. 'Fighting?' he managed finally. 'Who wins?'

'We both do,' she said. 'But if there was a panel of judges, it would be a close call in my favour.'

'And babies?' he asked, wiping away tears of laughter.

'Then we both lose. Especially when it comes to sleep.'

She had an answer for everything. She'd always had an answer for everything. But her saving grace was humour. Even when she spoke sharply, her happy nature shone through. His high-rise breakfast, the telling off for owning an improving hand, the knickers scene – all these examples of her true temperament had amused him. 'Seven years ago, you turned me down.'

'Yes, I did.'

'Why?'

'Because Ellen wanted you. She raved about you day after day, then I met Mr Wonderful, and all was well. Till he ran away, the rotten coward.'

Frank glanced at his watch. 'Right. Don't ever dare to turn me down again, madam. I'm as strong-willed as you are, so I may well turn out to be your Waterloo. We've a table booked. Let's call in and see the dragon.'

She pretended to gulp. 'Does she breathe fire?'

'Only on Saturdays when I top her up with paraffin. It's Wednesday. She'll be out of fuel.'

The 'dragon' had been sitting at her window for what seemed like weeks. He was messing about with that Polly Kennedy, who'd been engaged to a Greg somebody or other, who had abandoned Polly after her brother's accident. There was no chocolate in the house. Christine Lewis had promised to buy no more even if Norma screamed for it.

Inside, she was screaming. So loud were the internal shrieks, she didn't notice the car until it pulled into the driveway. Ah, so his hand must be better, then. When he left the car, Norma noticed the bruising. Yes, he'd fought on behalf of an urchin, hadn't he? Oh, no. The girl was with him. She was very pretty, but her eyes were quick with street wisdom. This was a daughter of the slums, and Frank deserved better. Norma turned away from the window. Her heart was doing somersaults, and she'd better get to that stupid doctor's surgery for a blood test.

The front door opened. She couldn't breathe properly. He knocked on her private door. 'Mother?'

'Come in,' she managed. Her son was a gentleman, so he stood back and allowed Polly Kennedy to enter first. The girl was lovely, with a healthy head of dark brown hair and bright blue, sparkling eyes. She had a neat figure, and Frank had seen her naked, because he'd written about her.

'Mrs Charleson,' Polly said.

'Ah yes. I remember you.'

'And I remember you, of course.'

'Yes, I'm sure you do. You run a rather basic cafe on Scotland Road.'

'And a hairdressing business,' Frank said.

A short silence ensued before Norma referred to the article in the newspaper. 'You weren't raised to hit priests in any circumstances.'

'I wasn't raised to kick nuns, either, but cruelty to children is intolerable. Billy Blunt could have died.'

'Frank saved his life,' Polly said. 'Almost broke his hand doing it.'

Norma continued to stare at her son. 'Going somewhere nice?' she asked.

'Shepherd's Crook,' he replied. After a second or two, he continued. 'Polly was Ellen's best friend, if you remember. We're getting engaged tonight, and Polly wants to wear Ellen's ring.' He watched while his mother's face drained of colour. Would she speak her mind in front of Polly?

Norma hung on to her temper, though it was no mean feat. It was all planned, all mapped out. Elaine Lewis had read Frank's interview in the paper and had offered to introduce him to lawyers who might be interested in pursuing the rights of children. But he was about to fasten himself to a second ill-bred waif. This one seemed feisty, cheekier than her friend had been.

'Are you all right, Mother?'

Her eyes narrowed. 'Yes, thank you.' She looked at Polly. 'And how is your brother?'

'Still in a wheelchair, Mrs Charleson, still doing the very basic cooking in our very basic cafe.' Polly felt cold, as if she were standing in front of an open refrigerator. It was Norma Charleson; she chilled the air around herself.

Frank's mouth twitched, but he dared not laugh.

'So when you marry, who will care for him?'

'We will.' This from Frank, who seemed mildly amused. Norma's system continued to howl for chocolate.

'Cal's getting stronger all the time,' Polly said. 'He still goes for treatment every week.'

'If you'll excuse me,' Norma said haughtily. 'I want to listen to something on the Home Service.'

They left. In the church-like entrance hall, Polly leaned on a cold wall. 'How have you managed to put up with her all these years?'

'Practice,' he answered. 'And selective deafness. I copied my dad, more or less.' He led her into the sitting room and asked her to wait while he went upstairs. She sat and looked through the fireplace into the dining room. It was a fascinating and unusual cottage, but she couldn't settle in the chair. Mother Moo was just a few paces away; did she want *that* as a mother-in-law?

Standing at a window, she looked out at Little Crosby Road. Frank was adorable, yet Polly knew there would be trouble. A part of her wanted to run away now, before he came back, but such cowardice was not acceptable. Greg and Lois had buggered off without a word; anyway, Frank knew where to find her. Above all, he deserved an explanation.

He returned, his face almost split in two by a very wide grin. 'Got it,' he said.

She simply stared at him.

'Polly?'

'Get me away from here, please. Now.' She turned, walked out of the house and stood by the car. Frank opened the passenger door, and she sat in the vehicle. As he walked round to the driver's side, she wondered what the hell she was going to say, because she loved him, but ...

He pulled out of the drive and parked further up the road. 'What is it?'

Polly inhaled deeply. 'I think we should wait, because of Cal. We don't know what he's going to need if he gets back on his feet. And I want the two of us – Cal and me – to stay where we are until we know the extent of his recovery.'

'But we can still be engaged,' Frank insisted. 'And that's not the real reason, is it?'

She offered no reply.

'Answer me, Polly.'

'It's one of the reasons. You know the other one. It's sitting back there in its little annexe. I'm sure she hastened Ellen's sudden and swift death, Frank. She aims for the weakest, which was why she treated poor Ellen so badly. I may be sturdier, healthier and cheekier than she was, but she never managed to hate your mother. I do hate her. And no matter where we go, she'll find a way of wrecking our lives, mine in particular.'

'But–'

'But I have a brother, and he's precious, and not as strong as he used to be. If she gets my back right up, I'll kill her, and what use would I be to Cal if I hanged or got a prison sentence? She won't let go. She's cunning, devious and a thorough bitch. Watching her just now, I could see the wheels in her head turning. No. She will not wreck Cal's life by wrecking mine. I am sorry, so sorry. I hadn't seen her for years, and I'd managed to forget how evil she is.'

'She's my mother.'

'She's your problem, then. I love you. I also love my brother and myself. She bullied and upset Ellen, who was frail, and she would try the same with me. I appear strong, but I'm still human and breakable. Within two minutes of walking into her room, my hands were itching to strangle her. Basic cafe, basic food. Who does she think she is? While she's alive, I can't marry you. Cal is my family, and he comes first. Take me home.'

'You love me?'

'Oh, yes.'

'Then you'll cope. Many women don't like their mothers-in-law. We can move far away from her—'

'Great. Then I'd feel guilty when she got sick or died. I'd blame myself for the rest of my life for keeping you away from her. Can't you see? No one can ever win. She triumphs no matter what.'

Frank started the car. But he didn't go over the moss towards the Shepherd's Crook; instead, he drove the woman he loved back to Scotland Road.

'I'm sorry,' she said, breaking a silence that had lasted several miles.

'Go to your brother,' Frank answered. 'I shan't bother you again, not yet, so don't worry. If you don't love me enough to tolerate my mother, then we must stay apart for a while. Because I can't look at you without wanting to hold you, and you aren't good enough for me at the moment, Polly. I expected better from you.'

She cried for hours that night. Never before in her life had she felt so alone. The other pillow smelled of him. She slept holding that small echo of Frank, breathing him in, mourning him. 'I buried my chances,' she whispered. 'And I let the old cow win.'

Five

Polly glared sternly at the image in the mirror. She was furious, upset, frightened, lonely ... 'I just don't believe you, Kennedy. You knew full well what his mother was, yet you still managed to be shocked, you damned fool. If you'd thought about it, you'd have realized she wouldn't have improved with age. Nobody ever does. You're pathetic, turning down the man you love all because his mother's a witch.' How could she live without that smile, without the touch of his hand on her arm, those daft breakfasts, his poky little car and her one pair of sensible knickers? He'd taken her to see his mother to test her mettle, to face Old Cow and prove that she could manage the situation. 'I failed. Just a little test, and I failed.'

He was her everything, yet he couldn't possibly be that, because of Cal. Till the day one of them died, Polly's twin would be high on the agenda; only children of her own could be allowed more importance. But she still didn't want a life without Frank in it.

So was she pathetic or was she principled? When she'd looked into those cold, calculating eyes, she'd seen icy fury and grim determination. There was something very, very wrong with Frank's mother. It was as if she couldn't reach anyone, touch anyone, feel sympathy for another person. She wasn't real. She was her own creature, a person she had built from imperfect spare parts purchased from some unscrupulous scrap merchant.

Norma Charleson would have given up becoming disabled, would have risen again like the phoenix to do as much damage as possible. Cal had to be safe. Could Frank have put a stop to his mother? He'd never managed to keep her away from Ellen, had he? Poor Ellen, so happy, so lively, so dead.

The disabled act had been invented to keep Frank at home. Mrs Moo, doing her best to look incapable, had balanced everything on her son's broad shoulders, keeping him busy and in charge. She no doubt believed that was enough, that he needed no personal life, no contact physical or emotional with a woman. He was her slave, and she intended to maintain her hold over him.

Polly removed her makeup. She'd been lying on the bed holding his pillow for hours, and she'd only just changed into her pyjamas. No pretty nightdress tonight, because he wasn't here. He would never be here again. Never was a long time, but Cal had to come first. As for the idea of visiting Mrs Moo for Sunday tea, for Christmas and other occasions – well, Frank would have been forced to go alone, and that was a very poor basis for marriage.

She hadn't been so thoroughly angry or confused for many a year. It was partly connected to the engagement ring, she supposed. It meant a lot, because it was from Frank, but it was also part of Ellen. She could not have accepted that particular ring at this particular time. Might she have accepted a different one, a new one? Perhaps a new one might have been less meaningful, and she might have given him a chance to put his mother in her place.

Deep down in her core, well below the emotional stuff, she knew she had done the right thing. She'd watched poor Ellen doing her best, cleaning and baking because Mrs Moo was coming. How much longer might Ellen have lasted without the old cow in her life? What might the dreadful woman have done to Cal's chances of recovery? Cal's main problems were undoubtedly physical, yet his state of mind needed to be positive if he were to make the best of any chances that might come his way.

For the whole night, she vacillated between despair and righteousness. Frank was the love of her life and she had chased him off. Again. Cal was her twin, and he deserved to be protected from a situation that might easily have become unhappy. And if Frank walked out on his mother for Polly's sake, that, too, could well have been uncomfortable. Oh, how she wanted him; oh, how she despised the woman who had given him life.

The card school had broken up hours earlier. Cal's attendant had put him to bed, and Frank had promised not to bother her in the near future. She wanted to be bothered. No, she didn't. Yes, she did. How could she manage to entertain two diametrically opposed opinions? Was she one of those schizophrenics who didn't know who they were or what they believed in? Why did life have to be so bloody complicated? Both pillows would be wet with tears by morning. And the bed had become a very lonely place.

Frank Charleson fared no better, while his mother, suffering already from chocolate withdrawal, was hauled over coals hotter than hell, and neither slept for hours after he'd finished with her at about two o'clock in the morning. 'This is not my fault,' she said repeatedly. 'Those people are just not civilized.'

'Not your fault? Not your fault?' He mimicked her voice. ' "You run that very basic cafe on Scotland Road, don't you?" Why didn't you just hit her in the face and have done with it? That poor girl has a twin brother in a wheel-

112

chair, and her best friend – my wife – is dead. You were the same with poor Ellen, criticizing her cooking and baking, hinting that the flat seemed difficult to keep clean, rubbing your knife and fork on a napkin before shunting food round the plate. You insulted my wife. You enjoyed causing her pain.'

'I have high standards, that's all.'

He laughed, though the sound arrived hollow. 'You ran barefoot from the Rotunda all the way to town on a regular basis, and you got thumped for stealing and shoplifting. Your mother was a washerwoman, and your dad cleaned windows. What's the difference?'

'I got out, Frank.'

'Hmmph.'

'Well, I did get out.'

'On my poor father's back, yes. He was the one who taught me not to hear you. He was a good dad. You are a selfish, greedy, overweight, lazy, nasty woman.' Frank seldom lost control, but his temper seemed to have slipped its leash on this occasion. 'I came back here after losing Ellen because you were ill. You said you were ill and I, very stupidly, believed you. There's nothing wrong with you unless Cadbury's is a disease.'

She turned on the tears.

'Too late and too unreal, Mrs C. I love Polly Kennedy. When she met you again, she feared for her future with me. She even feared for her disabled brother because of the trouble you caused Ellen. Now, listen for once in your stupid little life. I am going to marry her. But first, I have to get away from you. The business books are in my desk, and everything is up to date. Collect your own rents and arrange your own property repairs. I have other plans.'

He left the annexe, but she followed him. 'All this is yours now, Mother. You'll be able to live the life you deserve, I suppose. Tomorrow, I leave your house.'

'But you mustn't. I can't manage the business—'

'Then employ someone who will, because I am done here.'

'Where will you go?' she cried.

'That's for me to know and for you to wonder about.' Norma stumbled onto a sofa. 'How can you be so cruel?'

He glared at her. 'Look in the mirror if you want to find my teacher.'

Norma folded her arms. 'I speak my mind, that's all.'

'And I am speaking mine. You don't like it, do you? One rule for you, and another for the rest of us, it seems. Well, Polly speaks her mind, as do the rest of them down there. You are known as Old Cow or Mrs Moo. Many people hate you, Mrs Charleson. They know your beginnings, and they don't appreciate the airs and graces.' He walked away. 'And don't follow me upstairs,' he called.

Only now did Norma Charleson break down genuinely. She had no one. Her husband was dead, her son was on his way out of her life, she'd had no time to make friends up here ... Christine Lewis. All she had in her life was Christine Lewis, whose daughter would have been so suitable for Frank. He was an idiot. He should be looking to marry up, not down. What could she do? Oh, what could she do?

Upstairs and still in a fury, Frank crammed his clothes into suitcases. Among articles awaiting washing, he found Polly's knickers and pictured her sliding down the door jamb as she watched him donning them. 'My trophy,' he said, packing them into a carrier bag alongside other items that needed to be laundered. 'I'll get you back, madam. You shall be reunited with our underwear and with me. This isn't over.'

He lay on his bed and thought about Polly. He remembered their teenage years, afternoons at the swimming baths, table tennis at church youth clubs, dances, concerts, trips on the ferry over to the Wirral, just the four of them at that stage, Polly and Ellen, himself and Cal. Polly had been difficult to read, because she acted daft and hid her emotions, but he'd seen regret in her eyes when she'd turned down his first proposal. 'I should have persevered.' Yet he knew it would have made no difference, as Polly Kennedy's mind had been made up.

He rolled over and hugged a pillow. She'd turned him down for Ellen's sake, because she'd known that Ellen adored him. Polly was a selfless girl who set great store by her friendship with Ellen. She could not have broken her best friend's heart for all the tea in China and all the coffee in Brazil.

'But she's broken mine for Cal's sake. She didn't want my mother within a mile of Cal, and I can see why. But I'll dig us both out of this pit and make a happy marriage if it kills me.' Where would he live? He didn't know. What was more, he didn't care.

Eugene Brennan knew that if he didn't get out of this place, he'd go completely crazy. After a couple of days punctuated only by faint echoes of tedious Gregorian chant, a doctor visited him, giving him a rare opportunity to communicate. 'You are keeping me here against my will,' the priest blustered. 'Why? Why am I in this terrible place? The silence is murder – nobody says a word. This is solitary confinement. Prison cells are bigger than this hole.'

The visitor was infuriatingly calm and uninterested. 'You'll know about prison cells, of course. You gave up your free will when you injured that child. In order to keep you safe, we have certified you insane. As soon as you are through this controlled withdrawal, you will be transferred to a psychiatric facility.'

'Controlled withdrawal?'

'The drugs are helping you.'

They were doing no such thing, because he wasn't taking them. 'I need a bath,' he snapped. 'My clothes are ready to crawl off my back.'

'And you'll get a bath when you become less aggressive. We have to keep the good brothers safe, and your behaviour hasn't been exactly exemplary.'

It was a waste of time; the doctor didn't give a moonshine for this patient.

Father Eugene Brennan's second visitor was a solicitor. He wasted no time in coming to the point. The child had survived after a considerable amount of surgery. Billy Blunt was on the mend, though he was tormented by dreadful nightmares and seemed slightly withdrawn. 'His parents have sought legal advice, and they are being encouraged to bring a civil case against you and the Church. Financial compensation will be sought.'

'What?' the priest roared. 'The boy's a thief.'

'He's seven, small for his age and affected by your behaviour.'

'Whose side are you on?'

'I'm paid to be on yours. They say you kicked him.'

'I fell over him.'

'Witnesses will say you kicked him. So an insanity plea is our best course. The prosecution will also send doctors to assess you and they may well find you competent for trial. The Church has decided that you must answer, by the way, so you will not be spirited off in the night. You have one chance of avoiding court, and that's by proving mental instability. There's quite an uprising in the Scotland Road district. Father Foley is back, and St Columba's parishioners are insisting that he makes sure you face justice from the dock. Just be grateful it's not a murder charge.

You broke the boy's ribs and an arm, punctured a lung and damaged one of his kidneys.'

'I fell over him.'

'Two or three times?'

'And you're my lawyer? Go away and find me somebody sensible.'

'Gladly.' The man shuffled his papers, pushed them into a document case and left. When he had gone, nothing happened; no key turned, no hooded head showed at the grille. Brennan listened and waited for a few seconds; the brothers had a tendency to creep about in their open-toed sandals. He pushed the door outward, looked left and right. The main door to the outside world and freedom was at the right side down a long corridor. He had no key. As this was a facility for alcoholics, all doors would doubtless be locked.

Like a good boy, he closed the door silently and sat in his hard chair reading the missal. Let them think they could trust him with an unlocked door; he knew the way out and, for the moment, that was what mattered. He jumped up and opened the door fractionally. This way, the monks would see that the door was clearly open and that the incumbent had remained in his cell by choice.

When a hood finally appeared at the door, Father Brennan was mouthing silent words from his prayer book. He continued to read after the door was locked. If one of them lingered, he needed to look good. To finish his little performance, he took a rosary of brown wooden beads from his pocket, kissed the figure of Christ and began to count his way round the decades. They could stop fearing him. He would be good, would win a bath and, perhaps, a walk in the grounds.

He was going to escape.

*

Ida Pilkington (sweets, newspapers, tobacco and everybody's business) was in cahoots with Harriet (Hattie) Benson, who was fruit and veg with some cooked meats and canned goods. At seven in the morning, Ida was at Hattie's door. There was a problem. In truth, there were several problems, one of which was parked upstairs in Ida's second bedroom above her shop. Situated as they were one each side of Polly's Parlour, the two women kept a couple of eyes on Polly and Cal.

Hattie, just back from the wholesale market, opened the shop door. 'I'm thinking of going into bread and milk,' she announced apropos of nothing at all. 'And a bit of cheese.' She noticed her friend's face. 'Eggs. I might do eggs. What's up, Ida? You look like you lost a quid and found a penny. Get in here while I sort my stock. What's up?' she asked again.

'Don't ask.' Ida squeezed her large body into the shop. 'Here, let me give you a hand with that lot. I'll put the King Eddies over here, and the Pipers next to them. Ooh, Hat. I'm that upset, I keep regurgitating.'

'Well don't regurge yourself on me spuds. That sack there's for Polly's stews and pies, so leave it where it is. Right. What's up?' Hattie asked again.

'It's him.'

'Who?'

'Him. He's back.'

'What, Brennan?'

'No. Polly's him.'

'Frank Charleson?' Hattie asked.

Ida stopped in her tracks. 'What's been going on when I wasn't looking?'

'Oh, nothing much.' Ida never missed a trick, but she was behind the door on this one, Hattie realized. 'Look, Ida. We both have things to do. You should be selling newspapers already, and I—'

'There's a lad helping me,' Ida said. 'Now, this has to be a secret.'

Fruit and veg stared hard at tobacco and newspapers. Where secrets were concerned, Ida was as much use as a colander with oversized holes. 'The lad's a secret? Why is the lad a secret? You're making no sense at all.'

Ida puffed out her cheeks. 'I wish you'd listen, Hattie. He's hid up my stairs in the back room.'

'I'll listen when you stop talking broken biscuits. Who've you got hidden upstairs? If it's the lad, how can he sell stuff from up the dancers?'

The older woman straightened her spine in preparation for a momentous delivery. 'Greg Johnson. Realizes he's made a mistake, and he's come back for Polly. I'm in a right pickle, Hattie. I acted automatic, like.'

Hattie sat down abruptly on her behind-the-counter stool, while Ida lowered her bulk into the shoppers' chair. 'Hell's bells,' Hattie said.

'I know. Anyway, he's got a job in Liverpool, didn't like London one bit, and he's decided he belongs with Polly. Haven't we trouble enough on? More than half of us will miss Mass on Sunday in support of young Billy and his family, none of us knows where bloody Brennan is, now this bloke turns up out of the blue. I feel like joining a nunnery or finding a little house in a big field.'

Hattie didn't know what to say, and that was unusual. If Greg stayed with Ida, the whole area might know by this afternoon. Perhaps that was what Greg wanted. Ida was famed far and wide for her total lack of discretion.

'What shall I do, Hat?'

'Don't ask me for a start till I've thought about it. We all know what Polly suffered when he walked out on her. I was glad when she got angry, cos that seemed healthy. She's off to the hospital this afternoon with Cal, so the cafe will shut at about half past two. You know how she

119

runs about and does jobs enough for three people. Don't tell her today, that's all.'

'OK.'

'And don't tell anybody else, either. Where is he now, the waste of space?'

'Upstairs getting ready for work with some insurance firm in the Liver Building. I told him to go out the back way.' She paused. 'There's something else, Hat. Cafe's shut till tomorrow – there's a notice on the door. Urgent family business, it says. Blinds are down, door's locked, no brekkies and dinners today, queen. I'm wondering if she already knows he's back. She might be hiding for all I know. Oh, I've no idea what to think.'

'Bloody hell, Ida.'

'I know. That's why me stomach's gone bad. If that poor girl knows I've got the man in my house, she'll feel hurt. When he turned up, all I could do was hide him quick.' She paused. 'Urgent family business. What does that mean?'

'She never closes, Ida. No matter what, she carries on.'

'I know.'

'It has to be something big.'

'I know.'

'So either she realizes he's back, or Cal's taken ill, or she's taken ill—'

'I know.'

'Stop saying you know. We don't know nothing. But we do. We know she doesn't need messing about by that Greg one. Get rid of him. Tell him you need the bedroom for storage; say any bloody thing, but get shut of him immediately if not sooner.'

'Well, I don't want to be rude, do I?'

'Yes, you do. Tell him to piss off sharpish.'

'I can't say that, Hattie. I try not to do that kind of swearing.'

'Then I'll come and say it for you tonight when he gets back from work. Go home and make some toast, love. That's what I'm having. I'll miss that nice get-together we all have in Polly's of a morning, a bit of a chat before the day takes over.' She paused. 'How does he look?'

'Who?' Ida asked.

'Who do you think – the coalman? Greg Johnson, of course.'

Ida shrugged. 'The same. Good-looking, but a bit shifty round the eyes. I don't trust him, never did. His eyebrows nearly meet in the middle. Er ... why did you mention Frank Charleson?'

'Eeh, Ida, I've no idea. Me mind's all over the place some days. I just thought they seemed to be getting on all right just lately. Course, he's been a friend of hers and Cal's for donkey's years. Wishful thinking, I suppose. He's one of the few good enough for our Pol as far as I'm concerned.'

Ida opened the door. 'What's going to happen to us, Hattie? When we're all split up and divided? Can you imagine any different way of living? Can you imagine life away from Scotland Road?'

Hattie shook her head. 'No, I can't.'

'Will we go to London and stand outside Number Ten?'

'Yes, we will. Go back now, Ida. Get a bit of breakfast.'

Alone, Hattie locked the shop door and retreated to the kitchen. Her kitchen and scullery area were knocked into one big room, and she preferred it that way, because she could hear if some early or late shopper came along. She turned on the grill, cut a couple of doorsteps and shoved them under.

Later, as she sat chewing toast and supping tea brewed in a giant mug, she allowed her thoughts sufficient rein to wander. There'd been a moon without cloud cover the night before last and, as she'd walked back from the dustbin, she'd seen them through a bit of a gap in the curtains. So beautiful they'd looked together, like a pair of naked statues brought to life in a Scotland Road back bedroom. And Hattie had come in to sit and cry in this very chair. Frank and Polly were a match made in heaven. Oh God, she had to get rid of that rat Greg Johnson.

Again, she wiped away a few stray tears. She couldn't tell Ida, couldn't tell anyone about Frank and Polly. And now, the cowardly Greg was back, but he was too late. Polly Kennedy had found her man. Johnson mustn't be allowed to spoil it, the lily-livered idiot. She stood up and ran outside, through the back gate and into the alley. And she was just in time. He closed Ida's gate, walked past Polly and Cal's and found Hattie Benson blocking his way. 'Hello,' he said.

'Goodbye,' was her terse reply.

'Oh?' His eyebrows raised themselves.

She grabbed the front of his jacket and his tie. 'Pack your stuff and bugger off,' she spat. 'There's a mood round here these days. We don't put up with people who hurt people. We're sending one chap in front of a judge, but you . . .' She took a step closer to him. 'I'll have your eyes for ollies. The kids can roll them in the streets. Ollies, marbles, whatever you want to call them. Stay away from Polly Kennedy.' She removed her hand from his clothing. 'Ooh, look. I've left a deposit, a little bit of butter on your tie. Go back and change it, pack your bag while you're there. Come round here tonight, and there'll be a gang waiting for you. That's a promise. Some of our lads are good with their fists when it comes to looking after good folk like Polly and Cal.'

In her own yard, she leaned against the gate and shook. It wasn't fear; it was fury. She remembered the day of Cal Kennedy's accident as if it had happened yesterday. Months he'd spent in hospital and convalescent home, while his twin sister had given up her dream, the chance to work her way up at the best hairdresser's in town.

After a matter of weeks, Polly's Greg and Cal's Lois had done a disappearing act. Pol had visited her brother every day, while several Roaders had gone to see him once or twice a week, but nothing had been heard from the vanishing ones. And Greg had turned up out of the blue just when Polly seemed to have discovered a real man, one who'd been under her nose for years. Some people wanted killing. One of them was Greg Johnson.

Ida and Hattie got on with the business of the day. Each found herself listening for sounds from the cafe that separated them, but neither discovered anything to report. It was a hospital day. An ambulance would collect brother and sister later on, and the anxious neighbours were forced to wait. Neither was good at waiting, but there was no choice in the matter. People walked past both shops in search of breakfast, but they didn't linger. *Family business*, the notice said. It was a mystery.

'Right.' Cal Kennedy had had enough. 'You've been crying so hard, your eyes look like piss holes in snow. So the cafe's shut because you're not fit to be seen. You'd better tell me what's going on before I burst into flames.'

'I don't want to talk, Cal. If I talk, I might start crying all over again.' She was lying on the sofa with a tea towel over her eyes. The towel was wrapped round cubes of ice, and she was depending on these to reduce the red and swollen status of her eyelids.

'You think I notice nothing, but I know Frank stayed here.'

The towel was removed immediately. 'We had plans,' she offered after a short pause. 'And you were included.'

She picked up the towel and put it back to work. 'Then I met his mother again.'

'Oh.'

'Oh is right. She pushed my bezzie mate towards death, always running her finger over furniture looking for dust, giving her recipes to improve her cooking. She . . . humiliates people, belittles them. "You run that very basic cafe on Scotland Road, don't you?" she said to me. And I looked into those horrible, dead eyes and I got rid of him.'

'Then you're a fool.'

Once more, Polly uncovered her eyes. 'Listen, you. If he'd stayed away from his mam, that would have been my fault. If he'd visited her, I wouldn't have gone with him. And I wouldn't want her near any home of ours. She's evil. She's another Brennan, except she kicks with words. And I'm telling you now, her tongue's soled and heeled with clog irons. I wouldn't care, cos she's as common as muck, but she thinks she's the bee's knees just because their house is posh.'

'You love that lad, Pol. Somebody like me that studies life without taking a big part in it sees things. Once I walk again – and I will walk again – I'll be grateful in a way for this full stop I've been through. It's made me think. He's for you, Polly, and you're for him. And nothing will change that, ever.'

'Hmmph.'

'Never mind "hmmph", you're letting Mrs Moo win and you bloody shouldn't.'

Polly covered her eyes. No way would she cry again. 'Shut up, Callum.' The use of his full given name was a warning. Mam had used both syllables whenever her son had been out of order. Polly knew she was a fool; she also knew she'd still have been an idiot had she accepted the proposal. It was a lose-lose situation. She wondered how Frank felt today. He loved her, but he had to work for his mother ... or had he? Whatever he decided, he needed to do it without Polly's interference.

'One way or another, I'll set you free from me,' Cal said quietly.

'What? What do you mean?' Yet again, she removed the towel from her face. He was standing on uncertain legs, hands flat on the bed. She shot up and held him while he lowered himself into the wheelchair.

'See?' There was triumph in his eyes.

Breathless, Polly stood over her brother. 'Do that again, and you'll need no more treatment, because I'll bloody kill you. Slowly, they told you. Take care, or you'll do damage. Just keep still while I do my eyes.' She returned to the sofa. 'Cal?'

'What?'

'Well done.'

'Thanks.'

'But no more. Remember, I'm twenty minutes older than you.'

'OK. But I could murder a cup of tea.'

She gave up. She would wear sunglasses.

Billy Blunt was free from drips and transfusions. He was eating soft foods like soup and rice pudding, and his injuries were less painful, but he wasn't himself. Doctors advised the family to wait until he was healed and home, but Fred and Mavis had already looked into their chances of winning a case against Brennan. The lad had always been full of life and mischief; even with a bad dose of measles, he'd managed to wreck his bedroom while playing pirates. A light had been extinguished, and he had black semicircles under his eyes.

The headmaster had visited the ward with Billy's form teacher, and they'd both noticed the change in character.

After expressing the hope that he would improve, they promised to stand by the Blunts. 'We'll have a fuller picture when he's back at school,' the head teacher had opined.

Fred's brother Johnny had found a firm of lawyers who would take the case and, if they lost, would ask no fee. If they won, the Church would pay them and the Blunts. Although money might not heal Billy's mind, it would buy him a little holiday house in the country or by the sea.

During the day, the child was quiet, but his nights were torture. In his dreams were the fat priest, the black dog and the inability to move, and Billy's screams had become part of the environment. Staff did not want to over-sedate him, as his breathing had already been compromised in the attack, yet they were forced to calm him with mild medication.

'Brennan has to pay,' Fred whispered. 'I'll go to work now, Mavis.'

She kissed her husband. 'See you later, love.' So began another session for Mavis Blunt, a long, slow daylight time when she would not leave Billy's side for a second except to relieve herself or get food and drink. This was her Billy, yet not her Billy. He was all that mattered.

Wearing her best sunspecs and Sunday clothes, Polly Kennedy steered her brother towards physiotherapy. She had cancelled the ambulance; the walk would do them both good. Grateful for sunshine, she realized only too well that everyone would wonder why she wore eye protection inside the building.

'Take them off,' Cal said.

'Listen, you. Who's the driver here? If I turn left and go through a few streets, there's a big old river.'

'You're going to drown me?'

'I'm thinking about it. More trouble than the plague, you are. Anyway, sunglasses are this year's absolutely necessary fashion item.'

'Who said?'

'I said, so stop giving me lip. Ah, here we are.' She pushed him into the department. 'Who wants this?' she shouted.

'I'll have him,' a nurse called. The pretty girl waited while two men in white coats greeted Cal.

Immediately, Polly noticed that the back of her brother's neck was rather pink. He was the only person she knew who blushed on his neck. She handed him over to the therapists, but the thank you she got for going out of her way for Cal was typical. 'You're all right,' he announced to the staff. 'She's not mafia, though I'm not sure what she keeps in her locked violin case. The disguise is because she's been crying.'

But Polly let it all pass, because there was chemistry here. The nurse fancied Cal and he fancied the nurse. Yes, he was getting better and yes, Lois didn't matter any more. Tenderness in the young woman's face betrayed her inner feelings, and Polly's lip trembled. She had better not cry again, or she'd be wearing sunspecs right through Christmas. 'I'm off to the ladies' room,' she shouted before backing out of the department.

But there was no peace to be had in the washroom, because the nurse was hot on Polly's heels. 'I'm Linda,' she said. 'Linda Higgins. And you must be Polly. He thinks the world of you, does Cal.'

Polly removed the glasses and displayed her condition. 'All over a man,' she said. 'Crying myself stupid over a bloke.'

'Oh, tell me about it, because I've had my fair share. They're not worth it, Polly. Born with two brain cells that migrate to their trousers sooner or later, an appetite that would put an elephant to shame, and no ability to laugh at themselves.' She paused. 'Your brother's a bit of an exception, though.'

'Will he walk, Linda?'

'Lap of the gods, love. But I wanted to get you on your own before I ask him, because you're with him at home, so you have the bigger picture. We've got him the chance of some training at a place called Second Start. There are blind people, others in chairs like Cal, and they get taught small motor skills like soldering and assembling radios. Just one day a week.'

Polly thought about the proposition. 'He has a job. And ...' She chose her words carefully. 'He doesn't want to be different. Cal's not soft; he knows he's disabled, but he loves cooking. It's simple basic stuff, a fact that was pointed out to me lately. We had to get everything in the kitchen lowered for him. He goes to the pub, has his friends round to play cards. This is going to sound terrible, but he doesn't want a label. As far as possible, the Scotland Road people have kept his life as near as they could to what it was.'

Linda nodded. 'Thanks, Polly. I thought the answer would run along those lines, which is why I came to you first.'

Polly looked at herself in the mirror; the swellings were reducing. 'He stood up this morning.'

'Without assistance?'

Polly nodded. 'Used the bed. He's determined.'

'Then I take back lap of the gods. I've seen people walk when X-rays have proved it impossible. Oh, I hope he does it.'

'You like him,' Polly said.

'Oh yes, I do. We're warned not to get involved or fond, but it happens.'

'He likes you. I can tell, because the back of his neck went red.'

Linda laughed. 'You and I are the two people he wants to walk towards.'

Polly bit down on her lip, reached out and touched the nurse's hand. 'Don't mess him about, please.'

'Like Lois did? He told me all about her. No way, Polly. It's not in my nature.' She left the washroom.

Polly sat in a cubicle. A spark of hope flickered in her chest, and it wasn't all selfless. If Cal could be happy and safe, if a strong woman minded him, Polly would be free. With no twin to worry her daily, she'd be able to manage Mrs Moo. Cal had been her weakness and her strength, because he was vulnerable, yet good company and an excellent worker. The solution to her problem was cause for some sadness. It was ridiculous; she would miss her twin. Life, she concluded, was a series of double-edged swords, while her thinking had set itself on a loop by now, repetitive and annoying. She was getting nowhere.

'Yes, I'm still in the same place,' she whispered. 'But sitting on a hospital lav.'

She went to wash her hands. It was time to look at her brother.

Breathing was suddenly difficult for Polly, and she stopped dead in the doorway. Cal couldn't see his sister, because he was walking away from her. He was walking. She clapped a hand over her gaping mouth. Strong arms on parallel bars took much of his weight away from lower limbs, but he was definitely moving. He was walking towards Linda, a white-coated attendant at each side of him outside the bars. The left leg dragged a little, but the right foot was doing the job well.

When he reached the end, the two men turned him

and placed him in the wheelchair. Even from the door, Polly could see sweat pouring down his face. She watched while Linda dried him. If only he could take the girl dancing or to the cinema; if only he could go for a drive up to Southport or Formby. 'Slow down, Pol,' she ordered herself in a whisper. She must be patient.

She ran through a maze of equipment to her brother's side, knelt on the hard floor and hugged him.

'I'll call at your house soon,' Linda promised her. 'I'll show you how to help Cal exercise while he's lying down or sitting. And seeing that you run a cafe, you can feed me, Cal Kennedy.'

Polly grinned. 'Is the back of his neck red, Linda?'

'A bit.'

'Then we have a problem. Come on, O sweaty one. Let's get you home and hosed down.'

But Cal wasn't going home. 'I want to see Billy,' he said.

'You smell of sweat,' his sister accused.

'And you've got red eyes. What is this – some kind of competition?'

Linda stepped in. 'I'll push him, Polly. Follow me.'

They wandered through what seemed like miles of corridors, all green and cream, all smelling of disinfectant and floor polish. Linda and Cal looked so right together. Polly ached for Frank, but she wanted her twin settled, too; wanted him to have the chance of love and a life as near normal as possible.

Frank would be back; she had no doubt about that. And with her brother safely out of Norma Charleson's reach, Polly would manage Frank's mother. Probably. Possibly. She really must stop jumping the gun.

Mavis Blunt was pathetically grateful for company. Billy, sitting up in bed, was playing one-handed with Dinky cars on his wheeled over-bed trolley. Cal joined him while Polly kept Mavis company. Billy's mother shared all her worries about her youngest boy. 'He's gone nervy, Pol,' she whispered.

'I'm not surprised. No child should go through what he suffered. He'll get better, though, won't he?'

'I hope so. He's always been so lively, even cheeky. It's the nights, though. Terrible dreams, he has. We have to keep our voices down now – he hates being talked about.'

'Don't worry, Cal has him occupied. Two kids together, eh?'

They looked at the boy. He was smiling. Cal was causing multiple pile-ups on the trolley. 'Fire engine, Billy,' he called. 'And the ambulance.'

'You've a lovely brother, Polly.'

'And he seems to have collected a lovely nurse. Don't say anything.'

'I won't. Go and grab us a cuppa, Pol. The longer I sit, the more tired I get. There's a little kitchen for visiting parents – make one for Cal, too.'

Mavis watched Cal playing with her little lad. There were cars everywhere. An off-road race was taking place on the bed. 'You're cheating,' Billy cried. 'You went in reverse, and that's cheating.'

'I play poker, you know,' Cal said. 'Now you've lost the Morris Minor. You did that on purpose, William Blunt. That's my best car. You're the cheat, not me.'

Polly returned. 'Cal's nurse is making us a brew. Says she's off duty. Linda Higgins, she's called, very nice-looking. Cal's neck will go red. Just you watch.'

The two women giggled when Linda entered with a tray. Cal's neck did seem rather colourful. They noticed how the girl's hand lingered on Cal's arm.

'Now stop it with the cars, both of you,' she advised the males. 'This tea's hot, so no playing cars for a few minutes.' She sat with the two women. 'Your brother's good with children, then.'

'He's still a kid himself. Everybody likes Billy, though. He's a good lad.'

'Your eyes are red,' Mavis said. 'Are you all right?'

'Don't worry about me,' Polly answered. 'It's only a man. It won't kill me.'

They drank their tea before leaving Mavis to her lonely vigil. Cal asked Linda to have a word with the medical powers, because the boy needed to come home for his mother's sake. When Cal and Polly were in the ambulance, Linda waved them off.

'Wedding bells?' Polly asked.

'Who knows? I'm making no changes till I can walk properly without bars and two big bruisers watching out for me. What about you?'

She shrugged. 'I'll wait till you walk me up the aisle, babe. Never mind that now. We've half a ton of spuds to peel for tomorrow's dinners.'

Christopher Foley, priest for the parish of St Columba, did his duty. To God, he owed one Mass per day, and he had done his Mass at nine o'clock, when the totally dedicated attended church no matter what. But when eleven o'clock came, he was seated on a stool at the church gates, cigarette in one hand, mug of Typhoo in the other.

'Aren't we having Mass?' a lone, anxious parishioner asked.

'Go to St Anthony's, Mary. I'm with the pickets.'

'Oh.' She walked a few paces before turning back. 'Can a priest picket?'

'I may be a priest, Mary, but I'm still a bloke. I happen to believe in God, my flock, and all Christians everywhere, no matter what the shape of their faith. Billy Blunt's from a good Catholic family, and I let them down by going off and leaving everything in the hands of Eugene Brennan.

I see he hasn't improved. So I'm keeping company with the objectors, and I'll get a pint with them later in the Holy House. Go on, now. You have to be there before the introit, or you'll have missed Mass.'

She scurried away. Still existing in splendid isolation, Father Foley continued to smoke and sip at his tea. They had better come. The way things were, he stood out like a boil on the face of humanity. He could have gone for a round of golf instead of sitting here like something in Lewis's window. Ah, here they came, jagged ranks walking out of step behind Frank Charleson. Frank described himself these days as an escaped Catholic, but he remained a very close friend of Christopher Foley.

There should have been nothing funny about this strange and unprecedented occasion, but the priest and Frank found themselves almost doubled in the gutter with laughter. Some of the men carried cards. Each card bore a single capital letter. They were to stand in order until the press arrived, but their idea of order was not exactly tidy.

They began with EWWATNBERNANN, rearranging themselves into WE NAWT REBNNAN, then standing like naughty children while their headmaster, Mr Frank Charleson, snatched away the letters and redistributed them correctly. He looked at his companion. 'Father Chris, how dare these people complain about their children's spelling?'

'Oh, shut up.' The shepherd of the somewhat ungainly flock was hugging himself. He was in pain because of the laughter, and he'd lost his fag and his tea. 'Where did you find these ... these poor creatures?' he managed.

'They're yours,' was Frank's answer. 'And your parenting skills are a bit poor, Father. See? That one in the middle has his B back to front. I don't know why I bother. How can we ask respect from the press with a back-to-front

B?' He produced a shrill whistle. 'Oi, you with the legs. Turn your B the right way round.'

'What's wrong with me legs?'

Frank didn't know. 'I think you may be standing to attention, but your trousers are at ease. Pull them up a bit, we've photographers coming.' He returned to his ordained friend and fellow poker player. 'Have you seen Billy?' he asked.

'Oh, yes indeed. Grand little lad, but he has the night terrors, and his mother says he's not himself at all. I offered up Mass for him earlier. This has been taken all the way to Vatican, or so I'm led to believe. The cardinals weren't best pleased, so I think they've gone as far as the Holy Father with it. One of the bishops was heard to say that the Church is like a garden, and we need to do some weeding and pruning. Aye, it's a sad business.'

'How was retreat?' Frank asked.

'The nineteenth hole was pure luxury. Do you think they'll pull me up like some old dandelion? After all, I lied and said I was going away for a week of contemplation. If I did contemplate, it would be round about the seventh, because there was one hell of a rise to it and a bunker nearby the size of Southport beach. Ah, here they come.'

There was no shouting or swearing; apart from spelling, Frank had trained his troops well. He explained that the neighbourhood would not rest until Brennan stood before judge and jury, that no one wanted blood, but Billy should be compensated for his suffering, as should his family. 'There will be a civil suit as well,' he said. 'All decent people, whether lay or ordained, want the man to explain himself to the parents of that little boy. Do not visit young Billy with or without cameras. He's damaged, and not just physically.'

Journalists scribbled notes, while photographers did

their job. When the very civilized meeting was concluded, everyone began to wander up towards Scotland Road. Picketers from other churches joined them, as did more reporters from various newspapers. By noon, every pub on the road was filled to bursting. Frank lingered on the pavement with his pint. Diagonally across the road stood Polly's Parlour. It was closed on Sundays. On her one day off, she cleaned the place from top to bottom while poor Cal sat in his chair feeling guilty.

'She got to you, then?'

'Oh, hello, Chris. Yes, we got to each other and broke commandments. Then she drew a line under my bloody mother.'

The priest took a long swig of Guinness. 'Ah, your mother.'

'Polly's worried for Cal.'

'Ah well, your ma wasn't exactly kind to young Ellen, was she?'

Frank shook his head. 'I left home.'

'Did you now? And where are you living?'

'Bedsit in Bootle. And my stash of junk's still in lock-up till I find a shop with accommodation attached. I have to win Polly back, Chris. You'd better get busy with the rosary beads and the holy water, since we seem to need some level of intervention.'

Christopher kept his counsel. He knew Polly well enough, while Frank was one of his best friends, but Norma Charleson was a different kettle of squid altogether. She seemed totally self-centred, as if she couldn't entertain feelings for anyone at all. Her husband had been her ticket to a better life, Frank was a decorative, intelligent son, and she was the centre of the universe.

'Chris?'

'Sorry. I was just thinking about your mother.'

'No wonder you look depressed.'

The priest laughed. 'She's watching us, you know.'

Frank looked round. 'No, she won't come here till the rent needs collecting.'

'Not your mother, eejit. Polly Kennedy. She was at the window in her little hairdressing room. Go and knock on the door.'

Frank shook his head. 'It's not time yet. I have to sort my life out, Chris. And there's Cal. You know Polly has a strong sense of duty. Those two had good parents and an excellent upbringing. And twinship keeps them close, although she does make sure everyone knows she's the elder. She won't ever let him down.'

'I dare say you're right. Come on, let's away inside and get a drop of Irish. It'll all work out well, I'm sure.'

Six

Norma Charleson owned no sunglasses to hide swollen eyelids, no self-control to help manage her outbursts. She simply stayed on her chaise, wept, drank tea, wept again, ate her frugal meals, wept and got angry with everything and everyone. The good news was that her sugar level was nearer the mark and her urine contained no ketones. She felt rather weak, but this was a period of radical adjustment, and that damned fool of a doctor was pathetically pleased. He still refused to give her strong painkillers for her arthritis, so her opinion of him remained unchanged.

Christine Lewis didn't know what to do, because the housekeeper understood full well that chocolate was her employer's medicine. It was not without side effects, as the woman had gained stones in weight, was diabetic with neuropathy in legs and feet, but chocolate was the only thing that improved the mood of the woman who now wanted to be Norma rather than Mrs Charleson. Her job was hell on earth, and Christine longed to go home to her ancient, miniature house.

Yes, it was time to look for alternative employment, but could she leave Norma Charleson in this condition? Even if the woman did stage some of her behaviours, she was clearly unfit to be left in total isolation. Sometimes, a conscience was a heavy weight to bear.

'Will you stop cleaning for a minute, Christine? Every

time I look at you, you're attached to a duster or a damp cloth. Just sit with me for a few minutes, please. I can't stop crying. I don't think I'll ever stop, because Frank's broken my spirit completely. My own son, my flesh and blood, did this to me. My poor heart's all over the place with palpitations.'

Christine sat. 'You're not the only one who's been through this sort of thing. Elaine's a good girl now, but she was a silent, broody teenager for a while after Jim died, and not too wonderful during the university years.' Did Norma have a heart? She seemed to care only for her own comfort, and she hated change. She was also afraid of being alone at night in a house that was so dark at the back, so exposed. The spiral staircase to the upstairs garden room troubled her, and she locked herself in the annexe if Frank wasn't at home.

'He's twenty-six,' his mother moaned now. 'This isn't a teenage tantrum, because he hates me – he practically said so. I don't know where he is. I have to know where he is.'

'He'll come back, I'm sure, Norma.' Frank certainly had a heart and he wouldn't leave his mother in this state, surely? Even from a practical viewpoint, an address to which mail might be forwarded should have been left behind.

'You don't know him. He's stubborn like his dad. Charlie used to go days without saying more than a few words to me.'

Christine sighed. It sounded as if both men in her boss's life had worn internal armour in order to protect themselves from this impossible woman. 'Do you want me to go to that cafe you told me about and ask if Frank's there?'

Norma was suddenly quiet. She needed to think about that. She needed to think about rent collections, too, and then there was the maintenance side of things. Some of her properties were scheduled for demolition, but the rest needed to be kept in good order. She must buy more, too ... 'Make a pot of tea, Christine. Saccharin for me, and just a drop of milk.'

The housekeeper went to do as she'd been told. Frank seemed to be in the Scotland Road area, as his photograph was plastered across several newspapers together with his plea for children's rights. He'd been picketing with other people, one of them a priest who objected to the behaviour of his temporary replacement. He was quoted, too. 'All we want is peace of mind for a little boy and his family. My church and school are places of safety, yet this terrible thing happened in the grounds.' The poor man could lose his parish for speaking his mind, as few bishops liked their priests to broadcast opinions. It was rather like Parliament – three-line whip, go in, you're a free man, but vote as we dictate.

Meanwhile, Norma's mind was in top gear. But when it came to actual gears, her car hadn't been touched for months, so that definitely needed to be first priority. Christine had a licence, but she owned no car. If the Morris could be serviced and returned to working order, perhaps Christine might do the collecting for a little extra money. Once her own health had improved, Norma could take over.

Christine returned with the tea.

They sat and sipped while Norma's train of thought reached the station. 'Look, if I get the car working, I'll lend it to you and pay for petrol. Shopping would be so much easier and cheaper if we didn't pay delivery charges. And if you'd like to earn extra, there's another job you might like to consider.'

The housekeeper listened. Sitting and listening had been her main job for a few days now. She was being invited to become an employee of Charleson Holdings.

Her function would be to collect rents, note complaints and pass the list of required repairs to Norma, who would then send a firm of builders to mend the roof, the guttering or whatever required attention. 'And it's not a job for life, my dear; it would be just until I'm better and fit to handle things myself.'

'Er ... yes, I suppose I could do that. But I'd need maps, because I'm not familiar with many areas of the city.'

Norma nodded. 'Of course, I understand.'

'Are they widespread?'

'Well, I do try to concentrate on clusters when purchasing, but that's not always possible. There's Scotland Road and the streets either side of it, a few nearer the river, some in West Derby, Bootle, Litherland, four in a terrace near Sefton Park – oh, I'll get you a list. I would be so grateful. And you may use the car for yourself, too.'

'Is it all right if I think about it until tomorrow? I'm not ungrateful, but I have to be sure that I can cope with so much responsibility.'

'Of course you need to be sure. Another drop of tea, I think.'

While pouring more of the cup that cheers, Christine realized that her companion's tears had dried at the speed of light. She was solving her problems, and Frank had disappeared completely from her thoughts. What Norma Charleson needed was a servant, and a blood relative had no more value than the next man or woman. Where were people like Norma made? In some well-hidden engineering factory? Because she wasn't quite human. Christine knew someone else who was similarly uncaring when it came to other people, but she didn't want to think about Elaine just now.

The housekeeper told herself inwardly to try to find Frank, mostly to get his advice about the business. His mother had done nothing during recent years, and Frank could turn the tenants into people, would be able to give advice about who paid willingly and who didn't.

The day blundered on unsteadily. Problems were doubled because Norma had gone from one extreme to another. Thus far, she had eaten all her meals, snacks between meals, and chocolate almost continually. Now, she was taking herself right to the edge in the other direction, so she wasn't making full sense on occasion. The doctor had spoken to both women about the testing of new drugs for type two diabetics, but they were not yet available. All the woman had was a system that tested urine.

It was a disease in which, for the most part, the patient needed to be her own doctor. Until now, Norma had lived in a make-believe world where nothing could touch her. Christine felt that so drastic a change was dangerous, so she tried one more time before going home. 'If you don't eat enough, you'll collapse. It's called hypoglycaemia. Your brain pinches every last bit of sugar and you feel OK, but suddenly, your brain runs out. So, these are glucose. Keep them by you at all times, even in the bathroom. If your thinking alters, take one. If you have difficulty when walking, always take glucose.'

Tears again. 'You are so kind to me, like the sister I never had.' This was genuine thankfulness; Norma truly believed she had found a friend at last.

'And you are losing weight already. If you look after yourself, we'll be off to Liverpool or Southport on a shopping spree to get you new clothes.'

The tears stopped immediately. 'Oh, I'd love that.'

'Good. So keep yourself steady, stick to the doc's diet sheet more or less, and your clothes will be hanging off you in a few months. It will be a new beginning for you.'

'Thank you. Thank you so much.'

On her way home, Christine decided that she knew

what was wrong with Norma Charleson. At the age of fifty-two, she remained a child in many respects. She was still the centre of her own universe, hungry for food and attention. Her relationships were few and difficult; she wanted praise, approval and pampering. The mood swings might be attributable to her physical illness, though she used tears as a weapon, as might a five-year-old.

'And I'm all she has.' That was a sobering thought.

Linda Higgins and Polly were moving furniture in the living room behind the cafe. In order to help Cal exercise, there needed to be space all round his bed, which had lived until now against the wall under the stairs. While the women worked, he shouted directions from his wheelchair in the doorway. 'Don't forget space for my wheelchair' and 'Don't drop the bookmark, it's keeping my place just before Jack the Ripper strikes again' were just two of his many orders.

'Will you shut up?' Polly yelled. 'You're not a traffic cop down town. What about my couch and sideboard? They were our mam's and I'm not parting with them.'

'Why don't you just stick me in the backyard under a tarpaulin?'

'Don't tempt me, brother. But can we afford a tarpaulin? Linda, is he worth the price of waterproof covering?'

Linda called a halt. 'You'll have to put the sideboard against the wall where you walk through from the cafe to the kitchen, so you'll need to do a bit of a swerve. There is plenty of space for his wheelchair between the end of the sideboard and each doorway.'

'How do you know?' Polly asked.

'I measure by eye, the same as when I'm making clothes. And if you put some sort of protective cover on the sideboard instead of over your brother in the back-

142

yard, you can leave the dirty dishes on it instead of walking through and cluttering his precious kitchen every time.'

'I never said my kitchen was precious—'

'Shut up,' chorused the women.

Cal chuckled inwardly. He'd been under his sister's thumb since the accident, but now she was collecting troops. Some of the torture they were planning to inflict involved two people. If Linda was at work, he'd be at the tender mercies of Polly, plus Hattie next door or any passing stranger who looked soft enough to be dragged in. Oh, life was so bloody wonderful.

They emptied the sideboard and lifted it into its new position. It was Utility, so it wasn't large and wasn't heavy. Linda straightened her spine. 'We'll be the ones needing treatment,' she said. 'Right, handsome. Take yourself into the cafe, then get back in here and see if there's room for your chair to turn.'

'I'd never have thought of that,' Polly admitted.

'True,' her brother said. 'Never thinks about her poor crippled twin.' He did as ordered and managed the turn. 'See? I'm an expert in my field.'

'If we had a field, you'd be out to grass,' Polly said.

'Another four inches towards the kitchen, because his turn was a bit tight,' Linda ordered. 'Now, do the same with the other door, Cal,' she suggested when the sideboard had been edged along the wall.

He manoeuvred his way into the back kitchen and out again. 'God help you two when I can walk,' he said. 'I have every intention of running you ragged, so just you wait and see.'

'Empty promises,' Polly said. 'Ignore him.'

The sofa finished up facing the foot of Cal's bed. 'Do I have to sit looking at him?' Polly asked.

'No,' Linda said, her voice trembling with contained

laughter. 'Lie down, head on cushions, watch television. Or send him to the pub. Failing that, stick him outside as he suggested. You might even fit a small shed out there.' She positioned his bedside table. 'Right. Your wheelchair will fit at the other side, and it can be moved while the exercises are going on. Give Polly one bit of trouble, and I'll tan your hide, Mr Kennedy.'

'More empty promises,' he grunted. 'I'll go and make coffee for the workers.'

The girls repositioned the sofa and moved the television table an inch or two. 'There we are.' Linda clapped her hands. 'Done, but not dusted. You can do that later. He's looking well.'

'I can hear you,' Cal shouted. 'My hearing wasn't affected by the accident.'

'Nor was his brain,' Polly said loudly. 'He's still as daft as ever.'

Linda, suddenly exhausted, threw herself on the sofa. 'I've brought the exercise instructions. They're in the fruit bowl. The first time, I'll partner you and perhaps Hattie will watch.'

'What am I? The bloody cabaret?' called the voice from the kitchen.

Polly marched to the connecting door. 'Listen, they wouldn't want you at the Rotunda on a wet Friday even if no other acts turned up. Your muscles have shrivelled up like Mother Bailey's gob, and she's older than God.'

'She has a lot of worry, Pol.'

'So she should, running a secret brothel everybody knows about. But your legs need building up, so you won't be a star turn or even a Punch and Judy show. We need to strengthen muscle, hopefully without damaging nerves. But I'm telling you now, you are getting on my bloody nerves, so I'm going next door to look at Hattie's cabbages, then you can do your worst with bubble and squeak.'

Alone for the first time ever, Cal and Linda sat at a small table, she on a conventional chair, he in his usual means of transport with the brake on. The bigger table, Mam's best, had been given to Ida Pilkington, whose brother's Alsatian bitch had chewed part of a leg off her Utility dining table. Balanced for months on *Wuthering Heights* and a child's illustrated dictionary, it was now consigned to Dusty Den's scrap and rag yard, and the Kennedy table took pride of place, a ten-year-old aspidistra acting as its centrepiece when no one was eating.

They both missed Polly. She was the buffer, the surface from which their light-hearted remarks were bounced. Embarrassment held them back when no one was with them.

'You've a lovely sister,' Linda said. 'I really like your Polly.'

'She keeps me going, and she's a damned good worker.'

There followed a short, awkward silence. 'I think you'll walk, but you may need a caliper on that left leg.'

He agreed. 'More feeling in the right one,' he confessed, 'though I have had some pain in the left. Wait and see, eh?'

The conversation was stilted, and there was very little eye contact.

'You seem to have good neighbours,' she said. 'Helpful types.'

'We're blessed,' he answered. 'Ida Pilkington is newspapers, tobacco and sweets; Hattie Benson's fruit, veg and all kinds of bits. Jimmy Nuttall does fish, tripe and cooked meats, Ernie Bradshaw's a baker. Jack Fletcher, he's a costermonger, and we've loads more, every one of them a diamond.'

'I live in Waterloo,' Linda said.

'Posh?'

'Not really. Mam needed a bungalow, because she lost her legs when Bootle was bombed.'

He put down his cup. 'I'm sorry, love. Was that what made you become a nurse?'

Linda pondered for a moment. 'I think I always fancied nursing. But I suppose with Mam being the way she is, I felt drawn to people with mobility problems. I'm sure you've noticed folk asking whoever's pushing you whether you need something. Mam's funny. She always tells people she's there and she's not daft, and orders them to talk to the organ grinder. She says any monkey can push a chair.'

'I like the sound of her.'

'Yes. She rather likes the sound of you. She's talking about forming a union, the National Union of Disabled.'

Another silence ticked by. 'You've talked about me?'

Linda nodded.

'To your mother?'

'Yes. She'd like to meet you. Your neck's gone red.' Polly was right – he did blush all the way down to his shoulders.

'So has your face.'

They burst out laughing simultaneously. Like teenagers, they giggled and held hands in the centre of the table that separated them. It was the beginning of something, but neither understood what the something was. At last, they were trying to look at each other, and fingers tightened their grip slightly. Was this going to be love? Whatever it was, it remained young and needed nurturing gently so that it would get the chance to discover its own identity. Meanwhile, each enjoyed the stumbling company of the other, and life was worth living.

*

Hattie had hit the sherry. This didn't happen often, and it was seldom a pretty event. Her specs were crooked, her hair was a mess, while her pinafore was definitely inside out and covered in debris from stock in the shop. 'Come in. Sorry I've not cleaned up proper, but I'm a bit out of sorts, like.'

'Hattie,' Polly cried. 'What's happened?' To drink a significant amount, Hattie had to be upset.

'See,' Hattie said, though the word arrived as 'She', 'them teachers has said what they seen ... what they saw. So everybody's against him. He's had it, Pol. E'cept for God being on little Billy's side, Brennan could have ended up hunged.' She hiccuped loudly. 'Sorry 'bout that. I had tongue for me tea an' it repeats. Yes, it repeats.'

'You're repeating now, Hattie. Don't drink any more, love.'

'I re ... member you when you were a little kid. So you can't tell me what to do, Polly. I'm forty ... can't remember ... but I am, denny ... deffy ... dennifitely ...'

'Forty-three.'

'Is it?'

'Yes.'

'Must be past bedtime, then.'

'Yes.'

'And I wasn't joking with him, no way. Put butter on his tie, I did. He never come back, did he? I told him to bugger off, and off he buggered-ed. He did. Cos I shown him I meant business. Oh, yes. Went off like a whipped dog, tail between his legs.'

'Who did?'

Hattie tapped the side of her nose, though she almost missed her target. 'That ... at's for me to know and you to ... I said there'd be a gang waiting if he did bother coming back. Got a job down the Liver. In ... surance.

Bad man, Polly. Bad man.' She emptied the glass in one huge gulp. 'I think I feel a bit sick.'

Polly was at a loss. 'Did your husband come back?'

Hattie screeched with drunken laughter. 'Did he fu—Funny you should ask, but no, not him. If he come ... came here, I'd stick a knife in his doodahs. Useless. He drinks, you know. Terrible trouble with ale an' whisky.'

'Yes.'

'I can't stand them what drink.'

'You probably can't stand at all, Hattie. How much have you had?'

'Is ... it's only sherry.'

'Deadly stuff – that's fortified wine. Sherry's strengthened with brandy.'

Hattie blinked stupidly. 'I don't like brandy.' Another few hiccups crashed upward from her diaphragm. 'I hate brandy.'

'You're drinking it.'

'Sherry.'

'Has brandy in it, Hat. Let me make some tea.' Polly walked to the cooker. By the time she returned, Hattie was snoring. Oh, the poor woman would wake with one hell of a hangover.

The visitor placed a clean glass and a jug of water on the table next to her inebriated neighbour. If Hattie woke with a thirst, that would have to do. After picking up the sherry bottle and pouring its meagre dregs into the sink, Polly went home. She had intended to leave Linda and Cal for longer, but sitting with a sleeping drunk wasn't her idea of fun.

When she entered the living room, her brother was asleep in his newly positioned bed. Linda had gone. Never mind, she told herself. The evening had been different, at least. No hairdressing, just the shifting of furniture.

But who the heck was Hattie talking about? She'd got her knife into somebody, that was certain. And whoever it was had better keep his distance, because Hattie plus sherry formed a lethal combination.

By the time Billy was released from hospital, the schools had closed for the long summer holidays. Friends visited and signed the plaster on his arm, but he didn't seem interested. When questioned by his peers about the attack, he offered no answers. Small boys, always eager for excitement and colourful tales, gave up after a few days, and Billy was left alone. He didn't seem to notice the lack of visitors, didn't appear to care.

The nights remained terrible. For Mavis, it was like having her newborn baby back, since Billy slept now only during the hours of daylight. His bed was brought downstairs, and Mavis rested on the sofa between screaming fits. For once in her life, she was glad that her older children had left home.

Fred, a bus driver, needed to be alert for work, so he remained in the marital bed with cotton wool in his ears while Mavis shouldered the bigger burden. She, too, had to take naps during the day, so meals were thrown together and housework suffered. The poor lad had to get through this.

A district nurse called daily. Dissatisfied with the child's emotional health, she sent in a psychologist, who insisted on seeing Billy alone. 'No distractions, no inhibitions,' he whispered to the child's mother. Mavis went to sit in the parlour. This room was used only for visitors and at Christmas, so it advertised the fact by smelling empty. It was stale, unwelcoming and damp even in warmer weather. She had better start opening the window in summer and lighting a small fire in winter months.

Would Billy get well? Had a bang on the head sent him mental?

'Billy? I'm Dr Shaw, but you may call me Dr Pest.'

Billy looked the intruder up and down. 'Why?'

'Because I'm a pest.'

'So am I.'

'All right, then. We have much in common, you and I. I'm Pest Senior, and you're Pest Junior. I'm the good-dream doctor.'

Billy's mouth twitched. 'Bad dreams,' he said. 'I get bad ones.'

'I deal with those,' the doctor said. 'Nurse Jenkins told me you were tormented. So I've brought a trap. Not for mice, you understand, but for nightmares.' He lowered his tone. 'Don't lend it to anyone, especially grown-ups. It doesn't always work for them.'

'Why?'

'Because they stop believing in magic. Now, you'll be one of only three children in Liverpool to have a trap. And if you wake up screaming, blow the bad dream up towards the feathers. Make the feathers move by blowing hard.'

'Is it a bird?'

'No. Did you want a bird?'

'I want a dog, but not a big black one.'

'I didn't bring one of those, sorry. Now, take me through your terrible dream. Speak through the middle of the trap. It was made by native Americans. Even the adults believe in magic over there.' He took the dream-catcher from his bag.

Billy gasped. 'Spider's web,' he said. It was a huge circle with smaller circles dangling from it. Each circle, big or small, was filled with intricate, open threadwork. Tiny mirrors and feathers completed the piece.

'No bird was killed, Billy. These feathers were shed

naturally and collected by the people who made this for you. Right. Tell the dream through the biggest hole in the biggest ring.'

Billy gave his nightly torture to the open centre of the largest hoop. Feathers moved as he spoke, while tiny, weightless mirrors shivered and turned whenever the doctor's hand moved. And it moved regularly while the boy told his nightmare. But doctors shouldn't weep or get angry, so the man fought his feelings and tried to remain outwardly unaffected.

'So that's why I don't want a big black dog,' Billy concluded.

Dr Shaw nodded. 'I can understand that, son. Now, you may have to do some blowing. Bad dreams sometimes need help to disappear completely through the big hole, and blown feathers quicken the process. The smaller gaps hold your good dreams in the webbing and save them up. Right, get comfortable and stare into the dream-catcher.'

Billy was an easy target. Within seconds, his eyes closed; all he could hear was the soft voice of a kind man. The black dog was not a threat; it was a rescue animal. The bad, breathless man in black was locked up and would never again be seen in these parts. School and church were good places filled by good people.

'And when I count to three, you will wake and feel happy. You have a lovely mother. Look after her. One, two, three.'

Billy woke. 'Did I fall asleep?'

'Not quite. Life will get better for you, I promise. If you need me again, I'll come back; we pests should stick together. Ask your dad to hang the dream-catcher on a string over your head. Good lad. Bye for now.'

The doctor joined Mavis in the parlour. 'Well, you can be proud of him, Mrs Blunt – he's a brave little soldier.'

He explained about the dream-catcher and the myth attached to it. 'It must be hung over his head so that he can blow the feathers, but not near enough to touch him. I hypnotized him for a very short time. Now, it's a case of crossed fingers for all of us. Please tell the nurse everything that happens, and she'll pass it on to me. I'll show myself out.'

The anxious mother returned to the bedside of her little afterthought, born fifteen years after the last of the older ones. He was holding the dream-catcher and blowing on the feathers. 'Look, Mam. It was made by a Red Indian just for me. It helps to stop the bad dreams and saves the good ones.'

'Ooh, that sounds clever. Would you like something to eat?'

'I want a dog.'

Mavis bit her lip. 'With chips?'

'No. With a collar and lead and a bed and his own dish.'

'Ooooh.' She folded her arms. 'We'll have to ask your dad, love. They need walks on grass, and we haven't got grass yet. We might have grass when we move.'

Billy thought about that. He didn't want to move. Living on Dryden Street meant he could fall out of bed and into church or school within five minutes, because St Anthony's was on the corner. 'Do we have to move?'

'Yes, love. The houses are being pulled down before they fall down.'

Then he asked the question that had fallen from the lips of thousands of adults. 'Why can't they build new ones here?'

She didn't go into details about the Home Office wanting rid of Catholics because Catholics did the loot in 1919. It was only a rumour, anyway, and possibly slanderous. 'They want roads, not houses, Billy. They want big, wide roads with nobody living on them.'

'That's daft,' Billy said.

Mavis's heart fluttered hopefully. It looked like it was time to send for Cal Kennedy, because Billy loved him. In fact, most kids responded well to Cal. Perhaps that was because he lived in a chair and was nearer to their level in height. Was her special boy on his way back?

'I can get me dad's bus with a dog,' he said. 'He can drop me off at a park, then pick me up on his way back. It'll have to be a little dog. And I can walk to Everton Park; it's not that far.'

'I'll ask your dad.'

'Promise?'

'I promise.'

He smiled. Whenever he was ill, he got some of his own way. 'I'll have toast and jam, please.'

Mavis, once she reached the kitchen, forgot that she was no longer a Catholic and blessed herself at the sink. This was the first time Billy had demanded anything. 'Please, God, give me back my son. Holy Mother, intercede for me,' she whispered. Toast. Doorsteps, of course. Billy was getting better.

The cafe was unusually quiet. Lunch was cottage pie (scouse, with a covering of mashed potato), meat and tater pie (scouse under pastry), scouse with red cabbage and beetroot, or a choice of new offerings of chicken pie or paella. Cal had been reading again, and he'd got hold of prawns and chicken at cost from Jimmy Nuttall. 'They're not saying much out there,' he said to his sister. 'They don't like change, do they?'

Polly pushed damp curls off her forehead. 'Ah well, maybe some do. Them that had your paella want more, and there is none, and them that didn't try it want to, but it's all gone, because you didn't make enough. I told them

153

you were testing, and you'll make more next week. You, brother, are a cook. No, you're a chef. I'll go down town later and get you some cookery books before my girls arrive for their hair doing. Brilliant first try, Cal.'

He beamed. He had a lovely girlfriend, a great sister, and he was a chef who was learning to walk.

Someone tapped on the open door between cafe and living room.

Polly turned and left the kitchen. It was Hattie. From the cafe, whispers arrived. 'She's gone in' and 'She's going to tell her'.

'Polly?'

'What?'

'Can I come in?'

'For a minute, yes, but I've stuff to do.'

Hattie perched on the edge of a dining chair. 'The sherry,' she began. 'I had to have a drink to wipe his face out. See, Ida had gone and hid him in her back bedroom, but I told her not to say nothing. Then I put butter on his tie and got rid of him. But I'm not rid in my head; I keep seeing the bugger.'

'With butter on his tie?' Polly asked.

'Yes, and a few fleas in his ears. I told him to piss off and off he pissed.'

'You said as much when I visited you. You were very drunk.'

'But he's real, Pol. He never came back up here, like, after that first morning when I seen him, but he's in town working at the Liver in insurance or some such job. I'm the only one with the guts to tell you.'

Polly sat down abruptly. 'You mean Greg, don't you?'

Hattie nodded. She pushed a piece of paper towards Polly. On it were written the words *Lois is back, too. They went to London together and came back together, but they're*

*not together like boyfriend and girlfriend. This is wrote
down so I don't upset Cal.*

'Do you know where he's staying?' Polly asked, her
voice weaker than usual.

'No idea at all, queen. Ida's first thought was to drag
him in and hide him – you know how you are when
you've just had a shock. Then she told me, and I sorted
him out, but of course, she went and told everybody. You
know how she is.' She mouthed the rest. 'Only yesterday,
I seen Lois walking past the piano shop, and I put two
and two together, cos he'd already said to Ida that they
travelled to London together, but not like boyfriend and
girlfriend. Looks like they come back together, too.'

'What are you whispering about?' the chef called.

'Women's stuff,' Polly answered. 'So mind your own. I
want four banoffee puddings and two chocolate sponges
with custard.'

Hattie nodded, picked up the incriminating piece of
paper and returned to the cafe. She sat with her friends,
nodded again and whispered, 'It's done.' They didn't know
she'd seen Lois, and she was saying nothing. Let somebody else see her; let some other poor soul carry half the
burden. Frank Charleson hadn't been round in a while,
but Hattie still nursed the hope that her favourite girl
would marry Frank instead of the prodigal creep.

'You think the world of Pol, don't you, Hattie? The
daughter you never had, eh?'

'That's right, Ida. I promised her mam you and I would
look after her.'

'Once you got rid of your owld feller.'

'Do you know, love, I never got nothing out of
him. Bag of chips on a Friday, a smack in the eye of a
Saturday night, loads of sweaty socks, and grime on his
collars that thick I needed holy water and a papal blessing
to shift it.'

'I know, kid. There's not one of them to mend another. Bloody men? They should be locked up, most of them.'

'Greg mustn't get her back, Ida. She's too good for most, so definitely a sight better than that yellow-belly.' As for Cal, well, he had collected a pretty nurse, so to hell with Lois Monk, but Hattie kept that to herself.

When the dinner-time crowd had left, Polly started to clear up. Linda had been right about the sideboard; covered in heat- and damp-proof material, it was a good halfway mark for dishes and debris. He was back, damn him. And Frank was staying away because ... 'Because I'm a fool,' she told a pile of dinner plates.

'He's turned up, then? The bad penny, I mean.'

She jumped. 'Has that wheelchair got crêpe tyres? Sneaking up on me like that while I'm all of a dither – yes, Greg's back.'

'If I could walk, I'd kill him.'

'And a lot of use that would be, our kid.' She made the decision there and then. If Hattie had seen Lois, others would see her, and the news should come from Cal's sister, his one and only living relative. 'Cal, Lois has been seen, too.'

He parked his chair. 'Well, she'd better not waste my time, Pol. I'm not in the mood for folk who don't know whether they're coming or going.' He picked up his book and carried on reading about the malpractices of Jack the Ripper.

His sister, up to her elbows in washing-up water, considered spinsterhood. It wasn't a pleasant prospect, but it was a damned sight better than finishing up like Hattie, who had often sported a black eye, a cut lip, bruised arms. Polly retained no feelings whatsoever for Greg. The hurt had turned to anger, and the anger had dissipated like dew on a summer morning. He didn't matter, but he'd better not become a nuisance.

Someone knocked on the cafe door. 'We're closed,' the siblings called.

The tapping was repeated, so Polly picked up a towel to dry her hands and walked through. A well-dressed and pleasant-looking woman stood outside. Polly surveyed her through the glass before opening the door. 'Yes? Can I help you?'

'May I come in?'

'Of course.'

They sat at one of the tables. 'I won't keep you. I'm Christine Lewis, and I'm looking for Frank Charleson.'

'Oh?' This was the housekeeper, then. This was the one who danced to the mooing of the old cow.

'His mother asked me to collect rents for her, because Frank moved out recently. He's looked after the business for years, so I wanted to ask him a few questions, get some hints and tips.'

'He's not been here. I haven't seen him for a while.'

'Oh. Er . . .'

'What?'

'I thought . . . I just thought you and he were—'

'Well, we're not, because I can't stand the woman you're collecting rents for. When did he leave?'

'Not very long ago. It was a Thursday. Mrs Charleson said he'd been out with you the previous evening and brought you to see her. He drove you home and returned in a temper. She was very upset. Have you any idea at all where he might be?'

'She sent you.'

'No, no—'

'If I knew where he was, I wouldn't tell you. That bloody woman ruined my best friend's life and robbed her of years she might have had if she hadn't been mithered by Mrs Moo.' Polly lowered her tone. 'My situation's a bit like that; I have a vulnerable brother. He's not got a bad heart,

157

so he can't be killed like Ellen was, but he's unable to walk for now, and I want him in good spirits. That's why I turned Frank down, because I don't want her in my life or within a mile of my brother. So if Frank does come near, I won't tell you. Sorry, Mrs Lewis, but if he's cleared off, good luck to him.'

Christine Lewis found herself outside the shop; its door was locked, its blind was down, and window blinds were also being lowered. She suddenly began to approve strongly of Miss Polly Kennedy. The young woman should have hung in there with Frank. Because Polly Kennedy feared no one. She might have been Norma Charleson's albatross.

Somewhere outside Stone in Staffordshire, Eugene Brennan shivered in a barn. Staffordshire, if he remembered rightly when thinking of the geography of this godforsaken country, was not very far south of Cheshire. Chester, the county town, was a hop from the Wirral, which was a ferry ride or a long swim from Liverpool. He was going in the right direction. In truth, he would have liked to avoid Liverpool like the plague, but his money was there alongside other personal items he might need.

A pile of sacks that felt not too damp had to be his covering, while prickly hay, also covered in sacks, furnished him with a makeshift mattress. The right direction? He was wearing clothes stolen from a washing line, had spent money taken from a purse in some careless woman's kitchen, while the company he was keeping consisted of a bottle of Scotch and some scuttering things, probably rats. Oh yes, and he had killed a man of God.

He dozed. The day had been warm, but the night was quite chilly, especially in this aged building. Constructed from wood, it owned many gaps and loose planks. Courting the edge of sleep was not pleasant, because the dream threatened. Last night, in a deserted house in the middle of nowhere, he had lit a fire and slept in an old chair. Sleep was no place to hide.

The dream; oh God, yes, the dream. He was in his grey cell waiting for a grey man, one of many. A grey man himself, he was forced to wear the garb of a monk, as he had no change of clothing, and his own garments were being cleaned after his bath. The plus side to uniform was that he wouldn't be recognized immediately during his escape. On the wall over his bed, the pale shape of a cross lingered, but any incomer would not notice the missing Christ crucified, as the bunk was not facing the door in this cramped container.

The ordained priest lifted the weighty object and brought it down on the skull of one of the brethren just as the monk placed a tray on a tiny table. His victim did not fall; surprisingly, frighteningly, he turned to face his attacker. What followed would leave an indelible mark on the mind of Brennan, and an unsightly one on the face of the doomed brother.

An arm of the cross fixed itself in the man's sun-starved face. It broke his cheekbone, entered the eye socket and remained there. Brennan was welded to the spot, crazy thoughts running through a maze in his brain while he watched his visitor sink to the floor. It was an inside monk, because the skin was not weathered; other monks tilled the soil and grew vegetables, but this one clearly didn't. There was very little blood. There was very little blood because the first blow had stopped his heart. A dead man had managed to turn and face his killer. Had this been a miracle?

He bent over the still form and removed a leather belt. The key was his. He had the key at last, and he was a murderer. What he didn't have was the memory of inflicting the second blow. Had Satan made it happen?

Getting through the front door was easy; getting out of the grounds was not. A hefty man, Brennan took a while to climb over a wall and its added railings, but he finally managed it. As he hurried along a country lane, he heard a bell tolling. His victim had been found. The order would not be silent today, as its members would be forced to talk to police.

He left the lane and scurried through fields and hedges, climbed walls, dragged his exhausted body across a shallow stream. Water was good; dogs lost their bearings near water. From a washing line in the garden of a cottage, he stole clothes. In a copse, he hid the grey garment given to him in the monastery and donned ill-fitting trousers, shirt and cardigan.

Again, he travelled, trying to keep the afternoon sun to his left, as he needed to progress northward. From another cottage, he stole money and food. As a murderer, he would be hunted by every force in England. As a murderer, he might well face Albert Pierrepoint, the hangman who had dispatched those found guilty at Nuremberg. His face would be in every newspaper . . .

In the cold barn, he fell asleep eventually and relived once more the killing of a dedicated, decent man. But this time, Christ was made flesh, climbing off the cross and growing to full height. He stood in bloodied garments between priest and monk. 'Thou shalt not kill,' He said before disappearing from the scene.

Brennan woke screaming. He had broken a commandment that carried an extra clause: no confessor could forgive him, no priest would be able to cleanse his soul until he answered first to the law of the land. He was doomed. If he arrived at suburbs, his screams would definitely be heard. The owner of the off-licence from which he had bought whisky might well remember the oddly dressed man. He needed a beard. He needed to lose weight. Moving more and eating less, he would achieve the latter, while the former would take care of itself.

All this mess had been caused by a young thief who had entered sacred territory to steal from the vestry. 'All this for half a crown,' he mumbled. 'All this for a worthless young whippersnapper.'

Morning came. Bleary-eyed and weak, he staggered on, avoiding civilization, steering clear of cows and horses, as such animals were often accompanied by humans. Within a couple of days, he had become a man without a job, without a redeemable soul, without a future. Eugene Brennan was now a murderer on the run, a tramp, a vagabond. He might as well hang for a sheep. Billy Blunt, St Anthony's parish, Scotland Road, Liverpool. But before Eugene could go anywhere or do anything, the screaming had to stop.

Dr Shaw (Pest Senior) returned. He perched on the couch while Billy played on the floor. 'Right, Pest Junior. What's going on? I'm told you want to talk to me.' The bed had been returned to its rightful place upstairs. 'Do you still have the trap?'

'Yes.'

'And do you use it?'

Billy nodded. 'Yes, and it works. But the dream changed.' He put down a small fire engine. 'I'm getting a dog, but it's not long borned. When they get borned, you have to wait six weeks at least.'

'Is it going to be black?'

The child shrugged. 'It's a spaniel, I think. I don't care what colour it is, because the black dog spoke to me.'

'Did it?'

'Oh yes. Said he was on my side, a rescue dog, just like you told me. The fat man, the priest, ex-caped from where he was being kept.'

'I see.' It had been in all the newspapers, of course. The boy had probably read it or heard about it, since it was a nationwide sensation, the press having a field day with one man of God who had killed another.

'He had Jesus in his eye.'

'Who did?'

'The man who got murdered by the fat priest.'

Dr Shaw had spoken in confidence to a pathologist on the case, and the involvement of a crucifix was not yet in the public domain. Only detectives and a few medics knew the details of the murder. 'Anything else?' The psychologist tried to keep his voice level.

'Jesus stood up and spoke, something about not killing. Shalt is a funny word, isn't it? And he got the key – not Jesus, I mean the fat priest. That was how he excaped. The black dog told me. Anselm's a daft name, isn't it?'

A cold chill travelled the length of the visitor's spine. The dead monk had not been named for the general populace. The monks, one body in Christ, formed a contemplative order who scarcely spoke, spending their time with alcoholics and vegetables, quite a good combination in Dr Edward (Pest) Shaw's book. The brother as a free man had been Bernard Hughes, a Welshman from mining country in the valleys, but his order name remained a secret. Perhaps it had been Brother Anselm. A child would surely not invent such a name.

'Where's Brennan now?'

'In a shed.'

'Where's the shed?'

'How the heck should I know? The dog said what he had to say, then walked away. But I know something else:

162

he's trying to come back. Not the dog – *him*. But the dog will save me, so that's all right, isn't it?'

'No more screaming?'

Billy shook his head. 'I'll have two dogs. I'll have the real one and the dream dog, who says I must not be afraid. All I wanted to tell you is that Father Brennan's got out of where he was, and the dream trap works. See, the dog wasn't snarling at me, was he? He was snarling at him.'

'Yes.' Pest Senior had a telephone call to make. He needed confirmation that a Brother Anselm was dead. 'Send for me if you need me again, Pest Junior.'

'I will. And I'm going to call my puppy Jumble. He wore a grey frock with a hood on it.'

'Right.' The second reference was presumably related to the monk's habit. If Edward told his immediate colleagues about a dog that talked and a child who 'saw' events in his sleep, he would end up in a special ward for the terminally confused.

'He made dinners, that monk. Cal makes dinners. In the cafe called Polly's Parlour.'

Edward Shaw said his goodbyes and left. He stood outside and scratched his head. Sometimes, the mentally ill were misdiagnosed. And somewhere among the thoughts of Billy Blunt, divine intervention must have occurred. There could be no other answer, so he nipped into St Anthony's and said a prayer. It was best to be on the safe side, just in case ...

Seven

Polly was a bit fed up with her famous whistle, since it took effort, and she felt weaker without her special man, so she pinched Cal's football referee's Thunderer, a famous brand known to teachers and players of soccer nation-wide. It still needed a lot of breath, but it was easier than her own version.

'Bleeding hell.' Ida shoved a finger in an ear and riddled it about. 'That'll clear your catarrh and wax any day of the week. Polly?'

'What?'

'Do you want us all deaf?'

'Eh? I can't hear you. Now, I know you're all up in arms, but my second sitting'll be arriving before you lot have stopped chuntering. He escaped, the police are after him, there's nothing we can do but wait, so shut up and eat up.'

Jimmy Nuttall spoke up instead. 'Just shows he could have killed little Billy, though. If he can kill a man of God, why should he worry about murdering a kiddy? Well, our Colin works on a farm near Maghull, and he keeps shot-guns for when foxes come for the chickens. I'll try to borrow a couple and some ammo.'

Cal appeared in his wheelchair. 'You'll do no such thing, Nutter. We've enough on without guns, thanks. You could miss him and hit the wrong person. Do you want more children in beds down the ozzy? Just leave it, all of you, unless you want to put somebody on a slab in the morgue or in a wheelchair like me. Stop the daft talk.' He went back to put more bacon under the grill for second breakfasts. Polly shouldn't have to deal with all that trouble alone. Frank should be with her. Frank would be with her, preferably sooner rather than later if Cal had any say in the matter.

The shouting and arguing reduced in volume to near-whispers. Hattie mouthed to Ida, 'If I had a gun, I'd bloody shoot him, and I wouldn't miss, believe me. Right between the eyes, too.'

'We've got our rounders bats,' Ida replied. 'Battering him to death would be a lot more satisfying after what he done to that monk. A bullet's less personal, isn't it?'

Hattie grinned. 'You're evil.'

'I know, but I'm lovely with it.' Ida stood up. 'Come on, folks, let Polly get on with her second lot of breakfasts. Me and Hattie promised we'd look after the twins, and we will. So bugger off.'

The two women waited until all customers had gobbled their cold food and gone. 'There you are, love,' she said to Polly. 'Onward and upward, eh?'

Polly, standing in the doorway that separated home from work, smiled weakly. Not without Frank. There could be no upward without him.

Elaine Lewis made her way across Liverpool's business sector. There was some confusion or delusion regarding a search on a house purchase she was handling. Because she was a stickler for detail, she needed to check a very quaint clause attached to a property in a suburb where, apparently, anyone could drain land through its garden without permission and with no duty to make good any damage to said garden. Suspecting that the rule was no longer relevant, fourteenth century at the latest, she intended to investigate immediately before alarming her client unnecessarily.

In truth, she was very proud of herself for having discovered the ancient law. If it was still applicable, which she doubted, the new purchaser would need to insure his land against all possible eventualities. She had to visit a firm that held mediaeval law documents in its heavily guarded crypt, after which she intended to inform the vendor's solicitor regarding the results.

Then she saw him striding towards her, and her mouth was suddenly dry. Oh, he was incredibly handsome. Other women passing by looked at him more than once, and she didn't blame them. Grey suit, dazzling white shirt, dark tie, good shoes, the confident, steady walk of a man on a mission. Mum said he had beautiful green eyes. The hair, dark brown, was thick and slightly wavy. She felt silly, like a blushing schoolgirl who had just at this moment noticed boys for the very first time.

It might be better to introduce herself now rather than standing back to wait for the two mothers to invent an occasion at which they might meet. Anyway, he appeared to have left home, so the chance of any prepared gathering sat somewhere between remote and impossible. 'Here goes,' she whispered before approaching him. 'Frank Charleson?' she asked. 'Son of Mrs Norma Charleson?' His eyes were indeed beautiful, a clear and unusual shade of green. The only slight imperfection was a small bump on his nose, which was forgivable.

'Guilty, though I plead insanity,' he said. 'She drove me mad twice over and I'm only just out of treatment.' He stretched out a hand, making the fingers tremble. 'See that? Steady as a fractured rock. I am cured.'

She paused briefly. The man was endowed with

humour. Used to males who trod the dried-out corridors of justice, she came across levity very seldom in the course of a working day. 'I'm Elaine Lewis. My mother works for yours. She's the housekeeper at Brookside.'

'So you're the lawyer?'

'Guilty as charged, but totally sane for the moment.' She didn't feel sane; she felt dithery, wrong-footed and slightly alarmed. Control was slipping. Control was vital.

'Never mind, we can't all be blessed with lunacy. Yes, I know Mrs Lewis.' He shook her hand. 'I don't want to be rude, but I have an appointment to discuss the buying of a property, so I must hurry before someone else snaps it up. It's a bit of a gem.'

She took a card from a pocket. 'There's my work address. If you need any conveyancing, I'm your man.'

'That's a very pretty dress, sir,' he said, smiling down at her. 'But my mother must not know my whereabouts.'

'A lawyer is like a priest,' she told him. 'I guard clients' secrets with my life. Good luck with the purchase.' She walked away. He was looking at her; she could feel the heat of his eyes on her back. According to Mum, Frank was involved with a woman who ran a cafe on Scotland Road. Mum had met Polly Kennedy and seemed to admire her spirit. But Polly hated Mrs Charleson and had refused to talk to Mum, who was now rent collector for Charleson Holdings. In Elaine's opinion, Frank could do better if he wanted to play.

She was taken to the crypt, where she was shown the law. F replaced S from beginning to end, and it dated back to when the suburb had been farmland. The house currently being sold had replaced a pair of farm labourers' cottages that had been torn down long ago, so the law could be disputed. Yes, Frank might do a lot better, as long as he didn't get serious.

After returning to the office, she sat for a while and

begged her phone to ring. Not her type? Perhaps she should take a look at the competition; Polly was reputed to be pretty. Pretty Polly? That was parrot-speak. Oh no, here came Lanky Laithwaite. He hung round like a bad smell, and she was fed up with his persistence. Bob Laithwaite was a good-looking chap, six feet and four inches in height, and he kept asking her for a date. She was excellent at excuses and lies, so maybe she should aim for the bar and wear wig and gown with pride. This chap was definitely marriage material, but she wasn't, not yet, anyway. She wanted to play for a while before accepting rings, ball and chain.

'Doing anything over the weekend?' he asked, the tone attempting and failing completely to be casual.

Bob was a full partner, and she was mad not to take him on. But he was as dry as the parchment in that crypt. He would keep for a while, she hoped. 'Sleeping,' she replied. 'I have every intention of courting the rim of coma.'

'Alone?'

Lord, that was near the bone for him; it was almost funny. 'Yes, alone. I've been feeling rather run-down lately.'

'Then let me take you out for a pick-me-up. You can't possibly sleep from Friday night until Monday morning.'

'Bob, I can do anything I like. There will be patches of wakefulness, I suppose, because one must eat and so forth.'

'Can't I be the so forth? I think I make a very suitable so forth. I have the height, the clean-cut looks, hand-sewn Italian shoes, all my own teeth, no tonsils or adenoids, and a very good car.'

Elaine found herself smiling. There was more to Lanky than had met eye or ear thus far. 'No. Go away and solicit – that's how we earn our crust, as you well know.'

'I'm soliciting you.'

'Yes, you are. Find something more interesting to do.'

'I find you interesting.'

'But not doable.' That was very near the marrow, never mind the bone, she thought.

'I shall persevere, Elaine. Take that as a warning. Shall I commit my intentions to paper?'

'And I shall be looking for work elsewhere.' She shouldn't have said that to a partner in the company, even if he was a junior. But he was laughing at her, and his eyes twinkled when he laughed. Was she about to travel from famine to feast? Did she want a permanent male fixture in her life, or was she simply trying to offload her virginity? Whatever the case, she could not simply pause and collect two men in one day. Though she wasn't sure that Frank had been collected . . .

Her telephone rang. 'Who? Oh yes. Yes, of course. Put him through, please.' She looked up at the man in front of her. 'Hello, Frank. Really? So good of you to think of me . .' Bob's eyes, so recently twinkling with glee, were suddenly cold and flat. 'What? Oh, I knew you'd get it. Congratulations on that. Yes. All right, I shall pull out all the stops. See you in the Liver at eight, then.' She replaced the receiver.

'One rule for him and another for me, eh?'

'Pardon? Oh, you mean Frank. No, no. My mother works for his, and he's buying a business, needs the conveyancing done quickly. We've been friends for many years. He has a fiancée, I believe.' Yes, she should be a barrister, since she was an excellent conveyor of decorative untruths. Bob's face was alive again. 'We'll have lunch next week,' she promised.

'Lunch is business,' Bob complained.

'We are business,' she reminded him. 'We work together, so it mustn't get complicated or messy.'

'I don't mind messy,' he said. 'Messy can be fun in the right company. We could make mud pies at the Mersey's edge, go panning for gold in Wales, try potholing. There are many ways of getting dirty.' He walked away.

Elaine stared at her blotter. She'd been a wonderfully good girl, such a dedicated student, no boyfriends, no sex, no university societies, few distractions. Her single aim in life had been to become a lawyer. Well, she'd made it, and it was time to pencil some fun time into the schedule.

Frank might be a pretty toy, but Bob, if she could coax him right out of his shell, was satisfactory husband material. Love? It was for idiots who walked starry-eyed up and down the aisle towards disaster in both directions. Marriage, managed properly, was a partnership, almost a business. Sex was for discreet recreation; sex with a husband was for procreation. And she disliked children intensely.

Frank Charleson loved brats. Newspapers had printed his plea for lawyers to specialize in their protection; perhaps she might find someone to help him with that. After all, he wasn't marriage fare, so she wouldn't end up as his brood mare. But she wanted him to be her first, and she was determined to continue to get what she wanted. She wondered briefly whether Bob 'Lanky' Laithwaite planned to have a family, since he was the type she intended to marry. Oh, never mind; that could go in the pending tray. Anyway, she might run to one child as long as someone else reared it.

Bob wandered back. It was clear that he had sod all to do. 'Did I leave any briefs in here?' he asked.

'No. But I always keep a spare pair in my locker.'

'Double cotton gusset?' he asked, his tone deadly serious.

'No. All right, then. Dinner. Time and place to be arranged. Go away.'

He sniffed, shrugged and swivelled.

She watched as he stalked off. Even his back seemed

to be smiling. Bob was tall, educated, strong and rich. She would certainly marry someone like him. But first, she wanted excitement, variety, imagination.

Elaine Lewis knew she would be considered a cold fish by most. Everything came from the head rather than the heart, though there was one exception to that rule. She adored her mother. Nothing could ever happen to Christine, because Elaine was unable to accept the concept of a world without Mum.

But what Elaine could not know was that she owned an extra flaw, one she had not yet encountered, a major glitch deeply embedded well below her carefully constructed suit of armour. It was a weakness so profoundly rooted that she had not yet faced it, but it was about to come to the surface and overcome her to the point of no return.

She filled her out tray, emptied the in and left a few non-urgent items in pending. She would go home early, because Frank Charleson wasn't pending; Frank Charleson was tonight.

Ida closed the shop for five minutes. She went out the back way, ran past the Kennedy yard and entered Hattie's. With her spine against Hattie's closed gate, she stopped to draw breath. Who would have thought it? And just as everything seemed to be going so well, too. Gleeful about her new knowledge, she had come to confide in her close friend.

She edged her way through the kitchen-cum-living area. Hattie was serving in the shop, so Ida was forced to wait. 'I could be losing custom meself,' she whispered. Hattie was having a conversation about which spuds were best for roasting, which to use for scouse, which for chips.

The shop bell tinkled and Hattie came through, visibly

startled when she discovered that she was not alone. 'Blood and guts, Ida, you frightened me halfway to death. It felt like I was having a heart attack. Who's serving in your place while you're here?'

'Nobody. I've had me day's big run on newspapers and ciggies. But I had to come, cos I seen somebody else, not just Greg.'

Hattie folded her arms. 'You've clapped eyes on Lois at last, then?'

Ida blinked stupidly.

'Polly knows she's back,' Hattie said.

'Has she seen her? Has she been to the cafe?'

'No idea. Lois has been back in Liverpool a while. I saw her round about the same time as you gave Greg a room and I told him to bugger off. They probably travelled north together.'

'But you said nothing about Lois.'

'I did. I told Polly and she told Cal. You thought I'd warned her about Greg, but I told her the lot. I believe Cal just carried on reading, wasn't bothered, so that's all right.'

'But . . . but you didn't tell me, did you?'

'No, I didn't. You keep as many secrets as I keep race-horses, Ida Pilkington. It's like leaving a baby to be looked after by a shark. People will notice her hanging about, so they don't need telling.'

Ida's face was several interesting shades of red. 'Oh,' was all she achieved.

'You know they all call you News of the World, don't you? If they want people to know what's going on, they tell you, because it saves them the trouble of putting folk in the picture. If they want people not to know something, they tell me or someone else who can be trusted.'

Ida sat down. 'Am I really that bad, Hat?'

'Well, yes, but you can't help it. I mean, look at our

lives, love. We live alone, work alone most of the time, and I get through by listening to the wireless, a bit of knitting, some reading and the odd night at the pictures. And I got legless on sherry not too long ago, so I've got me faults, queen. None of us is perfect, see? People don't hate you. They just have to be careful what they let slip.'

For once, Ida couldn't think of a single thing to say.

'And it's not just you, either. The washhouse has always been full of gossips. You can go in there with your sheets and towels, but when you come out you've a lot more than your washing to carry, because you know who's pregnant, who's dying, who's had a hysterectomy, who's carrying on behind their husband or wife's back. Still, at least we've got one another, you and me.'

'For how long, Hattie?'

'That reminds me – there'll be a meeting soon about the London trip.'

'Are we going? To London, I mean?'

'Oh yes. We are definitely going.' She joined Ida at the table.

Ida spoke. 'This is the only place we've known, isn't it? From the Rotunda to town, Scotty has been our life. And they're going to split us up.'

'No they're not.' Hattie's face was grim. 'We'll have a two-bedroom place and share like the sisters we've nearly been. The buggers won't grind us down. We'll lose a lot of people, but we won't lose each other.'

'We'll lose our Polly, though.'

Hattie placed a hand on Ida's. 'She'll go anyway. No way will that precious, lovable girl avoid marriage. And even if she goes up in the world, she'll never forget you or me.' The shop bell jangled. 'Go back to your job while I serve whoever that is.'

Ida left through the backyard. She felt rather deflated and not a little embarrassed, because her news was not news. Other people's lives were of interest to her, since she had so little of her own. But she could learn from this; it was never too late to learn. In future, she would keep her mouth buttoned. Well, she hoped she could . . .

As she passed Polly's, a shriek of mixed laughter reached her ears. The three of them were at it again. Polly and a nurse were helping Cal with exercises. 'Let him walk,' she prayed, 'and give my Polly wings.'

Polly was literally rolling about on the floor. Sometimes, laughter was too painful to allow a person to remain upright for more than a few seconds. Linda, doing her utmost to maintain a professional and more dignified attitude, excused herself and went upstairs to the bathroom.

'I told you I'd be the bloody cabaret,' complained the victim on the borrowed hospital bed. His own bed was in storage at Hattie's, since it had been slightly too low for his torturers. 'It's not funny. And I can't help it. None of it's on purpose, you know. See, if you hit my knee like that, my foot shoots up of its own accord. Reflexes. Linda says these odd reactions are proof that my reflexes are coming back.'

'You kicked me.'

'Yes.' He grinned broadly. 'And I kicked her as well, so it's nothing personal. I mean, I wouldn't kick her deliberately, would I?'

'But you'd kick me?' She scrambled to her feet and gave him the dirtiest of her extensive collection of looks. 'You're a swine, Cal Kennedy.'

'Look, I'd kick you because that's what sisters are for. I've had to stay ahead all our lives, what with you being twenty minutes older and bossy with it. Wait till I'm up and about under my own steam, lady. See how you like having your legs pulled out of the hip sockets. Black and blue, I am.'

'Liar. There's not a mark on you.'

'But I feel the pain.'

'So do I. This isn't my idea of a hobby, you know. I'd sooner stick pins in myself than listen to you moaning while we try to get you better. Men are nesh. A woman gets a cold, but a man gets double pneumonia. We stick a plaster on a cut and carry on, but a man ends up with bandages and a sling.'

He closed his eyes. 'Mam always said nesh, didn't she? If we acted ill on purpose. Or if we moaned about being cold. "Yer nesh," she used to shout.'

Polly sat on the bed and held his hand. Many seconds passed. 'It was cruel, Cal. Both of them two years apart, bloody cancer. I miss them.'

'So do I, Pol.'

'Good job we were too old for the orphanage.'

Each tightened the grip on the other's hand. 'Oh, I don't know,' he said. 'Strawberry Fields is supposed to be nice. They get ice cream and holidays in Blackpool.'

She laughed. 'Freedom's nicer, love. We've not been so bad together, have we? Except for your accident, of course.'

There were breaks in his voice when he answered. 'I wouldn't have wanted to live through it except for you, Miss Polly. You've been my hero, babe. And here, this place and all the people rooting for me, that's helped a lot. But best of all, you've been a lighthouse on the rocks. The cafe, the cooking, feeling useful, getting adventurous with prawns and long-grain rice ..' He smiled, though his eyes were wet. 'My salvation.'

'You're a born chef, Cal.'

'I will be. When I get my legs back, it's cookery school for me, our kid. Night classes to start with, and then, when they ..'

'I know. When we have to move, you can go to day college.'

On the stairs, Linda Higgins listened to them, smiling as she realized how deeply they loved each other. An only child, she had never experienced the power of sibling love or sibling rivalry, and she was starting to understand what she had missed.

Fortunately, she had good parents. Dad worked from home in order to be with his wife, who needed constant care. His clients understood that the mountain must come to Muhammad, so they brought their books to him. When Linda had a day off he visited businesses, but for the most part bookkeeping was done in his little office in a corner of the bungalow's kitchen. So Linda was happy, though she was beginning to see what she had lacked.

Her love for Cal grew daily. They hadn't said much about it, but it showed. Polly saw it. Polly always went missing after an exercise session, running upstairs to tidy the hair salon or popping next door to see Ida or Hattie. Ida, a famous gossip, had elected herself surrogate mother to the orphaned twins, while Hattie was Ida's second string. Cal would walk, but Polly wouldn't tell them yet, Linda thought. She wiped her eyes and re-entered the boxing ring. 'Have you two done fighting?' she asked.

'Yes,' they said together.

'Just out of interest, who won?'

'She did. She always does. I should have fought my way out in front of her. That twenty-minute gap gave her an unfair start, and I've been paying for it ever since. How I've suffered.'

Polly sniffed and stalked out to put the kettle on.

As she waited for it to boil, she thought about Mam and Dad. He'd gone first, the gentle giant who had worked damned hard all the days of his life. Mam had never picked up after the bereavement, and she had given up her beautiful ghost two years later to breast cancer. The dreadful losses, with Mam's death followed three years later by Cal's accident, had welded the twins together. When daydreaming, she imagined two houses side by side, Cal and wife in one, herself and . . . and Frank in the other. Or perhaps one big house for all of them.

Frank. She should have accepted him, because she loved him. And the silly bugger had gone missing.

Where was he? Mrs Lewis collected rents, while Frank seemed to have disappeared altogether. She missed him as badly as she might have missed a limb. He was the other part of her; he was her completion. His mother wasn't his fault. Oh, why wouldn't he come and talk about things? 'And why am I such a bloody fool?' she whispered before carrying the tea tray through.

They were holding hands again. Cal deserved Linda, and Linda was good enough to deserve him. Oh well, that was fifty per cent of the family sorted out – possibly. As for herself, she would get by. Full-time hairdressing once again, onwards and upwards, except for Frank. No one else would be acceptable. As for Greg and Lois, well, they didn't stand a cat in hell's chance.

'Elaine, aren't you going to be late for your meeting?' Christine called up the stairs. Her daughter was taking rather a long time to prepare herself for an evening business chat with a man who was not her type. The unmistakable scent of Chanel No. 5 drifted down to the ground floor, and Christine gasped when her little girl appeared at the top of the flight. 'You are certainly dressed to impress,' she said.

'For a couple of gins in the Liver? I don't think so, Mum. This is a business suit, white blouse et cetera. So what's different?'

'The et cetera, dear daughter, being sky-high heels, that wonderful patent leather bag, your hair loose and flowing and half a pint of Chanel.'

'It's a briefcase containing legal pad and pens for notes. And my hair's been scraped back all day, so I'm giving it a rest. The shoes make me feel confident and you're exaggerating about the perfume – quarter of a pint at most.'

'You are beautiful.'

Elaine struck a pose, one hand behind her shining blonde hair. 'And he does have lovely green eyes – you were quite right.'

Christine swallowed. She dreaded losing her girl. 'Is romance in the air?' she asked.

'Flirtation, libation and pork scratchings, I imagine. He's a fabulous piece of decor, no more than that. I shan't be late.' She kissed her mother and went out to the car.

As she pulled away from her parking space, Elaine waved.

Christine watched, sighed and waved back. She loved her only child, but she knew Elaine very well, because they spent hours talking. There was something about the girl that worried her mother. The clever, well-groomed and beautiful lawyer was almost cynical when it came to men; some were toys that could be thrown away or passed on to another owner once outgrown, while others, steadier and wealthier, formed an assortment from which one might select a life partner because of his position and riches.

She closed the front door and went to sit in the cosy living room. Looking up at a wedding photograph, she smiled at Jim. There had been a deep, abiding love in the marriage, and Elaine was the result, so why hadn't she been born full of that love? Her childhood had been happy, she'd liked school, made friends, enjoyed the usual pyjama parties and birthday treats. She'd taken riding lessons, had a pony for a while, and then ... and then, university.

University had changed her radically. 'The girls are prostitutes and the boys are clients, though I'm not sure about payment,' she had announced. 'I shall keep my head down, do the work and get a first.' Younger than the rest, she had sailed through her degree on a definite first-class ticket, before moving into law. 'What's she up to now, Jim?' Frank was attractive ...

In the kitchen, Christine washed dishes and concentrated further on her daughter. She was probably still a virgin, but tonight, she was advertising herself. Frank was likely to be a toy, yet he loved Polly Kennedy who, though very different from Elaine, was equally lovely in appearance and definitely the more approachable of the two. 'Don't make a mess of your life, Elaine. And marry for love. You must marry for love.'

The Liver, a very old pub on the corner of South Road in Waterloo, was untypically quiet. At twenty minutes past eight, late but not indecorously so, Elaine Lewis strode in at business pace. She expected him to be waiting at the bar, but he wasn't. Frank Charleson was seated with three men of advanced age, and he was playing dominoes. He probably fitted in anywhere and everywhere, she told herself before ordering a gin and tonic.

She knew he'd seen her, because her peripheral vision was excellent, and she never missed a trick. He'd raised his head, glanced at her, then carried on playing the game. Cool customer, then. Well, two could play games, even if one lacked bits of wood with dots on. She took her drink to an empty table. 'I've some work to catch up on,' she called in his direction. 'I'll be over here when you're ready.'

She scribbled a draft letter to the lawyer on the selling

side of the property threatened by that defunct law. The game of dominoes continued. After a further fifteen minutes, she looked at her watch. Ah. She had been twenty minutes late, and he was preparing to leave his companions at precisely eight forty. So Frank had kept her waiting for exactly the same length of time. This was a form of communication that went beyond a business relationship. He had noticed her, then.

He sat down. 'You were late. I don't do late.'

'You do. You pay back by being as late as I was. Now, this property you're buying, do get a full survey first.' Businesslike was the way to go. Her hair drifted as if by accident over a shoulder and tumbled onto the notes. He bought her another drink, but she asked for orange juice, as she was driving. A trip to the Ladies gave him the opportunity to see flawless legs made more glamorous by high heels and black stockings.

She returned and carried on with business. The address of the property was noted, as was the solicitor representing the seller. There was a large shop downstairs, some storage to the rear, and a three-bedroom flat above. 'You'll be living there?'

'Yes. The business will be advertised as Aladdin's Lamp or Aladdin's Cave. I thought of Curios and Curios-er, but people might not get the Lewis Carroll allusion.'

'And you'll be dressing up as Aladdin?'

'Only in private.'

She rewarded him by showing him perfect teeth behind a broad smile. 'We all have our guilty secrets, I suppose.'

Frank studied her while she scribbled. Despite poise and panache, she failed to conceal the fact that she was available. Very much a man of the world, he had not been celibate since Ellen's death. Polly was still his indisputable future, he hoped, but until she saw sense, he remained available at a level that didn't really matter.

Elaine stopped scribbling and looked up. There was a modicum of desire in those unusual eyes. 'I'll start the search tomorrow, make sure the property is clean in legal terms.' She handed him another card. 'That chap's a good surveyor. If you need a structural engineer, he'll let you know. We'll keep this one out of my office so that I can give you special rates. After all, we're almost family, aren't we?'

He realized that she had an agenda, and he was on the list. For several seconds, he knew how a rodent felt in a cage with a motionless snake that would kill when hunger enlivened it. The warning bell was clear, but her beauty was undeniable. 'Thank you,' was all he said.

She packed her bag. 'You'll be able to go back and play now.'

'Not my favourite game, Elaine.'

She stood. 'Do you have a favourite game?'

'Doesn't everyone?'

Each maintained eye contact with the other. But as Frank stared at her, he saw Polly's face in the space between them. 'Still, since dominoes is the only game in town, I'll get back to it. I'll telephone you in a day or two.' He returned to the protagonists' table.

Outwardly unfazed and inwardly seething, Elaine Lewis left the scene. He desired her, but something or someone stood in the way. It was Polly Kennedy, who probably stank of bacon and black pudding or perm lotion and peroxide. Sitting in the car, she gripped the steering wheel so hard that fingernails dug into her palms. What was the matter with her? She'd always been so controlled and so . . . so indulged.

Oh yes, she'd wanted a certain doll, and she'd got it; she'd demanded riding lessons and a pony, clothes, makeup, perfume, private digs well away from her peers at university, and somehow Mum had come up with the goods. Christine Lewis, left comfortably off because of her husband's insurance, was by no means rich, yet her daughter had been spoilt.

'I want him,' she said to herself. Her body had responded automatically; even with a table between them, she had become aroused. This had never happened before, so was it as a result of her decision to pencil in fun time? Oh, it was so annoying. For the first time in almost twenty-three years, she felt at a complete loss. Like a window shopper, she had picked out what she wanted, though it wasn't going to come to her easily.

There was another way. At university, she'd watched it work. A girl would come clean by going 'dirty', an adjective much bandied about in the union bar. A female would proposition a boy and shrug if she got nowhere. Very rarely did that happen, since most men when offered sex without complications snapped it up. It was nothing to do with love; it was about feeding a type of starvation that would not be appeased by food.

Could she do it? Was she capable of begging Frank Charleson to relieve her of her virginity? Apparently, men liked the idea of being the first, but this one was possibly suffering from the disease named love, a chemical imbalance that occurred several times in the lives of most people. Suicides, murders and mental instability often resulted from the illness, as possessiveness and jealousy lay at the core of it. 'Never,' she muttered as she pulled into traffic on Liverpool Road. 'Love is for birds and idiots, not for intelligent women.'

'You're early,' Christine commented when her daughter walked in.

'There wasn't much to do. Oh, and I can't tell you any details about where he's settling, because I promised, and anyway, it would be unprofessional. Although it wasn't discussed, I get the impression that his mother's lost her place on his Christmas card list.'

'She thinks so, too.'

'Right. I'll have a bath and get changed.' Elaine started up the stairs.

'Did you like him?'

Elaine paused halfway up the flight. 'He's all right. Played dominoes with some old men, bought me an orange juice. He's very attractive.'

Christine slid back into the living room. There had been an edge to Elaine's tone, a quality that expressed disappointment, almost dismay. The beautifully dressed young lawyer had reached out for a plaything, and had failed to acquire it. Frank Charleson might not have had a university education, but he was a real man, a gentle person with ambition and charity occupying equal space in his soul. She sat and looked again at the wedding photograph. Was Frank too good for Elaine? Was it possible that Christine's perfectly polished daughter was substandard in some way?

There was something else, too, something Christine could almost smell beneath liberal applications of Chanel. No. She laughed at herself inwardly. It surely happened only to animals. Had Elaine been a canine, she might have ... No. But yes. It was as if Elaine had come into season at last. Oh, dear. Christine went to make a cup of tea. Sometimes, her thoughts were too ridiculous, too fanciful.

Upstairs, Elaine was beginning the first of many difficult nights. In the past, she had seldom contemplated her level of sex drive. It had been the main concern of many colleagues at university, but she had eliminated it from her life. She wanted a first with honours and a passport into law. Those who had been taken up by the social agenda and by finding a partner had emerged with lower seconds, which might just open a door into teaching, and she was sure that they'd all lived to regret the neglect of books and essays.

Was she a late developer? Why were these feelings so intense? He was just a man with a shop to buy. Was she normal? Did other women experience such vivid and graphic imaginings? And he was in every one of them. How had she expected the evening to end? In a hotel room between silk sheets, champagne on a bedside table, strawberries in a dish? Why him? Why not Bob Laithwaite? How could she, a woman totally devoid of experience, judge Frank to be amazing and Bob to be ordinary?

'Questions, questions, bloody questions,' she said, beating her pillow with every word. There were no answers except for one. Elaine Lewis began to suspect that she was oversexed and needful. She must find a way to get some relief. But it had to be Frank.

Earlier that same evening, Polly and Cal had experienced a different kind of discomfort.

They finished their meal and listened to the news on the Home Service before Polly went to wash dishes. She expected just two hair clients tonight, which was just as well, because she felt tired. Helping her brother was hard, exhausting and worth every minute, as he was definitely on the mend.

Hattie and Ida were the pair on tonight's agenda, and they were always good fun, though not intentionally. Between them, they came out with many inaccurate and hilarious statements, asked several daft questions and provided Polly with a great deal of entertainment.

But they arrived early and via the rear yard.

'We had to come,' Hattie babbled. 'I seen them and Ida seen them.'

Ida echoed. 'She seen them and I seen them.'

Cal glared at the invaders. 'I could have been having a bed bath.'

'Well, you aren't, so shut up,' Hattie snapped. 'They keep on walking past your front door. Everybody's watching them. You have to face up to this, young Kennedy clan.'

Polly dried her hands. She had no need to ask for the identity of the people at the front door. 'Hattie's right. Time we got this over and done with, Callum. We can't have these poor folk walking up and down Scotty making fools of themselves every night, can we?'

'No, it's a shame,' he said. 'Feel free to stay, ladies, seeing as I'm not having my bed bath at the moment. We could do with witnesses to stop me from strangling somebody. Polly?'

Hattie and Ida stood open-mouthed while Polly helped Cal out of bed. With one arm round her shoulders and the other on a crutch, he hopped over to the sofa. 'Well, that's a nice surprise,' Ida cried. 'We know you've worked hard, because we've heard you two and that young nurse screaming and laughing.' She dried her eyes. 'Will you walk proper again, Cal?'

'I hope so, Ida, though my left foot doesn't seem to know what the right's doing. Linda says nerves join up as and when they like, but there was a bit more damage to that leg. Anyway, never mind me. Just stop crying and look tough. We don't want Lois and Greg wearing our pavements out, do we? So they have to be frightened off, and your tears make us look soft. Come on, now. We have to be hard. Dead hard.'

Ida wasn't good at dead hard, but she did her best while Polly combed her own hair and applied a bit of powder and lipstick. 'Do I look all right?'

'You do,' said Hattie. 'Now, I'll go out the back way and into my house. When I see them, I'll knock on this wall.

Then I'll come back as if I'm getting my hair done. But don't worry about our hair, eh? Ida?'

'No, don't worry about our hair.'

They should have been on the halls, Polly thought. Ida and Hattie had no idea of how funny they were. Just lately, Ida had started to repeat almost everything Hattie said, because she was determined to stop being a gossip. She'd have had less trouble teaching a goldfish to samba, but she was making an effort, bless her.

Hattie dashed out. Ida, Hattie's shadow, was not uncomfortable in the Kennedy home, as she had looked after this pair of twins since their late teens. But she was nervous. Greg Johnson and Lois Monk were unforgivable, and Ida was afraid of rows. She'd been a bit shaky since a direct hit on Bootle had taken out her sister, two nieces and a nephew and, though she loved a good gossip session, she was seriously terrified by any kind of fighting; even a vigorous verbal exchange could upset her, though she was good at speaking her own mind when riled.

The knock on the wall arrived. Polly dashed through the cafe and flung open the door. 'Get in here,' she ordered. 'Showing us up, pacing about like a pair of kids up to no good.' A foot tapped as she waited, arms akimbo, face creased into a frown. 'Now,' she snapped. 'Come in unless you want to spend more weeks trailing round in circles like Hansel and bloody Gretel.' In truth, they currently imitated a pair of statues, though their sculptor deserved few congratulations.

They stepped in, and Polly bolted the door. 'My brother's through there, Lois. I think you may want to explain to him why you bolted without a word while he was trapped in hospital. You wrote him off, didn't you? Well, he's on the mend and almost ready for a Cordon Bleu education. Do go in, dear.' These last four words were delivered in Polly's posh voice.

When Lois had left the cafe, Polly took the bolts off the door and threw it wide once more. 'Out,' she told her ex-lover. Shocked, the man stood his ground uncertainly.

'Listen, you,' she continued. 'Yellow-bellied, lily-livered no-good bundle of trash – shift yourself now before I remove your face. There's no excuse for you. Your mother wants a slap in the gob for bringing you into the world.'

He opened his mouth to speak.

'Don't you dare talk to me, Johnson. This is a time for listening, not for conversation. You said all you needed to say by getting the London bus. What if I became ill or crippled? Would you put two hundred miles between us if I was run over and bedridden? So shut your gob and make yourself scarce. Come near here again, and you'll be met by a posse.' She pushed him through the door and made it secure once more.

'I love you, Polly,' he shouted, his mouth against the opened letterbox. 'I made a mistake. Everybody makes mistakes.'

She sat at a cafe table, her legs trembling, a headache threatening. Greg would get no second chance; even if she managed to forgive him, her heart belonged elsewhere. Was she as guilty as Lois and Greg had been? She'd seen Frank off because of his mother, and that wasn't fair, either. Yes, everybody made mistakes.

Lois emerged from the living room. 'Your brother's language hasn't improved,' she said. 'And if you'd had one more old crone in there, you'd have had the three witches.'

Polly pulled herself together and tutted. 'Oh, I'm sorry, Lois. Was he rude? That'll be because he's improving daily and soon he'll be enrolling at college to become a chef.' She shook her head in mock sadness. 'He's getting above himself, love. Oh, speaking of love, he's fallen for one of his nurses who supervises the physiotherapy department.' She achieved a rather tight smile. 'Actually, she's just been made up to departmental boss, a sister. And she loves my brother and would never, ever walk out on him.'

Lois blinked rapidly. 'Where's Greg?'

'Outside. He's been shouting through the door. Will you leave now, please? You two should stick together, because you've a lot in common. Take the top bolt off. I'll sort the door out when you've gone.'

When the cafe was secure, Polly returned to the sitting room where Cal was explaining about muscle development. He looked at his sister. 'All right, our kid?'

She nodded. 'Just tired and a bit of a headache coming on after putting the rubbish out.'

Ida rushed off to find aspirin and water.

Polly noticed that Cal's face was rather pale and drawn.

'Your brother was marvellous,' Hattie said. 'He asked where he'd seen her because her face looked familiar. Then he stood up and told her to— Well, he used a word I've never said.'

Ida came in with Polly's headache cure. 'Here, queen. I got you two, cos you've had a hard time.'

'Stress,' Hattie said.

'Stress.' Ida handed over glass and tablets.

Cal joined in the charade. 'It'll be stress,' he said, his tone wearing no particular expression.

It was in this moment that Polly knew beyond a shadow of a doubt that her twin was one hundred per cent back. Perhaps it was because he could stand, or it might be attributable to getting rid of Lois forever. But it was likely to have something to do with Linda and real hope for the future. The little devil inside him had been revived. She swallowed her aspirin and thanked God.

As the weeks passed by, Brennan became a very credible Irish tramp. At the beginning, he wondered whether to acquire pencils and paper so that he could write DUMB DUE TO THROAT SURGERY, but he didn't need to bother. There were many Irish people in England, especially working on farms, so he simply blended in and adopted an accent nearer to Western Ireland than to his home a few miles from the city of Dublin. His love for the land had never left him; he belonged here.

He even found occasional company of a kind, gypsies who fed him and listened to his prepared life story. An orphan, he had been raised by monks in various parts of Ireland, and he had stowed away on a ferry years ago. He had no papers, not even a birth certificate, so he lived the itinerant life.

As he lost weight and became stronger, clothes stolen in the early days hung off him, and the man he saw reflected in window glass bore no resemblance to the priest on the run. He had acquired a rucksack that contained all his worldly goods: towel, soap, toothbrush, whiskey, scissors, knives, a spoon and clothing filched from washing lines.

Still in Staffordshire, he wandered in all directions, certain that those hunting him would believe he had left miles between himself and the monastery, but he was cleverer than they were. With a full beard and in a working man's clothes, he was just another farmhand who laboured for food and minimum wages, but he felt well and drank less than he once had, since he needed his wits about him.

Sleeping remained a problem. When employers offered accommodation, he refused it, because he dared not risk screaming out in the night while others were within hearing distance. He continued to sleep in barns, derelict houses, empty stables, sometimes in woods while the weather remained good. He dared not think about winter.

Even autumn would be difficult, as he already felt the cold during summer nights.

Eventually, he would get to Liverpool and retrieve his few belongings, though he doubted he would be able to return home to Dublin. The jungle drums within the church were no doubt being hammered to death, yet the newspapers seemed to have calmed down a little. The fact remained that he had murdered a true servant of God, and retribution would be sought.

Eugene Brennan was unforgivable.

Eight

Apart from the absence of musical instruments, he was a wandering minstrel. There was a song about one of those, but he'd forgotten it. He wished he could forget Brother Anselm, but he couldn't and probably never would.

Casual jobs were easy to come by as long as he didn't mind walking, and he was getting used to travelling on foot over considerable distances. 'You can do it, Gene,' he urged himself often. He tightened his belt, though the braces were an absolute necessity, since his girth seemed to decrease with every day that passed. His beard grew, the skin on face, neck, hands and arms turned brown, and he drank less.

He did window-cleaning as long as the householder owned ladders, he mowed lawns, weeded beds, exercised dogs, fed chickens, wrung necks, pulled feathers, removed innards and trussed poultry ready for ovens. On a few occasions, he drove a tractor, walked cows home and even managed to talk a bit of sense into a partially broken horse. This was the life he had given up for the sake of his mother, who had wanted him to become a priest. Eugene Brennan was a farmer to the core, and he ought to have remained a farmer.

But he couldn't stay anywhere just yet. Every evening, he had to find shelter in an isolated place so that no one would be disturbed by his noisy dreams. They weren't as bad or as frequent as they had been, yet he dared not take a chance on being recognized and captured. What did he say when he screamed, how much did he give away? He had no idea.

So he wandered on, the man with no name, the minstrel with no music, the priest with no parish. He had few choices. All he could do was move on and on and on . . .

'You messing about up your sleeve again, Charleson? Does your determined separation from the faith turn you into a cheat and a liar?' Father Christopher Foley pretended to glare at his mischievous friend whose poker face was totally unreadable. 'I am beginning to despair of you, Francis.' He placed his cards face down on the table and buried his head in his hands. 'Who can a man trust these days?' he moaned.

Four males were seated round the presbytery dining table, every one of them welded to his top-secret cards. They were playing for money, which made this very serious business. An inveterate gambler, the much-loved man of God played to win, though his features were too mobile and expressive for poker. 'You're up to something, mate,' he accused, releasing his face and awarding Frank a dirty look. 'There is mendacity in every line of your body, every pore of your skin.'

'That's a big word for a Friday night,' Johnny Blunt grumbled. 'This is worse than work, Fred. Our foreman couldn't hold a candle to Father Foley, and he's a walking dictionary since his daughter got into university to do English literature. Gone all posh, he has, except for his thick Scouse accent.'

His brother voiced his agreement. 'Mend-a-city? It's what we had to do starting ten years back after the Germans buggered off leaving a load of holes all over the place. Like a giants' flaming golf course, it was. But we mustn't get Father here on the subject of golf, or we'll be here till a week next Thursday. He'll start going on about his putter not putting properly and the holes on the course being too small for his balls.'

'Me? Me mendacious? Me cheating with cards up my sleeve?' With his expression arranged in innocent mode, Frank threw in his hand, cards facing upward for all to see. 'Listen, Chris. You were the one a few months ago who found an extra queen of hearts in one game. Fred and Johnny here were witnesses, weren't you? Remember? He produced it with a flourish, and I already had it in a royal flush.'

'Surrounded by liars and fools,' Chris mumbled.

'Selective amnesia?' Frank asked. 'You remember, Fred and Johnny?'

'Yes,' chorused the brothers. 'It was disgraceful,' Johnny added. 'You wouldn't expect it from a priest.' He paused for a moment. 'Mind, Father Brennan's worse by a long chalk, may he rot.'

Tormented and heavily outnumbered, Chris Foley stood up. 'You're all talking a pile of hogwash. I do not cheat. Well, very seldom, anyway. And would I steal pennies from my close friends? Would I?'

'Oh, sit down, holy Joe. I can still hear you to this day,' Frank accused. Then he carried on, his Irish accent spot-on right. ' "Sure it must have been put away by accident in the wrong pack, for the backs of the cards are all the same, so." You, Father Foley, are a dishonest pastor and a very poor advertisement for Catholicism.' He turned to the other two men. 'Blamed his housekeeper, and she's a better Catholic than he is. Mind you, that's hardly diffi-cult when you think about the way he carries on. They've better Catholics than Chris stuck in prison cells all over the place.'

The cleric sat. 'And you are mocking me, Francis. Just think of the wonderful man who is your namesake. Francis of Assisi is a worthy saint who abandoned the grand life to care for the poor.'

Fred Blunt put his ten-pennyworth into the mix. 'You shouldn't have thrown in, Frank. That's a good fistful of cards. You had a few possibilities there. And we know you wouldn't cheat.'

Frank spoke again to his ordained cardsharp pal. 'Hang on, Christopher. I am named after Francis Xavier, who went about brainwashing folk in Asia for no good reason whatsoever. Francis of Assisi could charm birds from the trees, but he's nothing to do with me. So stick that in your porridge and eat it.'

'Are we done?' Fred asked. 'Me and Johnny thought we'd go for a pint in the Holy House. Fancy a few drinks down the Newsham, Frank? Or the Throstle's?' There was no point in inviting their host, as he was on duty for three parishes tonight. If required, he would deal with the baptism of a frail newborn or the blessing and anointing of a dying person.

'No, thanks. I need a word with my so-called Father Confessor here. He has whiskey and a spare room, so I'll stay the night. Mind, he's the one who should be confessing his sins, the cheating old monkey. It'll all catch up with him one day. What's that saying? Something about your sins finding you out?'

The two brothers left, their backs shaking with laughter. Frank and Chris spent ten minutes making supper in the kitchen: scrambled eggs, which represented the complete breadth of Frank's culinary skills, placed eventually on toast cremated by the resident priest of the parish. He scraped it over the sink, muttering all the while under his breath.

'You swearing again?' Frank asked. 'You'll go to hell on a handcart if you don't cut that out.'

'I'm speaking in Gaelic, which doesn't count. Anyway, what's the craic? I can see the worry bursting out of your eye sockets and pouring down your face. You look like a month of wet Sundays in Blackpool.'

'You don't half talk a load of tripe, man. Speaking of food, let's eat, then I'll moan when I've something in my belly.'

Chris said grace, after which Frank answered with a perfunctory 'Amen'.

They ate in silence. A friendship as close as theirs did not require constant chatter; each was comfortable in the presence of the other. Frank, a lapsed Catholic, experienced no trouble in accepting his closest friend's position in life, while Chris held firmly to the belief that Frank, a man good to the bone, would not be turned away by Pope Peter on the Day of Judgement.

After their frugal and somewhat crisp repast, they lounged in the living-room armchairs. 'I feel bloated,' Chris complained. 'Were those eggs all right?'

'Till I put the arsenic in yours, yes.' Frank scratched his head. 'I can't stop thinking about him. The bastard's still out there on the loose somewhere, and goodness knows what he's up to. I shiver every time my mind wanders to young Billy and that poor brother. What a career Brennan's had, from priest to murderer in a few weeks.'

Chris shook his head and sighed heavily. 'I blame myself, you know. He's always been difficult and quick to temper, but my passion for golf resulted in the near death of poor Billy and the killing of a monk. I shouldn't have handed over the reins to a man I dislike and for whom I never had respect. If he'd been decent in the eyes of the Church, he would have had his own parish years ago.'

'Oh, stop it. You didn't know he was going to turn completely crazy, did you? You needed a break. Everybody wants a change from time to time.'

'I told the congregation I was going on retreat, which I suppose I was in my terms. But instead of prayer and meditation, I won just short of a hundred quid while playing golf. That's gone into the Turnpike Fund, by the way.' He paused. 'Where the hell is he, Frank? This is a relatively small country, so how far can he get without being noticed? He's not an item you could miss, for he's built like a brick outhouse and has a face only his mother could love.'

'No idea. If I had an inkling, I'd be on his tail, believe me. But you are in no way responsible for what he is or where he is. Did he leave any belongings here? Might he come back to collect his stuff?'

'He left two missals given to him by his parents at confirmation and ordination, money, a chequebook, and clothing. Oh, there was his father's fob watch and a photo of his mother in a little silver frame. I wonder what those poor people did to deserve a son like that one?' The priest sat deep in thought while seconds ticked by. 'His belongings are locked in a repository safe in central Liverpool, so if he does return here, there'll be nothing for him.' He shivered. The man had a key to this house. Perhaps he'd lost it? Oh, he'd better have lost it.

Frank laughed, though the tone held little merriment. 'There's your altar plate, chalices, patens and so forth. A man needn't go far in Liverpool to dispose of them for melting down. Don't look at me like that, Chris. If he can kill a monk with a crucifix, he can empty your tabernacle without a qualm and steal your ciborium, the one you and the parish saved for all those years. Oh, and hide your mother's silver tea service while you're at it in case he gets in here.'

Chris nodded. He would need to make sure that his tabernacle, the central point on the altar, would be locked. 'What else bothers you, O faithless dolt? I can tell your brain's in overdrive, because your headlights are on full beam. Yes, those eyes are aglow with devilment.'

'Polly Kennedy to mention but a few. My mother. A temptress who might put Eve with her apple and her snake to shame.'

'Your mother's become a temptress?'

'No. Mrs Moo? She looks like a barrage balloon in a frock. I just delivered three women for you. Mother is a lost cause, sadly. Polly turned me down because of what my mother did to poor Ellen, and the temptress is my solicitor.'

'She solicits like a lady of the night?'

'Not that old joke again, Chris. She does legal soliciting.' He told his friend about the shop and flat on Rice Lane, his store of second-hand furniture and trinkets, his desire to set up his own business well away from Charleson Holdings. 'It was to be for me, Polly and her brother. A good start in life for the three of us, or so I thought. Now, it feels like just another pipe dream, though I don't know why, because I'm going ahead with it. I suppose nothing's as good without Polly. Without her, I'm only half of me.'

'She misses you sorely, Frank. It's not over. She had other stuff to think about is all.'

'So there's hope? God, I hope there's hope.'

Chris grinned. 'And this solicitor is tempting you into a dalliance of some kind? Or will she want a wedding ring? Take care. You know, marriage is like a card game. You begin with two hearts and a diamond or three, and you end up wanting a club and a spade. Somebody intelligent wrote that. I know for myself, anyway. I watched my brothers and feared for their sanity, especially once the breeding started, ergo I escaped into celibacy at the earliest opportunity, because it was a terrifying sight altogether.'

'So you've never been with a woman?'

'I didn't say that, did I?'

'Ah.'

'Take off the smile before I wipe it with the back of my hand. When you're old enough, I'll tell you stories fit to curl your hair. My past might well make a lurid novella or the tale of a rebel saint. That's for me to know and you to ponder until I choose to talk.'

Frank's grin widened. This wearer of vestments, mediator for the forgiveness of sins, speaker of Latin, baptizer of infants, comforter of the dying and bereaved, was probably the most normal man he knew. 'The bloody solicitor had me going, Chris. If she'd undone another button on that blouse, I might have jumped on her. Instead, I played dominoes, so at least I'm not banned from the Liver. Not just yet, anyway.'

'Ah, but they take just about anybody in there, Frank. They've let me in a couple of times, which goes to show how low are their standards.'

'Will you shut up and listen? I've slept with Polly twice. Once was just sleep with some giggling and a sore hand from hitting Brennan, the second allowed certain additional privileges.'

'And? So this is Confession? Will I get my stole and a rosary so you can do your penance?'

'Oh, give up, please. I wanted to say it's different when you love the woman. Better, more meaningful.' He let it all pour: his feelings, Polly's borrowed knickers, Ellen's engagement ring, his mother's nastiness. 'I was on my way out of Brookside anyway, if I'm honest. I've been collecting stock for ages, tucking it away in a unit near the Dock Road. But all Polly could see was the woman who murdered Ellen. Old Moo didn't exactly take a knife to her, but she was always buying her cleaning products – "do try this on mirrors and windows, dear" – or cookery books. Ellen shrivelled and died. She would have died anyway, but perhaps not quite so early – who knows? My mother gave her every encouragement to shuffle off this mortal coil.'

Chris poured two doubles into tumblers. 'There you go, lad. I know you don't want *ego te absolvo*, so this will have to do. Sins shrink when you're inebriated – take that from a serial offender. There's nothing like a drop of Irish to help you feel saintly. Just drink that, and I'll polish our haloes later while you tune the harps.'

Frank stared into the amber fluid, twisting the crystal in his hand so that light bounced off it. 'Elaine Lewis practically placed herself on a Sunday serving platter with garnish, roast spuds and three kinds of veg.'

'No apple in her gob?'

'No. She reminds me of a film star. Very polished.'

'Like glazed ham?'

'Shut up.'

Chris sighed again. 'I remember young Kathleen O'Gorman, so I do. She was lovely. Brown as a berry from the summer sun, blonde streaks in her long, flowing hair, that special twinkle in her bright blue eyes, lips like rose petals, and the way she walked . . . oh, she was nearly the death of me, but.'

Frank offered no comment, as he didn't want to stop the flow.

'We were engaged, you know. And we'd lie there in her bedroom planning a future to embrace at least four children, one a priest, one a nun, the rest teachers.' He lowered his head and shook it sadly. 'But it was not to be, Frank.'

'Because you gave yourself to Christ?'

The head continued to move from side to side. 'Not at all.'

'Then why?'

'Because her mammy was our babysitter, and we were all of six years old. When she heard us talking about bridesmaids, she fell in a heap laughing and moved me into another room. We were the talk of the town for weeks, all the biddies standing about gossiping, pointing at us and laughing. So we broke off the engagement. Oh, life was a vale of tears for at least a week, perhaps ten days to a fortnight. Then I met Tildy Byrne, whose brother owned a real cricket bat and wickets.'

'You were a philanderer in your youth, then.'

'Indeed, I was fickle. Then at eighteen, I saw the light. Well, I thought I did, but it might have been just a full moon, and me in a mad phase. And here we are now drinking the good stuff and worrying about your lawyer and the buttons on her blouse. In my considered opinion, the world does not improve.'

They sat for ten or fifteen minutes in the silence of Chris's unimproved world. These two outwardly very different men existed on the same wavelength. For both, faith was a shot in the dark at best, a curse at worst. Frank had walked away, but Chris struggled on, fighting to believe, urging his flock to trust and love a God with whom he often lost patience. He broke the silence. 'I should have been a train driver,' he declared.

'Why?'

'Well, it's the same thing entirely. You shove a load of people into pews and drive on. There's no choice, no diversions unless some great decider shifts the points. And you carry on with the gauge set for you, the lines fixed for you, onward all the way to the buffers. And if you try to change direction, every part of the train is derailed, and you're all buggered. I am that driver.'

'A shepherd often leads from behind.'

'With a dog to help him. You know, I fancy a Kerry Blue bitch.'

'Who's she? One of your bridesmaids?'

'It's a dog, you fool. Good Irish stock, strong and pig-headed like meself, but with a better sense of humour altogether. And better hair, too.'

Frank grinned. 'I hear young Billy got a pup.'

Chris borrowed the same grin. 'He showed me when I went round there.'

'Did he?'

'Aye, he did, so. Proud as Punch, the lad was. Nice little thing, the puppy, a leg at each corner, waggy little rudder at the back, friendly face. Spaniel, I think. They're talking of having it neutered. You might like to consider that yourself if the soliciting continues.'

Frank laughed. 'It's the betraying of Polly that bothers me. I have an over-developed sense of guilt and duty.'

'She turned you down, man.'

Frank eyed his companion harshly. 'Are you encouraging fornication?'

'I am not. All I'm saying is there are worse things, like killing a brother with a crucifix. Anselm was his chosen name. I bet they're all starving in Broughton Abbey, because he was the cook.'

'Damned shame. Still, they won't have to eat your burnt toast.'

'Frank?'

'That's me.'

'Just live your life, try to pray, try to accept your mother and attempt to get her to treat Polly with some respect. As for your other problem, do no harm. I'm ten or more years older than you, and I have a different perspective. Like all the other animals, we were given a powerful sex drive for a reason.'

'So we're animals?'

'Absolutely.'

'With souls?'

'Apparently.'

Frank drained his glass. 'What do you believe in, Chris?'

'Like I said, start by doing no harm, then try doing some good. This priest business is no walk in the park, believe me. As you said, I'm the shepherd. But some members of my flock are holier than I am.'

'No, I asked what you believe in, not how you function.'

The older man pondered. 'God's there and He's good. All the bad in the world is created by man, because he makes the wrong choices. Jesus is Messiah. Mary's His mother, but I hope she went on to live the normal life until she found her Son pinned to a tree, bless her. It's some of the other stuff I have trouble with. We should all have a degree of difficulty, or our faith would be too easy, and God gave us brains. If He'd manufactured us to sit back and accept, that would have no value, so He forced us to think and worry and choose.'

'Get us another drink before we turn serious or sober. But first, what do you think of Rome?'

'The Sistine Chapel has a lovely ceiling to it. It certainly wasn't painted by Liverpool Corporation. Other than that, no comment. Give me the glass, and it's my turn to tell you to shut up.'

They talked well into the night about baptisms, swiftly followed by Extreme Unction and death for mother, child or both, God's involvement with such tragedies, abortion, war, birth control and Polly Kennedy. Polly seemed to be Frank's best subject.

'So you'll be asking her again to marry you, I take it?'

'Yes, once I've established myself on Rice Lane. Or maybe before that. I've been carrying the ring for weeks.

I thought I might turn some of the downstairs storage into a place for Cal, somewhere more spacious for his wheelchair and so on. It's very cramped in their living room, you see.'

Chris sipped his whiskey. 'You haven't heard what's happened, then?'

'Heard what?'

'The lad's stumbling about on his feet again, leading his sister a merry dance. Mind, Polly's wonderfully happy about it. Oh yes, he's making grand progress. Frank? Dear God be my witness, I never meant you to cry, son. But don't be ashamed, because men do cry. If you'd seen the shape of me at the end of *Brief Encounter*, you'd have screamed for a lifebelt. As for Charlie Chaplin's *Limelight*, an ambulance turned up with police outriders and the lifeboat was launched.' He crossed the space between them and placed his left hand on his friend's head, blessing him with the right.

'Sorry, Chris. Polly told me there was a chance, because of him celebrating pain in the legs.' He dried his eyes. 'Sorry about that,' he repeated. 'I'm glad for him.'

'Away with your bother. This is an emotional time for you. Callum Kennedy's a better man than most of us, and he deserves to get well. Polly should be on the receiving end of better fortune, too. I never saw anyone working harder than she does. And there's a young woman on the scene, a nurse from the physiotherapy ward at the hospital. I think romance is in the air.'

'You're right, of course. Men do cry. I saw my dad cry more than once. Mother's fault, no doubt. Thank you, God. While you're at it, do you do removals? Only I've a pile of stuff needs shifting from the Dock Road up to Rice Lane.'

Chris chortled. 'Is this you praying at last?'

'It is.'

'One-nil to me and the Almighty, then, for this was a match played on God's own ground.'

'You cheating again, Father?'

'I never cheat.'

'Of course you don't.'

Chris laughed. 'I have to get my fun some way, Frank. That's my excuse, and you must live with it or leave me to it.'

'Another drink?' Frank asked.

'No, for I must away to my bed, or I'll be staggering about at tomorrow's early Mass as drunk as a lord after the hunt ball. Get to bed yourself, forget the blouse buttons and concentrate on your one true love and her brother. Goodnight and God bless.'

Frank sat for a while. Polly had turned him down because of Mother's treatment of Ellen; she had been worried about the possible undermining of her brother's positivity. Mother was in the past, and Cal was recovering. 'All I have to do now is get settled and make money. Easier said than done, but I'll give it my best shot.'

Norma Charleson was improving at a steady rate of knots. Moving more easily and becoming markedly more level in temperament, she seemed to react well to her diabetic diet. The silly doctor was pleased with her; he had also informed her that chocolate, poisonous to many animals, was equally toxic for humans if consumed in large quantities. 'Well,' she said as she and her companion looked through rails of garments, 'the poison must be out of my system by now. What do you think of this skirt? Oh, never mind, I've bought one very similar in brown, haven't I? There's no point in going wild until I've lost another couple of stone.'

She and Christine Lewis were in Southport at a shop

on Lord Street that catered for larger women, as Norma had reduced her weight to the point where she needed a different size of clothing. But since she was only halfway to her goal, she intended to provide herself with just a few items which would form what she termed her interim wardrobe. 'I hope it's worth it, Christine. God knows I could kill for a cream cake and some chocolates. Diabetes is so restricting.'

'Yes, I have to admit that it seems difficult.'

When the purchases had been made, they went to a rather nice coffee house for elevenses. As elevenses was just coffee, they didn't stay long. 'Even my shoes feel bigger,' Norma complained. 'But they'll have to do. I've spent enough for one day.'

Christine drove. Christine did almost everything these days, but her wages had increased, so she tolerated the extra burdens. She cooked, cleaned, washed, ironed, shopped and collected rents. But she was tired and ill-prepared for Norma's mood changes which, fortunately, were becoming less dramatic as her dependence on chocolate decreased and she began to take some pride in her appearance. Underneath the rolls of fat, a good-looking woman was fighting to get out.

'Shall we pop into Liverpool, Christine? We could wander round the Walker Gallery.'

'If you like.' The 'Norma' still grated slightly, but she was practically forced to use it. Christine Lewis was in another difficult position, too. Elaine was doing Frank's conveyancing, but she couldn't say a word about where. Elaine was also trying to capture him, but not for keeps, since she intended to marry someone dull from the business sector; or a doctor might do. So Frank could well be hunted, caught, used and released. Like Norma, Christine had just one child, and that child danced to music few could hear.

'You're quiet,' Norma said.

'A little tired. Don't worry, I shall buck up shortly.'

'Do you want to turn back?'

'Oh, not at all. Driving is a pleasure.' Norma had not treated Frank well. He had been a poorly paid servant, no more than that. But there was no excuse for Elaine, since she'd been treasured from birth, yet she was turning herself into a person scarcely recognizable by her own mother. There were no arguments, but Christine found that she was becoming increasingly uneasy in the company of her daughter. Like Norma Charleson, Elaine owned what Christine termed calculating eyes.

'Let's just drive round for a while,' Norma suggested a little too casually. 'It's such a lovely day, too nice for lingering in an art gallery. Let's watch the world as it goes by.'

The driver shrugged internally. This woman was looking for Frank again. For the third or fourth time, the car would circle the city, a suburb or two, Scotland Road and the Everton area. So Frank was missed by his mother. Although she had failed to appreciate the true value of her son, the newer Norma Charleson appeared to be developing the ability to feel for someone other than herself. 'He's a big boy, Norma. He'll be all right. Don't waste time worrying about a man in his late twenties.'

Norma sniffed.

'He'll be fine,' Christine repeated reassuringly.

'Oh, I suppose he will. It's just that I'd like to know where he is. There's something very unsettling about not knowing where the offspring is. You're sure he's not with Polly Kennedy?'

'Absolutely. People keep asking me about him when I collect the rent. He's very well liked in Scotland Road, and I get the distinct impression that I'm a poor substitute. They'd love to see him again.'

'Yes, he's popular, because he has a tendency to make friends of the tenants. He married one, and seems to want to marry another. I've learned something, Christine; we can do nothing and must do nothing if and when they decide to marry someone we see as wrong for them. Frank blames me for Ellen's death, though I had never been told in detail about her condition. In my clumsy way, I was trying to help. So that's another thing I discovered – don't help and don't hinder. I may be getting on in years, but I'm still happy to learn.'

Christine nodded her agreement. There was no help for Elaine. Also, there was no sign of Frank. They travelled homeward, where Norma would have salad and chicken, after which Christine would go home and endure a pleasant evening with her daughter.

The only trouble was that Christine scarcely knew the person she had reared. But everything must remain happy on the surface, since she dared not speak her mind. She was living with a stranger, while Norma, doing her best to be kinder and gentler, would spend the evening alone. Life was hard for both women.

'I bought you that scarf you liked, Christine. The colour suits you well, so I thought you should have it.'

'Oh, that's so kind of you.'

'You're a very pretty woman, you know.'

'So will you be when you lose a bit more of the weight. We do all right together on the whole, don't we?'

'We do,' Norma answered. But nothing would be right till she found Frank.

Daniel the spaniel, who had not been christened Jumble after all, was fighting with a bone twice his size. He was black. Because of the dog in the dream, Fred had deliberately chosen a good, strong, black pup. Mavis had worried, but he'd told her to calm down, because Billy had to learn that not all black dogs were nightmares.

'I still have the dreams,' Pest Junior informed Dr Pest Senior. 'But the dream trap changed them. The big black dog gets the fat man, and the fat man goes away. Only he isn't fat any more.'

The doctor sat down. 'Where is he when you see him in the dream, Billy? Is he on the playing field near the school?'

Billy shook his head. 'He's got a tractor. I've got a tractor. It's a Dinky. Daniel has to get injections against distemper. I thought it was paint, but it's a dog illness as well. My arm's nearly all mended, so I have to go back to school in September, but I can't take Daniel.'

Mavis led the doctor into the kitchen. 'He has the sight,' she whispered. 'My mother had it, and it's a damned nuisance. I mean, she couldn't pick a Derby winner, but she knew everybody's business before it happened.'

'I don't believe in that stuff, Mrs Blunt.'

She put him in his place right away. 'That makes no difference and doesn't matter. It'll happen whether you believe or not. If Billy says Brennan has a tractor, he has a tractor. See, I've wrote down everything he said. It's here.' She reached for an exercise book. ' "Sleeping in a wood, very cold. Slept in a barn with rats. Screaming in the night with bad dreams like I had." Billy said all those things. I wrote them as he said them. Brennan is thinner because he's working on the land.'

'Where, though?'

She shrugged. 'When it comes to geography, our Billy can find his way to school, church, the chippy and the sweet shop. To him, a farm is a farm, grass is green and a lot of trees make a wood. Just you mark my words now, Doc. Brennan is living rough and sleeping rough. He's likely going from one farm to another and labouring. Oh, there's a bit I didn't write down, so I'll do it when you've gone. He's grown a beard. It's a different colour from his hair, reddish with grey mixed in.'

Both stood and listened while Billy laughed as he tumbled about with his new pet.

'He loves his puppy,' the doctor said.

'So will I when it stops dirtying in the house, little bugger.'

The psychologist excused himself and went to play noughts and crosses with his patient. Billy was a sweet boy who improved daily. But second sight? It was a load of codswallop. Wasn't it? So . . . so how had the boy known the dead monk's name?

Ida stood up. 'Look, you lot. I don't care if I get there covered in coal dust, horse muck or molasses, as long as I get there. The wotsit . . . Industrial Revolution was up here as much as anywhere, and our mams and dads and grandfolk were part of it. And it was a dirty business. They sit there, them government idiots, on posh green benches and use big words so working folk won't know the plot, so why be respectful or respectable? I'll go on a coal lorry if it'll get me there in one piece.'

Others jumped to their feet and cheered.

Encouraged by her few moments of fame, Ida blossomed. 'Which port in this country carried every bit of ammunition through its docks in the war?'

'Liverpool,' her audience shouted.

'And whose dock workers worked like dogs day and night to get the guns and shells and grenades through?'

'Liverpool's!'

'And where did a lot of those too old or too young for war dock workers come from?'

'Scotland Road!'

'And which people are going to be torn apart as a big thank you for jobs well done?'

'Scotland Roaders!'

'What do we want?'

'Homes, not roads!' These three words were chanted repeatedly.

Frank Charleson, chairman of the Turnpike committee, sat at the front with the board. His right hand 'man' and deputy chair was seated next to him, and he loved her. Having kept his distance for a while, he was acutely aware of Polly's presence. Father Chris Foley, Fred Blunt, Hattie Benson and Denis Davenport formed the rest of the committee, though several self-elected people attended the meetings. This was an open session at which anyone could have a say.

Frank stood up and held up a hand. 'Right, calm down. Father?'

Chris Foley unfolded his arms and raised a hand. 'No rioting, please. I get enough of that on the golf links in Southport. We go in whatever transport we can muster. We make no trouble on the journey, and we make no trouble in London. The petition will be handed over by Polly and Frank to the police outside Number Ten. And we stand there in Downing Street packed like tinned sardines and we say not one word. We do not laugh; nor do we cry. There is something quite menacing about a crowd that remains in total silence. They won't forget us in a hurry.'

The audience clapped. Anyone who forgot this lot wanted his or her head testing.

'And we go not as Catholics and Orangemen. Our fellows from Everton, some of whom will lose their homes and businesses, will be with us. We travel as citizens of a free country and a great city that speaks its mind and shames the devil himself.'

The main door of the school hall flew inward and crashed into a stray chair. The gathering turned as one man to see Jimmy Nuttall (tripe, fish, cooked meats and skinned rabbits) trying to regain control over his breathing. He bent forward, hands on his knees, until he found some oxygen. Slowly, he unravelled himself into a more or less upright position.

Chris Foley walked the length of the room to support him. 'What in heaven has happened to you, Jimmy? You look like you've seen a ghost.'

'I want Fred. It has to be Fred, Father,' gasped the new-comer.

'Come away in with you, then. Lean on me. Try to stagger on, Jimmy, and hand over the burden, whatever it is.'

Jimmy managed the length of the hall. 'Fred,' he gasped, 'they found his body. They're pretty sure it's him, but he's . . . well, he's been there a while and animals have had a go at him. Police can't do fingerprints, cos . . . er, there's not enough there. They would have took prints, then tried to match them up with stray traces at Columba's and the monastery, but it's no go. The hot weather has . . . well, you know.'

The colour drained from Fred's face. 'But they're certain it's him?'

'There was a rosary underneath him and a half-empty bottle of Scotch.'

'He drinks Irish,' Chris said.

'But Scotch is easier to come by,' Frank commented. 'He'd drink anything he could find, I'd bet.'

Polly burst into tears. They hadn't got him. He had escaped his comeuppance by dying, and the courts would never prosecute.

Frank gathered her in his arms and put his mouth to an ear. 'Don't you dare weep like this on our wedding day. I carry our pair of knickers wherever I go. Pray I don't use them as a handkerchief to dry your eyes here and now.' He released her and turned to Fred. 'If he's dead, he's dead, and that's it, finished and done with.'

The place was so quiet that a feather, let alone a pin, would have made noise when landing. Mavis walked to the front. 'It's not him,' she said clearly. 'Who told you, Jimmy?'

'A bloke with a son who works for the print shop that sets the *Liverpool Echo*. The man they found – well, what was left of him – had been fat before he started to rot. Brennan was always fat.'

'He's alive,' she insisted. 'Billy sees him when he's asleep, but it doesn't frighten him any more. Brennan is thinner, he's drinking less and he's working in the fields. Can they not get an idea from his clothes? Or from his teeth?'

Jimmy answered in the negative.

'Did the body have a beard?' she asked.

Jimmy's shoulders rounded themselves. 'The head's missing,' he said after a pause. 'Carried off by a dog or a big fox, more than likely. The clothing's shredded, fingers chewed off, but they found booze and a rosary. As far as they can work out, there's a skeleton that would have been Brennan's height if it was all there, with some flesh and an amount of human fat. The rest has gone, even the feet.'

Mavis looked at Father Foley. 'I'm not a Catholic any more, but you are. And I may as well warn you, we'll still be suing the Church, because if we lose, we pay nothing, and if we win, the Church pays the fees, too. So, Father, if this God of yours can talk to grown-ups who're going to be saints and all that, can't the same God talk to a child in his sleep?'

'I believe He can,' was Chris's answer.

'You are wrong, Jimmy,' she said. 'He is still alive and kicking. Now, I'm going across the street to be with my son, who has the same sight my mother had.' She turned and addressed the people in the main body of the hall. 'What they found is not Brennan. Ask my boy.' She stalked out.

Fred made his apologies and followed her.

Frank stood up. 'Right. I'm sorry this is a bit like church, but please put anything you can afford in the collection box by the door. We'll convene again in three weeks from tonight.' He reclaimed his seat. Beneath the sound of scraping chairs and conversations, he spoke to Polly. 'You pregnant?'

'No.'

'Good. I would have needed to alter the grand plan.'

'What grand . . . ?' She was wasting her time; he was talking to Father Foley. She gathered up notebook and biro, lifted her handbag and walked to the door, pushing a folded ten-shilling note into the box. The bottleneck crush in the foyer was beginning to clear. A hand crept round her waist. 'You made me jump,' she accused.

'I remember,' he said. 'Best night of my life so far, that was.' He led her to his car and opened the passenger door. 'In you get.'

Untypically, she did as ordered without question.

He joined her, started the car and drove off at speed. 'Where are we going, Frank?'

'Somewhere quiet. I've got your ball and chain.'

'What?'

'Ellen's ring. Then I have secret surprises to plan and carry out, so we'll be married in a few months when I've done what I have to do.'

She grinned. 'Don't I get a say?'

'No. My mother's out of the picture, and I understand Cal is much improved, so less vulnerable. I'm making a home for all of us, him included, though I hear he may have plans of his own.'

'If you'd take the trouble to visit, you could see for yourself.'

'Still Miss Clever Mouth, I see.'

'Of course.'

He found a quiet spot near the river, and they held hands like a pair of children while watching the sun's glorious au revoir. And he asked again. 'Will you marry me, Polly Kennedy?'

She wore a thoughtful expression for a few seconds.

'Well, madam?'

'Can I have a big fridge and a washing machine?'

He burst out laughing; she was going to say yes. 'All right.'

'Can I have two children, preferably one girl and one creature, a proper sideboard, the *Beano* and *Dandy* delivered every week?'

'Yes. Though when it comes to the gender of kids, I can't make a firm promise. As for the comics, we read one each and then swap.'

'Fair enough.'

'Is that a yes, Polly?'

'Of course it is, you great lummox. I should never have allowed Mrs Moo to get to me.'

He took the ring from its box and polished it with the borrowed knickers. 'You get a good shine out of a double cotton gusset,' he announced seriously.

Polly blinked away a tear. Ellen had been so proud of her aquamarine with its four tiny diamond attendants. She held out her left hand, and he placed the ring on her finger. 'Frank?'

'Yes?'

She turned and held his face between her hands. The kiss she bestowed upon him asked nothing but gave everything; it was sweet and innocent, yet quite professional at the same time. 'I love you, Charleson. But you didn't leave home for my sake, did you?'

'For my sanity,' he answered. 'Which you will need to be assured of, so I left for myself, for you, for our daughter and our creature, for Cal, for my own business and our home. By the way, I love you, too.'

They stayed for a while under dusk's blanket, inventing their own language for their own love, saying the silly, private words that would accompany them through the rest of their lives. She didn't mind about fridges and washers; he was to have the *Beano* first, since he preferred it to the *Dandy*. Chris Foley would marry them, but in St Anthony's, which was Polly's church. Any girls and creatures would be raised as Catholics, as that was their mother's faith, and he would attend church with the family for their sake.

Huddled together for an hour in his too-small-for-anything-interesting car, they began their walk through life. Inevitably, they eventually strayed into the territory of others. 'What do you think about Mavis Blunt and what she said?' Frank asked.

'I don't know what to think. Mam and Dad were in my dreams long after they'd died. But Mavis seems so sure that what Billy sees is real.'

'She says her mother was sighted, Pol.'

'Yes, I know.'

'Was she sighted?'

'I think she was. I remember old Mrs Mahoney telling me to look after Mam and Dad. With hindsight, I think that might have been a warning without actually telling me they were dying. I don't have the answer about what I believe.'

'You're in good company. Even Father Chris gets confused on that score, and he drives the bloody train. Oh, he's invited us both for a meal next Friday, but only if you say yes to my proposal. He says you're a sensible girl except for loving me.'

'Cheeky monkey.'

'Exactly.'

'What do you mean by driving the train? Is he moonlighting for the railways?'

'I'll explain when I have a week to spare, but do you really think any clown would let him anywhere near a steam engine? He'd get excited if he was given a toy train, never mind the Flying Scotsman.'

'Aw, he's lovely, though, Frank.'

'My best mate. He's the only bloke I'm completely open with, and his sense of humour's great. And another thing – he's wise. Underneath all the laughing and gambling for pennies, he's one clever bloke. He would have been a great dad.'

'So will you.'

'I bloody well hope so, kid.'

They sat a while kissing and canoodling before he began the drive back to Scotty. 'Poor Mavis,' Polly sighed.

'And poor Billy, poor Fred,' Frank added.

'Nothing we can do for them,' she said as they parked outside the cafe. 'But you can do one thing for us. Come in with me now and tell Cal we're engaged. He's missed you. We've both missed you.'

When they walked into the living room, Cal was vertical and using a pair of crutches. 'Hiya, mate. Where the hell have you been?'

Frank swallowed a lump of emotion. 'You've come on

a bit, Callum Kennedy. I've been abandoning my mother, living in a B and B where my landlady has all the charm of your average rattlesnake, collecting some of my wares and parking them near the docks, preparing a flat and a shop, gambling with Chris and the Blunts, playing dominoes in the Liver pub, running away from a woman who wants to get into my drawers ...'

'I don't,' Polly laughed.

'I wasn't talking about you. It's the lawyer handling my conveyancing.'

'Well, she must keep her hands to herself. If anybody's handling your details, it should be me.'

'Nymphomaniac,' Frank said solemnly.

'I'm not one of them.'

'No, but she is. I reckon she could make a fortune if she put herself in Mother Bailey's hands. Classy, you see. Shove her in a boudoir with silk sheets, and she'd make a fortune.'

'Don't be making our Polly jealous,' Cal advised. 'She's bad enough as she is. When Linda's here, they turn into iron maidens.'

'Don't worry, Cal, I'll take this one off your hands and chain her to the sink. I've got a place. And there'll be a flat for you on the ground floor if you need it.' He looked Polly up and down. 'Show him your ring.'

Once again, she did as she was told. 'It was Ellen's,' she explained. 'I asked for it. I wanted her to be a part of our life story.'

'Congratulations, both of you. But I won't need the flat, because Linda and I will be in a bungalow next to her mam and dad. Mrs Higgins needs help since she got bombed and lost her legs. Makes me feel grateful.'

'You're getting married, too?' Polly laughed. 'We could have a double wedding.'

Cal shook his head. 'No. Let whoever marries us deal with one set of trouble at a time.'

She blinked. She would miss her twin terribly, but she would have Frank, and he was her whole world. Oh, and it would definitely be a double wedding.

Nine

At the first breakfast sitting, Ida, though seated, was on her soapbox. 'We need representation for all of us shop-keeper folk,' she said. 'The trouble with having a business or a proper job is that we can't stand for election in case our shops go down or in case we can't find another job when we get voted out. So who gets into the Commons, eh?' She stood up.

No one offered a reply, so she motored on. 'Our members of parliament are supposed to be there for our sake, that's why it's called the Commons. But what are they? Bloody doctors and lawyers, because they know they'll always get a job again if they lose their seats. There's a few teachers and dentists, too, because they feel safe. And they speak for us? What do they know about ordinary folk? They want to build roads into the city, and that's their excuse for moving us on. Oh, they're always jawing on about what they call eventual redevelopment, but that's a load of old soap. Bessie Braddock got in and made her mark, so why not Polly or Frank or Den?'

Polly yawned. After a late night spent talking with Frank, she needed sleep. Her man was looking tired, too. 'Are you going to eat that breakfast or paint a picture of it?' she asked him.

'Well, I'm not standing for Parliament,' was Frank's reply.

'I can hardly stand at all,' she told him. 'My legs aren't even related to one another this morning.'

He pretended to glare at her. 'You've no stamina.'

'And you have? You look as if you've been awake all night.'

'No comment.' He was busy thinking about moving all his stock from the Dock Road store. 'I have to go soon,' he said.

Ida continued. 'One of us has to try to get elected,' she insisted. 'Polly?'

'No chance.'

'Frank?'

'Ditto.'

'What about you, Den?'

Den said he couldn't leave his horse before adding, 'You do it, Ida. You're the one on your feet and mouthing off.'

She sat down again and ate her breakfast. Nobody seemed to listen to sense. Nobody wanted to go to London as a politician, either. Oh well. She dipped a soldier into the yolk of an egg. 'All the king's horses and all the king's men couldn't put Scotty together again.'

'Don't gab with your mouth full,' Hattie advised.

Ida shook her head. She might as well talk to the bloody wall.

By the time Eugene Brennan discovered the news about his sad and lonely death, he'd been deceased, decapitated, without feet, and a few manual digits short for several weeks. It was an interesting experience, and it pleased and disturbed him no end, taking him to the brink of hysteria when he read some of the tragic details. He had decomposed, and animals had made off with bits of him, leaving no feet, no head and no fingerprints. That part caused a few shivers, though he still managed to smile at the ludicrous claims.

He counted his fingers, touched his head and glanced down at his shoes. 'All present and correct. I do very well for a decomposed person. However, I must compose myself now and take advantage of this situation. Or would that be recompose myself?' He looked round the shed in which he had been sleeping; there was no longer a need for him to hide. Sheds, barns and derelict houses were all about to become things of the past. The nights were cooler, and winter wasn't too far away; he was safe. The dreams and the screams could stop now, surely? They must, because he would soon need shelter.

'Eugene, sorry to give you this terrible news, but you are no longer among us. I wish you Godspeed and a happy eternity. Amen.'

Thus providence shone on him just as September peeped over the horizon, when he found a pile of old newspapers in a stable at the farm where he was currently employed. As he read through the pages, he learned that a decayed piece of humanity had been discovered in Derbyshire with certain pertinent parts missing, and Eugene Brennan had been nominated as ex-occupier of said mouldy, fingerless, footless and headless residence. MURDERING PRIEST FOUND DEAD. Quite a headline.

He devoured every syllable of one article which went into great detail regarding his crimes, which still shocked him to the core. The drink had done that. A bottle a day kept reality at bay. He had kicked a young thief and had killed a Brother Anselm. Perhaps if he'd taken the pills in the abbey, he might have acted very differently, but he had been in full withdrawal and out of control. Even so, murder was murder, and his soul was beyond retrieval. Prayer proved almost impossible for a while, though he still had the odd few words with the Almighty. Begging for forgiveness would have been a waste of time. 'I'm a sinner, Lord, but there were mitigating circumstances, mostly the drink.'

He sighed heavily. The taking of a human life was a sin not forgivable in church law, so he had no chance of redemption. Being excommunicated bothered him more than he might have expected. He finished reading and threw down the newspaper. 'Mammy and Daddy were Catholic and I was a priest. But I wasn't a good one. And now, I'm dead. They were so proud of their son.' A tear rolled down his face; he was mourning himself, yet laughing at the same time.

They'd retrieved a rosary and a half-empty bottle of Scotch, so his name had been attached to the remains, as it was believed that the dead man had been overweight and a drinker. 'But I am a shadow of my former self, idiots.' Fitter than he had been in years, he suddenly had the chance of never being discovered. The nomad lifestyle suited him perfectly, though he was no longer dependent on it; he could now come and go as he liked, because he was completely free at last. Had his own mother been alive, she would scarcely have known him.

He was dead! 'Death makes life a lot easier,' he said to himself. Many itinerants were without papers like birth certificates and passports. They worked for low pay, gave no tax to the government, and were usually well received by builders or farmers, who were pleased to find a way of working sites or land using cheap manpower.

Physically and mentally, Eugene Brennan had changed in many ways. There was something about labouring that satisfied him and kept him away from the bottle during hours of daylight, when he was given good, home-cooked meals as part of his pay. He still drank in the evening, continuing to consume a little more than was clinically acceptable, but working in the fields seemed to help burn off the effects of alcohol. After all, he was a descendant of a heavy-drinking farming clan, so he needed no training, since he already possessed the necessary abilities to drink and to farm. As for the strength he had lacked during priesthood, it came back quickly and with some discomfort, though the pains were not as intense as he might have expected.

Well, he could move on to the southern part of Cheshire now. By the time he got to Liverpool, he would be someone else altogether. Did he need to go there? Yes, he did. All he had of Daddy was the watch, and the only bit that remained of Mammy was a faded picture in a silver frame, and he nursed over-sentimental and half-imagined memories of his parents. Then there was his money. He'd left over a hundred pounds behind, which now represented the total extent of his personal wealth, as the rest was in a bank account he dared not touch, dead or alive.

Also, he'd managed to hang on to the key to St Columba's presbytery, although it would still be necessary to break in, or to make the place look as if someone had broken in. Other items should disappear; if he removed just his own things, Eugene Brennan might be resurrected. But above all, he wanted to walk among them like the invisible man, to see the child, Father Christopher Foley, Frank Charleson and the rest. He would see them, but they would never notice him.

Being dead became very satisfying as time passed. His confidence grew daily, and he was able to spend his wages on a few items of clothing and some decent drink. A bottle lasted at least two days, so he was definitely on the mend. He chatted in shops, played darts in pubs, and found that the nightmares were finally leaving him. Dead men couldn't dream and, as he was safely defunct, he had no need to worry about Billy Blunt or Brother Anselm, since he had a different name, a changed body and a thinner, bearded face. This promised to be a brand new and promising beginning.

The name was easy. He took his surname, changed an N to a D, and became Brendan. It was an effeminate moniker, but it served a purpose. Surname? Mammy's maiden name had been Halloran, so he chopped it down to Hall, and there he was, a new man, a phoenix reborn not in fire, but in a pub with a glass of Irish in one hand and the stub of a cheroot in the other.

Oh, this was the life. The priest was dead, and the new man should now seek a woman. A woman would make him more normal, just one man in a crowd with a partner by his side. Did he want a woman? He had no idea. In his fifties, the only fleshly torment he endured was the need for whiskey.

How did a man get a woman? He wasn't handsome, but he was less ugly than he had been at his heaviest. Muscle had begun to replace flab and he was nicely tanned from working outdoors, while the trimmed beard disguised a weak chin. Although declared dead, he would feel even safer in the company of a female. And he'd nothing to lose at this stage. Compared to murder, intercourse with a female, should it be required, seemed a very poor relation in the extended family of sin.

So, it was a case of onward and upward as he made his leisurely way through the country towards the county of Cheshire. He was given rides by gypsies, by people in lorries, even by a deliverer of bread and a seller of coal. Conversation was possible at last, though he remained a poor, orphaned Irishman who had been passed from pillar to post, from orphanage to foster homes, never loved, never cared for. 'So I invaded England to get away from all that,' was the last sentence in his well-worn monologue.

In the south-eastern portion of Cheshire, he landed on his feet. Away from the main farmhouse, where he found himself, stood a caravan, and this was to be his home during harvest and for longer if he stayed on. He could take a bath in the main house as long as he gave notice, while the outside lavatory in a brick building was all his, and he could wash his hands at the outdoor tap in the farmyard. Oh, life was improving, indeed.

He had a home. Reassured by the farmer's wife that he would not be asked to share his caravan with another labourer, Brendan Hall settled in immediately. There was electricity wired in from the house, a good bed with clean sheets, a sink, a cooker, a table and a padded bench. After a couple of months on the road, this was the life of Riley.

Mrs Acton, the farmer's wife, had taken his word when it came to his list of skills, but he had told no lies. He could milk, he could churn, he could bring home a herd. Ploughing, planting and harvesting he had learned as a child. Root crops and top crops were all the same to him; he was capable of retrieving anything. 'But I can foretell neither rain nor sun, Mrs Acton. Over those two extremes, only God holds sway.'

'I'm Gladys,' she said.

'Then I'm Brendan. Pleased to make your acquaintance, and thanks for the job and the caravan. I'm grateful to you, so.'

He worked twelve hours a day every day. As well as helping locals to bring the harvest home, he swilled the yard, mended farm machinery, unblocked drains, fed pigs and hens, even slept with a shotgun by his side in case foxes should approach chicken coops in the night. Mrs Acton came to depend on him, and there was no sign of her husband. She pretended he'd gone away to a series of stock auctions, but one of the casual farmhands put that right. He'd buggered off.

'He buggered off,' said Paul Cropper casually as he sat in the yard with Brendan over soup and sandwiches one sunny lunchtime. 'Went with a younger woman from the stables over to Beresford's Drift. Play your cards right, and you could be in with old Gladys. It's her farm, not his. Well, it's her dad's. He still lives upstairs, bad health, getting on in years. She's a nice woman and you're a good worker who knows what he's doing. It's a match made in heaven, because you're about the same age.'

'Children?' Brendan asked casually.

'No.' Paul swallowed the last of his tea, belched and stood up. 'She couldn't have them, and she's past the age now, about fifty, I think. I've worked here on and off since I was a lad, and looking back, remembering what my mother said, Mrs Acton was heartbroken over it. He wasn't bothered, but she was. When it came to adoption, he didn't believe in it. Anyway, I reckon she's better off without him. Take my advice, Don. Get your feet under her table, treat her well, and you'll be out of that caravan in quick sticks.'

Like most people, Paul Cropper called his co-worker Don rather than Dan, which represented the second syllable of the chosen name. Perhaps it was as well, since Dan Hall rubbed close shoulders with damn all. As they left the barn, Don looked over his shoulder. It was a fine house and a valuable farm. Oh, and she was a good cook.

The paperwork was done and dusted, seals set, ribbons tied, deposit paid, and the searches and surveys were all finally completed. This was the end, and Elaine Lewis was in the dumps. She wanted Frank Charleson and, for as long as she remembered, she'd found little difficulty when it came to achieving her own way. He looked at her sometimes with what she imagined to be desire in his eyes.

He looked, but he never touched. As this was to be her biggest effort so far, she had dressed to ensnare him. She was graceful, beautiful and perfectly packaged.

She had the keys to the Rice Lane property, and this was probably the last occasion on which she would have a legal and practical reason for seeing Frank. Today, Aladdin took possession of his cave or his lamp, depending on which name he chose to adopt. He would do well. Although not an overbearing man, he owned a quiet strength and the sort of dedication that said a great deal about his character.

They were meeting for an early lunch, because as from noon the shop and the living accommodation were legally his, and she would hand over the keys. She had been wrong about him, since his entrepreneurial skills were going to become legendary. This was husband material after all. So it was possible to marry for love, then. Because insofar as Elaine Lewis was capable of concentrating on someone other than herself, she had formed an attachment to the man.

He had taken seriously none of her attempts to entrap him. After the meeting in the Liver pub, there'd been a dinner in a crowded restaurant, then an evening in the communal sitting room at his Bootle bed-and-breakfast place, and today was to be their last supper. Yes, it was only lunch, but there seemed to be a finality stapled to it. Reasons for meeting him had been used up; from now on, she could be no more than a customer in his shop.

A shadow loomed over her desk. She didn't need to look up. 'Hello, Bob,' she said, patience etched deeply into the words. 'And how are you today? Overworked again?'

'Those aren't your usual work clothes,' he accused her. 'You look ready for a wedding party or a visit to Buckingham Palace.'

'That's because this is fiesta time,' she replied. 'My

childhood friend moves today, so his mother, my mother, he and I are going out to celebrate at lunchtime.' The lies slid out so easily.

'Ah. Might you bring a friend?'

She laughed.

'Well?' he asked.

'No, I think not. It's a landmark in our lives, so no one outside our circle would appreciate its significance. Frank and I have always been close to our mothers. And our mothers will now look after each other all the time.'

A clock on the wall ticked. 'Why? Are you moving away from home, too?'

'Soon.' She had scarcely considered it, but it might be a good idea. 'Finding somewhere decent for the right price could be a long job,' she said.

'I could help. You'd have no trouble getting a mortgage. I shall keep my eyes open.'

'Thank you.' She looked back at their dinner date. He had chosen the wines and had even ordered her food along with his own. But she had stopped the waiter in his tracks and asked to see the menu for herself. Bob needed a great deal of training, it seemed. Could she really be bothered to teach this man that a woman had a mind of her own, that the days of male superiority had ended a few decades after the death of Victoria?

'That's a beautiful dress,' Bob said. 'The colour suits you very well.'

'Thank you. It's one of my favourites, too.'

He stared through the window at the Liver Building, saw the river glistening behind it. 'Will you marry him?'

'Er . . . no. Have you heard of familiarity and contempt?'

He nodded. 'And I've noticed the glow on your skin when you're going to meet him.'

'It's makeup.'

'Ah. Will you marry at all?'

She was getting just a little bored with the inquisition. 'No idea. But if I do, I shall be with a man who recognizes that a woman is born free. He will be clever enough to know he's with a clever female.'

'So you're clever?'

'Oh, definitely. Oxford at seventeen, here by the age of twenty-two, first-class honours, now law. There's nothing average about me, Bob. I can read menus and make my own choices. I am in control of my own life, so I don't really require a husband, since I want no children.'

He took a few seconds off, as he needed a rest. Elaine was desirable, but she was also hard work. 'Ah,' he said eventually, 'so you're the boss?'

'Yes.'

'Well, boss, your bra strap's on display at the top of your left arm.' He stalked back to his own office. It was time to give up on her for a little while.

The fury that rose in her throat was not commensurate with his remark about a bra strap. She seethed. He was a dolt, and she hated him immediately. The fact that he'd walked away without being dismissed was annoying enough, but a bra strap? He might be a partner, but he should keep questions and opinions to himself. She could get a job anywhere in this city, anywhere in the country.

In the powder room, she sorted out her strap, checked stockings and shoes, repaired her makeup. It was a beautiful dress, in a gentle turquoise shade, made in lace on top of silk of a similar, though subtly different colour. There was no silk on the arms, where flesh without bra strap now showed through the openwork. At her throat, a darker turquoise hung from a silver chain; this was echoed in a bracelet, though her earrings were plain silver studs. She was stylish; she was perfect, and she was probably looking for another job.

Meanwhile, Frank Charleson leaned casually against a

wall outside the newly opened bistro in which he would buy lunch. It was a place that served meals representing many countries, and the novelty made it popular with younger moneyed folk. At this end of town, close to the business sector, a restaurant like this should thrive.

He was waiting for Elaine Lewis for what he hoped was going to be the last time. She was fashionably late, as usual, and he was running out of patience. There was something dangerous about her, an occasional flash of fury in displeased eyes, a sudden straightening of the spine, the tapping of perfectly manicured nails on a hard surface, a frown deep enough to interfere with faultless good looks.

But Frank had arrived armed to the teeth on this occasion. Today was Nurse Linda's day off, which she usually spent with her mother, but she was standing in for Polly through the midday period. Polly, inside the bistro, studied the menu while Frank waited for his lawyer. All she knew was that Elaine Lewis was a manhunter who simply wouldn't give up on Frank, and she accepted the fact with equanimity, because he was gorgeous and the poor woman could scarcely be blamed.

Elaine arrived. She was stunning, and her attire was immaculate.

As ever, Frank admired her beauty. She was like a perfect statue into which breath had been pushed by a force that was not benign. 'Ah, good,' he said. 'Are you going on somewhere afterwards?'

'No. I wore this just to please you. I know you appreciate pretty things.'

'Delightful.' He led her into the bistro and to their table. 'Elaine Lewis, this is Polly Kennedy, my fiancée.' Polly was beautiful inside and out. Her personality shone from her face, because she had never been a statue. She smiled expectantly at the vision before her. 'Hello, pleased to meet you at last,' she said. 'Thank you for all you've done for us.'

Although Elaine often congratulated herself on her sangfroid, she didn't realize that her immediate reactions gave her away to people who looked closely. For us? She had done nothing for this young woman. Her eyes narrowed slightly, and the smile she offered resembled a silent snarl from a member of the cat family. She shook Polly's hand, placed Frank's keys on the table, and remembered another appointment back at the office. 'So sorry about this,' she said rather quickly. 'It slipped my mind completely until I was on my way here. I mustn't lose a client.'

Polly closed her gaping mouth and watched the woman rushing out into the street. 'There's something wrong with that one,' was her delivered opinion. 'Beautiful, but not quite with us.'

'I know. She's unreal. There's a creepy side to her. What are you having?' he asked, seamlessly altering the direction of their conversation.

'That stringy stuff looks interesting. See that woman over there sucking it up? I'll have string.'

He grinned. 'You'll need knitting needles with that, Pol. Or a crochet hook.'

She shook her head. 'It's spaghetti, I think.'

'Have you had it before?'

'Only out of a tin with tomato sauce. But there has to be a first time for everything.'

He studied his darling girl. She wore a simple pink and white summer dress with a tiny bolero. Apart from a bit of lipstick, she appeared to be free of makeup. Polly wasn't one for spending hours on her appearance, though he might have bet his last quid on Elaine Lewis staring for an age at the reflection of the person she loved most of all.

'She dressed up for you, Frank.'

'I know. She always has done, so she must have noticed my perfect good looks before we met. I know she recognized me from the start when she stopped me in the street, but her mother does work at Brookside five days a week.'

'Perfect good looks? If your nose was a ski slope, there'd be broken legs all over the place. Other than that, you'll do, I suppose. You have sexy eyes.'

He lowered his tone. 'Madam, your knickers are with me. I happen to know that they concealed several freckles on your bum. To have freckles in that area, you must have exposed yourself to sunlight.'

'And?'

'And you're a loose woman.'

'Fair enough. Seeing that you're paying, I'll have smoked salmon and avocado to start.'

'Avocado's an acquired taste.'

'So are you, but I managed.'

This was normality; this was what Frank needed in life. Polly was strong, feisty and beautiful; she joked, laughed at herself, loved her brother, was unafraid of hard work and would be a good mother. 'I love you,' he whispered.

'You'd better, because I am sick to death of bloody timewasters. Hattie's veg man let her down last week, something to do with a gearbox. I didn't know he had one, because he's definitely brainless. Without an engine, why would he need gears?'

Frank burst out laughing.

'Well, he's as thick as a piece of Stonehenge or the Great Wall of China.'

'You're a terrible girl, Polly Kennedy.'

'And you wouldn't want me any other way, so shut up!'

Oh yes, this was his Polly, the right one for him. She definitely had an engine in full working order, and her transmission was as smooth as a baby's backside. 'You're going to be a lot of trouble, aren't you?' he asked. A bundle of naughtiness wrapped in sunshine, she was.

'With luck and a good following wind, yes, I'll do my best to bring you up properly. A woman's first child is her husband.'

He lowered his tone yet again. 'When can we have another go at splicing the main brace, Captain Kennedy?'

Polly awarded him a severe look. 'Dangerous business, that. Sailors had to be drunk to take it on, because the enemy always aimed for the main brace.'

'But I'm not the enemy, sweetheart.'

She shook her head. 'You were bad enough one-handed. God help me now you have both. I suppose I could emigrate. New Zealand sounds nice, or I might try Canada.'

Frank carried on laughing.

'What's up with you?' she asked.

'Rice Lane is as far as you're going.' He ordered two smoked salmon with avocado, to be followed by two portions of spaghetti bolognese. It was time to try something new.

She didn't even know where she was. Liverpool was supposedly familiar territory, though there appeared to be bits of it that Elaine Lewis had never visited. The shoes were killing her. She bought plasters in a chemist shop, and found a coffee house where she ordered coffee and a couple of items that imitated croissants, since she hadn't eaten anything today and couldn't face much.

In the ladies' room, she removed stockings and applied plasters. After replacing the stockings and shoes, she stared in the mirror for several minutes. Compared to her, Polly Kennedy was very much an Eliza Doolittle.

She washed her hands and returned to the cafe to pick

up her coffee and croissants. Frank didn't want her, but Bob Laithwaite did. He was sitting at a table with two cups of coffee, that couple of croissants, jam, butter, and an encouraging smile.

She sat opposite him. 'Have you been following me?'

'Yes.'

'Why?'

He decided to speak plainly. 'Because I want you.'

'Oh, stop it.'

He leaned forward. 'I have your measure, Elaine. You want him, but he's already spoken for.'

Elaine frowned. 'What are you talking about? I told you he had a fiancée. I left them to it, because Frank's mother was taken ill this morning, and my mother is caring for her. As soon as they've eaten, Frank and Polly are going to visit his mother. I didn't want to play gooseberry, so I left, bought plasters for my heels, then remembered I'd had no breakfast. When I've eaten these so-called croissants, I shall go and see my mother in case she needs help with Mrs Charleson, since I have no appointments until late afternoon.'

Bob leaned back in his seat. She was a seasoned liar, yet he remained fascinated. He had met many pretty women in his time, but this piece of physical perfection was unique. She was definitely a natural blonde, as her hair was a mixture of many shades, much darker underneath where the sun's paintbrush had failed to penetrate. Her eyes, clear and blue, were large and defined by dark lashes, whose colour was probably achieved by the application of mascara. She had full lips, high cheekbones, wonderful skin and arched eyebrows plucked and helped along by pencil. So she was definitely that rare thing – a true blonde.

'Stop staring at me, Bob.'

'I can't. You're too beautiful. But I saw straight away that this person, this Frank, was in your sights. Today, you came to the office looking like a princess, and I knew you'd dressed for him. What do you want from him, Elaine? He's bought a junk shop and you're chasing him?'

Still ice cold inside, she continued with her untruths. 'I told you, it was going to be a party, so I dressed up in something new. Then illness struck poor Mrs Charleson, who has diabetes, high blood pressure and arthritis, so I left Frank and Polly to themselves, because it was no longer a party.'

'I saw you when you came out,' he said. 'You try to keep your expression deadpan, though you never quite manage that. You were upset, angry, unable to walk properly and totally unlike the Elaine Lewis I know and care about. Normally, you are under control.' Was she ever normal, he asked himself.

She sipped her coffee and chewed on a bit of bread that bore no relationship to the croissants she'd eaten in Paris. 'I was worried about our mothers,' she said after swallowing the dry, tasteless bap.

'Then you should have returned to the office, picked up your car and driven home. I sometimes think you manage to lie even to yourself. It's not a wasted tendency in a lawyer, but you do have your limits. You hit a brick wall today, and you're unused to that, right?'

She stared hard into his eyes. 'In my village, there's an old lady who uses a saying that always makes me smile. When a person talks rubbish, she tells him or her it's all a load of my eye and Betty Martin. I have no idea who Betty Martin is or was, but do you know her? Because you're spouting a heap of waste material, Bob.'

Seconds slid by before he spoke again. 'What's wrong with you, Elaine? What are you searching for?'

She smiled, though her eyes remained chilled. 'A new job,' she replied.

'Why?'

'To get away from you, since you seem to be the one searching. Following me today is not part of your remit. In fact, I could probably lodge a complaint about it. As you are a junior partner, I could go above your head and tell the seniors that you are harassing me.'

'But you won't.'

'Won't I?'

'No. It's a family firm and they're both my uncles. My name's different, because my mother is their sister, and her surname changed when she married.'

Elaine clicked back into brain-only mode. The Spencer brothers were both middle-aged bachelors, so there was a chance that Bob might inherit the firm when they died. She tried to calculate the value of this man, but it wasn't easy. A law firm was as good as its staff, and they had the best, since they had her.

'Are you working out what I'm worth in the long term?'

'No. I'm wondering whether to put another plaster on top of these.'

'For extra padding?'

'Yes.'

'Then the shoes are too big.'

'They didn't have my size, but I loved them, so . . .' She shrugged. 'A girl has to suffer if she wants to look good.'

There were two sides to her, Bob thought. On the surface, she was calm, collected and stunningly lovely. But inside, a tiger waited to get out, and she was probably great in bed. A sensible and educated man, he nevertheless had no idea of the true extent of Elaine Lewis's faults. Blinded by her beauty and amused by the teenage tendency to lie her way out of trouble, he assumed that she would settle and mature in her own time. After all, she was only twenty-three, a good seven years younger than he was.

He left her and brought his car to the front of the

building. 'Shall I take you home or to your friend's mother's house?'

'Back to work,' was her answer. 'My car's there.'

They sat in his vehicle. 'You make life up as you go along, don't you?' he asked without waiting for a reply. 'Like me, you're a spoilt only child. Like me, you've been indulged all your life. Am I right?'

'Almost.'

'And he's one that got away.'

She recognized an equal. He knew her because he knew himself. 'Yes.'

'Why him?'

She counted to five before replying. 'I needed him to be my first. There's something about him. Smouldering eyes for a start. He has a gentle nature and a sense of humour. But a woman could drown happily in those eyes.'

'Why not me?'

'I have absolutely no idea. Perhaps the familiarity breeding contempt applies to you, because we work together and you hang round like an unsavoury smell on the landing.'

'And you're a virgin.'

'Oh, shut up, Bob.'

He drove. 'You fascinate me,' he said. 'So beautiful a woman, yet such a naughty child.'

She didn't answer. Her main need was to be alone, since she found it difficult to concentrate when in company. All this needed thinking through, so isolation was required. 'Bob?'

'What?'

'Will you see to my appointment? It's a Mr and Mrs Crompton, quarter past four, just a couple of codicils. I need to go home before I get too tired to drive.'

'One condition. Dinner tomorrow night, and I'm cooking.'

She waited until they were parked outside the office before answering. 'You want me to come to your house?'

'Yes. I shall pick you up at your place at six o'clock so that Mrs Lewis can see I'm not a monster. Then I'll take you away, feed you, ply you with good wine and, if you wish, you may be my dessert.'

'What about my pudding?'

'That would be me. But only if you're agreeable. I have no stomach for rape.' He took keys from the ignition. 'Or we could have baked Alaska instead.'

'Then whip up your meringue, Bob, because you're not going to be my first.'

'Really?'

'Absolutely.'

He lit a cigarette. 'Pity, because I'm rather good at it. I can show you glowing letters of commendation, a gold medal from the Olympics, two first-class degrees, one second and one third. But I was drunk at the time when I slipped to third, and she was wearing some terrible perfume that reminded me of bathroom cleaner.'

Elaine refused to be amused. She needed to think. She needed to be away from here so that she might sort out her mind, get her thoughts in order, sum up the day. Because this was how lawyers worked. The facts must be laid out on paper with the possibilities in the next column. This man seated next to her must be analysed, good points and bad. And Frank ... Frank didn't want her. Ways to get to him, ways to get to her, that Pygmalion character who was incapable of comprehensible speech, guttersnipe, servant in a greasy cafe patronized by others of her ilk.

'Elaine?'

'He could do so much better,' she whispered, almost unaware that she had spoken.

'You were considering him as a husband.'

Once more, she did not reply.

'Why? He's just a shopkeeper.'

'I'm going home.' She stepped out of his car and walked to her own.

He followed her, of course. 'See you tomorrow morning, then,' he said.

'If I come back.'

He was about to tell her how silly it would be to leave without notice, but she jumped into the driver's seat, turned the key and roared past in reverse, missing him by just a few inches. 'Fiery,' he said to himself. But he was worried. Both uncles were pleased with Miss Lewis. She was efficient, pleasant and decorative. If she complained to them about their nephew's behaviour, they might react badly.

He turned and walked towards the offices. This was not his finest hour. If Elaine made trouble for him, Spencer and Spencer would have Laithwaite by the throat. He prayed that she would return tomorrow. Whatever else was wrong with her, she was excellent at her job. Bob Laithwaite would sleep badly tonight.

The first removals van arrived. Polly jumped up and down in the middle of a huge, empty shop and clapped her hands in glee. Their life was in that big vehicle outside, and she had helped choose it. They had almost new dining furniture, an ex-display suite for the living room, a brand new bed and second-hand wardrobe, dressing table and tallboy. This was many, many birthdays rolled into one. 'I'm excited,' she yelled.

'Are you? I hadn't noticed.' They were both filthy. After scrubbing floors, cleaning cupboards, washing windows, laying carpets and chasing each other with wet mops for over three hours, they looked as if nobody owned them.

He watched her. Even when she was in a state worse

than Dusty Den Davenport's cart, she was bloody gorgeous. 'I wish you could move in here with me, Polly.' She wouldn't leave Cal yet. He and Linda were head over heels, but Cal had vowed that he would walk into that blooming bungalow; he would, too. The twins were stubborn, pushy, determined people.

She went upstairs to supervise the removals men. Frank helped to carry some pieces, listening all the while to her changing her mind. 'Try it under the window ... put it at an angle ... be careful with that table; it needs a new hinge on one of the drop leaf thingies.'

'Behave yourself,' he whispered when passing close to her.

'Shut up, you.'

'And remember your promise.'

'Excuse us,' she said sweetly to the men. She drew her beloved to one side. 'I am going nowhere near that fire-breathing dragon. You're doing all that on your own, by yourself, without me.'

'I know. But it won't be breathing fire when you get there.'

She waited until the men had left to fetch another lot of furniture. 'What if it wakes up when we least expect it?'

'It won't.'

'Are you sure?'

'Positive. As long as you don't prod it.'

'Have we got soap?'

'And towels. Don't you dare back out on me, Kennedy.' She looked him up and down. 'One grunt or grumble out of that monster, and I'll be in Seaforth. You'll recognize me, cos I'll be stark naked with a new tattoo on my bum. I got the freckles joined together and covered up.' She stalked off, head held high, so high that she tripped over the edge of a carpet square. 'Bugger,' she snapped.

'Which tattooist's been meddling with my fiancée's bum?'

'None of your business.'

'All right. I'll hang these curtains.' He fiddled with rings and looked almost absently into the road below. She was there. The bloody woman had followed him. Determined to carry on no matter what, he hung the first curtain. She was getting out of her car. Damn and blast, would he ever be rid of her? A conversation was taking place between Elaine Lewis and Roy, the chief removals man. She gave him a parcel, returned to her car and drove off, rubber screaming against the road's surface. The Victorian dwellings and shops on Rice Lane might well lose the will to live if people drove like that.

At five minutes to six, the job was completed. Roy wandered upstairs for the final time, received his money and a generous tip, and handed over the final item just before leaving. 'A woman passed this to me, said it's a house-warming gift. Anyway, we'll meet you tomorrow at nine o'clock and fetch your shop stuff. Thanks, boss.' He touched the neb of his obligatory cap and left.

When Polly entered the flat's living room, she found Frank seated on the sofa with a package beside him. 'Is it a bomb?' she asked.

'Something like that. My beautiful, sick lawyer was across the road in her car. She gave this to Roy, said it's our house-warming present.'

'Oh.'

'Oh indeed. It's as if she wants me to give her attention, pay court, prostrate myself at her feet. I'm no doctor, but she has a mental problem of some kind. She frightens me halfway to death.'

'Don't you dare die, or I'll kill you.'

'Hmmm.'

'Open it, Frank.'

He looked at her. 'I do dragons, you do parcels.'

She picked it up. 'Heavy,' she said before putting it to her ear. 'Not ticking. What *is* she after?'

'Me.'

'For what, though?'

'Sex, I think.'

'Is she what Ida calls a sex mechanic?'

'No idea. But what I do know is that she's not normal. And her mother's such a nice, ordinary, decent woman. Elaine's like a fabulous house, a stately home beautifully decorated, but with no foundations. When she tumbles, a lot of people will suffer, her mother most of all.'

'Heck. You're dead serious, aren't you?'

'I am, love. She scares the bejaysus out of me, as my old granny used to say. My dad's mother, she was. Straight over from Ireland, mad as a hatter, the best kind of gran to have.'

Polly tore off the wrapper, opened a box and whistled. 'Oh, good grief. This must have cost over twenty quid. Lead crystal.' She lifted out a bowl. 'Your solicitor has what they call an agenda, babe.'

He looked at the gift. 'She can have all the agendas she wants as long as she takes my name off her list. Put that back in the box and stick the box in the sideboard. I'm sure it's lovely, but I don't want to look at it every day. Remember, I'll be living here all the time.'

She did as he asked while he went to deal with the fire-breathing dragon, an item installed in the bathroom by the previous occupant. It was a very clever idea when it came to delivering hot water, though its temperament was sadly unpredictable. The bath was enormous, and would accommodate both of them. He grinned ruefully. They were as filthy as a pair of chimney sweeps, so the water, now clear and clean, would probably be soup within minutes.

As he turned off taps and silenced the water heater, he felt a sudden chill. She was out there in the alley. How did he know? He left the bathroom and went into the kitchen where a jar of white-out stood prepared to cover the shop windows while he sorted through his wares and decorated some walls. Although the bathroom had patterned glass in its windows, he painted all of it. He didn't want Elaine Lewis to stand and watch shadow theatre while he and Polly lived their life.

'Frank?'

'Yes, love?'

'I'm making the bed.'

'OK. The dragon's asleep and the water's lovely.'

They sat in brown Windsor soup giggling like a pair of children. 'We'll be no cleaner, Frank.'

'OK. Get that old towel in the corner and wrap yourself in it while I play St George.'

She climbed out of the bath, covered herself in the ancient, striped thing, then ran to the door, where she stood and watched.

He pulled the plug, allowed dirty water to escape, blessed himself, then tackled the monster. It coughed, heaved, spat, and ignited with a bang. 'You haven't got a tattoo on your bum,' he said while clean water flowed.

Polly tutted. 'And he charged me three quid. Said it wouldn't hurt. No wonder I felt nothing. It was supposed to be a heart with Frank written through it, so you'd know I love you from the heart of my bottom.'

He laughed. 'Aren't you a romantic little thing? Come on, let's be having you, mucky minx. I'll have the tap end near the dragon again.'

The second lot of water fared better than the first.

'Are you superstitious?' she asked.

'No. Why?'

She shrugged. 'Well, should we get rid of her present?

Will it bring bad luck? Remember Mary Murgatroyd, used to live in Rachel Street? She was superstitious. Wouldn't refuse to buy from a gypsy, never walked under a ladder, wouldn't bury her husband on a Friday.'

'Really?'

'Really. Mind, he didn't die till the Saturday, so it was just as well. Her mother-in-law— Stop laughing, cos I'm dead serious here, Frank. Her ma-in-law gave her a statue with evil eyes that followed Mary wherever she walked. The family had no luck till she smashed it accidentally on purpose.'

'Where is she now?'

'Dead.'

'That's a shame. How did she die?'

'Avoiding a ladder; she went under a bus.'

They were both reduced to exhausted laughter. It had been a long and difficult day, so they dried themselves off and went to bed. He ordered her never to have a tattoo, as he wanted her to live to be very old, and wrinkly tattoos were horrible. They talked about Cal, who had banned his sister for the whole night; Linda was staying with him. 'I wonder if he'll manage it?' Polly said.

'No, but she will.'

'Ah. Will we?'

'Oh, yes. I just have to ... I want to put the bolts on in the shop.'

'Why?'

'People notice removal vans. Burglars and vagabonds are always on the lookout. I'll be back, so keep my place warm.'

It wasn't quite dark. He pulled on a robe before creeping down the stairs and into the shop. A white blind covered the glass in the door, and he saw her shape in the recess porch. She was ill, very ill, and he should feel sorry for her, but he couldn't manage that, because he seemed to be her prime target. What did she want? This was obsession at its very worst, and he might well be in need of another lawyer in the near future. He heard a key in the lock.

Leaping forward, he shot home top and bottom bolts. The noise made her run, but he carried on as if he hadn't noticed her, switching on lights and picking up a bundle of firewood for the flat.

'What I want is a locksmith,' he mouthed. She'd probably had the keys copied. No. She'd definitely had them copied. Why was she here? Had she wanted to spy, to listen while he made love to Polly? Was she considering arson or some other means of destroying what she couldn't have? Was she going to hurt his girl?

He went through and bolted the back ground-floor door, deliberately re-entering the shop and moving round so that she might see him. She mustn't know that he'd noticed her. Like a wild animal, she needed to feel free of hunters. How the hell would he get a lawyer to defeat a lawyer? And what crime had she committed?

When he returned to bed, his precious Polly was asleep. Never mind. She would still be here in the morning, wouldn't she?

Ten

At last, Christine Lewis gained Polly's confidence. After a particularly heavy second breakfast sitting, she was even invited to muck in with clearing up, and she didn't mind. In truth, she was very happy to help with the drying of dishes while Polly sat and washed at Cal's lowered sink. 'It's a hard job for you, Polly. But your brother's a good cook, or so I'm told.'

Polly was happy to agree. 'As soon as he's on his feet properly, he's going all cordon bleu, reckons he and Linda might travel to Paris for a course in continental cookery. Naturally, I'd have to warn the President about the invasion, because Linda and Cal together are an army. God help us all if they manage to get as far as Germany.'

'And what about you and Frank?'

'Oh, that's dead exciting, Mrs Lewis. He's got four antiquated Singer sewing machines, dolly tubs, possers, tin baths and wringers. He's turning them into garden ornaments covered in climbers. He's opening the backyard as a garden centre, says he has green fingers.' She shrugged. 'He hasn't. They're usually black from messing in compost and fertilizer. Still, somebody has to love the poor soul, I suppose.'

'And that somebody's you.'

Polly laughed. 'I managed to whisk him away from your Elaine. She seemed very taken with Frank, but I'd already put my name down for him. We're having a fridge, a washing machine and two children. In that order, I hope.' She paused. 'How is Elaine?'

'Hard to say. She plays her cards very close to her chest.'

'Then she should join Father Foley's poker school, because it's a riot. He couldn't keep a straight face if you paid him, though my Frank has a very good poker expression, a bit blank. They all cheat. With Elaine being a lawyer, she might just manage to sort them out, injunctions and all that.'

When the dishes were done, they gave Cal his coffee and carried theirs through to the closed cafe. 'Polly?'

'Yes, Mrs Lewis?'

'Call me Christine.'

'All right, Christine.'

The visitor smiled. 'Mrs Charleson's changed a lot. She thinks before she speaks, and tries to be kind, and it's because of her diet. All that sugar was poisoning her, you see. Diabetes makes people rather unpredictable until they get a grip on the diet.'

'Right.'

'She misses her son, Polly.'

Polly shrugged. 'I can't think why. She's got you to do her running about for her, so why does she need him?'

'Because she knows she's done wrong.'

'Well, I'm not upsetting him while he's sorting out the shop. He'll come round in his own time, but if Mrs Moo looks at me with the evil eye, she'll get nowhere with him. Just give him some space. I know him well, and he won't be pushed. My Frank's a clever bloke.' There was pride in her tone.

Christine smiled. Her daughter had probably found that to be true. 'I'd better get on, Polly. Your rent book's on the counter. Be happy. Er . . . did you say Mrs Moo?'

'Sorry. I mean Mrs Charleson.'

The rent collector was still grinning. 'That name suited her. It no longer does. Bye for now.'

'Bye.' Polly finished her coffee. She would leave Frank to find his own way back to his mother. If that was what he wanted, of course . . .

She'd been angry for days, first with Bob Laithwaite for accusing her of being imperfect because a slipped bra strap was showing through lace at the top of an arm, then with Frank for bringing Polly Kennedy to the bistro. That was to have been her lunch, *their* private lunch, just the two of them. Was Frank Charleson afraid of being alone with her? Did he become disturbed in her presence, and was he afraid of finding himself incapable of resistance? It had to be something of that nature, because all full-blooded males found her exciting to the point where self-control became difficult. She was used to such occurrences, as she'd suffered unwanted attentions since her early teens until she'd learned how to kick a man or a boy in the male pride zone. As for being collected from home to be taken out to dinner by the junior partner – well, he had no chance, and she'd told him so.

Her fierce hatred for Bob had cooled slightly, though she still resented him because he'd managed to cut through her outer layer and discover a little of her inner core, the kernel she had hidden so well thus far. He wasn't the first to achieve that; it had happened years ago at Oxford when . . . But she had vowed that it would never again occur. It had been a dark place, a terrifying time during which she had been unable to communicate her fears to anyone. She had no friends. Friends were not essential; she had discovered that fact in her late teens.

She remembered sitting in her little Oxford flat and telling herself that everything in the world was grains of sand and specks of carbon, that the world was dirty, needed cleaning— Scrubbing, painting, washing and wiping, never managing to accept that her accommodation was clean. She'd spent a mint on bleach, scouring pads, sugar soap, paint and polish.

Then there was the rocking. Unable to remain still, the upper half of her body had moved forward and back, forward and back, until she'd concentrated and made it stop. Her feet took over at that point, tapping on the floor, while her nails drummed on tabletops, and she had fought with herself for endless weeks in order to overcome and remove those outer expressions of inner torment. She'd beaten most of it, though she still found her nails to be disobedient occasionally.

She could not go back to that, to the crazy time. Counting. She remembered counting all kinds of articles from the correct number of cornflakes for breakfast to tiles on the roof of a house opposite her bed-sitting room. There were halves of tiles, thirds of tiles, broken tiles, slipping tiles. The building needed a new roof. She could not have lived in a place with a roof like that one, yet she felt unable to advise the occupants of the condition of their property.

Oh yes, and the clusters of roses on that dreadful wallpaper. She'd painted the walls white just to be rid of the flowers she had counted repeatedly. The room had needed three coats. Wet paper had bubbled, so she'd pricked the bulges with a fine pin in order to allow air and moisture to escape. She'd regretted the white, because it showed up the rest of the room until she'd painted that, too. A white box. She had lived for twenty-four hours a day in a sepulchre whited not on the outside of the building as in the Bible, but internally. So the process had begun again, and the walls became a pleasant shade of dove grey.

Even now, she sometimes studied digits on car number

plates. If she found one or two whose numbers added up to thirteen, that was unlucky. The third made it a good day, but she had to stop counting at that point, or she would need to find another three thirteens. It was just a harmless habit, and she didn't do it often any more.

She would sew a couple of anchor tapes into the turquoise dress to make sure straps never again slipped into view. Oh, and she needed some insoles for the shoes to make them a better fit. Plasters on heels always looked very Saturday night at some grab-a-granny dance in an ill-lit and seedy hall that reeked of urinals. Plasters were the thin end of the wedge, the beginning of a short drive into utter chaos. In a notebook whose place of residence was the glove compartment, she wrote reminders about anchor tapes and insoles. It was best to be on top of everything at all times.

Polly Kennedy was Elaine's real opponent. Pretty enough in her cheap corner-shop frock, she couldn't hold a candle to an educated woman in a nineteen-guinea dress of real silk and fine lace. The girl had looked as if she'd come from farming stock: pink cheeks, tanned arms, the wide, innocent eyes of the ingénue. Elaine hadn't failed to see the ring, either, just a cheap aquamarine with a few diamond chippings stuck to its sides. It resembled a prize out of a low-priced Christmas cracker.

She was sure they'd had a bath together on the night Frank had taken possession of the property, since they were very much a couple; Polly needed to disappear from the scene so that Elaine might have a chance. If she just had a magic wand!

He'd painted over the patterned glass. Why? Did he have the ability to sense a watching presence in the alley below? As for the incident with the key, that had almost given her a heart attack. Had he known she was there? Did he think a few bolts would suffice? He didn't realize what he'd taken on, did he? She was a lawyer, she was clever, she was beautiful, indomitable, a winner. And according to a certain chap in Oxford, she suffered from narcissism among other personality problems. Narcissistic? She was merely pragmatic, unafraid of the truth, accepting of her own physical self, even celebrating it.

'But all the same, I'm not sure I'm normal,' she said aloud. No one normal should be sitting in a car while the man she desired was a hundred yards away and in bed with another woman. Had the dimwit psych doctor been right after all? Did she have a fault the size of the San Andreas running through her? No, she'd been a gifted and industrious student, and she was now a talented lawyer. The facade must be made stronger so that no one else would catch a glimpse of traits that might be termed weaknesses. They were not weaknesses; they were merely the eccentricities of the kind displayed by many with great brains.

Mum didn't know the full story to this day. The breakdown in Oxford had been kept from her; it was intensely personal and almost dehumanizing. Obsessive, the doctor had said. He'd visited her and remarked on the neatness of her temporary home. 'Do you feel compelled to be organized and tidy?' the man had asked after looking at a pristine kitchen, a well-scrubbed bathroom and her newly painted bed-sitting room. What was wrong with a place for everything and everything in its place? He'd noticed the three mirrors, too. Did she spend much time looking at her reflection? Stupid questions.

It was now almost two in the morning, and her mother would be wide awake and worrying. Her mother mattered, yet Frank Charleson loomed large in Elaine's list of priorities. She needed him. These were hunger pains, though they were not in her stomach. It was lust and it was a new feeling.

Anyway, what was so bad about having things in rows? What was amiss when a person stacked older items at the front, newer at the back of kitchen cupboards? She was methodical, that was all. Clothes in the wardrobes were divided by colour, then subdivided by type and length. A second wardrobe held work clothes, suits at one end, blouses at the other. She had never in her adult life worked at a cluttered desk. Her tack at the stables had always been the best kept, her pony the best groomed. She was scrupulously clean and always well turned out, and there was nothing wrong with any of that.

Obsessive? Perhaps this business was a little extreme, hanging about just to be near someone who had rejected her. The difficulties in Oxford had started in the same way when a lecturer she admired greatly had downgraded one of her assignments to an A minus. She'd hauled him over the coals, he'd described her to her face as arrogant, and she'd finished up having psychological counselling. 'Am I mad?'

Was she mad? Was she going to get worse with age? Or could she keep whatever it was under wraps and well out of view? She'd been judged to have a personality disorder, which term could, in her view, be applied to anything from ill temper to schizophrenia. Well, she heard no voices unless they were real and attached to humans. 'Am I mad?' she repeated. There was no one here to offer an answer, of course. 'I think I'd better go home.' She went home.

Brendan Hall, commonly known as Don, loved his little caravan. It was comfortable and it was his alone. Gladys Acton was good to him. She changed his sheets two or three times a week, made his meals and brought a mug of cocoa across at nine o'clock every night. Both needed to be early to bed. She was often up in the night seeing to her father's ever-increasing needs, while Don was out and about before dawn, since he was now the main farmer. Local farmhands respected and trusted him, since there was very little he didn't know about the land or husbandry.

He met the ailing father, even sitting with him on Sundays and reading to him from the works of Dickens, an author favoured by both men. Gladys Acton was immeasurably grateful, as was her father. Matt Mason had few new visitors. A nurse climbed the stairs daily, the doctor once a week, his daughter several times a day. The aged man's intellect remained sound, and he loved the newcomer's accent. 'Thank you,' he said each time a portion of *Great Expectations* had been read to him.

They discussed politics and religion, though for the most part they concentrated on farming. Don told Matt about potato blights in Ireland, the history of his country's farmers, his continuing faith in crop rotation. 'I come from an old-fashioned country and I remain an old-fashioned farmer. I worked the peat bogs, had a job in stables from the age of seven, learned to milk at the same age and got a kick on the leg for my trouble on the first day. Farm work seems to be born in the bone, even when the bone gets damaged by a cow.'

Matt agreed. Privately, he advised his daughter to keep hold of the new man. 'He'll work harder than your fellow ever did. He's worth his weight in gold. Make sure you feed him well and give him a decent wage.'

Several times, Don carried the old man downstairs, wrapped him up well, placed him in the wheelchair and pushed him up and down the least rugged of the lanes. 'Perhaps bees next year, Mr Mason, a few trays of bedding plants, some tomatoes ... we'll sell stuff from the gate on the road if your daughter agrees.' He was happy. This was the life he should have chosen in his youth, but Mammy had been so proud to have a son in the seminary.

Gradually, Gladys began to trust the new man. She told him the truth. 'My husband always had an eye for loose women, Don. He's got at least two kids, and I'm infertile, so neither of them's mine. There's one in Beresford's Green, another in Lowton, and he's run off now with a thirty-year-old from Beresford's Drift. It was a Beresford that owned the whole estate way back in the whenever, so that's why we have the Drift, the Green, and the Ring – there are standing stones in the Ring, but not as big as Stonehenge.'

Don tutted in the right places, nodded or shook his head as appropriate. She seldom left room for replies, but he was happy enough to provide punctuation. Gladys Acton was easy company.

'My husband was always a fool,' she said.

'So it would seem, Gladys.'

'When Dad dies, the farm comes to me. If I died, it would go to Eric Acton, or so he thought. Then I told him he was disinherited in favour of my cousin, showed him a copy of my new will, and off he buggered. I waited till after I'd altered it before telling him, because he might even have killed me and Dad for the farm.'

Don loved listening to her. She wittered on endlessly, but was seldom boring. After a few weeks he realized that she reminded him of Mammy except for the accent. There was something soothing about a female witterer. He was delighted when she invited him into the house. 'Not yet, while the weather's all right. But in winter, you can have a spare room. You'll be warmer in there. It'll be one that has its own log-burning stove.'

He remembered the words of Paul Cropper – 'You'll be out of that caravan in quick sticks ...'

Gladys liked Don. He asked intelligent questions, made

rough maps of the acreage, labelled areas R for root crops, T for top vegetable or fruit crops, and G for grazing. B and C were barley and corn, while a reversed R represented rape seed. He wanted to keep bees in the farmhouse gardens, and was preparing to clean out a greenhouse for tomatoes and bedding plants. 'We could get someone to sell them from the bottom gate next year if you agree,' he explained. 'Honey, tomatoes, flowers, spuds, carrots, cabbages – there's always passing trade from people having a day out in the countryside.'

She was thrilled to bits with him. If she'd married somebody like this, she'd have had a lot less trouble and a couple of adopted children. Don loved the land; he was made for it. He would never have left her; he would never have called her an ugly old bag. 'I'm glad you came here,' she said.

'So am I. I'm getting a bit old for the nomadic life. This is the first time I've wanted to stay in the one place.' It was also the first time he'd enjoyed life; gradually, he began to understand fully that he'd been in the wrong job. Had he stayed away from the priesthood, things would have worked out better for him. The need to go back to Liverpool was diminishing. It wasn't worth it just for an old photo and a watch, or just to walk about among those people without being recognized.

'Well, I feel glad that you ended up at Drovers. This is a very old farm, one of the ones sectioned off in the sixteenth century. It's got a proud history, and it needs a man in charge. There was a man in charge, but he's upstairs in the oldest part of the house on his deathbed. Thank you for spending time with him. My dad was the last real man here. Then you came.' She picked up their cocoa-stained mugs. 'Thank you for picking Drovers, Don. You're my right-hand man, and don't you forget it. See you in the morning, love.' She left.

Love. She'd called him love. Not since Mammy had anyone spoken to him with so much affection and gentleness. In a few weeks, he would be inside the house. According to Paul Cropper, all workers ate at the scrubbed table in the kitchen during winter, though family used the small breakfast room. It was a warren of a house with bits added on over the centuries: sloping floors, creaky boards, heavy doors, beamed ceilings, and a huge flag-paved kitchen with a bread oven in one of the walls. As long as Gladys Acton lived, Don Hall would have a fine, comfortable home and a job he enjoyed.

It wasn't difficult to imagine someone like Henry VIII in the larger of the two dining rooms, dogs at his feet, lords and ladies laughing while the king threw scraps for the hounds. It was a valuable farm, though it could never be Brendan Hall's, because Brendan Hall didn't exist. Oh, and he might as well change it to Brendon, since Don seemed to suit him.

He lay in his narrow bed and wondered how it would be to share with a woman. And she might get a divorce. Would she expect him to marry her? He couldn't marry anyone if he didn't have papers. It might be necessary to develop a wife in some faraway place, one he couldn't divorce due to Catholicism.

Life was complicated. He left it behind by falling asleep. A dead man didn't dream.

Smoke filled the hallway and floated out to greet the couple at the door. 'He's set the bloody place on fire again,' Frank said. 'And here we are, invited to celebrate our engagement while he causes a conflagration. Maniac!' He spoke to his closest friend when the door opened fully. 'What a smell, Chris. What were you cooking? A dead cat? Did you forget to skin it?'

The man in the doorway pretended to snarl. 'Sarcasm again.' He winked at Polly. 'Lowest form of wit,' he pronounced.

Polly, who had never before seen a priest in a flowered and frilled apron, stifled a chuckle. Father Foley's chin had a smut on it, while his hair stood on end like the spines on a hedgehog. He smiled ruefully. 'What a lovely evening this is in spite of everything.'

'Sorry,' Frank said. 'I thought this was St Columba's presbytery, but I can see I've skipped the funeral and come straight to the crematorium.'

'Don't start.' Chris wagged a finger at his friend. 'The fire's out, and your supper's in the backyard. Hello, Polly. Come away in, the both of you. We need to pray for manna from heaven, for there's not a bite to eat in the whole house. We could go to the Salvation Army, I suppose.'

Frank held out a hand. 'Cough up,' he ordered. 'I'm passing the collecting plate for a change. Fish, chips and peas three times, right?'

'Right.' Chris handed over a ten-shilling note. 'I want my change.'

'And don't set fire to my fiancée, she's hot enough already. Who did you cremate anyway, Chris? Anyone we know?'

'A close friend who used to be a chicken.'

'Sad.' Frank kissed his girl and went off to buy supper.

Polly was led into the living room where the table was set with a cloth that wasn't quite straight, an ill-assorted collection of cutlery, and three plates. 'You should have got my brother to cook for you, Father.'

'I'm Chris to my friends and to my enemies, of which number your Frank is currently one. He says I cheat at cards. As for your brother, how's he doing?'

'Very well, thank you. He walks up and down outside

the cafe every day on his crutches. I'm insisting that we have a double wedding.'

'Oh, I'll have to charge twice for that.' He rubbed his hands together like a ham actor playing Shylock. 'You're to marry at St Anthony's, but with me as the one in the frock at the front.'

Polly grinned. 'There could be three of us in frocks: me, Linda and you. So don't wear your best, or you might outdo the brides.' She looked him up and down. 'Your face is dirty, and your hair's standing to attention, Father Chris. I don't know what that is on your apron, but it's a funny colour. Have you been paddling in the Alt? It's a mucky river, that one.'

He looked down. 'No, it's just a bit of good Irish butter and a few drips off bacon. I covered the chicken in bacon to keep it moist. Then the chicken gave up its ghost a second time while I was out ministering to a very sick old man. When I got back, the house was all but on fire. In my job, we get the odd emergency. Emergencies breed, you know. One begets another, which goes on to . . .' Still chattering away to himself, he went off to clean his face, tame his hair and change his clothes.

Polly looked round the living area, which was typically masculine: no flowers, no colour, no imagination. The furniture was old but good, while a floor-to-ceiling library on two walls demonstrated this man's eclectic taste when it came to literature. He had three volumes on the birth of the Church of England, a shelf covered in Communism, a large tome on Haiti where voodoo and Catholicism rubbed shoulders, and several Bibles, plus volumes on Islam, Buddhism and Judaism. He clearly liked to know the opposition, then. Frank had described Father Foley not only as his best friend ever, but also as a man of huge intellect. 'He struggles with his faith, Polly. Even priests do that, so don't blame me for my battle with it.'

She looked at his authors of fiction. Shakespeare in his entirety filled a shelf, Dickens rubbed shoulders with du Maurier, Kipling kept company with Lawrence, Eliot and Agatha Christie, while Geoffrey Chaucer lingered next to Aristotle. Father Foley owned an original 1928 *Lady Chatterley's Lover*, published in Florence, Italy, and a small collection of Edgar Allan Poe's grim stories. So here was a priest with a mind broad enough to encompass and learn from just about everything. She replaced Oscar Wilde and picked up George Bernard Shaw.

Chris came back. 'Ah, you've met my friends, then. A motley crew, wouldn't you say? I doubt I've read half of them.'

'A mixture,' she agreed. 'But at least you keep pace with what's going on in the world. I see you've read about the Holocaust.'

'Just the once, Polly. My stomach heaved and I wept buckets. Pope Pius made love to Hitler while getting as many Jews as he could out of the danger zone. He became an expert in the ways of bribery and corruption. People thought he was on the side of the Nazis, but he wasn't. A good man. A very good man. What I don't accept is the fact that people knew what was happening. Not all Germans were for Hitler, you know. But to see what one dictator can do is frightening, because the Germans themselves were defeated by him. He shouted jump, and they jumped.'

Polly sighed. 'Well, we won.'

'Nobody wins in war,' he told her. 'It's death and destruction, more or less. It's one human flattening another's house and garden, but on a bigger scale. Man is the most territorial creature on the planet. Never satisfied with his lot. See, a tiger kills when she's hungry, but man kills because he can.'

The bringer of supper rang the doorbell. 'Here comes trouble,' Polly said.

'Will we leave him where he is?' Chris asked.

'No. He'll start breaking windows or kicking your door in.'

'True. I'm glad you have the wisdom to deal with him. Keep a chair and a whip to hand at all times.'

They sat round the table. Chris poured wine and toasted the bride-to-be and her beau while Frank doled out the food. 'God bless you both and God help Polly.'

'Hattie Benson was in the chippy,' Frank said. 'And she's found your bridesmaid. She was in the paper last Wednesday under articles for sale.'

'Kerry Blue?'

'Who the heck's Kerry Blue?' Polly asked.

'A dog.'

'That's not very nice,' the man of the house opined. 'She's probably quite good-looking in her own way.'

'Still a dog, though. Anyway, she comes with a stiff brush and a metal comb, and she needs grooming daily, even on Sundays. Very curly hair, you see. Because you're a priest and she's from a good Irish Catholic family, you can have her for free. Hattie answered the ad on your behalf. It's a full Kerry, blue-black with no white patches.'

'Is she ready?'

'Oh yes, she's waiting for you.'

The penny had dropped. 'So you want a dog?' Polly liked dogs.

Chris nodded. 'Oh yes, I do want one. Man's best friend, a sight better friend than your fellow here, who accuses me of cheating at poker.'

'My Frank never lies. If he kicks somebody, there's truth in his boots.'

Chris eyed his new female adversary. 'So you think a priest cheats?'

'If he says you cheat, you cheat.'

'Love is blind.'

Polly leaned across the table. 'If he says you cheat, you cheat,' she repeated. 'Just eat your chips and feel grateful. Frank may have lapsed, but he's agreed that his children will be raised in their mother's faith, and he'll even go to Mass with them.'

'Holy Moses, a miracle.' The cheating priest blessed himself before beginning to eat chips with his fingers.

'Not even civilized,' Frank commented.

'Shut up,' his fiancée commanded. 'It's his house, so he can do as he pleases. But if he cheats on you anywhere else, thump him till you've knocked seven shades of daylight out of him.'

Chris burst into laughter. Theirs was a marriage made in heaven; it was also proof that God had a sense of humour, because together, these two were hilarious. 'Ah, you'll have a fierce and funny marriage. Will you live above the shop? Will you work alongside this man in the shop, Polly?'

'No idea. I want to keep the cafe going for as long as possible. They're used to it, you see. And so much is going to be taken away from them; I haven't the heart to add to their troubles.'

Chris told them he'd met Billy's Daniel the spaniel. 'A grand young dog and a grand young boy. Billy still insists that Father Brennan's alive.'

They discussed the idea of second sight, though Frank begged Polly not to tell the tale of the deceased Mary Murgatroyd from Rachel Street.

'She wasn't sighted,' Chris said. 'Superstitious, she was. Billy's a different kettle altogether. He says Brennan's thinner, working on a farm and living in a little house with wheels. Only you can't always tell with children, lively minds and vivid imaginations. He still dreams about his attacker, but he's no longer afraid because the man isn't frightening in what Billy calls his new life. This child, you know, is different.'

'Do you believe in second sight?' Polly asked.

'I do, indeed. Many's the time I've come across it, and many's the time I've not listened. But in the case of little Billy Blunt, I cleaned out my ears specially, for that boy is right. Father Eugene Brennan is very much alive.'

Polly and Frank stopped chewing. They laid down knives and forks.

'I phoned the police in a place called Buxton, and they put me on to the right people. They found – well, we know what they found, and we are just now trying to eat, so we'll leave the details to one side. So I questioned the Derbyshire police about the rosary. Told them I was a colleague and asked them to describe it.'

Frank swallowed. 'And?'

'Dark blue glass. And it's a very small one, a child's, the sort that gets given to a little boy at his First Holy Communion and kept as a lifelong memento. Girls usually have white ones. Brennan's rosary is like mine, full-sized and made of brown wooden beads. He's been filling in for me these past seven years, and I never saw him with a child's rosary or with any rosary other than the wood and silver one. So I told the police that the body they found was unlikely to be Eugene Brennan. Whether they took me seriously I've no way of telling.'

'I can't finish this food, Father,' Polly said.

'It's Chris unless I have the back-to-front collar on. Billy Blunt's grandmother had the sight. It often leaps a generation. I had to grow out of my own stubborn and know-it-all youth before I accepted that small miracles happen daily among mortals who will never be saints. I bet the two of you every book in this room that the man is still alive. When I'm proved right, I'll pick something special out of your junk shop.'

Frank pushed his plate away. 'Chris, he's just an ordinary kid.'

'As was St Bernadette. Most of them don't get noticed, and many grow up and forget the gift. Some throw it away deliberately, and I understand them, I do, because it must be a burden as much as a blessing.'

Polly stared unseeing at the table. 'I believe you, Chris. Billy's a good kid. He wouldn't lie. He's simple. I don't mean stupid, I mean he's not a complicated little soul. He likes toy cars and trains and Tarzan of the Apes. He loves my brother because he was always lower down with being in the wheelchair, and Cal's good at crashing Dinky cars.'

Frank remained unconvinced. He wasn't sure about God, let alone the visions of children. But the rosary certainly provided evidence, he supposed, though no one could prove that Brennan hadn't hung on to his childhood keepsake. 'And they found Scotch,' he said quietly. 'He always drank Irish.'

Chris carried on eating, though his visitors had stopped. 'The Blunts are still intending to sue,' he said between mouthfuls. 'Whether or not Brennan is found, they'll sue the diocese. Our three teachers who were witnesses will be giving evidence about what they saw. I could lose them, and my school will be all the poorer. Good teachers, they are. But they're looking to disappear into the state system, which makes me sad. Mr Davenport will give evidence, as will you, Frank.'

Frank agreed. 'I'll tell the truth, Chris.'

'And so you should. You're not eating. Why?'

'It's the thought of him being alive in the world,' Polly answered for both. 'When we were told he was dead, that knocked everybody for six, because we wanted him to pay. But what if he hurts someone else's child?'

'He won't,' was Chris's answer. 'He has a new life. The way Billy put it was to say that the bad man stopped being a priest, and he's not frightening when he isn't a priest. I happen to know he was from a farming family and worked the land from childhood. He's had a renaissance, born again in his fifties, possibly labouring and living in a caravan.'

Frank swallowed some wine. 'You take Billy's sight seriously.'

'Indeed I do. As for the explanation, I can tell you now that many a young Irish lad took Holy Orders just to please his parents. I'm confessor to one who has three children, but I don't damn him, because it's his own life and his own soul. We all sin.'

'But would you forgive Brennan?' Polly asked.

'Ah, no. He's beyond the reach of my feeble powers. Assaulting a minor and endangering his life was evil. The murder of a good man is the same. He is accountable under the legal system as well as to God. I wash my hands of him. If called upon to testify, I, too, shall tell the truth.'

'Which is?' Frank stared at Chris.

'That I did wrong, because I knew in my bones that he was quick to temper. Others have complained, or so I discovered recently. He should have been removed from the locum list. The Church will be forced to compensate Billy Blunt and his family.'

'Doesn't that bother you?' Polly asked.

'Ah, not at all. The Church sins, the Church does penance. The individual and the whole body are one and the same. All answer to almighty God. And anyway, this is a celebration. Frank, you and I should share in the degradation of your lovely fiancée.'

'She doesn't do threesomes,' Frank replied with mock seriousness.

'Then we need a fourth.'

'For what?' Polly's eyebrows moved north by half an inch.

'Something sinful.' Chris grinned. 'You're not ready for poker, so it will have to be whist. For money.'

'I don't gamble.'

'You do now.' Frank went to get Cal. 'If he's drunk, we'll win a fortune,' was his parting remark.

Alone with Chris, Polly reminded him about Frank's burning ambition. 'He wants to find lawyers and politicians who'll be prepared to uphold the rights of children. The politicians will make the laws, and the lawyers will uphold them and represent kids in trouble, frightened of their parents, frightened at school, scared of not getting enough to eat.'

'And worse. There is much, much more abuse, Polly.'

She nodded. 'I know. So if you think of anything or anyone, let us know. That's his dream, and it might come true. Mine won't.'

'Really?'

'Really. The Turnpike March into Downing Street could be the biggest waste of time and money this century, since they won't rebuild here for us. It's going to be a dead zone. This will kill people as well as buildings, because they've lived here their whole lives, so this is where they belong. It's their hearts' home. Stick them out in the back of beyond away from town, away from Scotland Road and Paddy's Market, and loads of older people will give up and lose the will to live.'

'The houses are beyond saving,' he said. 'But the earth below them would take new ones. It's all tied up with roads and tunnels and bloody money. And yes, priests get angry and swear and ask God why stuff happens. We go to London. We go so they might think twice before bringing a giant hammer down on some other communities. We go because you pay the government to look after you and they don't give a damn.'

She agreed. 'We go because we can. We make war because we can. No weapons, but plenty of fury. And you're right, we are territorial. This is our territory, our road, our streets. The enemy is taking away our territory.'

He beamed at her. 'You'd turn the words of any man to your ends.'

'It's called being a woman. Our job is to confuse and confound you, even if you're a priest. You can blame God for that as well, because who took Adam's rib and made a woman?'

'That part of the Bible's figurative,' he protested.

'Stop digging, Chris. You've made a hole big enough to bury yourself.'

He wagged a finger at her. 'Ah, you're well able for Frank, all right. You'll get nothing done because you'll be arguing. Come away now. You wash and I'll dry. Let's see can we tidy up without breaking anything.'

The kitchen was smoke-stained, but Chris advised his companion that the housekeeper would see to it tomorrow. They washed the dishes without any further argument. Chris noticed that Polly's hands showed considerable wear, and he offered her a jar of his hand cream. 'Don't laugh. These hands dole out Communion, put oils of unction on the sick and baptize frail babies. They need to be smooth and gentle. Ah, here comes our company.'

Seeing her brother in an upright position was something to which Polly had grown used, but watching him here, out of context, caused a lump to form in her throat. It was suddenly so real and so moving. The left leg wasn't yet properly educated, but he had been assured that it would improve. 'Hiya, our kid,' he said. 'I'll have a double whiskey and Father's marked cards.'

'He's Chris when he's in an ordinary shirt and stuff, and he's Ginnie when in his pinny. It's fancy, with flowers and a frill.'

'Ginnie the Pinny,' Cal mused aloud.

'I have no marked cards, young man.'

'They're just a bit bent through being up his cassock,' Frank said.

Polly sat. 'Teach me poker,' she ordered.

'Ladies don't play poker,' was Chris's response.

Frank stared hard at his beloved. 'That's all right, then, because my Pol's no lady.'

Cal agreed. 'I brought her up well. Scotty's no place for a lady, so I made sure she was tough.'

Polly wrote down the basic rules and kept a poker face throughout. She won nineteen shillings and sixpence. 'Beginner's luck,' was her opinion. 'But Frank, you give in too easily. Chris, your face lets you down, and Cal, you're over-confident.'

The host sighed. 'Well, that's us told.'

Frank just laughed. The other two had no idea of Polly's true value. If he'd explained, they would have been told even more decisively, because his girl was a tiger. And he was proud of her.

'Which end's which?' Hattie asked her friend.

Ida considered the item on the floor. 'Well, the back end's just peed on your rug and the front's chewing a stocking.'

Hattie went to fetch a cloth and disinfectant. At this rate, she would be getting shares in Dettol and she'd be out of nylons. 'When's his birthday?' she asked as she mopped yet again. 'And it'll be his poor housekeeper who gets lumbered, just you mark my words, Ida. I've yet to see a man clean up after himself, never mind wiping up after a leaky puppy.'

'Tomorrow.'

'Eh?'

'You were asking about Father Foley's birthday. It's tomorrow.'

Hattie glanced at the clock. 'Can we do it now, love? Only I can't manage another night with Oonagh here. I'm running out of antiseptic for a start, and she attacks the legs on that chair. Poor little thing's teething already. My furniture will be legless, and it's not even my dog. Oonagh doesn't suit, does it?'

'Big name for an old astrakhan glove with feet, Hattie. You should have left it where it was and let him fetch it himself. It's going to be hard work, so let's take it to him now, get rid and wish him a happy birthday. I'll just go and get a couple of birthday cards from the shop, Hat.'

Alone, Hattie picked up the little Kerry Blue terrier. She was falling in love with the tiny dog. It was a happy soul, always a wagging rudder and a pink tongue ready to impart the canine version of kisses. It wriggled in her arms and chewed gently on a finger. 'When we go to Kirkby, me and Ida will have a doggy. Yes, we will, yes we will. But it'll be grown up and trained, cos me and Ida aren't as young as we were.'

They both dreaded leaving. They would be among the last to go, because shops along the mile served the local populace, and only when continuing became impossible would they move. The retailers on the mile should stick together and fight any eviction order until their services were no longer required by customers.

Ida returned with birthday cards and a box of chocolates. 'He has a sweet tooth.' She looked Hattie up and down. 'You like that little bugger, don't you?'

'That's why she has to go. If I keep her any longer, he'll have no chance of getting her. I keep moaning and saying life was easier without her, but ooh, I'll miss her. So when we move, we're getting a dog.'

'All right. You can see to it, though.'

'I will. But it'll be a grown dog, trained and everything.'

'Fair enough.'

They signed their cards and donned coats. Hattie tied a red ribbon on the pup's collar while Ida wrapped the box of chocolates in tissue paper. They began the walk towards what used to be the Other Side, where Protestants lived. St Columba's was close to the edge of Catholic territory, but emerald and orange were joined now in the fight against governments local and national. They even drank together, though all that would change on walking days, when the fun would kick off yet again.

Priests were quiet, God-fearing people on the whole. Father Brennan had been different, of course, but he was the exception that— Both women stopped in their tracks. Father Foley was chasing Polly across the school yard, and Frank Charleson was chasing Father Foley. 'Stop in the name of the Church,' cried the custodian of souls for the parish of St Columba.

'Run, Polly,' Frank shouted. 'I'll get him.'

Chris stopped running and gasped for oxygen. He doubled over, hands on his knees. 'She's got . . . she's got my dominoes.'

Frank howled with laughter. 'Just be grateful that's all she's got. Give up – you won't catch her.'

Cal was propped in the presbytery doorway. He noticed the new arrivals, stuck finger and thumb in his mouth and delivered a whistle fit to strip paint. Everyone froze. Everyone except Oonagh. She yapped and tried to jump out of her temporary mistress's arms.

Chris found enough air and walked to the gate.

Although none of his company lived in the parish, he was familiar with most who had businesses on the main road. 'Oh, gracious me, it's Kaybee. Or maybe just Kay till she grows a bit. Come away in, ladies.' Like many a customer at the cafe, he sang 'Polly, Put the Kettle On' till Frank joined him.

'You're in enough trouble as it is. Carry on singing that, and she'll have your testimonials, let alone your double six.'

Hattie handed over the pup. 'Be good to her, Father. Happy birthday tomorrow. Oh, she's not house-trained.'

'Neither am I. We'll be great together, so. Thank you both. Follow me.'

Somewhat perplexed, the new arrivals walked behind Father Foley into the house.

'I can smell fire,' Ida remarked. 'Where's Cal?'

Frank answered. 'The fire's out. God's servant here started it. Cal's in the kitchen putting the kettle on. Polly's in a mood.'

Polly entered, her nose in the air. 'You're right, Frank – he cheats.' She walked up to Chris, saw the pup and melted. 'Hello, gorgeous.'

'She still loves me,' said the priest.

'No, I don't. You cheat at cards, you cheat at dominoes, and you're a disgrace.' She removed the little dog from her master's arms. 'I'm keeping you. You don't want to live with the nasty man, do you?'

Hattie and Ida seemed bemused. They were from a time when priests weren't normal human beings, when God's mediators were grim-faced, harsh and unapproachable. And here was Father Foley in a bright orange jumper, fawn trousers and brown slippers, messing about like a kid at playtime. He was just an ordinary bloke.

'Polly, let me have Kaybee,' he pleaded.

'You owe us ten bob each,' she replied. 'Plus danger

270

money, plus interest for keeping us waiting to get our dominoes back.'

'They're my dominoes, woman.'

'Which you knocked on the floor accidentally on purpose. Then you mixed them up with malice aforethought.'

'I haven't got any of that; tomato ketchup, HP brown and a bottle of salad cream, that's all I've got. And you have my dog.'

'Thirty bob and you can have her back.'

'I don't want her back. I want all of her, front, back, legs, tail and teeth. Kaybee is mine.'

'Thirty bob.'

'Have pity on a poor ordained soul whose life is dedicated to the betterment of others, whose parishioners always come first, who—'

'Who cheats at cards,' Polly snapped. 'Here, have your Kerry Blue. Kaybee is from the initials, I take it?'

'Indeed.'

She pushed her face close to his. 'Listen, Chris. Once I get to grips with the rules of poker, I shall wipe the floor with you. I'm going now to help my brother with the tea.' Polly sniffed, turned and walked off.

Hattie and Ida perched uncomfortably on the edges of two dining chairs. They watched round-eyed while their host babied his puppy, listened when he spoke to the animal in nonsense. Daddy's little girl was happy; they could tell by the movements of that silly tail. Frank, Polly and Cal called Father Foley Chris, and it all seemed so wrong. Weren't priests supposed to sit and pray or study when they weren't out ministering?

Chris went and sat with them. 'Ladies, have I shocked you? I'm just a fellow who sometimes dresses up for God. In His house, I wear my best because He deserves it. Like you with your hats and gloves and newest rosaries.

Sunday best. But priests play, too. Frank's my closest mate. We fight like cat and dog – don't bite, Kaybee – but it's all in fun. As for Polly, she's a credit to you ladies, because I know you stepped in when their parents died. Anyway, apart from the getting married bit, we priests are just like everyone else.'

Ida smiled tentatively. 'I suppose you must be.'

'And we sin, so we go to Confession. You just have to give us room to be human.'

'Be as human as you like,' Ida replied. 'But I want two sugars in my tea, and a few biscuits wouldn't go amiss. Hattie has one spoonful and a drop of milk.'

The three of them turned their heads towards the kitchen door where a miracle stood. Cal, steadied from behind by Frank and Polly, carried a tray into the room.

Chris wiped his eyes. 'Thanks be to God,' he breathed.

'Amen,' chorused the two older women.

Eleven

Having a love life was all very well and good, but it didn't bring home the bacon on time. Polly opened the cafe ten minutes late, and five people fell in. 'Just a minute,' she said. 'I'm doing my best, because I can't be in two places at once, can I?'

Dusty Den Davenport removed his workday pork pie hat, Ida tutted loudly, Hattie handed over a few carrots for Flick, the butcher's wife gave Polly a couple of pounds of pork sausages and Jimmy Nuttall demanded to know why Polly was running late. 'We're all bloody starving here, Pol. It was like queuing in the war; it all flashed before me eyes, it did, no oranges, no bananas, Pasha cigarettes and saccharin instead of sugar. Nightmare.'

'Sit down and shut up,' Polly advised him quietly.

Ida sniffed. 'She's in love,' she said to nobody in particular. 'I've noticed this before in quite a few people. In love means broken clocks, no calendar and no chance of any sense. I'll bet anybody a pound to a penny that Frank Charleson's upstairs, because they're practically living over the brush.'

Polly glared at the woman who had been an excellent substitute mother to her and Cal. 'That's enough from you, Mrs Pilkington. Right, people. Cal and I overslept, so you'll have whatever he's cooked, like it or lump it. He's worn out with exercising, and I'm worn out, full stop. It's one of those days.'

More customers arrived. Polly went through to the kitchen and stood in the scullery doorway.

'Six ready,' Cal said.

Like greased lightning, Polly shifted into serving gear. She ran about with bacon, eggs, tomatoes and anything else that happened to arrive on a plate. Breakfasters bartered black pudding for a fried slice, an egg for more bacon, hash browns for an egg.

The taunting began. 'It's musical bloody plates,' Hattie complained. 'Has anybody got mushrooms or a bit of sausage?'

Polly paused for a moment and watched them swapping plates or items of food. They didn't mind. Had they minded, they would have said so, because nobody living in these parts was afraid of speaking his or her mind. Yes, Ida had pretended to chastise her, but that, too, was par for the course. All this would be lost. Her eyes felt prickly, but she mustn't weep. The bloody government was planning an autopsy on a living body, and there was no way of forcing the powers to rebuild here. The schools, whose standards were high, churches, shops and homes would all be crushed by Westminster's dirty boots.

Peter Furness, still breakfastless, stood up with his notebook. 'Miss Polly Kennedy?'

'Yes, Constable?'

'I'm booking you for loitering with intent.'

'I haven't got a tent.'

He licked his pencil. 'I'm booking you anyway, no fixed abode.'

'Please yourself.' She went to collect more breakfasts. God, she would miss this cafe.

*

Christine Lewis had travelled far beyond the merely worried and upset stage. Elaine was all she had; Elaine was the only person in the world she truly loved. Elaine had taken life by the scruff of its neck and shaped it to suit her ends. But Elaine was ... disturbed. This house, usually a happy place, had become more than sad. Christine didn't want to be here.

She sighed heavily, feeling as if she were dragging air from the soles of her feet. She was so damned tired, bone-weary and afraid. There was something very wrong with her beloved daughter and, for a while, Christine hadn't known which way to turn. She had many friends and acquaintances in the village, but it was a tiny place where gossip seemed to travel successfully through walls as thick as the trunk of a hundred-year-old oak, and Elaine must not become a topic under discussion. Nevertheless, something needed to be done, and help was needed, as this was all too much for one woman.

'Help me, God. Please help me. If only she would talk to me.' But there remained the terrifying possibility that Christine's daughter did not realize how altered she was. Out of her mother's reach, the young woman might not have any insight into her own condition, and if that were the case, how could the situation be remedied? How was she behaving out there in the city of Liverpool? One thing of which Christine was fully sure was that the people of Liverpool missed very little, if anything at all.

In truth, Elaine's mother had known for some time that her girl was different, but she'd managed to persuade herself that it was the result of years of complete dedication to study, the deliberate lack of a social life and the humdrum nature of her initial legal work. Describing her career thus far, the young lawyer had often depicted herself as an i-dotter and a t-crosser, though that had begun to change some weeks ago.

'She must notice how I look, hollow-eyed and scared.' The image in the mirror might easily have belonged to a woman in her sixties, and Christine was not yet fifty. Fear was painted into every line of her face, while her eyes were underscored by the dark stains that arrive with too little sleep and an overdose of anxiety. She was living with a person she scarcely recognized, and that person was her only surviving relative. 'She chooses not to notice, I think.' Or did she have a choice? Was Elaine in control of herself? Perhaps the girl had kept herself on too tight a rein during her years of education, and perhaps that rein had finally snapped.

Fortunately, some cases of litigation had started to trickle in Elaine's direction, while much of the conveyancing had been passed to a junior just out of university. The board of Spencer, Spencer and Laithwaite believed in starting youngsters at the bottom. Qualifications opened the door, but they meant nothing in the world of law, where the real learning began. She was moving up the ladder, so what was wrong with her? 'Do I want the answer to that question? Do I really?'

Christine prepared herself for her own job. There was just one person to whom she might turn, and that was Norma Charleson. Norma's weaknesses were known only to her housekeeper, so it would be a tit-for-tat situation. An unexpected friendship had developed, because each had come to depend on the other. Yes, it had to be Norma, who was not quite the dragon she used to be. 'If I don't talk to someone soon, I'll be ill, too.' With unsteady hands, she donned her coat and picked up the keys to Norma Charleson's car. Today. For some unfathomable reason, it had to be today.

When Christine arrived at Brookside, a slimmer and much fitter Norma was reorganizing the study in preparation for decorators. Now that she had the whole house, she spread herself out and did some of the cleaning on her better days. This was clearly a better day for her. She opened her mouth to speak to Christine, closing it immediately when she saw the expression on her face.

'Oh, Norma.' The housekeeper burst into tears. They flooded down her face like the contents of a small, tidal river. 'Norma,' she repeated.

Norma closed the roll top of the desk. 'Go and sit down in the living room for a while. Put your feet up on that stool. I'll pop the kettle on and make you a nice, hot cup of tea.' In the kitchen, she found herself actually worrying about her employee. She was usually so calm, so controlled and sensible, that this morning's behaviour had come as a shock. For once, Norma wanted to help for the right reasons. The concept of living without Christine was not a happy one, but Norma's need arose from the part of herself that needed a friend rather than a servant, and this woman was so easy to like.

Christine sat. Normally, the role reversal might have amused her, but this was not a normal time. When she closed her eyes, she saw her child's immobile face, the expressionless surface that failed completely to hide whatever was going on beneath the smooth exterior. She said little, ignored her mother's questions and remarks – surely that showed at the office? Surely her colleagues had noticed the change?

Norma bustled in bearing tray and tea things and chattering nervously. 'I always think a nice natter over a cup of tea is better medicine than any doctor can prescribe. Shall I tell you what he said yesterday?' Without waiting for a reply, she motored on. 'He said, "Mrs Charleson, you need to walk more to get your circulatory system stronger. Build yourself up to half an hour a day five days a week." Does he think I'm an Olympic athlete? Says I'll live longer if I get moving. With arthritis? He wants his head testing.'

She sat. 'Right you are, you've had your weep, I've had my moan, so it's your turn. Come on now, out with it. If you hold it back for much longer, you'll crack open like a volcano, and I've good carpets and rugs to think about.'

Christine dried her eyes. It tumbled from her, not necessarily in order, but she just let the words pour. 'Something happened at university, and she thought I hadn't noticed, but I did when she came home at the end of one term. She was counting things like marigolds in the garden and tiles in the kitchen, and she talked to herself sometimes. It was horrible, really frightening. But she seemed to snap out of it, and she's been fine ever since. I truly thought we'd seen the last of it.'

Norma poured the tea, her hand shaking slightly.

'She was counting peas last night. And she's rocking a bit.'

'Here, drink this.'

'Thank you. In her bedroom, she whispers to herself. I think she talks to the mirror.'

'And the counting of peas?'

'On her plate at the table. Then she has a bath, dresses up and goes out. Every evening, after our meal, she goes out.'

'Where does she go, then?'

'I think . . . and I don't know what makes me say this, but . . . I suspect it's something to do with Frank. Don't ask me why, but I get the feeling that she grew fond of him, though he didn't return her affection.'

'My Frank? Are they together?'

Christine shrugged before sipping her tea. 'She won't talk to me. She's always talked to me, even if it was just about which clothes she was going to wear or what we were about to eat. But she seems out of touch with me, out of touch with life. It's almost as if she's stopped being real.' What she didn't want to admit was that her daughter had begun to alter in her teenage years, after the premature death of her father. 'I think she needs help, Norma.'

'What? A psychiatrist? From what you've told me about Elaine, she'll never admit that she needs assistance, especially for something of that kind. Too proud by a mile, Christine.'

'I know. What am I going to do?'

'No, no. It's what are we going to do, love. I'm not having you traipsing about looking for her on your own while you're in this state. Let me think.' She thought. 'So, we don't know where she goes.'

'No, we don't.'

'And we don't know what she does or who she sees.'

'Correct.'

Norma stood up and paced about very well for somebody riddled with arthritis. 'So we need to know where, what and who.'

'Yes.'

'Simple. We follow her when she goes out. What makes you think Frank's involved?'

'She talks to him in her sleep, calls his name. But, no, we can't follow her, she'll see us. She knows your car, because it's at our house as often as it's at yours. And in spite of her condition, I think she misses nothing. Underneath all this mess, there's a very astute woman.'

Norma walked up and down again. 'Right. I'll get her followed. My dear departed husband believed I knew nothing about his mistress, but I think in the end I knew more about her than he ever did. When he found out I'd had them followed, and when I had her history printed out, he ... well, he didn't last very long. I know a good firm; a very good firm. They'll get to the bottom of this for you in next to no time, I promise.'

Christine blinked. 'Private detectives?'

'Don't you worry, dear, because I'll pay. She won't know they're there, believe me. They're true professionals.'

'Oh, Norma.' Christine jumped to her feet. 'I don't want all that.'

'And I don't want you worrying yourself into an early grave. Just listen to me now. I've never been what you might call a nice woman. I married a man who got me out of poverty, and I didn't appreciate him. His son – my son – hates me. But I know now, I understand what I was and what I can be if I try. And for some reason I don't understand, I feel that my new wisdom came from you. So I shall help you. Leave it all to me.'

'Thank you. I can't take as much credit as you think I'm due, because it's a lot simpler than that. You're fighting diabetes, and that illness carries depression as a passenger. Now that your sugar's balanced, so are you. But thank you for caring.'

'You've done a lot for me.'

'Even so . . .'

Norma smiled. 'What are friends for? Look, Elaine's probably going through a phase, something to do with work or even connected to Frank. I can tell you this – he won't hurt her, because it's not in his nature.'

'He hurt you, Norma.'

'I deserved it.'

'Elaine might deserve it.'

Norma shook her head. 'Trust him. Please, trust him.'

Christine bit her lip. 'It may be the other way round, Norma. She might hurt somebody. There's such a huge change in her, as if she's angry, agitated, unhappy, dissatisfied and trying to conceal all that. She may damage herself or someone else – I don't know. I don't know what I think, and scarcely know what I'm saying. But she isn't the daughter I've had for over twenty years. I'm living with a beautiful, empty shell of a girl I used to know.'

'It must be terrifying.'

'Yes.'

'Right. I'll get the phone book. This must be dealt with now. We'll need a recent photograph of Elaine and one of Frank, just in case she's involved with him. Another thing you must do is go to town and drop in on her at work, see how she behaves there. You can learn a lot by seeing a picture in a different frame.'

'I can't.'

'Oh?'

'It would be out of character. I'd never do that. She could be in a meeting with clients or with another solicitor.'

'But you're her mother.'

'Exactly. I belong at home in the kitchen or opposite her at the table. She lives her life in separate compartments, rather like most men seem to.' Christine wrung her hands. 'Elaine's already furious about something or somebody, and I'd hate it if she turned on me while she isn't herself. And she definitely isn't herself. I'm living with a stranger. I need only look at her eyes, because they go from glassy to hyperactive in seconds.'

'Just hang on a minute.' Norma opened a drawer in a small side table. 'Yes, here it is. No need to look through the directory, because I seem to have kept his card. Now, I shall make an appointment and start the ball rolling. The sooner we get to the bottom of this, the better it will be for your sake. The ingratitude of children can be boundless, as can their cruelty.'

Christine swallowed hard. 'I think it might be something she can't help.'

Norma picked up the phone. 'So you're definitely talking about mental illness here?'

'Possibly.' She didn't even like to skirt the concept of Elaine's being mentally ill, so she certainly wasn't going to discuss it in any more depth. 'I think it's more likely to be emotional.' Emotional? The girl seldom displayed any feelings. She wanted to marry for money, to remain childless – or child-free, as she termed it – and she was determined above all to be successful in an area over-populated by men.

Norma replaced the receiver. 'Well, the thing is, do you really want to know what she's up to? Will you cope?'

'I must. You compared me a few minutes ago to a volcano that might blow its top at any moment. We both know why I'm in this state. Well, my daughter would fit the same description, but I don't know why. She has shut down as far as I'm concerned, but her brain is on the move all the time.'

'The counting?'

Christine nodded. She had to talk about it, or she would be the one in need of help. 'The counting, the rocking, whispering to herself, talking in her sleep. She sometimes looks through me, as if she sees something beyond and behind me. I am so afraid. If she's had some kind of brain-storm or breakdown, I need to get help for her. The only way to reach the bottom of it is to find out where she goes every evening. She comes home at all hours, too.'

'And says little?'

'And says virtually nothing.'

'Though you've always been close.'

'Especially since we lost her father. She was Daddy's little girl. She focused so hard on her career that she's possibly forgotten how to enjoy life.'

Norma placed the card on the small side table. 'Look, let's drive up to the river and blow the cobwebs away. We don't need to talk much. But before setting up a meeting with the Pearson agency, I need to be sure that you're sure. Come on, I'll drive.'

Like many Liverpudlians, they repaired to the Mersey

when thinking became a necessity. There was something soothing about tidal water when it was in a good mood; it lapped against the shore in a rhythm that could be hypnotic, though it was a force to be avoided when storms arrived. Today, it was glassy and almost as still as a lake.

'Does Elaine ever come up here, Christine?'

'I don't know.' It was true. Elaine always did things correctly. She took her mother out for a meal on her birthday, spent Christmas with her, bought food for the larder, helped with cleaning occasionally. But she seldom gave of herself and rarely acted on impulse. Christine knew few details about her daughter's life. 'What I do know is that she did some legal work for Frank, and she began to change at about the same time.'

'Could it be my son's fault, then?'

'No. She's been like this before, but not as bad as she is now. And as you said, Frank isn't a hurtful man.'

'Sulking? Wants her own way? You've said before that she's spoilt. That's often the trouble when there's just one chick in the nest.'

Christine shook her head thoughtfully. 'It's gone beyond that. She's lost control of herself, and I hope that's not noticed at work, because the job props her up enormously. My daughter's a bit like an almost pure diamond with a huge flaw through its middle. Most of the time, it doesn't show, but if the light catches the gem in a certain way . . .' She didn't finish the sentence.

Gulls swooped over the bay, their raucous cries filling crisp, clear air. Dog walkers strolled along the sand while their canine companions chased each other into the river's flow. It would soon be high tide. Ebb and flow was inevitable, and nothing on earth could stop it.

'You're right, Norma. Without knowledge, we can do little.' And if my daughter's heading for some kind of collision, I need more information. Let's go back and make that phone call before I start dithering again.'

'Yes, dear. We'll have another cup of tea, then I'll make the call.'

They went back to Brookside and Norma managed to get an appointment with Mr Pearson. 'It will be all right, I'm sure,' she lied to her companion.

Christine heard the lie, and said nothing more. Only time would tell.

At the beginning of October, Billy Blunt was finally proved right. Due to the persistence of Father Christopher Foley and several police forces, articles discovered near the corpse found in Derbyshire were described by a group of travellers who had lost a family member. The rosary was outlined accurately right down to its colour and a bent crucifix, as was the clothing, tiny scraps of which had been retrieved. The deceased had been overweight, and he'd always carried a child's rosary given to him over half a century earlier by his parents. He had been a drinker, had wandered off from time to time, and had last been seen outside Buxton earlier in the year.

Chris and Billy lingered together in the rear doorway of the Blunts' house in Dryden Street. They were watching a pair of lunatic pups leaping about ecstatically in the backyard. Daniel the spaniel and Kaybee the Kerry Blue were as mad as hatters, and each deteriorated considerably in the company of the other. At this point in time, they were one fat, black puppy with eight legs, two heads and many teeth.

'That, Billy, is an example of pure joy.' Poor Kaybee was going to be neutered at the earliest opportunity, but the Blunts were wavering because of Daniel's pedigree. He had been earmarked as a potential stud, though according to Mavis, he currently looked as daft as a brush. 'I can't catch him,' she often complained. 'The only one he listens to is Billy, because he completely ignores me and Fred. If he breeds, his pups will be as daft as he is.'

'God bless the daftness,' Chris said as his Kaybee performed a perfect if unplanned somersault.

They returned to the kitchen while the dogs began their run-through. A run-through involved the whole house and both dogs. They dashed about at great speed round every room, often climbing stairs they had just learned to descend. Until recently, two whimpering idiots had needed carrying down to ground level, but they had finally worked out their own centres of gravity.

'So, Billy, you and I were right about Father Brennan.'

'Yes. You knew as well, didn't you, Father?'

'I did, though I'm not gifted like you are. For me, it was the rosary, while you knew because of your dreams. I'm just so sorry that you had to suffer.'

Billy nodded. 'But the funny thing is, no other dreams are true – it's just the ones with him in them. He's happy now.'

'Is he?'

'He has a different life.'

'And you've no idea where?'

'On a farm. Why do I dream true things just about him?'

Eugene Brennan had altered the course of Billy's existence. A little of the shine had peeled away from the child, as if the beating had robbed him of innocence. Fortunately, this young man had a solid core, as he came from a good family. 'Because God sent you those dreams in order to help the rest of us find him. When he's caught, the dreams will probably go away, since they'll no longer be needed.'

'So it's like magic or a miracle thing?'

'Indeed. Now, go and ask Mammy can you come with me up to the Parlour for a dish of Polly's scouse. We've been invited.'

'What about Daniel and Kaybee?'

'Your mother will mind them for us.'

'I heard that,' Mavis shouted from the parlour. 'You're leaving me with Laurel and Hardy? I'm trying to clean in here, and I'm getting nowhere while they get everywhere.'

The priest winked at his co-conspirator. 'Then I'll take Kaybee along, because we can go in the back way as guests.' He picked up his exhausted puppy. 'We'll be off, Mavis. You can mind Daniel.'

'Thank you very much. I've always wanted to spend time with the criminally insane. He eats clothes, you know. And rugs.' She stood in the doorway, a scarf tied turban-fashion over her hair, polish in one hand, a cloth in the other. 'The trouble with puppies is they're gorgeous, so you have to forgive them.' She sighed. 'Oh, all right, off you go. I'll mind the terrible twins.'

'Thanks, Mam.'

'And from me, too. Come on, son.'

Chris and Billy disappeared while the going was good. If Daniel sank his teeth into another valued item, Billy's mum might just call her son back. Priest and child turned right at the bottom of Dryden Street and continued along Scotland Road. 'We can go in the front door, as we have no dogs,' Chris said.

Lunch was over and the cafe door was locked. Chris knocked, and they were welcomed by Polly. 'Hello,' Chris said. 'I've brought the young man you asked for. His poor mother's stuck with two mad puppies, God help her.'

'Come through, children,' she said before putting an arm across Billy's shoulder. 'There's jelly,' she told him. 'And cake and biscuits and ice cream.'

'Whose birthday is it?' Billy asked.

'Nobody's. It's Cal and Linda's engagement party, but we wanted to make a fuss of you, too.' She showed her ring finger to Chris. 'Frank got me an eternity ring so that I wouldn't feel left out.'

'I should have brought my sunglasses,' Chris complained. 'That's bright enough to blind a man. I may require compensation.'

The small living room was crowded. Ida and Hattie were perched on Cal's hospital-height bed. Cal and his fiancée sat on dining chairs at the table, while Frank and Polly dished out the food.

'Hello, Billy,' Cal called. 'We've a favour to ask. Polly?'

Polly squatted down in front of the boy. 'We don't want any bridesmaids,' she explained. 'We decided against silly girls in daft, frilly frocks, but we'd like you to carry the rings. No stupid clothes, by the way. You'll be in a grown-up suit with long trousers and shiny shoes. Will you do that for us?'

'Can I have jelly without eating what Mam calls sensible food first?'

'Yes.'

'And ice cream without having butties?'

'Definitely.'

'And you won't tell Mam that I've not ate real food?'

'Promise. Cross my heart, Billy.'

'All right, then.'

So it was settled.

Only Chris Foley, Polly, Frank, Cal and Linda were familiar with the full truth. The weddings would be soon, because both women were pregnant. Ida, who had not quite managed to rid herself of the tendency to air her views loudly and in public, came out with the obvious. 'What's the rush?' she asked. 'You in the club?'

'Yes,' the girls replied in unison.

Ida blinked. 'Linda as well?'

'Linda as well,' Polly said soberly.

Ida chewed on her lip for a moment. 'But Cal can't do the ... I mean, he's not been able to ... how can she be when he's ... ? Are you sure?'

Cal shook his head very slowly. 'Ways and means, Ida. I might not have been able to, but she could. And soon enough I'll be back to—'

'Shut up, Cal. Small boy, big ears.' Polly pointed at Billy.

But small boy with big ears had discovered three colours of jelly, ice cream, Carnation Milk, condensed milk and cake. He was busy inventing rainbow trifle in a glass bowl big enough to hold several pints and was in a world all his own, though he was having difficulty in layering the jellies in a satisfactory fashion. Concentrating hard, he allowed the tip of his tongue to protrude from a corner of his mouth.

'Well, he'll be sick when he gets home,' Linda warned.

Ida continued undeterred. 'So your legs were good enough for carrying on before you were ready for walking proper, then?'

Polly stared at the ceiling. The damp patch that looked like a map of Africa had developed a few islands, and concentrating on it was vital in order to manage not to laugh. Ida was often funny, though she seldom intended to amuse an audience.

Cal's face was set in determined mode. 'Things can work in more ways than one, Ida.'

'Can they? Not in my day, they couldn't.' She sniffed in a disapproving fashion.

A strange noise arrived from a space next to the sideboard. Chris Foley, who was Father Foley today as the dog collar was in situ, was sliding down the wall like something out of a Charlie Chaplin film.

Frank folded his arms. 'What the hell's the matter with you now?'

The cleric continued on his downward journey.

'You're worse than a kid,' Frank told him.

'I was just thinking of the time I was encouraged to take up a missionary position. Like Cal, I was forced to decline.'

'I'm not inviting you to anything else. This party's for our ring bearer, isn't it? You shouldn't be let out of your house.'

Ida had no idea about what was going on. Billy scooped lime jelly off the floor and dropped it into the mess he was creating. Hattie dug Ida in the ribs and advised her to shut up. 'Don't say any more.' She lowered her voice. 'They did it with her on top.'

'No!'

'Ida, one more word, and I'll clock you with my handbag.'

'I never heard of such a thing.'

'Shut up.'

'But I—'

'Shut up.'

Ida shut up.

Chris struggled to his feet. 'The reproductive process alone is proof enough of God's sense of humour.'

This time, Frank crossed the small room. 'Listen, you,' he hissed. 'Any more clever talk, and you'll be banned from the premises.' He grinned. 'Mind, I suppose you're right.' The last five words were whispered.

Ida turned to her best friend. 'Do priests know about that sort of thing?' she mouthed.

'Course they do. Pull yourself together. You're making a show of me again.'

'Sorry, but I—'

'There's more than one way to peel an apple, love.'

'Oh.'

'And no gossiping about them expecting. If they wanted the world to know, they'd put it in the paper.'

'Under articles wanted?' Ida smiled, pleased to have asked a clever question. 'I won't say nothing.'

'Good.'

Billy's concoction was not a success. 'How do you make trifle?' he asked innocently.

'Not like that,' the females chorused.

Cal took a more serious attitude. 'You get sponge fingers or stale cake, raisins, put a bit of booze in to plump up the raisins and soak the cake, a few almond flakes, jelly if you like it, custard when the jelly sets, then cream on top.'

'Will you make one and let me watch? I don't mean today, like.'

'Course I will.'

The child fixed his eyes on Polly, then on Linda. 'In the club means babies,' he stated flatly. 'When are they coming?'

'In late spring or early summer,' Linda answered.

'Both of them?'

'Yes.'

The boy picked up a sandwich, forgot about babies, and ate sensible food. The news was out; in time, and if or when he remembered, Billy would spill the beans.

Resurrection from the dead was extremely painful. 'And friend to friend in wonder said, the Lord is risen from the dead.' Where had he read those words? He wasn't the Lord; he wasn't even a decent human being, because he'd lost his temper to the point where he had killed a brother in Christ. No, he hadn't taken his medicine and yes, he might have acted differently if he had swallowed the pills, but he'd put Billy Blunt in hospital before all that, hadn't he? Now that he could control his intake of drink, he was able to see what he had been, how he had been for many years. Had he married and stayed in farming, he might never have resorted to alcohol.

Strangely, he had turned to God lately, thanking Him for Gladys, thanking Him for a successful harvest, for returning Brendon Hall to the path he should have followed thirty years earlier. For the first time since childhood, he was happy. But the story was front-page news once more, with a young Brother Anselm's photograph sitting next to an image of Eugene Brennan: fat, unsmiling and a priest.

Gladys bustled in with scissors. 'You all right, Don?' she asked.

'I'm just looking at the *Herald*. Did you manage to get some kippers?'

'I did, love. Isle of Man, boned and ready. They'll do nicely for breakfast tomorrow with a bit of bread and butter.'

'Well, don't give your dad any. He could choke on even a small bone.'

She loved the way he cared for Dad. 'He'll have egg in a cup mashed up with crumbled bread and butter, as usual. As if I'd give him fish. Did you say you wanted me to cut your hair? Come on, let's be having you over here, mister.'

He sat still and obedient while she wrapped an old tablecloth round his shoulders and began to trim his hair. She liked sideburns, so he went along with her wishes and wore a stripe in front of each ear. His crowning glory was now completely grey, and that helped greatly when it came to disguise.

'Can you imagine a priest killing a monk, Don?'

He shrugged. 'Priests are people. People have limits, and he was an alcoholic. A shame about the brother, though.'

Gladys sighed. 'Anyway, as long as he doesn't come

here, eh? The whole of Derbyshire's on the lookout for a fat man with an Irish accent. I don't know about Derbyshire, but we get Irish travellers all over Cheshire looking for seasonal work. Some folk moan about them; I don't. Any man who'll do a day's work for a few bob and a dinner is worth his weight in dolly mixtures. And they're usually good for a laugh, being Irish.'

He belonged here. He was good with animals, great on the land, happy with his lover. Gladys was gentle, caring and undemanding. She accepted his 'wife' in Sunderland, was sad that he couldn't be divorced, though she was very happy with him. Her Don had been as nervous as a new groom, but she'd sorted him out and had told him repeatedly that she couldn't imagine living without him. This was the life, and he didn't want it threatened.

'Are you having your whiskey now?' she asked. The man was like clockwork; he drank two doubles every night, said his prayers, slept like a baby and was more than happy to help with chores in the house and garden once morning came and milking was completed.

'Yes please, dear.'

He swallowed a bubble of fear. He was well established at Drovers, and he blended in very well. As Gladys's 'husband', he was accepted in the village and neighbouring hamlets, always ready to lend a hand with a broken tractor or a hard birth if there was no vet to hand. In fact, he was treated as something of a genius in agricultural circles, since he seemed to know soil just by touching it and sniffing at a handful.

Gladys handed him his glass of Irish. 'So, miracle man, we'll be knee-deep in honey next year, will we?'

'What?'

'Oh, you've gone into one of your dreams again, have you?'

He swung round to face her fully. 'Am I talking or crying in my sleep?'

'No. I meant your daydreams.'

'Ah.' He took a swig of whiskey. 'Let me know if I start with the nightmares, will you? I've had them since I was a small child, and you'll have no sleep if they start up again. I know your dad's on morphine, but he'd be awake, too. I get loud.'

'Don't worry. I'll keep the caravan bed made up for you, and if you start shouting, I'll throw you out after I've pulled the little bit of hair I've left you with.'

He had to smile. Gladys was one of those people who made a person happy even if he was miserable. 'You're good for me, young lady. You've given me a job, a home and a reason to live. I've never before been so happy.'

'Then what's worrying you?' she asked.

'Nothing. I'm just a little bit tired is all. And your father's talking about his death and the hymns he wants at the service. It will be soon, he says.'

Gladys sat in the chair opposite his. 'He's been saying that for a while, but he is in the final stages now.' Her face blanched. 'I've never lived without my dad. He's been a massive part of my life and I can't bear to think of him dying. I just go from one day to the next hoping it won't be yet. It's just lying to myself, but that's how I get by.'

'We all have our mechanisms, our rituals that help us travel through the day. But remember, you'll still have me.' But would she?

'What's your mechanism?' she asked.

'Oh, I've several. You, the whiskey, the land, taking your father out, reading to him, being with you like an ordinary family man, no more running.'

'Running? Were you running?'

'No, no. I mean travelling.'

'I see.'

'We were chased off many a time. Some of the high-faluting farmers don't want gypsies on their land so yes, we ran. But here in the cooler evenings with a nice log fire and a good woman, this is perfection for me.' Gladys wasn't pretty, but she glowed and looked beautiful when he said certain things. She was small, round, strong and rosy-cheeked from years of toil. Except for her accent, she could have been the wife of any decent Irish farmer.

'I'm glad you came here,' she said before picking up her knitting. It was a cardigan for him, of course. Just like Mammy, she put him first, cooking his favourite foods, buying him new clothes and even cutting his hair. He was the husband she should have had, the child who had been denied her.

They made love that night. Gladys, grateful for any attention, was comforted, while he gloried in the joys of the flesh, however fleeting they might be. Whatever, it helped him sleep. But just as he drifted towards uncon-sciousness, a realization hit him. He loved this woman and didn't want to leave her. It would all be fine, he re-assured himself, because he looked nothing like Eugene Brennan. Gladys was his beloved, and nothing but death could separate the two of them.

Frank was hanging pictures on the rear wall when the shop door opened. 'I'll be with you shortly,' he called. He descended the ladder, turned and saw her. She was, without the slightest doubt, the most stunning woman he'd ever seen in the flesh. Like a Hollywood queen, she was beautifully attired; her makeup looked great and not too heavy, while the shoes and bag must have used up a month's salary. 'Ah, Elaine,' he said resignedly.

She stepped towards him. This was the day on which

she would take the bull by the horns, because the tension was killing her. He had to want her.

Feeling threatened without quite knowing why, he backed away a pace. He did know why, he reminded himself inwardly. This woman kept popping up all over the place, and he was one hundred per cent sure that she was one hundred per cent crackers.

'I thought I'd let you know that my company will be briefing prosecuting counsel in the William Blunt case against the Catholic Church,' she said. 'As far as litigation is concerned, I'm the new boy, so I do the legwork.'

The legs, too, were magnificent. She was a work of art, no less and no more, because the eyes expressed little. What had made her like this? Short of tearing her clothes off and lying on a huge bed surrounded by flowers, she could not have done much more to advertise herself as available to him.

'And I've taken on board all you said about lawyers becoming specialists in the area of ill-treated or deprived children. My seniors are considering that suggestion. I may take up arms myself in that discipline.' Every man wanted her. Why should this one be different?

'Good.' He wiped his hands on a damp cloth. She was mad. Although she was a good enough actress, she could not conceal her insanity from him.

'So we must have a meeting some time. And I need to see three teachers, a police constable and his sergeant, then a Mr Davenport.'

Frank dried his hands on the front of his overall. 'Fair enough, though we're rather tied up with wedding prep- arations just at present.' He watched the eyes again, and they seemed to glint slightly, like the surface of a dull, flint-type element. 'It's to be a double wedding. Polly and Cal are twins, you see.'

She pretended to study a few articles in the room. 'I

like your tantalus. Perhaps I'll buy that some time for a present.' Turning, she asked, 'When's the wedding going to be?'

'Three weeks.'

'Ah. Will your mother be there?'

'Not by invitation, though she wouldn't be turned away. She doesn't approve of my Polly.'

His Polly. Elaine must not allow her contempt for that wretched woman to show. This man, this beautiful example of humanity, was meant to have been Elaine's first. She had chosen him, but he refused to respond. 'You don't like me, do you, Frank?'

He felt riveted to the spot. 'What?'

'You don't like me.'

He shrugged. 'What gives you that notion?'

'You do. You give me that notion.'

He hated her. He hated her for making him nervous, for forcing him to be careful here, in his own property, especially when Polly was visiting. 'I have no strong feelings for you either way,' he lied. 'You're just someone I happen to know.'

'I always get the impression that you wish me far away.'

'Oh?' She was never far away, and that was the trouble. 'Yes.' She smiled, though the eyes remained cold.

'Elaine?' He arranged his words carefully. 'You may be the centre of your own universe, but you're not even a B road or a crease on my map. Polly is my life, and I'm no cheat.'

Laughter that bordered on the hysterical bubbled from her lips. 'You think I want you? Go and marry your greasy-spoon girl, because if that's what you want, that's all you deserve. I just considered you for a while as a possible source of entertainment, nothing more. But if you're so wrapped up in Miss Egg and Black Pudding . . .' she shrugged, 'then fun time is over before it began.'

'If you need to play, try Lime Street. You'll even get paid for it. Now, tell your employer that I will not talk to you. He must make me an appointment with someone else.' There, the gauntlet had been thrown down.

'As you wish.' She swept out, leaving behind her a distinct chill and the aroma of expensive perfume.

Frank panicked. Was she capable of hurting Polly? Was she mad enough for murder? If so, there were two of them on the loose, since Eugene Brennan was probably still alive. Both had cold eyes. Each was self-engrossed and self-indulgent. Polly had to be safe, as had Cal. Frank made up his mind there and then to move properly to Scotland Road. He would be here in the shop all day, but nights must be spent with Polly.

For a brief moment, he considered phoning Elaine Lewis's bosses, but what could he say? 'Your Miss Lewis sits outside my premises on Rice Lane almost every night' would sound pathetic, as might 'She's obsessed with me, wants me to bed her.' She wasn't having the bloody tantalus, either. He would give it to Chris as a gift for Christmas. He slapped a sticky SOLD label on one of the decanters and put the whole thing away in a cupboard. Miss Elaine Lewis could go to hell, where she would no doubt find suitable company.

He packed a small case with underwear, pyjamas, toiletries and clean shirts. There was a baby to protect, too. As head of a small family, he needed to be on guard against the decorative sepulchre who would be involved in the Billy Blunt case. The damned woman had lost her grip on herself; no, she was no sepulchre, no burial site, no whitened grave. She was more dangerous than what-ever was implied by that Biblical reference. Elaine Lewis was a powerful vehicle out of control.

*

Elaine seemed to have lost the ability to breathe. She sat in her car on Rice Lane and listened to her own rasping airways. Was this asthma? She'd never before suffered from it; her physical health had always been good, because she was a perfect specimen.

She didn't realize that this was a full-blown, adrenalin-charged panic attack. The day darkened, seeming to close in around her as if pushing her into the abyss. Did death feel like this? Was she going to shuffle off the coil at the age of twenty-three? After struggling to open her window, she managed to gain some oxygen, though breathing out wasn't easy, either. What if Frank Charleson spoke to the partners? He'd refused to deal with her. He knew, he knew, · he bloody knew!

What did he know? That she wanted his body to connect with hers? Or did he think she'd chosen him as a husband? Because the latter was the truth, and she had to face it. Did love make a person crazy? Did it interfere with the very basic and necessary act of breathing? Was she in love? If she was, it was an illness. A lecturer at Oxford had preached just that – it was a serious illness with the ability to interfere with all physical and mental functions. Many a first-class degree was reduced to a lower second because of love, he had insisted. Well, she'd managed to avoid that situation, hadn't she?

She calmed down slowly. Right. The most important requirement was self-protection. If Frank complained about her, she might lose her job, the very thing that defined her. He had to be stopped. How, though? More to the point, why was he choosing fried cod when there was high-grade salmon on the menu?

'Remember that love unreturned is only an inch from hatred,' the Oxford savant had continued. 'It is a well-known fact that most murders happen within families or as a result of unfulfilled sexual desire, which is almost always the basis for love between human adults.' And she had listened. After listening, she had found her flat and had isolated herself. Anyone who stared at her during lectures was awarded what she termed her evil eye. When accosted, she simply said nothing and walked away. Being labelled frigid was all right with her.

But here she was, sitting in a car on a road between rows of Victorian properties, some commercial, some residential, longing for a man who didn't want her. Why? What was it about this particular man? She saw naked desire in the eyes of most men, but nothing in his. Was that her problem? Had she homed in on him because instinct told her it would be a difficult job? Did she value the unattainable in order to prove that she could win against all odds?

Breathing became easier. She inhaled through her nose, exhaled from the mouth. It was all about control. Somehow, she would have to silence Frank.

A lawyer knew a great deal about criminality. First, though, she had to wait until the love became hatred. Did she have time for that, or would he speak to her superiors about today's altercation? Wearily, she drove back to the office. One point must be conceded: her first would be Bob Laithwaite.

Twelve

'I've bought us a brand new washing machine,' Frank said. 'It's great. Unusual, but great. It didn't look right in the middle of the living room or standing in our bedroom, so I stuck it in the kitchen next to the sink.'

'Right. I believe you'll find that's probably the best place for it, all things considered. It's where normal people keep their washing machines.'

'Yes, it seems quite happy where it is now, a neat fit between sink and fridge. It'll settle down given time, because I had a quiet word with it. Oh, yes, I taught it its position in life.'

Polly, who was suffering all-day exhaustion due to repeated morning sickness, lay on top of the eiderdown. 'Good for you. Does it have rubber wringers to get the water out of your clothes?'

'Clothes? What clothes?'

'The clothes you wash in it.'

'Oh, so that's what it's for? Hmm, I did wonder, because I had trouble getting into it, and those blade things mangled my feet. An hour and a half, I spent in Accident and Emergency. They said I was very lucky. Insane, but lucky. You see, I thought it was an alternative to having a bath.'

She awarded him a look fit to flatten a house. 'It's a good job I know what a clown you are, or I'd have you locked up. Stop acting the rubber pig, because my sense of humour's taken a few months off in Blackpool for rest and recuperation. It might not bother coming back at all if you keep being such a nuisance.'

'Well, the damned thing ate my shirts. It's a Hoover, so perhaps it's really for floors. Anyway, my poor clothes came out in ribbons, all torn to bits, no buttons and a very odd shade of grey. I must read the book of destructions before I have another go.' He shook his head sadly. 'Life gets so complicated, doesn't it? And that Oxydol doesn't half froth up. I nearly had to man the lifeboats. My whole life flashed in front of my eyes. I put a record on, music right to the end, like they did on the *Titanic*.'

In spite of tiredness, she laughed at him. He was clearly determined not to improve. 'You're supposed to read the instructions first, love. Don't make me start giggling again. I've breakfasts to face in the morning, and I have to get myself rehydrated by then. I'm going to charge this baby rent with a heavy deposit against damage to the building.'

'How long are you going to be like this?'

'Till my stomach moves south instead of living in my throat.'

'I'm doing your breakfast jobs,' he told her. 'You can serve dinners, because you've usually stopped throwing up by then. Ida says she's got help in the shop, and she'll come in and give you a hand for a couple of hours.'

'Ah.'

'It's very good of Ida to offer, Pol.'

Polly said she didn't mind Ida giving a hand as long as she didn't put her foot in it. However, she did mind her Frank neglecting his new business. She sat up. 'But your shop, sweetheart. Things don't sell themselves, do they? You can't just ignore a new business.'

'No matter. As I've said before, you come first. Mind, I am a bit confused about all this. You see, most things with moving parts arrive with an instruction manual and a twelve-month guarantee on parts and sometimes on labour. I know, don't start; I should have read the washing-machine stuff. But you get none of that with a woman. What happens if you seize up or need a change of oil? Where's your gearbox? If your engine gets flooded or your battery runs down – ouch, that hurt.'

'Thank your stars it's only a pillow. You never read instructions, anyway.'

'True. Shall I make you some toast?'

'Please, but not much butter.'

'Oh, and I've changed my name to George, thought I'd better let you know.'

Polly offered no reply.

'I killed the dragon.'

'Did you? Well done. But not the toast – I don't want that well done.' It was easier to eat food that tasted of nothing. 'George?'

'Yes?'

'Do we have hot water at the flat?'

'Yes. I bought a new dragon. This one came house-trained. It doesn't even spit.'

'Good. Go and get my toast.'

Alone, she stretched out again. Life was a little bit out of order, and Frank was worried about something. She hadn't pretended not to love him for half her life without learning the signs. Too bloody full of jokes and empty laughter, he was. On top of that, she had a life inside her and she'd given up hairdressing. Somebody was coming along tomorrow to buy all her stuff, and she was sad, because she'd been excellent at her job. 'I'll be a great mother,' she said. 'I can be good at more than one thing.' Furthermore, this baby would have a brilliant father.

Downstairs in the kitchen, Cal was making toast for all three of them. Linda was currently at home with her family, and the two men were deep in conversation. 'Is there a word for the way she is?' Cal asked.

'I can think of half a dozen,' Frank answered. 'Mad, creepy, tenacious, obsessive, bloody nuisance. She's also as gorgeous as any film star, and she uses her looks to wield power over men. What she doesn't understand is that most of us want to see a bit of furniture when we look through the windows. I don't mean she's thick, far from it, but I think she had her personality surgically removed. I can say in all honesty that I never met anyone like her before.'

'What's it like being a sex symbol, Frank? She must see something in you. Go on, tell us the secret.'

'Shut up. I've got the only woman good enough for me upstairs with heartburn and a bad attitude. I've made us a nice enough home in the flat above the shop, and it'll suit us fine till the baby's walking. After that, I'll let the flat and find us a house with a bit of garden. Well, that was the plan till Elaine Lewis turned up like a bad penny. There's something unreal about her. She's scary.'

'Hmm. And she's watching your shop and flat.'

'Yes.'

Cal buttered the toast. 'This is Polly's on the blue plate. Too much butter makes her sick. Elaine Lewis will know you're not living down Rice Lane now.'

Frank grinned. 'Never underestimate your own people, lad. I've a neighbour down there who's seventy if a day, and he sneaks in and messes about with lights and curtains. The wireless works, so he's got a bit of entertainment, and I've told him he can light the fire, but he has to keep checking front and back for a mad woman. As long as I leave him tea, milk, a box of biscuits, coal and kindling, he's happy to do the job for thirty bob a week. By the time I roll up for work in the morning, little Miss Sunshine will be at her office in the city.'

'What about your car? She'll see it's not there now.'

'But it is there. I'm using the shop van. I keep it in a garage nearby.'

'Right. Stick your toast and cocoa on that tray. Oh, and she'll find out you're here, by the way. And she'll soon know you're expecting a child, which could make matters worse.'

'I'll let people round here in on the problem by bringing the matter up under any other business at the next Turnpike meeting. They'll all watch out for her. If she has as much sense as I think she has underneath it all, she'll not tackle Scotty Road. Even Hitler couldn't frighten this lot. Ida would have her eyes out, Hattie might clobber her with that rounders bat she keeps for emergencies. And that's just the women. Yes, she'll have to watch out if she wants to poke about round here.'

'I agree with that. Some of the women terrify me, Frank.'

Frank laughed. 'It has to be just the women; very few Scotland Road men would clobber a female. Are you OK getting yourself to bed now you've sacked the attendant, or do you need me?'

'I'm OK, thanks. You see before you an almost upright citizen with a lot less pain. This wedding's going to be a scream. I've to walk Polly up the aisle with Linda's dad walking her, and after that I swap over and become a bridegroom. Mad. Linda's funny. She said there'll be a wheelbarrow in the porch in case my legs go on strike. I asked her what people might think if a man got delivered to his destiny in a wheelbarrow, and she said the alternatives are a general anaesthetic or a shotgun. Too clever for me, is that young woman. Mind, I'll sort her out once my legs start working full time.'

Frank carried the tray upstairs, treading softly so that he would hear if Cal fell. But Cal's mind was so strong and so set that he seldom stumbled. He was ready now for a made-to-measure support for his left leg, while the right needed no help at all. His spectacular progress had been supervised by Linda and Polly, though both insisted that Cal would have made it happen anyway.

He gave Polly her toast and cocoa.

She eyed him with distrust. 'Right, spill the beans,' she commanded.

'I didn't do beans, it's just toast with butter. How's my son?'

'She's fine. I'm the one suffering. Sit down and try to behave yourself.'

He perched on the edge of the bed. 'Right, here's what's happening.' He gave her an edited version of recent developments, holding back his own fears and his near-certainty that Elaine Lewis might well be criminally insane. 'She thinks she's God's gift, but she's like an empty diary, no appointments, no events and definitely no friends. She needs a few months in a mental institution.'

'Are you sure she's the full quid, Frank?'

'Educationally and academically, yes. I reckon her quids are guineas when it comes to her job and knowing stuff. But behaviour-wise, she's deficient unless it's business. It's been embarrassing, believe me. She drives past a couple of times a day, hangs about in her car at night. I might go and see her mother. Though I wouldn't like to upset Mrs Lewis, because she's a lovely woman. She's enough on her plate working for my mother.'

Polly agreed about Christine Lewis. Although everyone along Frank's mile had missed him, folk in these parts had grown used to their gentle, pleasant rent collector. 'Yes, she's liked round here, though her daughter sounds like one of those psychopaths. So what are you going to do?'

'No idea. She is a lawyer, remember. But she's got herself mixed up in the Billy Blunt compensation case, said I had to have a meeting with her. I refused, and that was possibly a mistake on my part. I suppose I knocked her off the pedestal she built for herself. Why she fixed her sights on me I've no idea.'

'You're handsome.'

'I know.'

Polly hit him again. 'You love yourself, too, so you're the same as she is.'

'Shut up and drink your cocoa.' He couldn't frighten her, mustn't have her worried, because he was here to protect her. The other bedroom, her salon, would be made into their sitting room, and here they intended to remain until after the birth of their child. His reasons were clear only to himself: he was staying with Pol because a crazy woman might just turn and try to hurt him, his fiancée, and anyone else connected to him.

He could well be endangering Polly and Cal by being here, but at least he was available and could keep an eye on the outside. The shop van was housed where horses had been kept for a hundred years or more, in stables down the road. His main problem was disturbed sleep. He seemed to have trained himself to wake several times in the night, and he would creep about looking out of back and front windows to check for Elaine Lewis. He should tell someone. Convincing police that a lawyer was crazy could be hard, though Peter Furness might listen.

'What are you thinking about, Frank?'

'How brains can't stop a person being crazy. Or how brains can make a person crazy. And what if she scares the old man who watches the place for an hour or two every night?'

'Is she dangerous?'

'I don't know. I may talk to her mother. If I do, I'll go softly, because she doesn't deserve to suffer.'

After a pause for thought, Polly asked, 'And Elaine?'

'Needs to be stopped, love. I've riled her by not doing

whatever it was she wanted. Just keep an eye open for her, eh? While I'm at the shop, be alert.'

'Alert's my middle name.'

He sighed dramatically. 'Some parents have a lot to answer for.'

She was cold to the bone. A wind had whipped up over the Irish Sea; even the inside of her car was chilled. 'How did you get here, Elaine?' she asked herself. The journey from Liverpool to Southport had not registered in her memory. Always, she had been in control. In her job, she needed to be streets ahead, because she was only a woman. 'Pull yourself together, Lewis.' She was furious with herself for showing all her cards to Frank Charleson. His refusal to want her had numbed her to the bone, and her thinking processes had been affected, as had her memory. Had she come here along the coastal road or via Lord Street? She had no idea.

She shuddered when she recalled the visit to his shop. Weakened by desire, she had opened herself to rejection. Her position at work might well be threatened if he reported her for harassment. Frank Charleson was determined to put a stop to her. He was fiercely protective of Polly, and he was fast becoming Elaine's worst enemy. She needed an ally.

'I have an ally,' she said.

Having sidestepped the attentions of Bob Laithwaite for some considerable time, having forbidden him to come anywhere near her home, she now had to do a complete turn, and he must become her first. He was handsome, intelligent, and not as boring as he had first seemed. But she would be breaking her own rules. Sex for pleasure should take place between a woman and a man she desired. Sex within marriage was merely a duty, and Bob was marriage material.

But her philosophy was already distorted, since she had made the decision that Frank could have fulfilled both roles. What she felt for Frank had to be ignored; what he felt for her must be addressed. She now had to admit to Bob that for personal reasons, she couldn't work with Frank. Perhaps the new boy might cut his teeth on Mr Charleson?

'You are a stupid woman,' she said aloud.

For a while, she sat and marshalled her thoughts into some semblance of order. 'There is but one small step between love and hatred,' she said. In three weeks, Frank would be married to his real childhood sweetheart. 'And I'll be stuck with Lanky Laithwaite.' He was malleable, at least. Frank was not about to reshape himself for her, was he? Whereas Bob ... Bob wanted her. His work was suffering, because his brain had moved south for the winter. Clearly, she was not suffering alone.

Elaine Lewis closed her eyes. 'You may be the centre of your own universe, but you're not even a crease on my map,' Frank had said. So he despised her. Rather too tired to summon up the energy required for temper, she kept herself on simmer. Mum knew there was something amiss with her. It was time to pull herself together with the help of a man who clearly adored her. That had to involve a sexual relationship she neither wanted nor needed, though the longing for physical contact with a man grew stronger every day. 'It should have been Frank.' It would never be Frank. He was lost, almost as finally as her father had been lost for eight years.

She concluded yet again that Frank Charleson might well complain and ruin her chances with the firm. He didn't want her involved with the defending of children and the upholding of their innate rights. He didn't want her anywhere near his and Polly's lives. She must stop this rocking; her personality disorder had to remain where it belonged, under her pretty shoes, trampled on, ignored, squashed to death. And she should go home. It was late at night, and Mum might even send for the police if she continued to go missing on a regular basis.

The threatened blot on her copybook needed to be erased before it soaked in and set. He had to be removed in case he got the chance to spoil her career. Murder? Did he deserve to die because he had refused to bed her? The answer was probably yes. It was rather radical, though, and what if she got caught? Oh, her weary mind was going too fast. Shouldn't having Bob Laithwaite as an ally be enough? Not if Frank submitted a complaint in the morning, she thought. Her brain was moving in circles; this had to stop.

She must go home, take herself up to bed and sneak out again. Her thoughts were becoming even further out of control. There was a can of petrol in the boot for emergencies. This was an emergency. It was regrettable, but she must remove Frank from the scene. He hated her, had rejected her, and the only way of preventing further difficulties involved petrol, a funnel, some rag and a match. This was a foolish and dangerous way to think, her sensible side was saying. What else might she do?

Her loud, uninhibited self was screaming for her to commit murder. Sense must prevail. There had to be another way.

Christopher Foley heard the bell at his front door. His housekeeper was outside with Kaybee, so he hastened downstairs before finishing his morning prayers. It was ten minutes past eight, he'd been up in the night ministering to the sick, and he wasn't dressed. After fastening the belt on his dressing gown, he opened the door, looked straight ahead, and lowered his gaze until it fell on a child. The child was Billy Blunt, and Billy needed to be at school by nine o'clock. 'Is this you leaving St Anthony's and transferring to us?' he asked. 'Because this school's not as convenient for you. Are you in trouble at all?'

'No, Father. What's a bothy?'

'A what?'

'A bothy. That's where he keeps all the newspapers with his photos in. He has a big suitcase thing hidden under planks of wood and stuff. In a bothy.'

'I think it's a Scottish word for a shed or a derelict cottage on a farm. Away inside with you before we both freeze to death. This is what my poor old mammy used to call pneumonia weather.'

Inside the house, Chris's housekeeper had just returned to light the fire. 'Thank you, Mona. Toast and tea for two, please. Where's Kaybee?'

'In the kitchen eating her breakfast.' Mona went off to do her bit of catering.

'Get near the fire,' Chris ordered. 'Shiver the winter out of yourself.'

Billy was staring at the priest. He was just an ordinary bloke like Dad, striped pyjamas under a brown dressing gown, slippers at one end, stuck-up hair at the other. 'You don't look like a priest. You look like an ordinary bloke.'

Chris smiled. Some of the cheek was coming back. 'Nor should I look like a priest, child. I dress up for God, not for my own amusement, and certainly not for a young visitor. Now, give me a minute, so.' He went to the bookshelves and flicked through the pages of a large volume. 'Scottish. It's a worn-out building on a farm. It's left so that any person may use it for shelter in times of need, like in a blizzard. So where did you hear it?'

'In a dream.'

'Ah.'

'He's not happy any more, Father. It's because he knows that everybody knows he isn't dead. She said the word bothy. Her name's ... I might remember it in a minute.'

'She?'

Billy nodded. 'Her name sounds like ... like happy.'

'Does it?'

'Yes, but it rhymes with bad.' He smiled broadly. 'Glad. He's storing farm things for her in the bothy, and that's where he keeps the box with newspapers in. He doesn't look like he used to look. He's stronger and not fat, and he's keeping bits from papers, bits about him not being dead.'

'And you've no idea where he is? Might it be up in Scotland?'

'She doesn't talk Scottish.'

'How does she talk?'

'Through her mouth, same as everybody else. Sorry, Father. She talks a bit Woolly, but not real Woolly. It's a quiet voice. She seems to be a gentle sort of person.'

'Not a Lancashire accent, then?'

Billy was a wise young man. 'You see, they can be anywhere. I mean look round here – we've Scousers, Chinese, Scottish, Irish, Italians. We've Polish people, too, and Jews who got here in the war – they talk like Germans.'

'Can you see the farm in your head?'

Billy was thinking hard.

'Can you see the farm, son?'

'Not really. I try, but it all goes away. Dreams do that. I usually remember just the talking. I'm sorry, only it's just him I see, and her if she's near him. She's nice. He's nice now, says his bedtime prayers, pushes an old man in a wheelchair and reads him stories. Don, he's called – I mean Father Brennan, not the old man. He should have been a farmer, you see. If he'd not been a priest, he would have been all right.'

Mona came in. 'There you are, Father. There you are, Billy. Wash your hands when you've finished, because you don't want jam on your school books, do you?'

Kaybee rushed in, knocked over the small breakfast table, grabbed toast and ran off with it.

Chris threw up his arms. 'Oh, my goodness. Animals have no commandments to break, Billy. That's why they're perfect. We can't be perfect, because we know right from wrong.' He was laughing. 'Do you ever wish you were a dog, Billy?'

'They don't live long. Anyway, my dad blames Moses, says he shouldn't have wandered off up mountains looking for stones with writing on.'

Chris dried his eyes. 'Oh, God, I love Liverpool,' he said.

Mona came back after chasing the dog. 'Father,' she said sternly, 'she's getting worse. I can't catch her. The devil himself couldn't catch her, I swear. And you'll need a new rug, because that one will never come clean.' She left in a darkening mood.

'We'd better clear up,' Chris said. 'Mona can be mortallious troublesome when she's riled.'

'I'll be late for school if I help you, Father.'

'Then I'll take you. A biretta's better than a letter from home.'

'Sounds like a poem.' Billy righted the table.

Chris scrubbed at jam with his handkerchief. Neither rug nor hanky emerged in a good state after his effort.

They tidied up as best they could, and Chris went upstairs to dress himself. It was a strange business, yet he had every faith in Billy Blunt's dreams. Eugene Brennan would be found.

They walked together towards St Anthony's. Chris

decided to catch Billy when he wasn't concentrating. 'Does the farm have a name?' he asked casually.

'Sounds like Rovers,' was the child's quick reply.

So a Don was living with a Glad in a place that sounded like Rovers. An old man lived in the same place. It was time to talk to the police again.

After hiding his van in an alley, Frank opened the door to Aladdin's Cave. Just one letter lay on the mat with *By Hand* inscribed in perfect copperplate on the envelope. He picked it up. It was from her. He didn't need to open it to know it came from Elaine Lewis, since he'd seen her signature often enough on correspondence connected to the purchase of the business.

Wondering briefly about poisons that might be absorbed through the skin, he carried the letter to the counter and opened it. She was sorry. She was ashamed. She was guilty of trying too hard. She accepted that his heart belonged elsewhere. She had behaved unprofessionally and immaturely, probably because she'd never imagined herself in love before. She begged him not to harm her career. She further implored him to write his account pertaining to the Billy Blunt case and send it to her. She remained sincerely, Elaine Lewis.

He picked up the phone. The instrument he had ordered weeks ago was working at last. An operator asked for a number. He got through to the firm's switchboard, then to Miss Lewis. 'It's Frank Charleson. I read your letter, and don't worry, I'm not going to spoil your life as long as you stay the hell out of mine. I shall write to you about what happened when I punched the fat priest.'

'Thank you. I just want to—'

Frank ended the call, and found himself shivering. Just a few syllables had fallen from her lovely lips down the wires and into his ear. But he knew her; by God, he knew her. The locks had been changed, so the key she had to this place had been rendered useless.

Women killed. They usually left their victims to die alone and choking on poison or in fumes created by fire, but they were capable. She was fit for just about anything, because she wasn't right, wasn't in one piece. It was almost as if that wonderful brain had a core solid enough to concentrate, pass exams and do her job, while outer layers had fragmented to the point where she was unable to control her emotions. She could kill. The neighbour needed to come and go quickly two or three times, or he might be ... Oh, God. Frank stopped shivering and got on with his day.

He had hung up on her. She'd had a really bad day yesterday, and had finished up so tired and muddled that the thought of murder had appealed, but oh no, she'd sat up for hours composing that wretched letter. On top of all that, someone was watching her. Her instinct for self-protection was always on guard, and she was definitely being followed. The pores on her arms and the back of her neck opened when she drove or walked through town. Why? Who?

Bob had to be dealt with now. To get his hands on her, he would doubtless sell his soul if necessary. She wandered down to his office and posed in the doorway. 'I've come to leave a deposit,' she said. 'If you're interested, that is.'

He blinked stupidly. 'What?'

'Stand up, idiot!' She closed the door. 'Come here.'

It hit her like a ton of badly stacked bricks tumbling from a lorry. When he touched her, she trembled. His hungry kisses took away her breath, and he had to support her, since her legs turned to jelly. If it was like this with Bob, how might it have been with . . . with the other one? Frank.

'Little minx,' he whispered between kisses.

She could do this. She could do anything at all if she put her mind to it. Yet this was not really connected to her mind. Relatively late in the day, she was discovering something about herself. Her body needed this. 'I'm a virgin,' she told him.

'Then it's time you got help.' His hands began to travel. 'We can't do this here, Elaine.'

'Then you must book a room for Mr and Mrs Whoever. I'll see you after work.' With enormous difficulty, she summoned up the strength to return to her own office. She had just learned something, and she didn't know whether it was good or bad. It seemed that she needed sex, and just about any donor would do. Interesting. At lunchtime, she would buy something exciting to wear. Frank Charleson could have his little lard-soaked caterer. Elaine Lewis was going to inherit a law firm by marrying the nephew. Well, she might just do that. On the other hand, there could be someone else just round the corner . . .

Richard Pearson placed a large brown envelope in Christine Lewis's hands. 'It's all in there,' he said, 'photographs included.'

Norma Charleson stared hard at her housekeeper. The poor woman was clearly on the verge of nervous collapse. 'So Elaine is behaving like somebody who isn't normal?' she asked.

'Well, yes, I suppose she is fixated, almost obsessed. But don't despair, because people do change, you know. I've caught many a man in a clinch with his extracurricular woman, and he's done an about turn, gone back to his family and stayed. Those who change partners are seldom happy. The problem for them is that when they ask their wives to take them back, it's too late. Elaine may just snap out of this pattern. Never give up hope, whatever the nature of the problem.'

'She's watching my son? Does he know?' Norma asked.

The man explained that Frank was currently living with Polly and Callum Kennedy, though he drove daily to his shop on Rice Lane. 'One of our girls had a cup of tea in Polly's Parlour. The main topic of conversation was Polly's wedding to Frank, though a lame man, presumed to be Callum, came through from the back and said something about the wicked lawyer getting to Frank first. Polly laughed and said Elaine was crazy.' He paused. 'I'm sorry, Mrs Lewis, but we write down anything that seems relevant.'

Christine, after placing the envelope on a side table, curled her hands over the arms of her chair. Elaine was a proud girl. She would hate it if she thought people were discussing her. 'My daughter's very clever,' she managed to say. 'It's just that . . . she changed when her daddy died. She carried on working at school, did very well, but she stopped completely when it came to enjoying herself. It was as if she had something to prove, and she's still working at it.'

Mr Pearson smiled reassuringly. 'She's probably having a late teenage. Perhaps she kept herself strong when her father died and missed out on the freedom years. They get crushes on people.'

'She didn't.'

'No, that's what I'm trying to say. She postponed her teenage. If she were fifteen, I'd take the way she's acting as part of the hormonal quagmire.'

This was a nice man, a good man. Christine liked him

straight away. He was one of the believable people who took his job seriously; if Elaine's behaviour had disturbed him, then Elaine's behaviour was abnormal or at least out of step with her chronological age. 'So she just sat there in her car?'

'For the most part, yes. But yesterday she went into the shop, and there were no other customers. After a few minutes, she emerged as white as a sheet. She seemed upset and angry.'

'Have you spoken to Frank?' Norma asked.

'Not in my brief, Mrs Charleson. Unless asked, I won't speak to anyone about the target. If I hear something, I'll make a note, but I have no time for private detectives who chatter here, there and everywhere.' He returned his attention to Christine. 'Your daughter has a good career and is extraordinarily clever and attractive. But she's obsessed where Mrs Charleson's son is concerned. As I said before, she's having her silly years relatively late.'

'She rocks, counts things and talks to herself,' Norma said. 'Christine and I act as confidantes for each other, so we have few secrets. But thanks for what you've done, Mr Pearson.'

He stood up. 'Richard. I'll leave you now. If you need me again, you know where I am. Stay here, I'll let myself out.'

Left alone, the two women stared blankly into the middle distance for a while. 'What must we do?' Norma asked finally.

'I'm going to Rice Lane,' was Christine's reply. 'Frank's a good soul, and he'll tell me the truth.'

'I'm coming with you.'

'And if he hits the roof?'

'I'll catch him on his way back down from the roof and batter him with my handbag.'

'Oh, Norma.'

'I know. I do know. It's a vale of tears. I'll get my coat.'

Christine, too shocked to feel much, found her own outerwear and handbag. It was too late to start worrying about involving poor Frank, too late for any kind of worry, because her plate was already full. Her perfect girl was not perfect, and Christine was focused on discovering the truth. There had to be help for Elaine, but would she accept help?

'Come on, then,' Norma called. 'Let's up and at 'em, Christine.'

They left for Rice Lane.

Neither of them could wait. Bob, having deliberately neglected to book a room earlier, marked himself and Elaine as having meetings in the city. He felt as if his ship had finally come in because she wanted him. Yet there was something not quite right about her . . .

Like most young men, he needed relief. If love arrived, it would be an accident, but he was prepared to take the risk. She was an ice princess with a volcanic core; the cold side of her, the one people saw on a daily basis, would prevent any repercussions in the workplace.

She was standing by his car. 'Where are we going?' she asked.

'To my house. We don't need a hotel, do we?'

'No, I expect not.'

He crossed the city, drove up Smithdown Road towards Woolton, and pulled into the driveway of a pleasant detached house named Cherry Hinton on the edge of the village. 'Here we are.'

'Very smart.' She got out of the car without waiting for him to open her door.

Bob smiled to himself. The little courtesies meant nothing to Elaine Lewis, because she considered herself the equal of any man. In fact, he rather suspected that she believed herself to be in a class of her own, above and beyond the rest of human mortals.

She liked the house. The furniture was good, the rooms spacious and airy, while even the gardens were attractive. The man clearly had an eye for the good life. 'Ten out of ten,' she said.

'I had help from my mother and a designer. Are you hungry?'

'Not for food.'

He led her upstairs. A sudden awkwardness hit him. She was out of context, she was in his house, and she now knew where he lived. Elaine Lewis had an agenda; she always had an agenda, since she seemed to do nothing purely for fun. 'My room's there,' he said when they reached the landing. 'The bathroom, should you need it, is through that door.' The warning bell continued to sound dully in his skull, but other senses, over which he had little control, overtook him. Why was he afraid? He had no idea.

She repaired to the bathroom and changed into the diaphanous item she had purchased earlier. Looking in the mirror, she saw a beautiful woman whose hair needed a quick tidy. So this was the big moment, then. She had read about it, and understood that women felt radically different after the first encounter. 'Don't dare to glow,' she advised her reflection. 'Do not go all happy and silly.'

When she entered his bedroom, he was naked under the sheets, and she stood in the doorway for a while just looking at him. He had a strong face, good teeth and a pleasant smile. 'Hello,' she said. She might pretend that he was Frank.

'Come here.'

She climbed into bed and they clung together. An experienced man, he had never before bedded a woman of

319

Elaine's calibre, so he was glad he had mastered the basics. Yes, she was a virgin, and no, she didn't weep. She screamed with joy, dug her nails into his flesh, wanted more and more and more than he could provide. For a first timer, she was bold, uninhibited and wild.

Bob was in good health, robust and eager. But three hours later, he had become comparable to a wrung-out dishcloth. 'It doesn't work that way, darling. A man needs a rest between bouts. We've already gone three longish rounds, and the referee's thrown the towel in twice. Look at me – I'm worn out.'

'I see.'

'Do you, though?'

'I suppose so. Women are more capable, then.'

'Some are. I'm sorry, but the male mechanism can't be altered.' She had definitely been inexperienced, so she'd told the truth in that area. 'Have you never been touched at all before? Honestly?'

'Honestly.'

'No kissing or fondling?'

'No. I was too busy collecting qualifications. My aim is to prove that this is no longer a man's world exclusively.' She kissed him. 'Don't you want to play any more? Shall we get the Monopoly or a pack of cards to pass the time until you recover?'

'Later. Let's go down and find something to eat. Did I tell you I'm an excellent cook?'

'No, you didn't. You go. I'll have tea and a plain biscuit.'

He left the room, dragging in his wake a dressing gown.

So. That was it, then, she told herself. She'd collected another problem because she wanted more. 'I'd need to keep two or three men, I suppose,' she said, plumping pillows so that she might sit up. Emotionally, she remained intact; physically, she'd had several experiences that might have blown her socks off, if she ever wore socks. It was

320

a good thing she'd waited, or she'd never have passed her driving test, let alone her degrees. Where was he?

Bob was sitting in a kitchen chair at the small breakfast table. He felt like an ailing stud horse that hadn't quite lived up to the mare's expectations. Elaine Lewis was lovely, exciting and bloody dangerous. 'I wakened a sleeping monster,' he mumbled. Perhaps it was because she was learning; he must have given her a good time, since she'd demanded two repeats. 'Or maybe it's part of her madness.'

He wasn't sure about why he'd labelled her slightly unhinged. It was probably down to facial expressions, or the lack of them. She was obsessive. Items on her desk were always in the same positions, no mess, not one quarter inch of misalignment. She visited the rest room at ten minutes past ten and at half past eleven unless telephone calls or visiting clients interrupted her routine. She ate each day at the same clean restaurant, kept spare stockings in a drawer in case she developed a ladder, scrubbed out her coffee cup and looked after her nails. During the afternoons, she went to the rest room at about three, circumstances permitting. Clothing and makeup were always perfect. It was as if she had stepped out of a painting, but had never managed to become three-dimensional. Multi-orgasmic? She went like an Arab filly in a flat race. So many similes and metaphors, because she wasn't real.

'Oh God,' he groaned, his head in his hands. Almost every man in the world imagined being with a nympho. But the one upstairs needed a bloke fitted with a jet engine and no brakes. What had he started? How might he rid himself of her? Would she slow down in time? He looked up. She was standing in the doorway wearing the wisp of a thing she'd bought for the occasion. He was an occasion, no more than that.

She tutted at him, stalked past and decided to make strong coffee. The man had no staying power; perhaps caffeine might wake him up. 'Are all men the same?' she asked. 'Do they fade away after a few minutes? Because if that's the case, I'll need stables where I can keep several.'

'You really are a cold, callous bitch, aren't you?'

Her hand stilled for a split second over the coffee pot. But she kept going, heaping in the grains until she thought the end product would be strong enough. 'I love my mother,' she replied truthfully.

'But you love yourself more, Elaine.'

She joined him at the table. 'I'm pragmatic, I suppose. And yes, guarding me has been a priority since Daddy died. My mother's a wonderful woman, but she doesn't have the strength he had. I look after her now. Whatever happens to me, wherever I go, she will be part of me. In a sense, the roles are reversed, since I am no longer a vulnerable child, while she weakens as she grows older.'

She poured the coffee into mugs while he found sugar and cream. He passed her the biscuit barrel and, for the first time, saw the child in her when she took off the lid. 'Gingerbread men!' she exclaimed. 'Mum and I used to make these.'

'I bake them for the children next door,' he said. 'Their mother's been ill, and their dad's a grand chap, so I make little cakes and so on for them.'

She liked that. It meant that he would look after her. 'May I have one?'

'Of course.' He watched while she bit off the head, almost feeling the pain on behalf of her little victim. She ate the head before breaking off the limbs and lining them up on the lid of the biscuit tin.

'The perfect crime,' she said. 'Evidence consumed.'

'Who did you just kill, Elaine?'

'A gingerbread man.'

'Really? Does he have a name?'

'No, don't be silly. Do you believe me capable of murder?'

He did consider it a possibility, though he offered no answer to her question. But he needed her to leave, as he didn't want her to sleep here tonight. 'When you've finished, get dressed and I'll take you back to your car.'

Unperturbed and without as much as the blink of an eye, she continued to consume her gingerbread. She had failed. This man would never want her again. She had to work with him, see him almost every weekday, yet he would never again stand at her desk waiting for crumbs of comfort. 'Would you like a leg?' she asked.

'No, thanks. I'll . . . I'll go and get dressed.'

Bob Laithwaite was not a nervous man. He had prepared briefs in defence of murderers, rapists and gangsters, and he'd never felt as chilled as this. But there was usually someone to hand during interview, a policeman or a guard who would come to his rescue if things turned nasty. Here, he was alone with a stunning woman and he felt strangely disturbed. Perhaps he was learning to recognize criminality, or perhaps his imagination was working overtime, but this woman scared seven shades of something out of him.

She was in the bathroom, probably dressing herself. He needed to get clean, to be rid of the slightest residue on his body, but he would have to wait until later. It was weird. The whole thing was absolutely incredible, as he had felt drawn to her like base metal being pulled by magnetism, yet all the while he had known that she was different. Oh yes, she was certainly that.

Again, she stood in the doorway.

'Elaine, why me?' he asked.

'Because you were there.'

'But you feel nothing.'

She shrugged lightly. 'I wouldn't say that.'

Bob fastened his shoelaces and stood up. 'I don't mean the physical. You, inside, whoever or whatever you are, you aren't human.'

'I'm a lioness,' she said.

'You're not normal. Now, go downstairs and wait for me. I'll drive you back to the city.'

The journey was made in silence. He felt affinity with women who sometimes described post-coital sensations as dirty, abused and cheap. The desire to scrub his whole body remained strong; he needed to be free of corruption. What was wrong with her? When would the cool facade crack, and when would she bring down the firm with her?

Elaine's cool facade papered over many cracks just below the surface. Frank hadn't wanted her, and this chap seemed distressed, disappointed, worn out and keen to be rid of her. The trouble with close encounters was that they were simply too close. There was no shelter, no clothing, no task behind which one might hide. At work, she dictated letters, answered the phone, saw clients, visited police stations and prisons. In a horizontal position and unclothed, a person was suddenly open to scrutiny.

Furthermore, Bob Laithwaite had woken something in her, and—

'Here we are,' he said.

'Thank you.' She left the car and walked to her own. She heard him revving and burning rubber in his haste to get away. This should not have happened. He was supposed to be totally in love, needful and lonely without her. He'd been her second choice, anyway, but where did she go from here? It seemed that no man would ever want her because she was perceived as strange. Was honesty strange? Was a strong sex drive strange?

Her body still tingled. She wanted more, but not with him. On top of all that, the idea of working alongside Bob was unbearable. Tomorrow, she would be ill; tonight, she would look more seriously at positions advertised across the city. Two men. Just two men, and both had become threats to her career. 'Never defecate on your own doorstep again, Elaine,' she whispered. She drove home. It was six o'clock, but Mum wasn't in, while no smell of cooking emerged from the kitchen. 'Curiouser and curiouser,' she said.

Then she picked up the paper and started to search in earnest for a new job. Mum would come home eventually, and Elaine had plenty to do in the meantime.

When Christine and Norma arrived at Aladdin's Cave, Frank was struggling with a Victorian tea table whose fold-down top would not stay up and act as a table, since its mechanism was broken. He also had a couple of customers who were browsing through sundry items retrieved from house clearances.

'Hello, Frank,' Norma said.

He froze, screwdriver in one hand, small tabletop in the other.

Christine walked across the floor and stood next to him. 'I need to talk to you about Elaine,' she whispered. 'And you'll find your mother somewhat changed.'

He glanced at his mother. She looked healthier, slimmer and happier.

Wonders never ceased, he decided. 'Would you two ladies care to wait upstairs, please? The shop closes in about an hour. Feel free to light the fire, and you'll find tea, coffee and biscuits in the kitchen.'

They climbed the stairs while Frank pondered Christine Lewis's words. She wanted to talk about Elaine. Why? And did she want the truth, the whole truth and nothing but, as was often said in courts? He decided to be completely honest, or Elaine's mother might get a worse shock later in life. By the same token, the girl could improve, though he nursed grave doubts in that area. It was something about her eyes, something about the way she spoke to people, as if she could not be bothered to imagine the effect her words might have on a recipient.

The two customers arrived with their spoils. Many young folk setting up home had begun to patronize the shop, because items like crockery and cutlery cost a lot less when purchased second-hand. Frank kept any silver locked away until someone enquired.

It was time to close the shop, time to face Christine and Mother. He locked the door, comforting himself with the knowledge that he would soon be back where he belonged, with Polly.

Thirteen

Frank, only too aware that he was literally scared of what was going to happen, drew himself to full height before ascending the stairs. He didn't know what to expect, yet he dreaded going up to the flat. Christine Lewis, for whom he had always held great respect, wanted some answers, though he could only guess at the questions. Usually a calm and controlled woman, she seemed very much out of sorts today. She was drawn, twitchy, and colourless.

He paused halfway up the flight. Living with her daughter for more than two decades had probably taken its toll, and he wasn't in the least way surprised by that concept. But he dreaded the inquisition. As usual, he would tell as near to the truth as he could manage without causing pain. How might he avoid hurting the poor woman in this situation? Oh, what a thankless task parenthood could be.

He looked over his shoulder and checked security, just as he always had since the night he'd found Elaine Lewis with her key in the lock. He hoped not to clap eyes on the woman for the rest of his life. The shop blinds were down, the door was bolted three times, but his mother awaited him in the flat. 'Let joy be unconfined,' he mumbled quietly. Oh well, it had to be done; Mother must be faced some time, and that time seemed to have arrived.

Norma Charleson disapproved of Polly just as

thoroughly as she'd disapproved of Ellen, so for Polly's sake he regretted having been found. But sooner or later he would have been discovered, as Liverpool was not the largest of cities, while advertising in local presses rendered him open to all comers. Never mind. He had better face the music, however discordant its harmonies. He flattened his hair, straightened his spine and entered the living quarters he had been forced to abandon because of sheer, naked fear of one young woman who was madder than the least sane of Lewis Carroll's characters.

His heart quickened as he placed a hand on the door-knob. They were talking quietly in the living room.

The pair sat together on the sofa, Mother's arm across Christine's shoulders. She appeared to care about some-body, then. Mrs Lewis seemed to have aged, while Mother looked decidedly younger and healthier.

He closed the door quietly. 'Sorry I was away so long, ladies. Those customers took a while to make up their minds.'

Norma looked up when her son entered the room. 'I made a pot of tea, Frank, but she won't eat anything, and God knows I've tried my best. She's been out of order for a while now, poor soul, since we started getting Elaine followed.' She patted Christine's hand.

'I see.' Frank placed himself in front of the fireplace. 'We all have to eat, you know. And you're quite slender enough, Mrs Lewis. Even your shadow will come out on strike if you don't take some food.'

Christine raised her head and smiled bravely at Frank. She'd missed him. He had two levels of humour, one dry, the other silly. He was a nice man, a good man, and she hoped that Elaine had not upset him too greatly. 'My daughter's gone strange, Frank. I feel as if I don't know her, and she barely talks to me.'

Strange? Stark raving crackers would have been nearer

the mark. 'Yes, she has been behaving oddly, Mrs Lewis. I wanted to talk to you, but was worried about causing any upset. She helped me with the legal details connected to the shop and the flat. But she wanted ... well ... she wanted more than money for services provided.'

'She wanted you,' Christine said, and the words were delivered not as a question. 'She's never had a boyfriend. At university, she put herself on one side, away from all the societies and college occasions. She missed out, because Oxford offers opportunities above and beyond degrees. There was a point where the sheer weight of work got to her, and she faltered slightly, but I thought we'd put all that behind us. What's she up to, Frank? I'm completely at a loss as to what to make of her.'

Both women gazed expectantly at their host.

He moved and sat in an armchair. There were no answers, yet he knew he must make an effort. 'She's looking for what she thinks she needs, Mrs Lewis. I don't doubt that she's a very clever woman, and I know she's beautiful, but she's no idea about real life and relationships. There's a gap in her makeup, as if she knows nothing about ordinary, day-to-day living. I'm sorry.'

'As am I,' Christine said. 'So she comes and waits outside every night?'

'Yes, she almost invariably arrives here,' he told her. 'She even had the key copied so that she might let herself in. The locks are changed and I keep the bolts on at the front. A neighbour comes in through the rear door every evening, closes curtains in the flat, lights a fire and so forth, but I tell him to look out for her and not to stay too long, so you're not the only one who's been having her watched. Because of Elaine, I can't even live in my own home. I stay with Polly and her brother when the shop's closed and after I've done my deliveries and collections.'

He paused for a moment. Could he say it? Should he? Oh, he must. 'Because for some reason I don't fully understand, your daughter frightens the living daylights out of me, Mrs Lewis. I've no idea what she's capable of, but I want her away from me and mine. She looked at Polly with disdain, then with sheer hatred. Polly is expecting our first child, and she must be kept safe.' He paused. 'And if Elaine tries to destroy me, she might hurt my neighbour instead, so I've had to make him aware of her obsessive behaviour. He will have warned other nearby residents, and gossip travels, but that can't be helped, because his bodily safety is more important than her reputation. Fortunately, I now have a phone installed, so we can summon emergency services if required.'

'You fear for your life?' Christine asked, her mouth remaining open after the question had left her lips.

Frank nodded. 'As I said before, she terrifies me. There's a special kind of coldness in your daughter. I regret having to say this, but for me, she's as hard and as chilled as the article that destroyed the *Titanic.*'

Norma blinked back some unexpected wetness; she was going to be a granny. 'Elaine sits in her car looking for you, Frank. We've been told about that by the detective whose people have been keeping an eye on her. And you think she could do something terrible?'

Frank had no idea, and he said so, because he might have been wrong. 'The fact is, we all have opinions and those opinions are not necessarily the truth. My truth and yours could be miles apart. We all make judgements that may often be wide of the mark.'

Christine nodded thoughtfully. 'When her dad died, something in my daughter died, too. She kept the grief inside, where it festered, no doubt.'

Without processing his thoughts, Frank simply reacted. 'Psychopaths are born, not made,' he said, wishing immediately that he could bite back the harsh statement. 'Again, just my opinion, but backed up by a little reading in the Picton Library.'

White-faced, Christine stared at him. 'What did you say?'

'I'm sorry. So sorry.'

'You think my daughter is—'

'Mrs Lewis, I'm no doctor; I'm just an ordinary bloke with a junk shop. All I know is she's different, absent, unable to connect at certain levels. That coldness of hers freezes my blood. But she does have control when it comes to her working life, so that's good. Yet at the same time, I'm afraid that one day she'll crack wide open and do something unspeakable. She's a mess, but it's not your fault. You're a good woman.'

Norma spoke up. 'You're frightening Christine, Frank. I didn't bring her here to make things worse for her. This woman's my only friend, son, because I've never been kind or gentle or generous like she is, but she's taught me more about life than ... than ...' She turned away from him. 'Christine, come on, let's get you home.'

'No, Norma. I've always valued Frank's opinion. He might not be an Oxford graduate, but he's a clever young man.' She dashed some saline from her cheeks. 'Frank, I don't know where to turn. What do we do next?'

'I wish I knew,' he said.

'So do I.' Christine wrung her hands.

Norma knew. 'We have to wait till it happens. Because no one would believe she's not normal until she does something or other. You read about stuff like this all the time in the papers, people who do things while their balance of mind's disturbed. For the most part, families and work colleagues had no idea that the person's mind was disturbed at all.'

'Nearly always suicides,' Christine mused aloud.

'She won't do that.' Frank went to make more tea. 'She'll look after herself at all costs, Mrs Lewis,' he said as he walked towards the door.

'Call me Christine. She is selfish. Correct in her way, but selfish.'

'Correct in that she remembers your birthday and buys groceries,' Norma said. 'That proves she does know the proper thing to do, so she's well aware of the difference between right and wrong. So it looks as if she falls down when it comes to relationships with people her own age. Perhaps she'll straighten herself out in time. People go through things. When Frank was born, I cried for about three months, didn't know where to put myself. It passed. He stopped having colic and I stopped the weeping.'

In the kitchen, Frank waited for the kettle to boil. The truth about Elaine was that she couldn't put herself in anyone else's shoes, was unable to sympathize with another person, to feel pity, to offer comfort, to give real affection. To a lesser degree, his mother had been like that. He warmed the pot.

According to the Bible, God had breathed life into the human animal. Elaine was one of the exceptions, and the fact remained that although she seemed cruel and thoughtless, it was possibly not her fault. She was rather like a telephone line with a break in it. But could she be mended? He pictured her sitting in a corner of some institution for the rest of her life; as bad as she was, surely she didn't deserve that? Yet everyone else needed to be safe. Oh God, was there ever a clear answer?

He returned with a fresh brew and some biscuits. 'Christine?'

She raised her head. 'Yes?'

'Running on fumes can harm your engine, so take a bit of fuel, please.'

'I can't. I'd be sick, sorry.'

He offered the plate to the other occupant of the sofa. 'Mother?'

'No thanks, Frank. I'm counting points to save my kidneys, apparently.'

'Good for you, Mother. Glad you got a grip on it at last.' She'd definitely lost many pounds and looked better for it.

'What can we do?' she asked her son yet again.

He explained that little could be achieved by seeing a doctor on Elaine's behalf, because doctors had to keep quiet about patients. 'You might register your concerns with him, but you can't make him treat her or talk to her about your worries. Talk to him, so that if anything does go amiss, he knows that you were anxious about her. Beyond that, I have no idea at all.'

'And when it's too late?' Norma asked.

'I know what you mean, Mother. But she's a law-abiding citizen who's also a successful solicitor, and her cleverness helps her to hide what's going on beneath the surface. The subsidence has started, and cracks have begun to appear, only she's broken no rules thus far. Until her foundations crumble completely, there's little to be done. It seems a pity that we can only hang on until she goes too far. If you try to reason with her, she won't even hear you.'

Christine agreed. 'She is deteriorating. I'm afraid, too. She looks right through me sometimes.'

Frank glanced at the clock, then at his watch. 'I must go shortly, or Polly will be anxious. She's having a hard time of it, morning sickness and permanent exhaustion. I just hope she's better for the wedding. It's an afternoon job, so fingers crossed ...'

'She'll improve,' Norma said. 'I couldn't keep a thing down for the first few months of pregnancy, but I learned after a lot of hit and miss that plain, semi-sweet biscuits settled my stomach. After that, I went mad for orange peel. I used to give the oranges to your dad or to neighbours' children, then sit there chewing on the peel. I knew a woman who liked apple dipped in malt vinegar. Pregnancy is weird. She'll stop the vomiting soon, so don't worry. Make sure she drinks plenty. Try her with some arrowroot biscuits.'

Frank frowned thoughtfully. Mother sounded almost normal and approachable. 'Will you come to my wedding?' he asked. 'You too, Christine, but not ... well, just you. I'll send invitations, of course.'

Norma's face lit up. 'I'll be there, Frank. Christine?'

'I hope so. But I seem to have a lot on my plate.'

'You do,' Norma agreed. 'She'll come if she can, Frank.'

'I understand.' He did. He understood better than most.

It was late, and evening was casting its thickening shadows, and there was no sign of her mother. Everything was going wrong, and the whole caboodle was beyond the reach of Elaine Lewis who, try as she might, was unable to control the world and its quirks. Mum, on the other hand, was organized and dependable to the point where she might be elected to supervise time zones right across the planet. So where was she? Predictability was one of Christine Lewis's many strong points.

Every evening, Elaine walked in from work to a welcome, a meal, and the kindest companion she had ever known. But Mum noticed things. Just lately, communication between the two women had become stilted, almost formal, because the younger one had been otherwise engaged, while the older had become ... What had Mum become? Quiet, worried, then almost part of the wallpaper. 'I've neglected the only person who cares about me. Right. I'd better go and find her, because I can't just sit here

334

going over and over what's happened, or I'll go mad. Men. Bloody men.'

There were no lights on at Brookside Cottage, but Elaine knocked and rang the bell anyway. So, wherever they'd gone, they were probably together. She walked round to the back of the house, but found no sign of occupation. What if— No. Mum knew absolutely nothing about the mess with Bob Laithwaite, so . . . so where? Mrs Charleson wasn't speaking to Frank, because he was going to marry the girl from the Scotland Road cafe, and— God, no.

She returned to her car. For a while now, she'd been followed. Not that she'd actually seen anyone, but her body had been on red alert, as if trying to tell her something. Frank? Had the two women and Frank got together? Would he run to his mummy for help because a nasty young woman had practically propositioned him? If that were the case, would her mother be involved? Where the hell were they?

As she drove towards Rice Lane, recent events played over and over in her head like a film at the cinema. First, Frank had dismissed her out of hand; second, a man who had worshipped her for months had consigned her to the waste basket, just another mistyped piece of work at the office. Now, her mother, always punctual to a fault, seemed to have altered the rhythm of life without leaving as much as a note of explanation.

After driving further along Rice Lane on this occasion, she parked and watched Aladdin's Cave. Her hands were shaking so badly that the car was rather less than parallel with the pavement's edge. Norma Charleson's vehicle stood outside her son's shop. The place was closed, but lights upstairs advertised the presence of a person or persons, and curtains were drawn. There was clearly a plot on. If her mother betrayed her by contributing to said plot, Elaine would have nowhere to turn. 'How can you do this to me, Mum? How can you help people to gang up against your only daughter? It isn't fair.'

The shop door opened. Norma and Mum stepped onto the pavement, Frank behind them as they walked to the car.

A white, searing hot fury cut its way through Elaine Lewis's body. It was a physical pain she remembered from years ago, when her father had died; she'd been angry with him for leaving her. Slowly, carefully, Elaine had placed her trust in Mum, and Mum had now turned on her. 'I'm an orphan,' she whispered. They had been talking about her. They'd had a meeting about her. They'd probably had her followed by a private detective . . .

Had they been there today, those followers? Had they pursued her and Lanky Laithwaite to his house in Woolton, and had they seen anything untoward?

This was betrayal on a huge scale.

Constable Peter Furness, off duty and in moleskin trousers with a sports jacket, was led into Father Christopher Foley's living room. 'They already think I'm mad because I'm a Woolly and don't talk like them. If I start clacking on about little Billy Blunt and his dreams, I'll finish up in cell three with a straitjacket. It's all right for you, Father. You don't have to go and make a fool of yourself. I'm the one who's being asked to act like a madman and send the whole station rolling about the floor in hysterics.'

'Oh, sit you down and be quiet, man. I'm a permanent fool; it's my greatest achievement so far.'

Peter sat. 'So the farm sounds like Rovers, she's Glad, could be Gladys, and he's Don. Staffordshire, Derbyshire, John o' Groats, back of the bus terminus in Burnley – where do we kick off? And who's the blooming referee for this stupid match? We can't get plain-clothes officers in on a kid's dreams, can we? We've no idea where the farm is, anyway.'

He took a measure of whisky from the priest.

'The child came here one morning, Peter, to ask me what was a bothy. Bothy is a Scottish word. Glad says she has a bothy, but Billy says she talks more like a Woolly than a Scot. It's possible that itinerant labourers named the place a bothy, but Billy didn't make it up, I'm sure.'

'And?' The policeman's eyebrows travelled up his forehead. 'Well?'

'Phone calls,' was Chris's reply.

'Whose phone?'

'Mine, for a start. We have to practise lying and pretending we've gained information in a more acceptable form. I'm reporting to you now the supposed fact that I took an anonymous phone call. A muffled voice told me that Eugene Brennan's thinner, living with a Gladys on a farm that sounded on the phone like Rovers, that he calls himself Don and keeps secrets in a locked box under piles of wood in a bothy.'

The policeman sighed and shook his head. 'Madness.'

'Then you and your fellow officers must make hundreds of calls till he's found.'

Peter took a sip of whisky. 'This is the first time I've been asked by a priest to break a commandment. Do you have a hit list while we're at it? I could knock off a few Protestants for you, blackmail some sinners, rob a bank.'

'Not just yet, thank you. Oh, and sarcasm doesn't suit you.'

'Neither does dark blue, but I'm forced to wear a uniform when on duty. Look. How come you believe the child?'

'Because miracles are not the exclusive property of people with haloes. 'Because he's seen things before,

337

always connected to Brennan who beat the daylights out of him. It's a gift. His grandmother had it.'

'Oh, for God's sake, Father—'

'It is, indeed, for God's sake. Father Brennan killed a monk after battering that poor child. We have to find him, so I've written down my statement about the phone call, and I know I can trust you to back me up.'

Pete drained his glass and stood up. 'I should have saved a drop so we could raise a glass and toast lying priests. I'm off. See you soon.'

'Wait a minute. Just listen to me. I was in my bed one night when there came a knock at the door. No one there. Just a shadow like a piece of fog beckoning me. So I got the oils and the stole and my little crucifix and followed this grey shape. I don't need to tell you any more, do I? Because I was needed that night by a man outside whose house the fog disappeared. But I'll never be a saint. Billy will never be a saint. Miracles happen. Messages get through. So take that lying message of mine and let it do its job. Behind the lie is a miracle, and don't forget that.'

'All right, Father.' Peter left the room, calling over his shoulder, 'I think we're both in the wrong jobs, Father Foley.'

Chris stayed where he was. If a policeman couldn't find a door he'd already used, there was no hope for anyone, was there?

Frank felt her presence before actually seeing her; an icy shiver crept the length of his spine. When the two women were installed in Norma's car, he bent down and spoke through the open passenger door. 'Don't turn round whatever you do. She's about fifty yards away on the other side of the road. Is the boot locked?'

Christine shook her head. 'No,' she whispered, shocked

and worried because the thought of her own daughter being in the vicinity made her feel physically ill. It wasn't right; she'd never felt like this before. Or had she?

'Right. I've an early Victorian sewing table inside the shop, so I'll carry it out and put it in the boot. Don't move or make a fuss. Don't cry, don't scream, breathe only if you must. Christine, you saw my advertisement in the papers, and you forced Mother to come with you because you wanted to make us speak to each other. Be calm. You've won a lovely octagonal table, anyway. The pedestal is hollow for the storage of knitting needles, and there are compartments under the hinged lid for all your other sewing requirements.'

When he had gone, Norma reached for her companion's hand. 'We're acting normally,' she said, shaking her own shoulders with pretend laughter. 'Where the hell are you going to put the sewing table in such a small cottage?'

'I'll find a corner for it, don't worry.'

'Are you afraid of her?'

Christine found no answer.

'Stay with me if you like. Pretend I'm ill.'

'Well enough to come shopping, though. Well enough to sit here shaking with laughter while she watches. No, we have to carry on as usual.'

Frank brought the small table and manipulated it into the boot. He returned to the passenger side. 'I think she's gone, but I won't look directly. Drive extra carefully because you may be shaky. Don't let her win. Don't let her rule you. If it gets too much, throw her out, and if she won't go, give the cottage back to the estate and I'll store your furniture while you sort yourself out. Off you go. Bye.'

Frank stood and waved till the car disappeared from view. Would Madam buy the story about a sweet, well-restored early Victorian sewing table? Probably not. Her instinct for self-preservation was well honed; Frank feared for both mothers. Yet he knew he couldn't follow the car, since that might prove to Elaine that she had been discussed.

He was powerless and angry with himself. If he'd sent the customers away and closed the shop, he could have seen Mother and Christine earlier, and Elaine would have been at work during that time. He would leave his car outside now, cut through a couple of streets and collect the van. Before setting off, he penned a note for Al, his neighbour. *She's been outside this afternoon. I suppose you noticed. Take care, because she's running out of patience. Custard creams in the barrel, digestives in the Jacob's tin, a bit of ham in the fridge if you fancy a sarnie. Frank.*

While double-checking locks he noticed the shadow of someone entering the open porch. The bell sounded. 'Who's there?' he called.

'Bob Laithwaite.'

'Who?'

'I work with Elaine Lewis. My name's Robert Laithwaite.'

Frank hesitated. Was this another of her tricks? And he needed to get back to Polly who, in spite of the apparently tough outer shell, was currently fragile underneath all the laughter and cheek. He drew back the bolts and opened the door. 'What do you want?' he asked.

'I need to talk to you about Elaine Lewis. May I come in?'

Frank stepped back. 'I can't stay; I have to get back to my fiancée, because she isn't very well.'

Bob placed his cards on the table both literally and metaphorically. 'That's my work number, and the other's my house phone. She's dangerous. I suspect that you've been on the receiving end of her attentions. I went through her files to find you. Have you been singled out for her special treatment?'

'Yes, I have. What about you, Mr Laithwaite?'

'Bob. I was foolish enough to bed her. Big mistake. On top of all her other little foibles, she seems to be a rampant nymphomaniac. There's something very wrong with the woman.' He eyed Frank up and down. 'We look similar, could be brothers. Anyway, to cut the opening paragraph short, my uncles are the senior partners in the firm, both bachelors who consider her to be the greatest discovery since the wheel. Nothing will persuade them to be rid of her. I don't know what to do. And I can scarcely put my finger on the truth, because it's just so hard to explain.'

'I know. She's not right, yet she's always correct. It's like trying to convince yourself and others that Michelangelo made a pig's ear of David. Look, Bob, I have to go and make sure Polly's all right. We're waiting for a phone to be installed so that I can talk to her without driving home, but there's a bit of a queue for phones. Come here for lunch tomorrow, one o'clock. We'll get privacy in the upstairs flat.'

'Thank you. I know you were her real target and that I was her second choice.' He opened the door. 'I'm a bit scared of her.'

Frank felt his shoulders sagging with relief. Someone else knew, and that someone else was a lawyer. 'See you tomorrow, Bob.' He repeated the ritual, snick down on the Yale, bottom, middle and top bolts shot home, all because of that bloody woman. And halfway up the mile, that stretch of Scotland Road owned for the most part by the Charlesons, the best girl in the world waited for him. He was late, and to hell with Elaine bloody Lewis. Polly mattered. While lights still blazed upstairs, he left his property by the rear door and walked towards his hidden van. What a life.

*

The cafe was closed, but full. Inured to the vagaries of Scotland Road residents, Frank parked his van in a disused stable and used his key to let himself in. Oh, no. Polly would have his guts for garters, because he'd forgotten a meeting of the Turnpike committee. In Polly's list of commandments, this was mortal sin. He smiled sheepishly before finding a chair near the door.

She was in charge, of course, standing at the front with her full teapot and her cheeky attitude. 'Did the wind change and blow you in the right direction, Frank? Glad you found time to be here before the end.'

'Sorry,' he mouthed, pleased to see Cal occupying an ordinary cafe chair. The committee had grown again, because ordinary members were too nosy to stay at home. Ah well, this was democracy.

'We've decided we can't do anything till next year,' Polly told him. 'I'm going nowhere till this baby's a few months old, and our Cal agrees about his and Linda's baby. You could all do it without us, I suppose, but the march started off as my idea, cos I was the only one who took the trouble to look at the history of this road. So we reckon October or November next year. Hattie?'

Hattie stood up. She'd canvassed one side of the road with all adjacent streets, while Ida had done the other side. 'Children will go to school halls for minding. Every teacher from every school has volunteered to look after kids. Each street has to elect two or three mums to cater for children too young for school.'

'And the old folk?' Polly asked.

'The same. They won't be neglected, you can bet your bottom dollar on that.'

Ida stood up. 'Can I say something?' she asked.

'Can we stop you?' was Hattie's reaction.

'Well, it's good news. Father Foley's been in touch with three firms that run charabanc trips. They'll need the date well in advance, but we'll have every coach and two drivers in each, because we're not stopping in London. This is the good bit – they'll do it for free and bring us home the same day. Well, I mean the same night, I suppose.'

'Thank goodness,' Polly said. 'That leaves us with money for food.'

'No need,' Jimmy Nuttall shouted. 'Those of us who sell food will cater and charge only cost. We don't want anybody losing out money-wise because of a march that shouldn't need to happen. And don't forget, we march on Liverpool after London. We'll need no food or transport for that.'

'Thank you,' Polly said. 'Now, all who have a business on or near Scotty, signs will be made for you. Each condemned business will identify itself in writing. Every street will have a sign, as will all churches and schools. Older children will carry those. We'll probably have priests with us, too, plus a few family members from Ireland and Scotland. Let's hope and pray that Father MacRae doesn't bring his bagpipes and drummer, because we want absolute silence. Let them think of us as louts, and let us teach them something.'

Hattie chimed in. 'As well as us not being louts, we're reminding them that they're liars and murderers. How many grannies and granddads will survive the clearances? How many have been told that new houses will be built here for them in time? The killing of Scotland Road was promised by the Home Office over thirty years ago, but we've no concrete proof. And concrete's what this bloody government needs; we should bury them in it.'

'Before they're dead?' Frank asked.

'Either way,' snapped Hattie.

Polly looked at the watch Frank had bought her. 'Any other business?' she asked.

And he simply couldn't do it. Frank had intended to bring up the subject of Elaine Lewis, but there stood Polly with a child in her womb, and Frank's throat was suddenly paralysed. He would need to tell individuals, and he would require a photograph of Elaine. Oh, that bloody woman! Why him? Why Bob Laithwaite, who'd seemed decent enough during their short encounter? Once again, Frank felt powerless. But he looked at his girl with her shining eyes and glowing skin, with her attitude and her cheeky little smile, and he felt emboldened. Together, they could overcome anything, please God.

The front window rattled. Frank rose to his feet and went to see who had dared to be later than he had. Pete Furness fell in, fingers curled round the collar of Billy Blunt's winter coat, which item was still attached to its owner. 'Mrs Blunt?' the constable called.

'I'm here.' Mavis folded her arms. 'Back to normal, is he?'

Pete fought for air. 'Tell you what, missus, this here lad can't half shift.' He puffed out his cheeks. 'I've put both our names down for next year's Derby, and neither of us will need a horse.' The accent continued to advertise his status as a son of inland Lancashire.

Billy's mother stood up. 'What the hell's he been up to this time?'

'Jumping buses,' was the reply. 'Jumping on while they're moving, jumping off while they're moving. There's a gang of these daft kids. I know how Chicago felt during prohibition, because we need eyes in the backs of our heads. The conductors are sick to their wisdom teeth, and the drivers daren't get any speed up in case a jumper dies. Everybody on board will be late home, dinner dried up, wife as mad as a cat shut in the dustbin with next door's poodle.' He released the young offender. 'One more time, Billy, and you're down the station for a caution.'

Billy, wearing a dark scowl and clothes that needed readjustment due to rough handling, tidied his outerwear. 'There's nothing else to do.'

Mavis bridled. She wasn't a big woman, but she bridled well. 'Constable Furness, there are other offences to be taken into consideration.'

'Oh?' Pete removed his helmet. 'Such as?'

'Fruit nicked from Paddy's Market, a new collar for Daniel the spaniel – don't know where the heck he got that–'

'Spending money I saved,' Billy shouted in eager self-defence.

'Shut up,' his mother ordered. 'Drinking his dad's beer, throwing stones at what's left of bombed houses, getting stuck in one of the cellars and needing folk to dig him out. Isn't that trespassing? And giving cheek, too. You've no idea of what we have to put up with.'

'Terrible,' Polly said, fighting a giggle.

Pete scratched his head. 'No wonder I'm losing hair, what with this daft hat and all the worry about bus jumpers and the like.' He winked at Mavis. Her dreadful child was on the mend, and that mattered more than any of the lad's crimes.

Frank followed Pete Furness out of the cafe and took him into the doorway of Hattie's shop. 'We have a problem,' he began. Without missing the slightest detail, he related the almost incredible story of Elaine Lewis. 'I don't know how far she'll go, Pete. There's another chap involved now, a workmate who got dangerously close to her. She's crazy enough to follow me here when she finds out I'm not living in the flat. People on Rice Lane are walking about with their eyes on stalks, worried about anything from broken windows to arson. She was there earlier, watching her mother and my mother in the shop. She won't like that. She'll think we've been talking about her.'

'Is she paranoid?'

'From what I've read, more narcissistic, thinks the sun shines out of her own belly button. I'll get you a photograph. See, few would believe me, because she's a brilliant lawyer, beautiful, well dressed, too bloody perfect to be true.' He paused. 'I fear for her mother. Her mother's always supported her, like most mothers do. If Elaine thinks Christine's stepped out of line ... People often hurt or kill those they love and trust most.'

'You shivered then, Frank.'

'Yes, so would you if she set her sights on you. It's a bit like hearing the purr of a big cat and waiting for it to change to a growl, then a lunge. She sees, she wants, she gets. What worries me is what happens when she doesn't get. Boiling anger? Retribution? Destruction?'

'Bloody hell, Frank. Can't you find a normal problem like pests leaping on and off buses? All I get from you is beaten kids, a murdering priest and a madwoman. And from your best mate, Billy Blunt's dreams.'

'I know. It's a hard life, eh?'

'It is. Get back to your lass. She's looking great.'

Frank nodded. 'Call in on her in the morning when she's heaving in the bathroom. She's very noisy with it.'

'She's lovely, Frank.'

'She is. I'll go and tell her you said so.'

Christine came to a halt in Norma's car, parking it as close as possible to the house. Elaine's car was already here. For a few seconds, Christine sat still and simply breathed. She had to become an actress, needed to carry on as if there was nothing bothering her, as if she'd been on an exciting journey of discovery with Norma Charleson. 'Come on,' she urged herself. Norma had wanted to accompany her on the last short lap of the journey from Rice

346

Lane, but, since that might have been judged by Elaine as unusual, Norma had been decanted at Brookside.

When a degree of equilibrium had been achieved, Christine forced herself to become an excited child. She left the car, dashed to the house and threw open the front door. 'Elaine?' she called. 'Elaine, come and look at my find.'

Several beats of time staggered by on weary feet. 'Elaine?'

'Coming.' The younger woman descended the stairs slowly. 'What?' she asked.

'I'll need help,' Christine gabbled. 'It's small, but solid.'

They walked to the boot of the car, and Elaine opened it. 'Isn't that a beautiful thing? It's what Victorian ladies bought when engaged to marry, a sewing chest. The pedestal's hollow for larger items, and there are lots of compartments under the lid for buttons, threads and so forth.'

'Nice inlay on the top,' Elaine managed. 'Where did you get it?'

'Ah, I'll tell you about that once we're inside. It was quite an adventure.'

When the sewing table had been placed in a corner away from all windows, they straightened themselves and looked at it. 'Better there,' Christine said. 'We don't want the wood bleached by sunlight.'

Elaine's eyes slid sideways towards her mother. 'Where were you? You're always here when I get home.'

Christine almost stumbled at this first fence. 'Darling, I have a life too, you know. You've been missing for many evenings and I've had to throw away good food twice. We're both free women.'

'Are we?'

'Yes, we are.' Christine sat down; her legs felt weak. 'Frank Charleson has opened a shop on Rice Lane – oh, but you know about it, don't you?'

347

'I did the conveyancing, yes.'

'Well, there was an advertisement in the local newspapers with a photograph of Frank in the doorway. He called the business Aladdin's Cave. Norma mustn't have seen the advert, or she would have said something. So I pretended we needed a small table for an empty corner, and managed to persuade Norma to come with me to look at the shop. She didn't know I was taking her to see Frank.' Lying didn't come easily, yet it had to be done. 'I got them back together, Elaine.'

'So that was your adventure?'

'Well, yes. Norma was up in arms about his engagement and stopped talking to him. As you and I already know, he stormed off and left home. It was beginning to look as if they'd never communicate again. We had a cup of tea in the upstairs flat, and they talked. She's going to the wedding.' Her beautiful daughter was not beautiful at present. That lovely face wore a creased, angry expression.

Elaine placed herself in the chair opposite her mother's. 'What did they talk about?'

'I didn't ask.'

'But you were there.'

Christine shrugged lightly. 'No idea apart from the awkward greeting at the start. I took my tea downstairs and rooted about till I found this little gem.'

'In the dark?'

'What?'

Elaine blinked rapidly. 'Er . . . I was there in my car. I'd been working on a will for a Rice Lane resident and was completing my notes. The lights were on upstairs, though not in the shop. Days are short in October.'

A quick answer was required. 'I was in the rear storeroom, Elaine. He keeps better pieces out of the public gaze, saves them for customers who want something special. When I went back upstairs, the two of them were chatting as if nothing had been wrong. So I'm very pleased about that and about my lovely table.'

Elaine announced her intention to cook a meal, left the room and began to peel vegetables. Mum was nervous. She'd been chattering away like a monkey striving to be freed from its cage. This had been one hell of a day. When questioned about the lighting in Frank's shop, Mum had blinked rapidly. Mum knew. She knew the will was a lie, knew that Elaine had embarrassed herself by throwing herself at Frank Charleson. 'I'm seeing Bob Laithwaite from work, Mum. We've kept it quiet because his uncles don't know yet,' she called.

'Isn't he a partner?' Christine asked.

'Junior, yes.' She wasn't seeing him. He, too, had rejected her. 'So that's where I've been in the evenings.'

'Right. Will you be bringing him home?'

'Early days. I'm looking for another position, because having a relationship with someone in the same firm can be awkward.'

'I suppose it might be, yes.'

Something in Mum's tone failed to ring true. Elaine set the vegetables to cook and placed two chops under a slow grill. Right. The decision made itself. 'There's a flat in town,' she called. 'It's above some offices on Hope Street. The sale fell through during conveyancing, something to do with a mortgage. I think I'll take a look at it and grab it if it's still available. Two bedrooms, bathroom, kitchen and a large living room. Time for me to set out on my own journey.'

She walked to the doorway, knife in her right hand. 'I need my own place, Mum. I hope you understand.'

Christine swallowed a lump in her throat. She mistook it for sadness until she realized very suddenly that it tasted of relief. Carefully, she answered, 'Well, I shall miss you.'

'I'll visit.'

'I hope you do, dear. And bring your young man.'

'If it works out, I shall do that, of course. It's just that I'm not sure yet. He's very keen, but I need to meet more people, don't I? Like the old saying goes, there are shoals of fish in the sea.'

The mother looked at the adult child, the perfect daughter. And she saw ice in the eyes, felt the chill on her own skin where Elaine's gaze rested. 'Don't worry about me. As long as I know you're well and happy, I'll be quite content.'

'Good.' She went to turn the chops. There was a hollow quality to her mother's voice, as if the woman had switched to automatic. Was she lying? 'Mum?'

'Yes?'

'Someone's been following me. In fact, I think more than one person's involved.' Once again, she stood in the doorway, but the knife had been replaced by a tea towel. 'Even though I'm working in litigation now, I'm scarcely dealing with society's underbelly, since I don't do criminal cases, so it won't be hit men. I wonder who would want to have me followed?'

Christine tutted. 'I don't like the idea of that. Who might it be? Does Mr Laithwaite want to find out whether you're being unfaithful?'

'I doubt it.'

Although her daughter's eyes seemed to be boring into her head, Christine maintained her poise as best she could. 'People look at you wherever you go, Elaine. You should be used to it by now. I've told you before to get a portfolio together. Fashion modelling pays well, and you'd have another string to your bow even if you played on it just occasionally.'

Deep in thought, the young woman returned to the kitchen. She should get out of Liverpool altogether, go to

London where life was bigger, where a person could do exactly as she pleased without being noticed. Yes, there were decisions to be made.

In theory, lunch was in the oven. In reality, Frank, very good with scrambled eggs, was trusting to luck. He had a book about it, so that should have helped. 1 tsp meant one teaspoonful, while 1 tbsp was one tablespoonful. Hpd was heaped, and level was a full word, at least, so he'd done his best with lamb (cubed, with fat removed), onions (chopped, though not too finely), carrots and potatoes (sliced thinly). Lancashire hotpot? He should have borrowed Cal.

It didn't smell too pleasant, but perhaps it would improve given time and a good following wind. Running up and down the stairs all morning hadn't helped, but customers came first. Had he put salt in twice? The gravy on which the potatoes tried to remain afloat seemed a bit lumpy. 'I'm a victim of my own success,' he grumbled, removing Polly's frilled and flowery apron from his person.

The shop was doing well. People came for miles to furnish their houses with decent second-hand stuff, since he sold everything from sofas to cruets, but the job left little time for cooking. When the shop was closed, he was often out delivering and collecting before going home to Polly. He worked seven days a week, so surely he could forgive himself for one failed hotpot?

Bob Laithwaite didn't say much. He stepped into the flat, sniffed the air and declared that the aroma was interesting. 'Different,' he announced, 'but definitely interesting. Is there a chippy nearby?'

Frank nodded. 'That's the end of my new career, I'd guess. I'm no Mrs Beeton with her household hints and separate twelve eggs. Separate them from what? Each other? Their mother?'

'Yolk from white,' Bob replied with mock seriousness.

'Bloody clever clogs bloody lawyers. Come on, then, chips it is.'

So chips it was. With half an hour to spare after their meal, they sat with coffee in front of a crackling fire.

'She's scarpered,' Bob said. 'Her mother phoned in this morning to say that Elaine had disappeared in the night with all her clothing. Terrible state, the poor woman was in. My uncles received a letter from Miss Lewis. Due to personal circumstances which she couldn't disclose without involving others, she has left the area and will send a post office address as soon as she is settled. She would be grateful for a reference. They're upset. She was good at the job.'

The two men were strangely comfortable together, almost as if they were related in some way. 'I'd prefer to know where she is,' Frank said.

'Same here. As long as her address isn't my bed. She's a rampant bloody nymphomaniac. And have you noticed her eyes?'

Frank nodded. 'Cold. Almost dead. It's like having a reptile in the room. She sucks the warmth out of all around her like a boa constrictor might. All that perfection stuff, never a hair out of place, not a crease in her skirt – unbelievable. My fiancée looks like a bag of pretty rags until noon, though she is pregnant. But Polly sets no store by fashion or neatness. She's real. Elaine's like something two-dimensional.'

Bob spluttered on a mouthful of coffee. 'There speaks a man who's never been used as a toy. Two-dimensional? Einstein's theory of relativity would have been seriously deformed if he'd had her to deal with. She treated me like some kind of wind-up doll or a wireless with the old battery needing a charge. If there'd been five of me, we'd all have been busy for about a week. Like servicing an express train, it was. I ran out of coal and steam.'

They started to laugh like a pair of schoolboys swapping lewd stories in a cloakroom after a game of football. But beneath their glee, a form of mild hysteria simmered. They didn't know where she was. A wild animal had escaped from a travelling circus, and no one knew where, when or whom it would strike. Frank wiped his eyes. 'Why are we laughing?'

'No idea.'

They hugged like brothers before Bob went back to law and Frank returned to the job of sanding down the legs of an ill-treated dining table. With a bit of varnish, it would be as good as new, and he would make three quid on it. Where was she? Where the hell was she?

1956

Fourteen

As wedding parties go, it was on the small and quiet side, though Brookside Cottage felt rather full by four o'clock in the afternoon. Caterers had set out their stall in the annexe, but the through living/dining room, although thirty-plus feet by fifteen, was packed with people. The two baby prams, together with Mrs Higgins's wheelchair, took up a great deal of space, as did the table layered in wedding gifts. People spilled into office and kitchen, while several sat outside in a warm August sun. The atmosphere was relaxed, and that suited bride and groom very well. It had been a happy day, and Norma Charleson was grateful, because this wonderful bride certainly deserved some joy.

The couple were pleased to be somewhat neglected, because they and their guests were so taken by two pretty, three-month-old baby girls. Both children had been born slightly prematurely in May; both had arrived noisy, healthy and sweet-natured for most of the time. In each, the Kennedy genes shone through, although Elizabeth Charleson was dark, while Catherine Kennedy was fair.

They looked like two stages in the development of a photograph, one positive, one negative, each perfect. Their features were a close match, yet the colouring-in and fine detail had been taken from different areas of the artist's palette. All who met the infants agreed that they were gorgeous beyond belief. Like most females of any age, Beth and Cathy revelled in the glow of praise. All they needed to do was lie back and coo, and everyone within their sphere became a sycophant. Life was good, and they were in full charge of it.

'They're cunning,' Linda had been heard to opine on such occasions.

'They're female,' was her husband's usual answer.

'Kennedys,' Frank often said, his head moving slowly from side to side in feigned resignation.

'Winners,' was always the last word from Polly. She was a strong believer in people power, especially when the people were female. Even Frank's mother had become an example of the strength of womanhood, since she had, of late, displayed marked symptoms of humanity.

Norma Charleson was head over heels in love with her granddaughter. Like many women, she entered her maternal phase on the birth of her son's child, but she took care not to lavish too many gifts. She had learned the hard way to think before she leapt, and she treated the cousins like sisters. Excellent babysitters, she and Christine often took care of one or both babies while their parents were elsewhere, and the new marriage would make no difference in that area. Oh, this was a truly wonderful day.

'Hello, Norma,' Christine mouthed across the room.

Richard waved and brandished a cake-cutting knife. He was waiting for the speeches to be delivered so that he and his wife might plunge the blade into the bottom tier of their cake.

Norma beamed. Christine looked stunning in a greyish blue suit with good accessories. Her new husband, Richard Pearson, was the private detective who had found out about Elaine's carryings-on. These two had fallen hopelessly in love. Both widowed, both settled in their solitude, they had been drawn together inexorably over recent months, and Christine had already moved into his house in Allerton at the other side of Liverpool, yet she would continue to work with Norma. The two women had grown close. Christine had taught Norma sensibility, while Norma had strengthened her housekeeper's backbone and helped her through her grief over Elaine.

Frank was here, of course. With him was a pleasant young man named Laithwaite who had worked alongside Christine's Elaine. A tall, slender woman stood by his side. Bob Laithwaite, like Frank, had broken his mother's rules, because the lovely creature next to him sold underwear and stockings in Lewis's. Norma smiled to herself. How silly were mothers? She included herself, of course. Ah, here came Polly with Hattie and Ida from Scotland Road. And chatting to the groom was that terrible priest, an adorable Irishman who divided his time between golf, God and poker. He was a character; the cottage was full of them. Norma was a fortunate woman, and she knew it.

Cal Kennedy walked well with the aid of one caliper and a stick, though his mother-in-law had left her legs at home. Yes, she could manage them with a pair of sticks, but not while drinking. Having made progress halfway down one bottle of champagne already, she had probably made the right decision by leaving the prostheses behind, since she was legless in more ways than one.

Oh, this was a happy house today. It needed to be filled by a family, and Norma had plans in that direction. She studied her son. Would he accept Brookside? She must speak to Polly. Polly managed him very well for the most part, while he seemed to enjoy pretending to be ruled by the bundle of mischief he had married.

Norma sipped champagne, careful to drink little, since alcohol was bad for a condition she was still learning to manage. She noticed that her son and Bob Laithwaite were quite similar in appearance, and might almost be mistaken for brothers. Norma liked Bob, but surprisingly, her favourite person apart from Baby Beth and Frank was the daughter-in-law whose provenance was a basic cafe on Scotland Road. Polly was amusing, kind-hearted, cheeky, direct and friendly. She was also an excellent wife and mother, bright, quite well read and very lovable. Frank had made an excellent choice after all.

Norma made her way to Father Foley's side. 'Any news?' she asked.

He knew what she meant. 'The wheels grind painfully slowly, Mrs Charleson. The official line is that the search continues, but the evidence isn't a lot to go on. I passed all the details along the line, and I'm sure Constable Furness did his best, but there's no idea of where to start – Brennan could be anywhere. Ah, excuse me a moment, because I must speak to your son. He's been on a winning streak recently, and I don't trust him.'

'Nor should you. He's a born poker face.'

She made her way across the room. There were people she didn't know, guests from the groom's side, but they seemed to appreciate the buffet, the champagne and the company. At last, she collared Polly. 'I'm moving out of Brookside,' she said without preamble, 'into a bungalow near your brother and Linda and her parents. You, Frank and the little one will perhaps like to live here. This is a house for more than one person. Christine will still look after me and Charleson Holdings, though she's more of a companion than a housekeeper these days. If you don't want the house, I shall let it to another family. It needs life; it wants children.'

'But what about—'

'You deal with him. This place is part of his legacy anyway, so what's the difference whether I'm dead or alive? Christine and I can help Linda's mother and father while Cal's on his cookery course. It all makes sense. Have a word with my son, please. Tell him it's what I want. He listens to you.'

'Are you joking or what, Ma? That son of yours is a law unto himself.'

Norma swallowed a giggle; Ma was an improvement on Moo. 'What?'

'He doesn't listen to me, so you're wrong there. Remember our wedding? I told him about forty-seven times to take the price off the bottoms of his shoes, but did he? No. And there he knelt with the stickers for all to see, a penny short of three quid in Freeman, Hardy and Willis's sale. He made a show of me. My husband listens to nobody, Ma. He's a pest.'

Norma chuckled. 'And Billy Blunt knelt on the floor to peel off the price tags, and the rings rolled off his cushion. Precious memories, Polly. Sometimes, the things that happen by accident, the occasions that go wrong, can be the happiest to remember. The tale will be told to your grandchildren. You married a man with a price on his feet rather than on his head. Legends arise from such mishaps.'

The younger woman took a sip of champagne. 'Tell you what, though. I'd love to live here, I would. Leave it with me. There's no rush, is there?'

'None at all. The bungalow's paid for, and I can move whenever I'm ready.' Norma glanced at the bride. 'Doesn't she look absolutely wonderful?'

'She does. Is she all right now? About Elaine, I mean.'

'Not till she finds the truth, Polly.'

'Is there truth where Elaine's concerned, though?'

'I worded that wrongly. I mean not until she knows the facts.'

'Still no word?'

'Not a syllable. Always so correct, always loved her mother, but she didn't send as much as a Christmas card to the woman who gave up everything for her. I nearly had to break Christine's arms to make her buy that bag and those shoes for the wedding, because her whole life's been about saving up for Elaine.'

'She left the day you both went to see Frank after the silence, didn't she?'

'She did indeed. And thank God for Richard, because he saved my best friend's life, Polly. He's poised to go ahead with the search, because he's sure Elaine will be based for most of the time in London, but Christine's hesitant. I sometimes think she prefers not to know.'

Polly glanced at the bride. She looked happy, yet there was a tiny speck of loneliness in her eyes. 'Bob Laithwaite says Elaine isn't practising in a law firm, wherever she is. They have lists, and she's on none of them, though she might have changed her name by marriage or deed poll. Or some big companies employ lawyers full time, so ...' She shrugged. 'God knows where she is.'

'It's a mess and no mistake,' Norma said. 'Now, you and I are going to break my diet. When they get on with cutting that cake, I'm having some, and you're getting it for me – just a small piece. Oh, will you tell Linda not to forget she's taking in a couple of skirts for me? Losing half a ton of weight's all very well, but it can be costly when it comes to clothing.'

Richard's older son, Alan, was the best man, while Frank, acting *in loco parentis*, had given away the bride. Their speeches were hilarious. Alan said he and Richard's daughter, Gillian, had been advertising their father in the newspapers for years. 'In the end, we were forced to pay in order to have him shifted from under our feet. Keep him away from paintbrushes and wallpaper, and don't let him cook or fix the car, because the man is a disaster. Christine, we wish you luck. Oh, and he snores.'

Frank wore his poker face. 'You may have noticed that

the bride is older than I am, and therein lies my interest, as I deal in old stuff, including some antiques.' The ensuing laughter was ignored by him. 'Oh, and she owes me money, but I shall not dwell on that until I twist her husband's arm later.

'I've kept Christine in cold storage for several months. Apart from a bit of touching up with varnish and the odd flick with a feather duster, she remains in her original condition, judged by Sotheby's to be a copy, not true Jacobean, just one of several made for Harrods in the early part of this century. The groom picked her out, left a deposit, and I now await settlement of the balance plus two tins of the aforementioned varnish.

'Richard, look after her. She may be a copy, but she's a gem that deserves a good, solid setting, which I'm sure you will provide. Christine, thank you for looking after my mother and me until I left to be with my glorious Polly, who gave me a lovely daughter. I wish you both well. Bridegroom, get your chequebook out, since I'll be collecting what's owed to me.'

'Quite the orator,' Norma whispered to her daughter-in-law when the applause subsided.

'He may need to be. He's been approached again about standing for the council.'

'Will he do it?'

Polly shrugged. 'No idea. He's in the Labour Party, because that's nearest to his beliefs. If we move here, I doubt he'll stand. This looks like solid Tory territory.'

'I suppose Labour would be his choice.' Norma, a staunch Conservative, kept further comment to herself. Remembering herself as she had been, alone, friendless and without her son, she was still learning to make room for people. Everyone had a selfish side; Elaine Lewis was proof that total selfishness was disastrous. 'How's the cafe doing?' she asked.

'Hilarious. I'll tell you when we've a week to spare.' Polly moved away to check on her daughter, who was due for a feed. 'Come on, pet, up we go.' She carried the child upstairs and into the room that had once been Frank's. As she breastfed Beth, a male voice travelled in from the landing. 'Who told you?' Ah, that was the bridegroom.

Polly listened carefully. She was lucky to have such good hearing, since the door was closed and this was a solid house.

'Chap from one of the Inns of Court in London.'

Polly moved to an ottoman nearer the door. Was the other speaker Bob Laithwaite?

'She's at the top of her game, so to speak, Richard. God alone knows what Christine would say. But there you are, she has been found. No need for you to contact your colleagues in London when Christine makes her decision. She lives in a court just off Kensington High Street, a mansion flat with many rooms, apparently. She won't be difficult to find.'

Yes, that was definitely Bob, Frank's friend.

He continued. 'Elaine was a damned good lawyer, a stickler for detail. All the chambers wanted her because she briefed so carefully. But she's well paid in her new career, lives in that huge flat with servants. So there you have it. When Christine's ready, she's in for a shock. I think she'll take it badly.'

'I'm sure she would, and I'd rather she didn't know. She deprived herself for the sake of that dratted girl.'

'Sorry, Richard. I suppose I've rather ruined your day, though you did tell me to keep an ear to the ground.'

They drifted away, leaving Polly with a guilty ear to the door. She wouldn't say a word. Ma was becoming a little too sensitive to be told half a tale. All Polly knew was that Elaine wasn't using her qualifications. If Bob wanted Frank to be told, he would do the telling himself. She addressed her curly-haired daughter. 'Just us then, babe. I know half a truth, and so do you. Unfortunately, we both know the same half. Bloody Elaine. Sorry. Shouldn't swear near you. Your dad is, of course, a different matter altogether.'

The door opened slightly. 'Polly? Are you in there, sweetheart?'

'Come in, Frank. We were just talking about you.'

'That's OK, because I'm your best subject.' He came in and closed the door. 'Now, don't get upset; we don't want your milk curdling, do we?'

She blinked. 'Eh? What are you on about now?'

'Elaine has landed.'

She blinked again. 'Elaine Lewis?'

'The very same. Have we any garlic flowers?'

'Oh my God.'

'I'm pretty sure God wouldn't want to be in the same room as her. She gets the local papers sent to wherever she's based in this country, so she saw the announcement and drove here this morning. She says there were traffic jams, hence she missed the wedding. Sent a card to Christine's cottage, but the place is empty, so Christine never received it. But the poor woman burst into tears of joy when she saw her girl entering the room. It was quite an entrance, too. She came, she saw, she conquered. Dressed like something from a Parisian fashion house. Very glamorous.'

'Oh my God,' she repeated before shifting the baby to the other breast. 'What's she wearing this time? Has she turned up dressed like the king's breakfast as usual?'

'Stunning. She's just started working as a model, but only for the better magazines, not the sort you and I might catch sight of in Ida's shop. When she walked in, Christine nearly fainted, and Richard had to hold her up. The silence was deafening. Elaine gave her mother a copy of her portfolio with all her European work in it, then tickets for Paris and the key to a flat she uses over there. Such drama. She outshone all of us, bride included. The whole thing has turned into a show with her as the only performer. Even her wedding gift is a celebration of herself, photos and permission to visit the place where she stays in Paris. Yes, it's all a look-at-me job. Typical.'

'Poor Christine.'

Frank smiled. 'She's over the moon. It seems she always advised Elaine to get a portfolio and do some modelling as long as she returns to law eventually. But, you know, I got the distinct feeling that very few of the guests were pleased to see Elaine. I'd go so far as to say they think Christine's better off without her daughter on the scene.'

Polly mulled over the conversation she had overheard. From the remembered tone of Bob Laithwaite's voice, there was more to Elaine than law and modelling. The half Polly had heard was not the juiciest part, but she would keep her mouth shut anyway. 'So all the girls are going to look like country bumpkins while she shines. She always makes me feel as if I need a bath.'

'You're lovely, and so is Linda. It's the difference between a living, breathing animal and a piece of glass-eyed taxidermy. And you both wear the glow of recent motherhood, so she can't hold a candle to either of you. God forbid that she should ever breed.'

'What's she wearing?'

'I think it's called ivory. A bit darker than white. It's shiny.'

'Satin?'

'Polly, I wouldn't know satin from synthetic, would I?'

'It'll be satin. Fancy wearing near-white to a wedding. It's all about her, isn't it? This beautiful house and the garden are her backdrop and she'll perform as the main attraction.'

'And that will always be the case, because it's the way she's made. In a sense, she can't help it, though I'm sure she knows the difference between right and wrong because of her intellect. We just have to be brave and keep smiling. I'll stay with you until you've finished feeding Moppet.'

'Her name's Elizabeth.'

'Yes, but she makes a lovely Moppet. You're in a bad mood now, aren't you?'

'Probably. The idea of having the lovely lunatic back isn't attractive. She'll only break Christine's heart all over again, and on the poor woman's wedding day, too.'

'She'll be gone by tomorrow, has to be in Milan by Wednesday. Don't worry about her – she's here to celebrate herself and show off how well she's doing. The look on my mother's face said it all; I'm just glad she has no gun, or Elaine Lewis might have been on the receiving end of half a dozen pellets. Come on, put your bosoms away and get downstairs. This has to be faced, my love.'

'I know.'

'Let's get it over with,' he suggested.

When they arrived on the ground floor, Elaine, with her mother and Richard, was posing for photographs in the rear garden. 'Good God,' Norma whispered to Polly, 'does she not tire of fashion shoots?'

'Hush, Mother,' Frank advised. 'We must do nothing to spoil the day for Christine and Richard.'

'No price on the instep of his shoes,' Polly said.

'You'll never let me forget that, will you?'

'No.'

'One mistake. I make one mistake, and you turn it into a pan of eternally bubbling scouse.'

'Here she comes,' Norma warned.

The vision arrived and placed herself in front of Frank. 'What a beautiful child,' she exclaimed. 'May I hold her?'

'No,' was Polly's terse reply. Little Beth would be the one in need of a wash if this terrible woman touched her.

After a second or two of embarrassment, Frank stepped into the breach. 'She's just been fed, and we don't want that dress ruined, do we, Elaine?' He walked her towards the wedding cake and placed her in a corner. 'Hurt Christine just once more, and I'll separate you from your breath, you evil bitch. Stay away from me, my wife and child, my mother, my brother-in-law, his wife and their baby. Stay away from Bob and his fiancée, because he's ready to wipe that false smile off your dead, unfeeling face. You are hated. Live with it.' He walked away, determination advertised in his stride.

Polly whispered to Norma, 'I know he's smiling, but he's just given her down the banks,' she said.

'Down the what, dear?'

'Sorry. It means he's given her a telling off. Look, she's counting to ten.'

'So she does feel things, then?'

'Only if they're about herself. The rest of us could lie down in front of a train, and she'd just send for a few mops and buckets and some men to clear the mess. She's here to celebrate herself, not her mother's wedding. Oh, Ma, I hope she never comes back for good.'

Elaine Lewis righted herself within seconds and returned to the garden. These bloody people. She'd driven all the way from London for her mother's wedding, had booked into an expensive hotel where she'd changed her clothes and where she would spend the night, and Frank bloody Charleson had insulted her. She looked for Mum. Mum was in the arms of her new husband. 'She's forgotten me already,' Elaine said under her breath.

But Bob Laithwaite hadn't forgotten. What the hell was he doing here, anyway? She approached him slowly.

'I'm a friend of Frank's,' he told her when she asked. 'We were both treated badly by you. You broke your mother's heart, never even bothered to let her know where you were. Be careful, by the way. Rumours from London's Inns of Court do travel northward. Just make sure that your partners have a lot to lose. But you've already thought of that, haven't you?'

He stepped back a pace, noticing that she seemed to have blanched slightly under the skilfully applied makeup. 'Judges and members of the Cabinet need to conceal their little peccadilloes. Don't worry, I won't say a word unless you cause any further damage up here. But be aware – one false move in this area of the country and I'll get the *News of the World* on to you. I know fashion modelling pays well, but I reckon the lions' share of your income is earned when you're on your back. Do we understand each other?'

'Perfectly.' She walked away and re-joined her mother. These people didn't matter; she could buy and sell them twice over any day of the week. Even so, she would be in no hurry to revisit Liverpool. Blackmail was a dangerous game, and she had no intention of courting its attention.

After the funeral of poor old Matt Mason, Don Hall saved Gladys a sad chore by devoting time to the sorting out of Matt's many effects. Good clothes and shoes went to the parish for distribution among the poor, the ancient mattress was burnt in the yard, while all paperwork was placed in a large biscuit tin with a picture of Buckingham Palace on its lid. Life insurance to the value of twenty thousand pounds was due, so Gladys would be comfortable for the rest of her life. Don was pleased about that.

God alone knew what would happen to him in the future, but he was relieved for the woman he loved.

Gladys was going through what she termed a 'gloom'. 'Glooms' happened after the death of a loved one and, according to Gladys, lasted for a minimum of six weeks. She was talking about bereavement, of course. 'Thanks for doing all the jobs for me, Don. I'll be hanging on to his books. Loved his leather-bound volumes, did Dad, Dickens most of all. We'll get a nice bookcase for them, I think. And all his cufflinks, keep them, and his *Book of Common Prayer*, also his photos.'

'Of course.'

'And his war medals, too.'

'I have them all, Glad. And I have the deeds to the farm. They're framed and under glass; he kept them beneath his bed. The place is called Kingsmead, isn't it? I'd no idea about that.'

'Yes, that's right. Kingsmead's its real name from hundreds of years ago.'

'Yet it's known as Drovers.'

She nodded. 'Wild boar got hunted in the woods for ages, and the kill was all piled up in the meadow. Kings or lords often led the hunt, then meadow was shortened to mead and stuck on the end after "King", because I suppose the king owned all the land in a way, especially when it came to hunting parties.'

'So why Drovers?'

'Well, when all the wild boar had been hunted, my ancestors allowed a path through the top of the meadow to be used by neighbouring farmers who drove herds to and from market. Drovers is the path, the farm was given the same name by locals, and it stuck. I doubt anyone could direct you to Kingsmead Farm, because that name's long forgotten. It's from the Middle Ages.' She gazed through a west-facing window. 'He loved sunset.'

'I know he did.'

'And Thackeray and Dickens.'

'Yes.'

'And the rides in his chair. He seemed to pick up no end every time you took him out. Fifty-four years, I had with my dad. There was nothing he couldn't do. When Jed Finlay got a burst appendix, Dad even ran the forge. Yes, he learned to shoe horses so that Jed would have a business to come back to. He made butter, bottled fruit, taught me to read and write, mended roofs, replaced windows, rebuilt barns. And he helped any other farmer who had trouble. Dad was one of nature's gentlemen. I don't remember my poor mother, but I shall miss him till the end of my life.'

'I know.'

She smiled at him. 'He loved you, too, said he was glad I'd got somebody decent and capable at last. And I know you loved him.'

'I did indeed. But look at it this way – he can have no more pain, so it's a blessed release in one sense.' He smiled and touched her face. 'Will you be all right just now for a short while? I've a catch loose on a chicken coop, and the bloody foxes are everywhere.'

'I'll be fine, love.'

Love. She often used that term of endearment. He went out into the evening sun and watched its rays as they disappeared to illuminate some other horizon. Don had loved Matt. The old man had been like a new father to him, full of praise and encouragement, always grateful for a walk outside, a chapter from Dickens, a drop of whiskey in his tea. 'You know now, don't you, Matt? You know what I am and what I did. No excuses. I was drunk when I hit the boy, and in full withdrawal when I killed the monk. I didn't take the pills, but that's a reason born of my stubborn ignorance. Your daughter will never be hurt by me. We miss you.'

He checked the coops. 'I'm sure one of those foxes carries a screwdriver,' he muttered. 'In fact, I bet the little devil has a full set of tools, saw included.' He actually liked foxes, but they were daft. A fox entered a coop, killed a chicken for supper, then, when the others started flapping and squawking, he killed them just to shut them up. No way could a fox carry twenty corpses, yet he never learned to stay cool. 'Keep quiet, girls,' Don said. 'In your case, it doesn't pay to advertise. Just concentrate on laying eggs, and no squawking.'

He sat on a barrel. Things had died down, nothing much in the newspapers since Eugene Brennan had been resurrected from the dead. Strangely, the silence frightened him. Stuff was going on beyond the limited reach of his senses, and he could only sit and wait. Yes, he was a different man, a healthier and happier man, but the fact remained that his fingerprints belonged to Father Eugene Brennan, whose marks had been left in the monastery and in St Columba's presbytery and church. The less he learned, the bigger the terror became. How would she react if or when they came for him?

Gladys. She was the best woman in the world, hardworking, dutiful, a good cook and not too demanding in the bedroom. He'd grown used to that business, but he wasn't a natural lover. She didn't seem to mind, though. The fact remained that he would have been adequate if he'd avoided ordination. Normal domesticity suited him. As for farming, it was his calling. How many sent for him rather than paying a vet? How many took his advice when it came to planning crops? 'I wasted my life, and all to please Mammy.'

Don Hall scarcely drank, while Eugene Brennan had always been a dipsomaniac. A bottle lasted over a week these days, yet he'd shifted one a day when at his lowest ebb. He wasn't yellow any longer, and the palms of his hands no longer glowed red like traffic lights on stop. Even his nose was paler. It was all down to Gladys, Matt and this beautiful part of Cheshire. He belonged.

But one urge dominated his psyche and his soul, and that was the need to confess. Guilt hung heavily on Catholic shoulders, as it was a weighty package placed there by teachers and priests when a child was still an infant. From the age of seven, Don had been aware of sin and its subdivisions. A venial sin might be eradicated by an Act of Contrition, but a mortal misdeed demanded a higher price, and he should pay it.

Yes, the hangman awaited him. The only person to whom he might confess was Gladys, and what would be the point of that? Unforgivable even by the ordained, he knew there was nothing Gladys could do to relieve him of the burden. He must continue to bear it alone.

He stood up. The coops were as secure as possible, while a grieving woman needed his support. She had to be cared for. The last words on Matt Mason's lips had been 'Take care of each other.' A man's dying wishes must be obeyed, and the taking care of Gladys was no onerous task. Don had to be strong for her sake until she recovered from bereavement.

He walked back towards the house and his daily dose of whiskey. She would have bottle and glass ready on a tray with his newspaper, and she might well have gone upstairs to run his bath. How much longer would he live the idyll? When would they come for him? Should he move on and save her from the grief? Many questions, but few answers.

As dusk fell, Elaine gave her mother a post office box number for mail. 'It's the only way,' she explained. 'I move about so much, so a friend picks up letters for me. If you mark the envelope urgent, she'll make sure I get the message as quickly as possible.'

'Are you leaving already?' Christine asked, her face displaying dismay.

'I must, darling. Have to be in Italy next week, and I've a million things to do, calls to make, appointments to keep. Be happy,' she ordered before turning to Richard Pearson, head of the Pearson Agency. 'Look after her, please.' He had probably been the chief of all the followers, and the smile she awarded him didn't touch her eyes.

'Of course I shall.'

Elaine had filled in the blanks. Another guest had told her that Richard Pearson was a private detective, and she still retained the memory of being watched and pursued. Christine had married the man who had shared with her a level of betrayal that was unforgivable. Bride and groom knew that Elaine had been obsessed with Frank Charleson. On top of that, her first bed partner was here with a very attractive woman. Everyone present probably knew the whole story. But far worse than that was the fact that Lanky Laithwaite was aware of her current lifestyle. If he knew, how many more here and in London held the truth? She couldn't stop, not yet, not until her bank balance became healthier. And there was the other thing – she needed sex like other people needed food. Being paid by the elite for her services added seasoning to the recipe.

She kissed her mother and, without awarding her stepfather a second glance, left the house in as slow and dignified a manner as she could manage. The urge to scream and rant bubbled inside her chest. She felt desperate almost to the point of no return, yet she managed not to explode. This was a feeling she'd experienced last year, when crazy thoughts about petrol and matches had skipped through her brain. She must remain calm, sensible and on the right side of her temper. But she also needed to be more careful in London.

What could Bob Laithwaite prove at the end of the day? That she entertained gentlemen with cocktails and dinner, that she enjoyed the company of intelligent conversationalists who might improve her chances when her modelling career was over and she returned to the law? Rumour? Did it have any real value?

A knuckle tapped on the windscreen.

She wound down her window. 'What now?' she asked. It was Bob Laithwaite, her second mistake, her first bedfellow. 'What?' she snapped.

'Four little words,' he said. '*News of the World*.'

Who would dare, she wondered. 'Really? I have no idea what you mean.' Would he go so far as to bring down members of the Cabinet, bigwig barristers, a judge or two? 'Keep guessing, idiot, because you couldn't be further from the truth if you tried. Yes, I entertain important people with their wives or husbands. Yes, my dinner parties are famous. Do you think I'd risk my own reputation and my own chances by walking on the wild side? When my looks fade and the modelling work peters out, I'll have the right contacts.'

He laughed. In a sense, the woman continued dangerously naive. 'Some of us who practise north of Watford do have influence, you know. And we aren't deaf.'

'I'm so pleased for you.'

'And I am warning you, Elaine.'

'Are you? And those you seek to destroy by your lies don't deserve such treatment. Feel free to talk to them and their families, since all are welcome visitors at my parties.'

Bob paused for a few seconds before replying. Perhaps she wasn't naive at all. Her dinner parties were likely to be great successes, because she was a perfectionist to the point of obsession, but what did her dinner parties hide? She had a great brain and was clever enough to work out that her body was worth money. The fashion designers of Europe paid her well, but men of real means probably paid more. She had made herself into a socialite, possibly with a male companion by her side, a stooge whose sole purpose would be to deflect rumour. But rumour had begun to seep northward and must be rife in the capital. 'How much does a high-class whore earn these days, Elaine?' It was fleeting, but he was almost sure that uncertainty visited her eyes until she blinked it away.

'Mum!' she called.

Bob stood back to allow Christine to take his place.

'Please visit us soon, Elaine,' Christine begged.

'I shall. But I must go now. Things to do, people to see. Enjoy Paris.' She drove away.

Christine spoke to Bob. 'Is she all right?' she asked.

'She's just as she was when she worked with me,' he replied truthfully.

Christine noted that the words had been chosen with care. Her daughter, successful in the world of modelling, a proven favourite in law, was not happy. Elaine seemed to have no capacity for happiness. 'Bob?'

'Yes?'

She breathed deeply. 'Did you have a relationship with her?'

'No,' was his immediate reply. 'I spent an afternoon with her at my house, but I couldn't . . . it seemed I didn't come up to scratch on her dance card. She's needful, very needful.'

'Oh? In what way?'

'In every way. She demands constant attention. That's just the way she is. Try not to worry about her. She looked beautiful today, didn't she?'

Christine nodded. 'All I want is for her to be happy.'

Bob just smiled. This good woman's wedding reception had already been disturbed by Elaine, and he wasn't going to make matters worse. 'She's having a great time, better than any debutante, always entertaining people, always travelling. I think she's as happy as she'll ever be, so stop worrying.'

'I'll do my best.'

When they returned to the house, the cabaret was under way. Mary Bartlett, the butcher's wife, had teamed up with Hattie and Ida, and all three were ruining 'Sisters'. Instead of the usual lyrics, they sang about their trades: 'When a certain gentleman arrived from Rome, all Ida had to offer was *Woman's Own*,' and later, 'Cauliflower, beans and ham on the bone.' It was tuneless, it didn't scan, and everyone loved it, especially those who had drunk more than a drop too much.

Linda's mother, drunk and happy, sang 'Danny Boy', which brought tears to many eyes. The tears were not born of emotion, though many of those present were sad to hear the murder of such a pretty song. Chris Foley rescued the situation by producing a harmonica and leading a sing-song.

Norma kept an eye on the bride. It seemed that the brief return of Elaine had not done much good, because Christine was quiet. 'If only she'd stayed away,' Norma whispered to her son.

'Snap,' he replied. 'My thoughts exactly.'

She decided not to leave the job to Polly. 'I've bought a bungalow. This house is now in your name, so do as you like with it. Polly would like to live here. She told me so.'

He grinned broadly. 'That's right, kick me in my weak spot, Mother.'

'Please live here, Frank.'

'We probably will, so don't start fretting. I'll have to let the flat.' He looked her up and down. 'You've improved in many ways, Mother. Thank you for the house. Polly will love the garden; so will Moppet when she gets mobile.' He shook his head. 'Imagine that. A mobile Moppet. When the screaming and nappies die out, the chasing around begins. I can't wait.'

'Oh, you'll be all right, son. Polly can manage just about anything, can't she?'

He blinked. Having suspected for some time that Mother approved of his wife, he was none the less surprised when she verbalized her opinion. 'She's capable. Keeps me in my place for a start.'

'You love her.'

'Always have, but she turned me down the first time I asked. And the second time, too. She finally married me for the *Beano*, the *Dandy* and a washing machine. I threw in a fridge, and made sure she was pregnant, so I had her cornered. It was damned hard work, believe me.'

Norma wasn't fooled. Polly's love for Frank was clear; it shone in her eyes every time she looked at him. 'You seem to have some sense after all,' she told him. 'Whilst I was obviously without any.'

'True, but you're getting there.' He looked round to make sure nobody was listening. 'What did you really think of Elaine?'

'The fashion model?' She shrugged. 'Something wrong with her. Christine deprived herself of all kinds just to get her through university.'

'I know. The ingratitude of children, eh, Mother?'

'It's more than ingratitude, Frank. She needs help.'

'Yes, she does.' He knew that only too well.

Chris Foley had seen enough coffins to last him until he needed one for himself. 'Whose bright and totally stupid idea was this?' he asked.

'Yours,' chorused Frank and Polly.

The priest mopped his brow. 'You should have had more sense than to listen to me. When did I last have an intelligent thought?'

Man and wife stared down at their paintbrushes. Polly scratched her head. 'Erm . . . Frank?'

'Give me a minute. I'm sick of this black paint. Er . . . he got the coaches to take us to London, had Kaybee neutered, decorated the kitchen after nearly burning it down. He must have had a bit of sense when he did those things.' They both paused to study the parish priest of St Columba's.

'I doubt he leaves the price on the bottom of his shoes,' Polly said.

'Do you want a black eye?' Frank raised his loaded paintbrush.

'Not today, thanks.'

'Or I could do you a red one if you'd rather.'

'Trying to give them up,' she said before turning on their ordained friend. 'You said it was multiple murder by the authorities. You said we had to have cardboard coffin lids, black on one side, white with red writing on the other. One for each street, one for each business, one for each church and school. You're on churches and schools, Frank's on businesses, and I'm on the streets.'

Chris shook his head sadly. 'Frank, you must get Polly off the streets. She's enough to do without selling her body for recreational purposes.'

Frank laughed. 'No, she's given it up, because they wanted change out of a ten-bob note. She wore out four pairs of shoes, but her mattress is still brand new, practically unused.'

Chris eyed the relatively new bride. 'Is she no good?'

Frank shook his head. 'She's rubbish. Except when she's with me.'

They all continued painting their miniature coffin lids. The London march was just weeks away, so Ida and Hattie were busy collecting signatures for the petition. Although their protest might have little or no effect, it was vital that parliamentarians understood that people had power.

'How's the cafe?' Chris asked.

'A riot,' Polly replied. 'Carla and her husband have moved in. Their surname's Cook, and customers were calling them Can't Cook, but Cal gave them some lessons. Hattie sometimes helps with breakfasts, so her shop doesn't open till ten o'clock, and Ida does dinners, because she has a lad who serves in the newsagent's. They've had the fire engines out once, but people kept going in for the entertainment value. At the start, everything was either raw or overdone, and the accidents continue, but it gives folk something to gossip about.'

Frank laughed. 'They'll keep going till the bulldozers arrive.'

'Did you hear about Jimmy Nuttall?' Chris asked.

'What about him?' Frank sat back on his heels. Painting in black was very depressing.

'He soled and heeled his boots with his first lot of bacon, said they lasted a lot longer than when the cobbler mended them. Oh, and he said the eggs were so hard-boiled, they'd have done as golf balls if they'd been a different shape.'

'Never mind the golf, Father Chris,' Polly advised. 'There's God and there's golf, and they both begin with G, but don't confuse them. Paint your lids.'

Chris painted his lids. Women these days were very bossy.

The lift attendant didn't think much of the newest tenant of Hogarth Court. She was a snob. Blissfully unaware of his own inverted snobbery, he scarcely looked at her whenever she encroached on his beautifully kept territory.

She settled herself on an upholstered bench, her feet resting on good Wilton carpet. Desmond was on duty today. He wore an interesting and rather regal uniform, and she approved of his existence, but he was too low down the pecking order to merit much attention. He closed the gates and pressed the button for her floor.

Desmond, used to lords, ladies, the high-born and the well educated, shared her unspoken opinion. She was merely middle class, which fact was displayed by her silence. Other residents spoke to him, allowed him to help with the carrying of shopping; they shared jokes and anecdotes, treated him like a human being. Members of the middle class were different. They looked over their shoulders at their ancestors, who were almost invariably working-class, and they feared a return to that status, so they gave themselves airs. Well, he knew what she was, and he had no intention of attempting to communicate with a beautiful slut.

He opened the gates and stood back while she lifted her suitcase and walked towards her own door. As ever, she moved gracefully, perfectly, every inch the catwalk clothes horse, the socialite, the beauty. But he knew what she was. He knew she had acquired a key to the back stairs, that it had been copied and that her 'customers' used it.

To keep things looking tidy, those same men brought their wives to supper or cocktail parties; on those occasions, they used the lift. He knew them, knew they were figures of importance. He also had friends in Fleet Street . . .

*

Alice and Mark awaited the arrival of Elaine. Mother and son, they worked for Miss Lewis and were well paid to guard her secrets. Alice was supposed to be the maid, while Mark played the part of fiancé to the owner of the establishment. Although his natural orientation lay in the area of other young men, he was happy to help Mum and Miss Lewis in their business.

Alice's real function was mostly secretarial. She kept the diary, lined up appointments, arranged bedroom equipment to suit each of Madam's clients, supervised cleaners and looked after her employer's many special garments. There were men who wanted chastisement, others who preferred a nurse or a schoolgirl, a few who needed straightforward and unadorned sex, a couple who required near-strangulation in order to be satisfied.

Alice admired her boss. She had a cool, pragmatic view of this area of her life, and was always ready to experiment, because she was one of the few who actually enjoyed the work. There were a dozen regular clients, all in dire need of absolute discretion, every one of them certain that they could trust Elaine and Alice. Mark, who lived elsewhere, was brought in for dinner parties, since he was a shield behind which Elaine could be concealed during such events. Fortunately, Alice was a good cook, so the social occasions were always successful.

Elaine came in.

'How was it?' Alice asked.

'Dim, small and boring. Hello, Mark. Get me a gin and tonic, large, no ice.' She dropped her suitcase and fell into an armchair. 'Still, I don't have to worry about my mother, do I? She's married a private detective, so she'll be well guarded.'

Alice nodded. 'The phone's been red hot. I told them to wait until the Milan show's over. Sir Naughty Boy was rather petulant.'

'Let them wait, Alice. They're so grateful when they finally get to see me. Am I packed for Milan?'

'Yes, indeed. Did your mother enjoy her day?'

Elaine took her drink from Mark. 'I think so. She was beautifully dressed, so it seems he can keep her in the manner to which I encouraged her to become accustomed. I made sure they didn't get this address. Can you imagine them turning up while I'm chasing Lord Whip-me through the flat? They'd have heart attacks, I'm sure.'

Alice chuckled. Even she retired to her own room when some of the clients were here. 'Did you give them the Paris key?'

'Yes. No one's in Paris for a month or so. My manager approved the arrangement. So.' She drained her glass. 'Hair, nails and facial Tuesday, rest day tomorrow. Must look my best.' She left and went into her bedroom.

Alice eyed her beloved son. 'We'll be all right,' she told him.

'Oh, will we?'

'Of course. She has as much to lose as anyone.'

'She could bring down a government,' he said.

'But she won't. She's a cool customer.'

Mark nodded. 'Needs no ice in her drinks because she's made of it.'

'Stop it. She pays our wages, so remember that. And don't tell any of your boyfriends about what goes on here unless you want to go back to a grubby bed-sitter while I serve my sentence in jail.'

'Don't worry, I'm not stupid. But I'm telling you now, Mother, she's sailing close to the wind. The comings and goings will be noticed.'

She nodded. 'Perhaps. But if I get wind of trouble, you and I will be two of the goings. I'm too old for prison. Off you trot now. Geoffrey will be waiting for you.'

He kissed his mother and carried Elaine's empty glass into the kitchen.

When her son had left the flat, Alice sat for a while, hands folded in her lap. She was almost sure that Desmond, who awarded Miss Lewis some strange looks, knew what was going on. He hated her. Should she mention that? Not yet. Alice's investment fund needed topping up, so she must take the risk. The Elaine Lewis Show had to go on; the main attraction enjoyed the work, anyway, liked dressing up, liked sex. Oh well. It took all sorts to make a world ...

Fifteen

'It's not just us, then.' Ida bit absent-mindedly into one of Hattie's apples. 'What?' she asked when the shopkeeper glared at her. 'Can you not afford a Cox's Pippin, then? It's coming to something if you can't let a friend have a bit of fruit.' She returned her ally's glare with compound interest. 'All right, all right, misery guts.'

Hattie folded her arms tightly. 'That's a top-layer show apple – I've polished it.' Like many traders, Hattie knew how to make her display of goods look attractive. 'If you were a kiddy, I'd be reporting you for shoplifting. Do I pinch magazines from your shop? Do I pay for me newspapers every week?'

'No and yes,' Ida replied. She rummaged in the pocket of her pinny and slapped a couple of pennies on the counter. 'And as I was saying, it's not just us on Scotland Road. They're threatening Egypt as well. There's been discussions and all that since Disraeli was in charge, but the French and our lot are going to start chucking some bloody big fireworks. It's in the papers all the time, something to do with a canal everybody wants to drive their boats through.'

Hattie nodded thoughtfully. 'Ships,' she said. 'It's a ship canal between two seas.' She pondered for a moment. 'Then there's all these White Russians,' she murmured. 'They're not even Russians; I think they're from Hungary.'

Ida emitted a long sigh. 'Poor buggers. It's Russia's fault, though. The Reds are messing about in somebody else's yard, then telling us, the French and the Israelis to leave that canal alone. I think Nasser sold it, so Egypt doesn't own it. Nobody likes Nasser, and some say our lads are looking to shift him while they're at it over the Suez Canal. The world's gone crackers.'

'Our Turnpike protest won't be noticed.' Hattie sighed. 'The government's more interested in money than people, anyway. Flaming Tories.'

Ida sat in the customers' chair. 'That's where you're wrong, queen. They're all the bloody same whatever the colour or cut of their cloth. They get corrupted. There's something soaked into all that fancy panelling and green leather down yonder, and it gets under their skin sooner or later like scarlet fever. It's the whips, too.'

'The whats?'

'Whips. A three-liner means you'll be dragged off your deathbed to vote. You go in at the start a free man trying to work for the folk who put you there, then you get whipped. Voting's up to you, but the big boys put pressure on.'

'With a whip?'

'A whip's just a bloke. Three lines is three lines marked under the order to attend. If you vote wrong, you're finished. It's just a different type of dictatorship.'

Hattie leaned on her counter. Ida was a great deal less daft than she usually appeared. 'Been reading again, love? And talking to our Pol?'

'No law against it as far as I know, Hat. I've got this library book at home called *Westminster, Mother of Democracy* – something like that. A Lord Somebody wrote it. It's opened my eyes, I can tell you that for no money. Democracy? They've no flaming idea. We'll be swept under the carpet like dead flies. See, we don't want them wasting lives and money over in Egypt, but we don't get a choice. Like I said, it's a bloody dictatorship hidden under a thick layer of ... oh, I don't know. Of pretending to be decent. Why should they take notice of Scotty Roaders?'

'Then why are we doing the march, Ida?'

'Because we can. Because there's no law stopping us. If we took farm animals with us, we could bring London to a full stop. As things stand, we'll be just another semi-wotsit on their bits of paper. Semi-colon,' she finished triumphantly.

They were silent for a few minutes, each contemplating the non-existence of real freedom. Ida, in revolutionary mode, was seething inwardly. She wondered whether the whole country could be persuaded not to vote at all at the next General Election. A nationwide strike would take some organizing, and some soft bastards would vote anyway. Hattie was pondering taxation levels. 'If we all refuse to pay tax,' she said eventually, 'they'd soon notice that.'

Ida nodded. 'Or if we refused to go out and vote ...'

'It won't happen,' they said simultaneously. They both grinned. After many years of near-sisterhood, each was attuned to the other.

'Polly's in today, so you don't need to be a waitress,' Hattie said. 'Mrs Moo's minding the baby.'

'They don't call her that any more.'

'I know. Polly's tamed her, got her trained. Mrs Lewis – I mean Mrs Pearson – had a lot to do with it, too. She thinks the world of our Pol now, does the old cow.' Hattie sighed. 'Still, I suppose it's just as well, because she baby-sits Beth for Polly.'

'It's all changing, isn't it, Hattie? There's a mood on round here these days, as if hope's dead. Little things like no hairdresser above the cafe, Carla plating up breakfasts and dinners, me having help in the shop so I can do the waitressing, you selling less stock, Polly and Frank living bloody miles away, Cal training to be Cordon Blue, Sergeant Stoneway retiring.' She lowered her head sadly. 'No matter what we do, it's over.'

Hattie shrugged. 'That can't be allowed to count, because we're going to London. Polly's worked hard at this plan.' She glanced at her watch. 'Come on, let's get our breakfast. God knows we've earned it. Politics is exhaustifying.'

Polly was radiant. The glow came from within, radiating outward to tint her face, brighten her eyes and make her dark curls shiny and bouncy. She'd imagined that things would be different after the arrival of a baby, but she'd been wrong. Frank continued affectionate, spoiling his wife to a point where she was sometimes embarrassed, because he wasn't afraid to show his devotion even when they had company.

And they often had company, since they loved entertaining friends, and the ex-Mrs Moo stayed with them a couple of nights each week. Norma Charleson doted on her granddaughter, though she usually remained in the granny flat until needed. However, she'd caught the pair of them canoodling on several occasions, and a sight that might once have infuriated her now made her smile. They were so right together, so deeply in love. And it showed in Polly even when she was away from Frank.

She was away from home this morning. Ida and Hattie arrived at Polly's Parlour. 'Look at her,' Ida whispered.

'I am looking at her, you soft girl. My word, she's happy. That's what a good marriage does.' Hattie's tone was tinged with sadness. She automatically raised a hand to her face, which had often sported bruising in the bad old days. 'She deserves him, Ida. And that lovely house and the baby. It's like watching a flower opening, isn't it?'

'Yes. A real English rose.'

The real English rose was currently demonstrating the sharp tips of her thorns. 'Jimmy, you asked for mushrooms. See, I've got it written down here.'

'That's not mushrooms; it's a number five.'

'Number five *is* mushrooms,' she enunciated slowly, as if addressing a deaf person or a young child. 'There's no time to write the full words. One's bacon, two's eggs fried, three's eggs scrambled, four's—'

'It's you what's scrambled, Pol,' Jimmy said, grinning broadly at her.

'Four's eggs boiled, five's mushrooms, six is black pud—'

'I'll have that instead.'

'You'll have the back of my hand, Nutter. And you'll be wearing your bloody breakfast if you don't behave yourself. You like mushrooms, anyway.'

He clicked his tongue at her and winked. 'You're lovely when your dander's up, Pol. I must try this more often. Thanks for the mushrooms and the floor show, babe. You should get one of them jukeboxes like they have in the milk bar, then you could show us how to bop.'

She bridled before flicking a tea towel at him. 'Entertainment's extra,' she snapped. 'Come next week, I'll be doing the seven veils dance, but yous will all be blindfolded and glued to the chairs.' She stopped, turned, then turned again. 'And number thirteen's weedkiller, so watch it.'

Jimmy scanned the whole room, a huge smile on his face. 'I feel sorry for Frank,' he announced before winking again.

The cafe door was flung inward. The subject of Jimmy Nuttall's sympathy stood on the step, his daughter in his arms. 'Here you are, Polly,' he called. 'You needed a joint for dinner, and there's plenty of meat on this one.' He passed the baby to Hattie. 'A bit of mint sauce, and she'll go down lovely with spuds and veg.'

Hattie cuddled the pretty bundle. 'He's right – she's very well upholstered.'

Frank stood back to allow his mother into the parlour. 'I've got the pram in the back of Frank's van,' Norma Charleson announced. 'Oh, he's lifting it out now. You can walk Beth about if you like, Hattie, or take her to your shop. I'll have a boiled egg, please, Polly. One slice of toast.' She sat down in the very basic cafe she had damned not too long ago and smiled at everyone.

'Coming up, Ma,' Polly replied. She swivelled on her heel and clouted Jimmy Nuttall again with her tea towel. 'Behave, or I'll set my Beth on you. She's got teeth now, you know, and I sharpen them for her.'

Frank returned after parking the pram outside the cafe. 'I'll pick you up in a couple of hours, Mother. Watch the pram; kids like the wheels for go-carts.' He winked at his wife. 'Next one had better be a boy. I'm out-bloody-numbered.'

'Oh, go away,' Norma scolded. 'You love being surrounded by women, and you know it. Shoo. Buzz off and build your empire; leave us to eat in peace, son.'

Ida stole Beth from her best friend and stood near the window to watch the pram.

Frank decided to go for the kill. 'Polly?'

'What? I'm busy, in case you haven't noticed.'

He blew her a kiss. 'I love you,' he shouted before running for his life.

The standing ovation brought more colour to Polly's cheeks. Three tens. Yes, she wanted three full English and a gun. 'I'll deal with him later,' she muttered to herself. OK, she needed to calm down and get three tens, and one four for her diabetic mother-in-law, plus just one slice of toast. She had to stop this blushing; she was a twenty-six-year-old mother, for goodness' sake.

The middle room, which had been Cal's, was now the living quarters of Carla, whose hair had been saved in the nick of time by Polly. Carla's husband, a Paddy's Market trader, also lived behind the cafe. He helped out when he could, but Carla was the mainstay, and she was improving daily. In Polly's opinion, this was just as well, or the whole neighbourhood might have gone down with food poisoning.

'All right, Carla?' Polly handed over the orders and watched Carla's modus operandi, which was unusual. Because of the lowered level of equipment, she used an office chair with wheels on. She scooted back and forth, always on the go, usually talking to herself while wearing a smile. For a few moments, Polly lingered in the doorway. This was her place, Cal's place. From the corner of one eye, she could almost see the hospital bed with a wheelchair parked to one side. Closing her eyes, she tried to imagine Scotland Road and its adjoining streets without buildings; no houses, no shops, no bustle. It was impossible.

She blinked and pulled herself up. The era was almost over. Cal was doing great. Currently waging war with flaky and choux pastry, he was studying under a pint-sized Parisian whose aim in life was to save England from ze blandness of feesh and cheeps. Cal did a wonderful imitation of Maître Henri. 'Fold eet, fold eet. Mon Dieu, zees is no a sheet for ze bed. Zees is art; we are eat avec ze eyes.'

'Carla?'

'What, love?'

'When it happens, when we're all gone, my Frank wants you to live over the shop down Rice Lane. No rent. You'll mind the shop while he's out, if you agree, and there'll be a wage. Leave Frank to do the plundering while you sell the spoils.'

Carla swung through a ninety-degree turn. 'Thanks, Pol.'

Polly swallowed a lump of anger and grief. 'We have to stick together, kid. It's only geography.'

'No. It's cold-blooded murder. They could build here, Pol.'

'I know.'

'But they won't, will they?'

'No. No, they won't, not for a good few years. It won't be a painless death, either, because the place will be destroyed a bit at a time.' And she was suddenly wrapped tightly in Carla's arms. 'Carla?'

'I'm scared, Polly. They can just hurt us like this even though we don't agree to it. Scotland Road's our home, three or four generations of history in it. I was born in Virgil Street, and so was my mam and her mam. There weren't enough chairs, so me and the other kids ate on the stairs. And we had so much fun with Uncle Jim and his accordion and our Eileen what sang like an angel—'

'And your dad, who sang like a dying horse.'

'And playing cards and dominoes. Remember hop-scotch and ball on the wall and long skipping?'

'I do.'

'Tig-tag and ollies, four glassies for one ball bearing?'

'Salt, pepper, mustard, vinegar on cellar steps,' Polly mused.

'Queenie-o, who's got the ball?'

'Yes. Carla?'

'What?'

'Your bacon's on fire.'

While Carla extinguished small flames, Polly sat for a few minutes in the middle room. She listened to the cook's colourful expletives, closed her eyes and thanked God for

Frank. He was naughty, happy and adorable. Ma Charleson had finally grown up, Beth was beautiful, and their home was spectacular. 'I'm one lucky woman,' she breathed. 'The luckiest. What about the rest of them, though?'

The orders arrived, and she carried them through. Ma would stay once her breakfast was finished. She would go through to the back of that greasy, basic cafe, would wash dishes, mop the floor and clean all surfaces so that Carla and Ida could have an hour's rest. There was good in everybody, though some mineshafts needed to be dug deep before a decent seam could be found.

When she'd finished doling out the meals, Polly started back to the middle room. Jimmy Nuttall blocked her way and planted a kiss on her cheek. Untypically docile, Polly returned the favour.

He blushed bright crimson. 'I should get double for that,' he shouted. 'The bet was I'd kiss her. Well, she kissed me back. Ten bob twice, I'm after.'

The owner of Polly's Parlour watched while Norma handed over a pound note. 'Well done,' she said. 'I thought she'd kill you.'

Polly's jaw dropped. 'Ma?'

'Yes, dear?'

'You're a terrible woman, as bad as the rest.'

Norma frowned. 'I always was,' she said. 'I just hid it well.'

Polly poured herself a much needed cup of tea. She couldn't beat them, so she joined them. And there wasn't a single mushroom left on Jimmy Nuttall's plate.

For Don Hall, the sun had ceased to rise. Whatever the weather, whatever the time of day, he lived in a permanent, bone-chilling darkness. It was the silence. It sat solid in his chest and his stomach like a lead weight, and nothing would shift it. Gladys had been fussing about with liver salts, vitamins and milk of magnesia, but no patented medicine offered a remedy for naked fear. He couldn't tell her, of course. Well, he had to tell her, but not in person. The clock was ticking, the calendar's pages turned, and he sensed that his time was almost up.

He stood near the hens he had nurtured and protected, spoke to them, had a word with pigs and goats. After gazing round at the land he had come to love, he set off on heavy legs to join Gladys for the last supper. There had been nothing in the newspapers, yet he knew that Drovers was, for him, situated in the still, quiet eye of a deadly storm; they were coming to arrest him. They would blow in at gale-force nine any day now, and the dreams were coming back again.

Gladys started on him the minute he stepped into the kitchen. 'You look terrible, love. You shouldn't be working, and I'm fetching the doctor no matter what you say.'

He held up his right hand in a policeman's *stop* signal. 'Tomorrow, Glad. You can get the doctor in the morning.' By then, it wouldn't matter; by then, it would be too late. He washed his hands at the kitchen sink, sat down and managed the soup. For a reason that eluded him, he ate most of his meal, including half a bowl of rice pudding. 'There you are,' he said. 'Stomach's picking up, so it is.' The condemned man had eaten heartily. She would miss him, and that thought hurt him as much as the idea of death.

'Thank God,' Gladys murmured. 'Because I don't know what I'd do without you. A godsend, that's what you are, Don.'

He blinked, then stared at her. She loved him. For the first time since Mammy, somebody loved him. That her love was almost unconditional was clear, yet how could it survive the knowledge that he'd half-killed a child and murdered a monk? He glanced at the mantel clock. 'I'm going to watch for foxes from the caravan,' he said, the tone almost too casual.

'You're not fooling me with your shotgun,' she replied, a smile stretched across her face. 'I've seen you feeding them, you daft lad.'

He felt the heat on his cheeks. 'Then they don't eat the chickens, do they? If I'm ever busy elsewhere, you feed them. They're hungry, that's all. I've one eating out of my hand, so.'

She stood, arms akimbo, in front of the kitchen fire. Round, short and rosy-cheeked, she looked beautiful. 'I'll let you out, then,' she announced, 'but only because you seem a bit better than you were. Who am I to stand between a man and his best friend, the chicken killer?'

Don walked to her and kissed her grey-streaked hair. '*Benedicta tu in mulieribus*,' he whispered.

'What?'

'Ah, just a bit of Gaelic nonsense,' he offered as translation of a sentence from the Ave.

'What does it mean?' she asked.

'Blessed art thou among women.' He meant every syllable of it. 'I'll go now. Get yourself off to bed, and don't worry about me or the foxes.' He left the house, pausing only to watch through the window as Gladys cleared the table. The strange calm accompanied him while he walked away. It had to be done. It was a sin, but who was counting? He'd already won a place by Lucifer's fire, so why worry about the final act?

The night was clear and cold, with a thousand stars shining down on him. There was a chance that those faraway suns shone on worlds like this one, so had Christ died on each and every one of those possible planets? Where did God fit in with endless space, endless time, and myriad Earths to save? Did it matter? 'I'll know soon enough,' he muttered.

In the bothy, he collected up all the old newspaper cuttings and photographs, packing them neatly into an attaché case. The world needed to know. These articles, together with the letter he'd composed for his beloved, would be found with his corpse. The idea of killing himself on Drovers land had been dismissed from his agenda, because she must not be the one to find him. Police would take the letter, but Gladys would receive it eventually. The strange serenity persisted. Even while he left food for Reynard and his family, nothing disturbed his mood. He would never again see his fox; he didn't deserve any happiness, so he was on his way out.

Back in the bothy, he picked up the implements he required before beginning the trek to common land. Half an hour later, he was where he needed to be, and he set out his altar and stripped off most of his clothing. Before facing St Peter, he needed to do penance in the vain hope of achieving repeal and Purgatory rather than hell. The whip he had made owned nine tails, and each tail had a sharpened hook affixed to its end. This was positively mediaeval, yet it had to happen. A bucket of ashes waited on the floor, a small shovel by its side.

'*Confiteor Deo omnipotenti, et vobis fratres,*' he began.

In the distance, campanologists practised their skills in preparation for Sunday, and he paused partway through his confession. 'For whom do the bells toll?' he whispered. It was time.

The night Fred Blunt stole (though he preferred the word borrowed) a Liverpool Corporation double-decker bus would become legendary among Scotland Roaders and their descendants. Fred needed three people, and they were a bit spread out. He collected Father Foley, Cal Kennedy and Frank Charleson. When questioned, he just told them to shut up, because they'd see for themselves when they all got back to Billy. 'Let me concentrate,' he demanded. 'I had a couple of pints earlier on.'

The trio huddled together in a vehicle designed to transport at least fifty people. It was cold, it was midnight, and a half moon glistened in a clear sky that offered no cloud cover to earthlings. Fred was driving like a lunatic. However, the lunatic was experienced in the driving of buses, so passengers had to place their faith in him, since no other choice was on offer.

'I was reading the Marquis de Sade,' Chris grumbled.

'For a priest, you don't half choose your reading list well,' Frank told his best pal.

Chris sniffed. 'Keep your friends close, your enemies closer.'

'You're just a dirty old man, and that's the top and bottom of you.'

'This is true, so. I should maybe give up the cloth and find me a good woman.'

Cal grinned lewdly. 'Father, you'd do better with a bad one if you're reading sadism.'

The priest whispered under the engine's noise, 'What the blood and sand is going on with Fred and this bus? We haven't even paid our fare.'

His two companions shrugged. Cal was still wrapped up in flaky pastry, and he had an exam at nine in the morning. Frank worried about Polly worrying. She had Moppet to look after, but Mother was there, so she wasn't on her own. Even now, he could scarcely believe that Pol had taken him on ... But heck – what was happening here? Why wouldn't Fred speak? Polly would have made him talk. Frank grinned. His Pol could get blood out of a stone – or gravy out of a brick, if she needed it.

397

'Would you ever look at the cut of him?' Chris asked Cal. 'Well and truly captured, he is. Captured and captivated.'

'So he should be. She's my sister, and he's a lucky man.'

'Till she chases me,' Frank said.

'Well, you've habits.' Chris was laughing nervously as the giant vehicle swung into Dryden Street. 'Pawing and nuzzling at her while she's ironing. She'll clock you with hot metal one of these days, mark my words.'

'She won't,' Frank told him. 'She says my good looks save me, and I must continue ornamental. I think she'll get me framed soon, or glued to a pedestal. Being so handsome is a burden.'

The vehicle shuddered to a halt. 'Right.' The driver turned to look at his companions. 'He asked for you three, so I got you. Father Foley, you're a man he trusts – same goes for you, Cal.'

Chris pointed at Frank. 'Sensible so far, but why does he need my idiot friend here? Is there a cabaret?'

Frank clouted his best mate across the shoulders.

'Now he's after striking a priest.'

'Shut up,' Fred ordered. 'Sorry, Father, but it's all to do with that feathered thing with mirrors on it. Dreamcatcher. Billy says it came through the big hole, and it wasn't a bad dream. He said it was a bit like watching an old film, all jerky and a funny colour. Mavis ran and fetched Hattie, then our Billy asked for yous lot. We want witnesses, because if my lad's right, Brennan's dead.'

This statement put an end to all the nervous jocularity. 'Dear God,' Chris breathed. 'Right, lads. Let's get inside.'

Billy was playing with his cars on the floor. It was the middle of the night, and it was great being up and about; it made him feel older, important.

'He's not upset,' Mavis said quietly. 'But I want you to

listen to him, then look out for the news tomorrow. It looks like Father Brennan died about an hour ago.' She reached and grabbed Hattie Benson's hand. 'Thanks for sitting with me, Hat.'

Cal entered on crutches. 'Hiya, Billy.'

The child looked up. 'Where's your tin leg?'

'It's having a rest. Linda says I should change our surname to Lipper.'

'Why?'

'Cal Lipper. That's my tin leg. Caliper.'

'Oh.'

Chris positioned himself near the fire while Frank got down to Billy's level. 'That's a fine fire engine.'

'It all happened cos I bought it with money for Mam's birthday.'

Frank shook his head. 'No, son, none of it was your fault. If it hadn't been you, it would have been some other child. Father Brennan wasn't well in his head.'

Billy thought about that. 'Dad says he was always pissed.'

Mavis looked heavenward and heaved a sigh.

'Did he, now?' Frank grinned. 'So what's the story? Tell Father Foley, eh?'

Billy raised his head and smiled at the priest. Father Foley was just another bloke who wore striped pyjamas and a tea-stained dressing gown in the mornings. He was real, and he gave fewer Our Fathers and Hail Marys for penance, so St Columba's was always packed on Confession nights. 'I've got a house in Blackpool,' Billy said. 'It's mine, just mine. I can have holidays, and other people can stay in it and pay me. But I can't have any of the money till I'm twenty-one.'

Chris nodded. 'You'd only spend it on Dinky cars and the like, so that's the best way.' The settlement had been made swiftly and out of court, because the Blunts had

399

decided that their boy had been through enough. 'What did you see, Billy?'

The boy frowned. 'Oh yes. I had to wake Mam up in case I forgot. You sometimes forget dreams,' he said, his eyes sweeping over all of them. 'He's dead. Father Brennan, I mean. He told me he was sorry, then the light came and he melted.'

'Melted?'

'Yes, Father. Like a snowman, but dressed funny. There was a big whip with hooks on it and I saw a bucket and shovel. He was wearing one of the things what Mrs Benson gets her spuds in.'

Hattie spoke for the first time. 'A potato sack?'

Billy nodded. 'And he was thinner and quieter.'

'Tell them the rest, son,' Fred urged.

'I've forgot it.'

Mavis took a small notebook from her pocket. 'The farm's real name is Kingsmead. It's in Cheshire – that's what Billy said. And Brennan's changed his name to Don and—'

'And he's been good,' Billy insisted. 'When he's a farmer, he's good, really nice and happy and he doesn't get pi– drunk all the time.' He paused, deep in thought for a few beats of time. 'He came for him, that monk with the daft name. He was there, too.'

Chris blessed himself hastily.

'And that's the last one,' Billy whispered. 'The last dream. I won't have any more, because they were Father Brennan's dreams and thoughts and I just shared them. Gladys Mason used to be her name. It's her farm. Can I have a jam sarnie, Mam? And he looked after the foxes. They'll miss him.'

'So you'd a conversation with him?' Cal asked.

Billy smiled at his friend who could now walk nearly

properly. 'No. I just listened. Sometimes, I could see what he was remembering.'

Mavis went into the kitchen. Hattie, tired after a hard day, made her excuses and went home. No one should ever doubt the sight of an innocent. The bad priest was dead, and she needed her sleep.

Chris Foley leaned on a wall near the Blunts' sideboard. Sackcloth and ashes, then. Eugene Brennan had not allowed Billy to see the flagellation, but those self-inflicted wounds, filled with ashes, had been covered by the time the child had been welcomed in to hear the apology. There was some good, honest guilt in the man. And if Brother Anselm had collected him, was there a chance of life eternal after a longish sentence in Purgatory?

Chris found himself praying for Brennan. Well, praying was his job, wasn't it? Praying, doubting, reading, studying, accepting the sins of man and carrying them back to the Lord. *Father, forgive them, for they know not what they do.* Jesus's words, spoken from the cross, asking for a blessing on His murderers, echoed in the mind of Father Foley, St Columba's, Everton, Liverpool. *So who am I to doubt the word of Christ?*

Billy dug his teeth into a jam sandwich. 'It's true isn't it, Father? Isn't it, Cal? Frank? My dream, I mean.'

'We believe so,' Frank answered for all.

Chris blessed the company before leaving to walk home; he was on duty till morning. Cal and Frank stayed for a few minutes just to make sure that the Blunts were all right. 'I'll call in tomorrow,' Frank said. 'I'd better go, because my boss is quite harsh when it comes to time-keeping. I hope she's asleep.' The three men left as Mavis took Billy back upstairs to his bed.

After dropping off Cal in Seaforth, Fred took his last passenger home. 'It's a queer world,' the driver said.

'You can say that again.'

'It's a queer—'

'Shut up, Fred. I feel as if I've been fried in batter and served with chips.'

'Sorry, lad. He asked for you three, said he wanted listeners.'

'Witnesses.'

'Yes.'

'Do you think he'll stop with this sighted business now, Fred?'

'I bloody hope so. It makes my flesh try to crawl off the bones. I just want the ordinary life for me and mine.' He applied the brakes. 'There you go, son. See you soon.'

'Ta-ra, Fred.'

The bus pulled away while Frank stood almost praying that Fred wouldn't lose his job for nicking a bus. He was up for promotion to inspector, but tonight's stunt might well put the kibosh on that.

Upstairs in the bedroom at last, Frank undressed quietly and slipped into bed, his right arm reaching out to cover the little bundle of mischief and joy who was his wife. She smelled of Silvikrin shampoo, baby powder and breast milk. She smelled of home. She *was* his home.

'Frank?'

'Go back to sleep, girl. I'll tell you about it tomorrow. I love you.'

She growled in her almost-sleep.

'Same to you,' he said.

Somebody was trying to knock the front door off its hinges. Hattie, who had stayed behind after keeping Mavis company while Fred went to steal a bus, was late this morning. She leapt out of bed, pulled on a dressing gown, pushed her feet into old slippers and stumbled down the stairs. Oh. It was Ida, of course.

Hattie drew back security bolts and opened the door. Ida, doing a fair imitation of a goldfish, carried a newspaper. So it was true, then. Father Brennan was dead and Ida had the evidence. 'Stop your noise and come in. What's up?'

Ida flew into the shop like an oversized bat out of hell. 'Are you not opening today? Are you all right? Is it one of them mind grains what you get sometimes?'

'Migraines, they are. No, I was late dropping off asleep last night. What's going on? Has World War Three kicked off without me noticing? Has somebody drained all the water out of the Suez Canal?'

Ida drew herself up. 'Don't talk daft; it'd fill up again, wouldn't it? You dig a canal near natural sources like rivers.'

Hattie folded her arms.

'Or seas,' Ida concluded.

'Been reading again, love?'

'I have. And you should see today's papers.'

'Is he dead?'

'Eh? Is who dead?'

Hattie looked up as if seeking divine intervention. 'Little Billy had one of them dreams. Is it in the papers?'

'You what?'

'Right. I'm putting the kettle on. Leave the bolts off in case anybody wants serving; it won't be the first time folk round here have seen me in the dressing gown. Mind grains? What next?' She walked through to the living quarters with Ida close on her heels.

'Why would Billy Blunt's dream be in the papers, Hat?'

'He saw Brennan in sackcloth and ashes.'

'No.'

'Yes. Fred came to get me about elevenish last night. He had to go and pinch a bus.'

Ida blinked. 'A bus?'

'Yes. You know, one of them big things with stairs, wheels, and no smoking on the bottom deck. Shut your mouth, Ida – there's one due in a minute, and you might be mistaken for a tunnel.'

Ida's lower jaw relocated itself, and her mouth set in a hard line before she spoke again. 'What are you on about, Hattie? I have to go waitressing in a few minutes.'

'The monk came for him.'

'Say again, girl.'

'The monk he killed with a crucifix came for him.'

'But he's dead.'

'They're both dead. Do you want a cuppa?'

'It's not in the papers.'

Hattie scalded the pot while her visitor dropped into a chair. 'They probably didn't find him in time for today's papers,' Hattie mused, almost to herself. 'Billy said a light came and they melted away like snowmen. He wasn't upset – Billy, I mean. But it shook the nerves of the rest of us, I can tell you that.'

'Who was there in the house?'

'Mavis, Fred, Billy, me, Frank Charleson, Cal Kennedy and Father Foley from Columba's. Oh, and the dog. It's a daft bugger.'

'Why wasn't I there?'

'Because we were packed like sardines.'

'Not because I gossip?'

'No. You've gone better with that, anyway. Billy wanted witnesses, and Mavis asked me just to sit with her while Fred pinched a number fifty-three.' She poured the tea. 'Here you are, Ida. Put yourself outside of that.'

Ida, who had virtually forgotten the reason for her visit, sipped from the cup that cheers. 'He took a double-decker?'

'He did. Billy wanted his grown-up mates round him.

He's always liked Cal, he respects Frank, and he seems to think the sun shines out of Father Foley's eyes. So Fred had to go trolleying all over the place to pick them up. It was quite a night.'

'But the little lad's all right?'

'Yes, as far as I know. Mavis is going back to church – she's gone all holy water and genuflecting near her statue of the Sacred Heart; Billy says it's all over now with these dreams, so there's just Fred in trouble. He was down for inspector, remember?'

Ida nodded. 'I do. That'd be another fiver every week.' She crossed her fingers. 'Anyway, you'd best take a look at this, Hat. Government ministers, high-up judges, some cops, a bank manager, couple of doctors, army officers and a Russian spy or something.'

Hattie wore a puzzled frown. 'What are you on about, Ida?'

'Elaine Lewis, daughter of Mrs Pearson what collects rents for Frank's mam. She's been running a house of ill-repute – well, a flat of ill-repute – in London. They call it a mansion flat. Kensington.'

'No. Isn't she a model?'

'That must be her day job,' was Ida's swift reply. 'She's got a maid what looks after her.'

'Let's have a shufty, then.'

And there, on the front page, was a photo of Miss Lewis in a beautiful suit. She was posing on the pavement attached to a long road at the bottom of which stood the Eiffel Tower. 'Bloody hell, Ida.'

'Bloody hell is right, Hat. Her poor mother. She put every ounce of herself into her daughter and saved every last penny she could scrape for that girl. Talk about a smack in the gob, eh? Mrs Charleson won't be best pleased, either, cos that Christine Pearson's her best pal. Her husband a grand chap, but he can't save her suffering all this lot. Break her heart, it will. What's the world coming to, love?'

'God knows, Hattie.'

'Does He? Well, we'd best pray for a miracle, then.'

Paul Cropper knocked on the back door. He opened it, and stuck his head through the gap. 'Mrs Acton? Gladys?'

When he got no answer, he shouted once more, then decided to get on with his work. For some reason or other, the herd had not been milked; nor had eggs been collected from the chicken house. Where the hell was Don? It wasn't like him to slacken off and leave the beasts in distress. Something was wrong.

As usual, the farm worker in Paul rose to the surface and dealt with practicalities. He lined up the Drovers cows, attached tubes, and allowed machinery to do the rest. When eggs had been collected and stock had been fed, he tackled the cleaning. It was getting light, so casual labourers were about to arrive; they always did jobs listed by Don. This was all wrong. By now, Paul and Don should be in the kitchen having breakfast. The casuals were always fed slightly later than the farm manager and Paul, Don's assistant.

He stood in the middle of the yard, his head cocked to one side. What was that noise? Bells. Police? Ambulance? Paul's blood suddenly pooled like a solid mass in the middle of his chest. The broom he had been using was transformed, since it needed to do the job of a walking stick. Cold fingers of fear touched every vertebra, every nerve. The bells were getting nearer; there was more than one vehicle.

He sat on the edge of the water trough. 'I don't know what to do,' he muttered. Should he run back to his family's farm and fetch his dad and his four brothers?

Mum might be needed if Gladys was hurt. A hand rose of its own accord and swept through his hair. There was little he could do until he found out the details of what was going on.

'Cup of tea,' he decided aloud. 'I need some sugar.'

The kitchen was colder than normal, too. In the grate, last night's fire remained damped and barely lit. He opened the damper to allow oxygen to flow, fed in some kindling and a small amount of coal, then riddled the ashes with a poker. Where was she? Where was Don?

Big Mac burst onto the scene. Big Mac, a Scot from a travelling family, was huge; people often expressed the opinion that he shouldn't really fit in a caravan unless he hung his feet through a door or a window. He seemed to fill the entrance to Gladys's kitchen. 'Mrs Acton's gone off in an ambulance. She collapsed.' He reached the centre of the room, placing a shovel-sized hand on Paul's shoulder. 'Don's dead, son.'

Paul blinked senselessly. 'Dead?' he managed finally.

Big Mac nodded.

'Are you sure?'

'Aye. We found him. I went for the police. When they came back bringing me with them in the car, Gladys was there near the body. My oldest sons had stayed with Don till I got back. It's a wicked mess, Paul, blood and flesh all over the place. I sent my lot home once the cops were there, told them they'd still get to work this week, but no dinners, because Gladys won't be cooking for a while. White as a sheet, Don was. So was she. They may keep her in the hospital.'

'But might he still be alive? Is there a chance?'

Mac shook his head. 'Nay, Paul. He'd ripped the flesh off his back with hooks on the end of a home-made cat o' nine tails. He'd poured the contents of Gladys's ash pit in the wounds, and he wore a couple of sacks pinned together, but we could see the damage where the material was torn. There's no way the man could have survived that. It looks as if he swallowed all old Matt's medicines after ripping himself to shreds. The empty bottles and boxes were all there.'

'But he gave the medicines back to the doctor.'

Mac shook his head. 'He said he'd given them to Nurse Barton, the big woman with the bike. Morphine, some of it. It was planned, Paul. He must have told the doctor one thing and the nurse another. He's been dead for a while, quite a few hours. I tried not to disturb anything, but I did touch a wrist to look for a pulse, and he was cold, very cold.'

Paul swallowed hard. 'Go and tell my dad, Mac. I'll have to stay and look after Drovers. Explain it all for me and get me some clean clothes. We can't have her coming back home to find dead animals and the place gone to pot.'

'The police will want to talk to you.'

'Yes.'

'Will I get one of your brothers?'

'If anybody can be spared, I'd be glad of the company tonight.'

Alone again, Paul folded his arms on the table and rested his head on his hands. Poor Gladys. That rat of a husband had walked out on her, and Don Hall had been her salvation. Now he, too, had gone. But why? He'd been quiet of late, but he'd never been a great talker. Tears gathered and poured, wetting Paul's fingers and the table-cloth. But tears wouldn't clear the yard or tidy the hen house.

He sat up. The fire was happier, so he riddled more ashes and stuck a shive of bread on the end of a toasting fork. There was work to be done, and a body needed fuel. For Gladys's sake, the Cropper brothers would keep this place ticking over. Big Mac and his family would help, as would many people from nearby farms. Toast and another cuppa, then the show would go on.

It was a sombre gathering at the house of Mr and Mrs Richard Pearson. Frank brought his mother, who was having a refresher course in driving so that she might take the reins of her property business once more. Still nervous about taking charge of a car, she sometimes relied on chauffeurs.

Three people sat in a heavily charged silence, because no one knew what to say to the fourth. Christine Pearson, mother to a woman who was now under arrest, sat still as a stone close to a fire that failed to warm her. The government, currently in crisis over Suez, was threatened by a beautiful girl, and the beautiful girl was Christine's fault.

Richard took Frank through to the back of the house. 'You know that chap who worked with her,' Richard whispered.

'Yes, Bob Laithwaite. Bob's become a good friend. He's liaising with the NSPCC over the Open Door project we're working on; it's for kids in trouble.'

'I'd like to talk to him, Frank.'

'That can be arranged. I'll get you an appointment with him. He's a good chap. He often comes for a meal at our house, brings his girl with him. You'll find him easy to talk to.' He placed a hand on Richard's shoulder. 'This is going to be like bereavement for Christine.'

'I know, son.'

'Bob took care to warn Elaine at your wedding. He told her that her goings-on had attracted attention. Try to hold yourself together, Richard. Christine needs you now. And get a doctor, because she may need help sleeping. As for feeding her – well, it won't be a walk in the park. But she's stronger than she looks. Anyone who could manage my mother before her epiphany proved the existence of backbone. Hang on.' He crept into the hall. Christine was crying. Frank treated himself to a sigh of relief. The dam had burst; thank goodness for that.

Norma, kneeling on the floor next to her friend, held on tightly while the sobbing worsened. Frank couldn't help displaying a tight smile. Mother's arthritic knees seemed to have taken a turn for the better. It was plain that she really cared for Christine, and that fact gladdened her son's heart for a few seconds.

Norma glanced at Richard. 'If it's all right with you, I'll stay the night. I know you look after her well, but sometimes, a woman needs a woman.'

Richard nodded his agreement.

Norma's attention shifted to her son. 'Ask Polly to pack me a few bits from the granny flat – underclothes and toiletries, mainly. She'll know what I want; she's a sensible girl.'

'Right, Mother.' He was proud of his Polly. She could probably deal with anyone from earls to tramps, because she made things happen and treated everyone the same. 'I'd best go and open up,' he said. 'I'll bring your things after closing time, Mother.' He retained the inability to offer comfort or comment to Christine. After shaking Richard's hand, he touched the weeping woman's hair. 'See you later, then.' His voice was gruff, because it strove to cover a plethora of emotions including sympathy, anger and a ton weight of frustration. He could offer no real treatment for Christine's wounds.

He sat in his van and cursed under his breath. How had such a lovely woman managed to produce a monster? From High Court to Cabinet via back benches, onward through police and embassy staff, Elaine Lewis had cut a swathe through England's capital. She was greedy, self-serving, narcissistic and mad. On top of all that, she was dangerously clever, though not quite clever enough, it would seem. According to press reports, somebody from the mansion flats had broken the story. It was probably just as well, all things considered. Perhaps further damage might have ensued had Elaine not been stopped.

He needed Polly. At times like this, she was both balm and anchor.

Before sallying forth to pick up some goods in Netherton, he took a detour and called in at Brookside Cottage. He gave Norma's request to his wife, who had been listening to the radio. 'Oh, Frank,' she breathed. 'How is Mrs Lewis – I mean Pearson?'

'Christine's weeping, love.'

'Good. It's best to let it out. Our Cal didn't cry for a week when Mam died. Tears are part of the healing. Come here, my lovely lad.'

They sat on the sofa, each clinging to the other. 'You read these things, or hear them on the wireless, but they're never about people you know, are they?' she said.

'It's our turn,' he replied. 'And poor Christine's.'

Polly planted a kiss on his temple. 'Never mind. Elaine never got to mess with your credentials, did she?'

He sniffed. 'She's a predator.'

'And I'm not.'

'No. You're just a pest, and I love you. Sometimes, I need to come home and tell you that.'

'Hmm.'

'Hmm what?'

'Glad I'm not at the cafe.'

'So am I, babe. Because loving you is no joke.'

'Except in the cafe.'

'Except in the cafe.'

She awarded him a dirty look, but it was never

411

collected, because he was dozing in her arms. To hell with the shop, she told herself firmly. Until Beth woke, she would hang on to her man, the beautiful soul who would always be her first naughty, adorable child.

Sixteen

'Wake up, Polly Poppet.' Frank had a Moppet and a Poppet to care for. The former was in Seaforth with Frank's mother, while the latter had ceased to be a morning person since giving birth to said former. He considered using a flannel dipped in cold water, but his little wife was capable of being quite fierce if provoked. 'Polly? Come on, sweetheart. Open your eyes and give your old man a smile. We need to get a move on, love.'

'No, leave me alone. It's the middle of the night.' She rolled over, taking a pillow with her. Cuddling this item, she drifted again towards sleep, grumbling softly as she tried to reclaim her rightful place as a resident of unconsciousness.

He walked round the bed and switched on a table lamp. 'Today is London day,' he said. 'I've run your bath. Open your eyes.'

' 'S not,' she replied. 'London tomorrow. Go 'way. I'm having a lovely dream.'

'It is tomorrow, love.'

'Is it?' At last, one bright eye glared at him. 'It's never tomorrow; it's always today.'

He couldn't argue with that.

'Where's Beth?'

'We took her to Mother's house last night – remember?'

'Oh. Yes. London.' She groaned. 'I'll have a bath when

413

we get back, because I'll want to scrape away the contamination.' She sat up, stretched, yawned and looked at the luminous alarm clock. 'Five o'clock?'

'It is. We leave Scotland Road at six.'

'We need our heads testing,' she complained before yawning and stretching again.

'It was your idea, babe.'

'Then I'll have the first appointment with the head doctor.' She looked him up and down. 'I love you,' she told him. He looked good in black. Actually, he looked good in more or less anything.

Frank laughed. 'Loved by a pest who's first in the queue for head testing. I love you, too.' Several times a day, they reminded each other that they were still young, still head over heels, and still needed one another. 'So I'd better be second in the queue for analysis.'

'You'll always be first in line for me, Frank. And you're blushing.'

'Is it a long queue?'

'Not particularly. Just you, Jimmy Nuttall, and Dusty Den's horse, though I'm not sure about Flick; I think he's only in it for my carrots and apples. Oh, and he likes the crusts off brown bread.'

'What about my friend Chris, then?'

Her jaw dropped slightly. 'Father Foley?'

'Oh yes. He said if he hadn't been ordained, I would have had serious competition. He's just a dirty old wolf in a priest's vestments. Now you're the one blushing.'

'I'm not.'

'You are.'

She threw the pillow at him. 'It's hormones,' she pretended to snap. 'And it's your fault. I'm expecting your son. I was going to tell you after London.'

Frank swallowed hard before sinking onto the edge of the bed. 'Oh, Polly,' was all he managed at first, hugging her closely. Seconds passed before he added, 'I know you wanted them close together, but this is a bit quick. My son?'

'Nobody else's, that's certain. I can tell it's a lad because I feel different from how I was with Beth. Remember? I was sick from the very start.'

He pulled himself together. 'Have you been to see the doc?'

'Not yet. I don't need to. I'll go tomorrow or next week.'

'But London. Are you all right for London? All that way, then standing there after the petition goes in?'

'I'm as fit as a flea. The real question should be, is London ready for us?'

He kissed her before lifting her off the bed. 'Get dressed.'

'Are you crying, Frank?'

'No. Stand on your own two feet, missus.' He set her down.

She knew he was shedding happy tears, but she left him to compose himself while she had a quick wash and donned funereal garb. She couldn't help grinning, because she guessed that a certain black, floaty nightdress was partly responsible for her condition. He'd bought the bloody thing for her, so yes, it was all his doing, bless him. She was delighted. If Beth couldn't have a twin, she could become a sister at a very early age.

'Are you pleased?' he called from the bedroom.

'About the baby? Yes, of course I am. Are you?'

'Yes. Very happy.'

She returned, pulling a dark navy blue sweater over her head. 'Wreaths?'

'Den has them. Chris has the coffins, Ida has the banners and I've got the petition; it weighs a bloody ton.'

Polly nodded thoughtfully. 'Do we trust Ida with banners? Do we trust her with anything?'

'No, but Hattie will keep her in order. I'll go and make a bit of breakfast.'

She placed a hand on his arm. 'Don't be worrying about this.' The other palm patted her belly. 'They'll both have a playmate, and they'll help each other like Cal and I did. A child needs another child. I'll be sleeping in chain mail after this one, because three's a crowd, four's a job lot, and five's a Sunday afternoon football team in the park, so you'll be rationed.'

'I've got a good tin opener, Pol. Oh, and some wire cutters.'

'I know, love. We'll have however many we're sent, eh? Go on. I want a bacon butty with HP and a gallon of tea.'

'No morning sickness?'

'I told you, it's a boy.'

He went downstairs. Polly sat for a minute on the bed, her right hand twisting Ellen's engagement ring. 'He's happy, Ellie,' she whispered. 'I'll look after him and keep him smiling. God bless you, babe.'

Richard Pearson gazed into the sad eyes of his exhausted wife. She had lost weight, and the charcoal suit hung loosely about her thinner body. 'We don't need to go, you know,' he said quietly. The whites of her eyes remained pink after days of weeping, and her face was creased with lines of worry. All he wanted was for her to be well and untroubled. 'We don't need to go,' he repeated. 'Polly and Frank will understand – so will the rest of them. You need rest, Christine.'

'I have to go, but I don't want to be on a coach with other people. As long as we get there by twelve, we'll be in good time. I'm sure a policeman will direct us to Downing Street. The press will be there, Richard, but they won't know I'm her mother. We can share the driving.'

'You're worn out.' He took hold of her hands. 'Have you changed your mind about having Elaine here?'

Christine shook her head. 'No, I have not,' she replied emphatically. 'I'm not going to look after her and make sure she answers the conditions of her bail, and you're certainly not taking responsibility for her. No, Elaine is not coming to live with us.' She drew herself up.

'But Christine—'

'She can go into a bail hostel with other criminals. I wash my hands of her. Plus, I won't have her anywhere near Frank and Polly, not after what Bob Laithwaite said to you. If she can threaten national security, imagine what damage she could do here in Liverpool. She's ... she's manipulative.'

'But will you live to regret not offering your support?'

'No. I'll either drop dead with shame or pull myself together and enjoy my happy second marriage.' She smiled wanly. 'What did you take on, Rich?'

'A good woman with a problem daughter. No regrets on my side.'

'You're my rock, darling.' She sat down. 'All that work her dad and I put into her, all that love and care and education. And there she is now, passport confiscated, bail conditions to answer, her ...' she swallowed a bitter taste, 'her clients suspended from their work, diplomats in bother, and she has the gall to expect us to take her in. When they asked her did she have parents to vouch for her ...'

'I told you, Christine. My staff could have kept an eye on her.' His private opinion was that Elaine should have returned to the north, since her erstwhile clients were people of influence, and a false passport might be obtained more easily if she remained in London.

Christine shook her head once more. 'Why should your staff have to do that? Why should we have journalists and press photographers outside our house? Let her loose on a city that deserves better? I don't think so. No, she made her bed and filled it with rich folk. Let her lie in it alone from now on.'

Richard placed himself next to his wife on the sofa. 'You deserve better, my love, but never feel that you're responsible for what she's done. Our kids are influenced by all sorts of people once they're out and about.'

Christine closed her eyes. Elaine had wanted a pony, so her wish had been granted. Toys, books, the latest fashions in shoes and clothes, holidays, trips to the theatre – the list was endless. 'She was indulged,' she told her husband. 'I should have kept her in check. She was spoilt.'

'As were my kids. We all do it wrong, you see. Think about it; we're amateurs, no training. All we can do is follow a template given by our parents, who were also amateurs. By the time we qualify for a certificate in competence, we're about seventy, and we're watching our own offspring while they struggle against the tide. Now.' He slapped his knees, stood and offered a hand to the woman he loved. 'Come. If we're going, let's get on with it.'

'Yes.' She had to make an effort and offer her support to those whose rents she collected. The tale told by Polly sat near the front of her mind, just behind Elaine and all the trouble she had caused. After the police strike and loot of 1919, the Home Office was believed to have decided to clear Scotland Road. While this was only rumoured, the threat had been relayed many times. The neighbourhood was to be flattened, and no new houses would be built. Stripped down to its bones, the plan amounted to a decision to divide and disperse Catholics. All the government of today wanted was access to tunnels under the Mersey. That was now the official reason, a decision that would break up families and shatter hearts. It just wasn't fair, and she must show her face today.

'Christine?'

'Yes, I'm ready. And thank you.'

'What for?'

'For being you.'

Gladys Acton remained sane enough to realize that she wasn't right in the head department. This was described by her team of doctors as awareness of and insight into her own condition. She would have been better without said insight, because her brain was full of pictures and information that made her wish she'd been deaf, blind, or both. Don had scourged himself before pouring a bucket of ashes on his wounds.

They brought her pills, and she swallowed her pills; they brought her food, and she swallowed her food. What she couldn't quite ingest was the news about Don's criminal history. It had filtered through and, of course, she'd seen his body with the flesh ripped off, with his wounds full of ashes from the fire, with sacks attempting to cover what remained of him. The medicines, Dad's medicines, empty bottles, empty boxes ... Don had planned it all carefully.

She ate, she drank, she existed. All farmers ate well, no matter what their state of mind. It was a hard life, and a body needed fuel to get through a day on the land. But she was not at home ... How many days had she been in here? When would she go home? Would it be home without Don and his efficiency, his kindness, his gratitude?

And she was with some very strange people. One old lady ate paper, while a girl who looked about twenty years of age rocked all the time. A woman called Sal walked up and down the ward every day, and another elderly female with a flourishing moustache threw food at members of staff. At least Gladys was noticing her environment, and her main doctor was arranging for her to be released very soon into the care of the Cropper family.

Here he came now. Small, earnest and gentle, he wore half-moon spectacles and a white coat that probably wasn't his, as it hung like a two-man tent from his slight frame. 'Hello, Gladys,' he said. 'You're looking better than you did.'

'Hello, Doc.'

He pulled up a chair and sat next to her bed. 'Mrs Cropper will look after you, and her son has organized a posse to deal with your farm.'

'Oh.'

'But I want to make sure you're ready, so I'm going to read something to you before we complete arrangements. If this upsets you too much, tell me to stop and we'll wait till you're ready. OK?'

Gladys nodded just once.

'It's from Don. A very decent policeman copied it for you – they have to keep the original as evidence for the coroner.'

Her heartbeat, driven by a sudden surge of adrenalin, quickened. 'Right,' she whispered.

'Don was a Roman Catholic priest, Gladys.'

'Yes.'

The doctor moved his chair closer to the bed. 'You know what he did – I mean his crimes?'

Again, she inclined her head.

'Well, I'm not going to dwell on that. It's been in every newspaper from Land's End to John o'Groats, so it's all in the public domain. He didn't tell you he was a priest.' These last four words conveyed a statement rather than a question.

'I didn't know.'

'Quite. Are you calm?'

420

'Yes.'

'Don't be afraid to ask me to stop, but I'll carry on even if you weep. I shall wait for the word stop.'

'All right.'

'Tears are good. They cleanse the soul and provide release for emotions of which we are scarcely aware.' He unfolded a sheet of paper and held it with both hands. ' "My sweet Gladys, I had no joy before you. I am an alcoholic who was in the wrong job for almost the whole of my adult life. Then I found you by accident and everything changed the minute I came to live in your house.

' "I am a farmer born and bred; it's in my blood, always has been. My mother guided me towards priesthood, and I was desperate to please her. Two women in my life have loved me; Mammy was one and you are the second. But I felt that Mammy's love appeared to carry clauses like some sort of treaty, and, though I realize now that she would have loved me no matter what, I allowed myself to be swept along a path that was not right for me.

' "Drink was my answer. I should have left the priesthood long ago, but I was usually too inebriated to organize the details. My temper was unleashed many times. Under the influence, I committed my first notice-able offence and was sent to the monastery. In withdrawal, I refused the drugs that were offered and we all know what ensued.

' "You looked after me, Glad; we looked after each other. You cut my hair, washed my clothes, made my meals, praised and scolded me. You sewed and knitted while I sowed and reaped. You held me in the darkest hours of night, and I love you. Please understand that I can't stay. I'm saving the hangman a job, I suppose.

' "Get the Croppers in, especially young Paul. You could bequeath the farm to them if your cousin doesn't need it. That's just an idea that popped into my head, but I thought you might like to consider it. Or you might sell it to them and find a nice little cottage for yourself.

' "I miss you already and I certainly miss your dad. He was a good man and I enjoyed his company greatly. Read this bit carefully, Glad. Make sure you go to Annie Cropper. She is a woman with a big heart and a large family. A way will be found to keep Drovers going. That Scots traveller – Big Mac – is an honest and useful person, and he has some strapping sons. You are not alone, my love.

' "When this is all over, think of me sometimes with kindness in your heart. I don't know where I'm going. God will decide my fate, because I have no way of wiping clean my soul. *Dominus vobiscum* – that's a blessing from my alter ego, who was not the best of men.

' "I remain, no matter what, your lover, your servant and your friend." '

Dr Evans raised his head. 'He signed himself as Don, then as Eugene Brennan.'

'Thank you,' she murmured.

'How do you feel, Gladys? My name's Tom, by the way.'

How did she feel? Like a car with no steering wheel, a ship without a compass on a cloudy night, no stars to show the way. 'I'm better than I was.'

'It's OK to cry.'

'Have I not cried, Tom?'

'No, but you screamed a lot. I believe you'll do your weeping on Mrs Cropper's shoulder. It's a friend you need, not me.'

She plucked at the quilt on her bed. 'So can I go home?'

'No. But you can go to Netherleigh and recover with the Croppers.'

'Do they want me?'

'They want you.'

Gladys continued to fiddle with her bedding. 'Do they know what Don did before he came to me?'

'Yes.'

'Does everyone know?'

'Yes. You must stay inside the Croppers' house until the press people get bored and bugger off.'

A slight smile played at the corners of her lips. Dr Evans swore. 'You swore,' she said.

The psychiatrist grinned broadly. 'That, my dear Gladys, was nothing. You should hear me when I miss a meal. Low blood sugar makes me go ballistic, as do Jung and Freud. Mine's a job you make up as you go along, trusting to instinct rather than to published sages. You were in shock. You were an easy patient.' He glanced across the ward. 'Get out while you can, before you start eating paper or wearing out the floor.'

'Or growing a moustache.'

The doctor emitted a sigh of relief. She was back. 'We'll send for Annie Cropper. She did visit, but you were out of it, under sedation. You're bereft.'

'Gloom time.'

'That's the one.' He shook her hand. 'I hope I don't see you again soon as an inpatient, young lady.'

'I'm over fifty.'

'So am I, but I don't brag about it. You'll be given medication, so take it. Your family doctor will prescribe further doses until you're completely recovered. See me in a week in the outpatients' clinic. You can bake me a cake in Mrs Cropper's kitchen. Are you a good cook?'

'I am.'

'Good. Then I may keep you as a weekly visitor for some considerable time. I like cake.' He turned on his heels and walked away.

Gladys blinked. She was going nearly home. What

should she make for him? Fruit cake, chocolate, Victoria sponge? Didn't fruit cake mean a mad person? Fruit cake it would be, then. He was a nice man, but quite mad in his own special way.

There it was, on a board outside the newsagent's shop. Elaine Lewis bought several dailies before sitting to read in a nearby park. The weather was chilly, so the park was almost empty, though London's streets continued their usual journey towards the commencement of their working day. LIVERPOOL COMING TO LONDON was the headline on the front page of a paper published for the masses, one she had seldom purchased.

A smaller line was printed below. *The Jarrow march all over again?* She perused the article.

While you read this, several coaches carrying angry people are making their way to the capital city. On this occasion, the demonstration is not about jobs; it's about the destruction of a community. Unlike the Jarrow revolt, today's event will involve many people too old to march from Liverpool to London.

Their collective belief is that the Home Office ordered the destruction of Scotland Road and all nearby streets after the police strike of 1919 and the resulting loot of shops in the city centre. Although residents accept that their homes are in need of replacement, they have failed to persuade the authorities to rebuild houses on the same land. Government officials adhere to their already stated intention to widen roads along the route to tunnels under the River Mersey.

Serious demolition began in the 1930s and was interrupted by the war. A number of residents have already been separated from extended family and placed outside the city on several new estates. Those people will be represented today by many who are not happy to live where there are few shops, inadequate public transport services and too few schools and churches.

Mrs Frank Charleson, spokesperson for all involved, drew our attention to the facts as she sees them. 'We've had many premature deaths among healthy but slightly older folk who have been moved out against their will. We are city people, and we are fourth-generation city people. We love Liverpool life.

'This road has been here forever. It was a turnpike through which travellers to and from inner Lancashire had to pass both ways. It remains cosmopolitan, friendly and Catholic. The name Scotland Road says exactly what it was – the road to Scotland. Horses were changed here, people rested and slept in inns here, and all were made welcome.

'Regarding the Catholic connection, I have several things to say. The standards in our schools are high and they have produced some remarkable people in the worlds of business and entertainment, the armed forces, the merchant navy and the House of Commons. Our churches are beautiful and special, and we are proud of them. No one suffers alone in these parts. The Protestants are with us, representing their own community on the Turnpike March, and will be supporting us all the way.

'Now, perhaps I shouldn't say this, since proof is hard to obtain, but here goes, because I may as well hang for the full sheep. In 1923, a junior minister in the Home Office was reported to have started the push for dispersal of Catholics in the area, as Catholics were blamed for the 1919 loot. That man became a very important figure in our country, and held high office within the Cabinet for many years. I shall not name him, as my possible slander would become probable libel once printed in your paper.

'So there you have it. We want homes, shops and schools, not roads.'

Her husband, Mr Frank Charleson, added, 'It's cold-blooded murder. Yes, the buildings are a mess, but this government is too high-handed by far. Widen the road, and rebuild here rather than ripping out our heart and stamping on it. My family owns property along a stretch of the road, and we'll be compensated up to a point, but what about the residents?

'Our clergy will be with us. Even Rome is behind us, but what the hell does anyone care? Are you awake, Anthony Eden, Sir? Because we certainly are. But don't be afraid; you won't need to read the Riot Act. After all, we're just looters, aren't we? Though we haven't committed any crimes recently. Ask at the local police station.'

Our reporter visited several shops and houses along the route. He found a good atmosphere, happy and humorous people and a solid dislike for the current government. Mrs Ida Pilkington expressed the opinion that there are too many near-Nazis in power, people who would be happy to bury Scotland Roaders in order to be rid of them. 'A bit like Cromwell's lot,' she said. 'Shall we make priest holes?'

Elaine folded the newspaper. It was a sensationalist rag, though it showed Frank and Polly in a good light. Both were bold orators. She still missed Frank. If Frank had chosen Elaine instead of Polly, life would have been so different. Or would it? 'It takes more than one to keep me happy,' she whispered, her breath clouding the chilled air.

426

'And the Charlesons have their baby.' Her head ached again; she should have bought shares in Aspro.

Frank and Polly had probably wanted a family. Elaine retained the belief that children were a waste of time, energy, money and education. What was the point of a woman going to university if she intended to breed? What was the point if she was going to be a whore or a clothes horse? She shivered, but not because of the weather. Her bones were chilled by the absence of hope and the clear knowledge that she had no future.

Mum might come to London with the throng today. Perhaps if Christine saw her daughter, she might relent and allow her home. In Liverpool, Elaine should be less noticeable, especially now that Mum had a new address. Plans down here in London could carry on without her presence; in fact, it might be best if she could be elsewhere when the new passport was produced. But was there really anywhere to hide on this small island?

South America, though. Who the hell wanted to live in Peru, Argentina or Brazil? She was a lawyer, damn it. She was a solicitor, a fashion model and ... and something else, something that had got her into deep, deep trouble. She was addicted to sex. Oddities had been catered for in her establishment, and they had provided more than money, since some of them had expected chastisement, and she had enjoyed that. What the hell would she do in South America? Learn the rumba, the samba, the paso doble?

She found a cafe and ordered breakfast. The Scousers were coming, and she would be nearby when they arrived. With no work and nothing to distract her, she could certainly spare the time. Her life was over; she had wrecked it herself, and she should have stayed in Liverpool.

While she chewed on tasteless toast, her mood

427

darkened further. She could well end up in prison. If she fled the country, she would never be sure whether she might be recognized, pursued, and dragged home by bounty hunters employed by criminals who had been badly represented by her clients from the legal profession. Having bedded judges, QCs and solicitors, she could well become a target worthy of capture, as her prosecution would almost certainly lead to the arrest of several City lawyers and politicians.

Was life worth living now? Probably not. Vladimir had been a mistake, since he had worked in an embassy, and the government was afraid that he might have gathered information through her, as she had also entertained members of the Cabinet. Yes, she was in a mess. It was time to collect the purple purse, just in case. In case of what? Well, she had to report to the police station first. After that, the day would be her own.

A cavalcade of seventeen vehicles passed through Liverpool that morning. Six were coaches, while the rest were cars, vans and lorries. They were photographed on Scotland Road by cameramen dragged from their beds at an unusual hour, and saluted in the city by people walking to work at this ungodly time of day.

Each coach had a leader in charge of food, drink and order. Father Christopher Foley was boss of the first coach, Polly and Frank shared responsibility for the second, Hattie and Ida were in charge of the third, while Den Davenport (minus his horse) supervised the fourth. Number five was under the watchful though humorous eye of Jimmy Nuttall, and the well-being of passengers on the sixth rested in the sensible hands of Fred and Mavis Blunt.

Coach six developed a problem while still in Cheshire.

The driver flashed his lights, and the message was conveyed down the line until the whole procession ground to a halt. 'What sort of noise?' the driver asked of a rear-seat passenger who had walked to the front. 'There shouldn't be any noise, because this coach is in perfect working order.'

'Like a banging. Like the wheel's loose or something.'

'There's nothing wrong with my bus. All these coaches were checked yesterday and there were no problems with any of them.'

'But there's a noise. Not all the time, like. No need for you to take it personal.'

Mavis glanced at Fred, and Fred glanced at Mavis. 'It's him,' they said in unison. 'Turn your engine off,' Mavis suggested.

In the relative quiet, everyone listened to the sounds emanating from the rear luggage compartment. 'The little bugger,' Fred snapped. 'We said nobody under the age of twelve, and even then, the names had to be picked from a hat. He's supposed to be with Carla till school time, then in Judy Greene's house after school. That lad's getting to be a law unto himself.'

The driver, muttering ominously about the possibility of exhaust fumes, leapt from the vehicle, closely followed by Fred and Mavis. Billy was dragged out and examined by the driver. 'He's fine,' he snapped. 'But we can't take him back, or we'll be late.'

'He's fine? Fine?' Fred roared. 'More like fined. No spends for you till Christmas; that might teach you to do as you're told. You've gone too far this time, Billy-boy.'

Mavis agreed with her husband, though she held her tongue for now. The teachers would be worried, as would Judy Greene and Carla, though nothing could be done about any of that. She grabbed the child's hand and dragged him to the front of the coach. Billy certainly knew how to embarrass his parents. 'Get in there,' she hissed.

'Sorry, Mam.'

'You will be, I promise.'

Squashed between his parents on a seat made for just two people, Billy remained silent. He was going to see London. He was going to see the house where the Prime Minister lived. The man who stole money from working folk lived next door, too. Billy might see the big clock and the bridge that opened and closed. Then there was Buckingham Palace and Nelson standing on a long pole somewhere, with lions lying near him but lower down.

But when true daylight arrived, what Billy and the rest saw on their way through England was more impressive than any mere city. There were hills and forests, fields where animals grazed, lovely old farmhouses with whispers of smoke curling from chimney pots. Passengers stopped chattering while travelling through their green and pleasant land. It was beautiful, especially where the greens changed and became the mellow tones of autumn.

Billy broke the silence. 'The leaves have gone rusty, Mam.'

'They're dying, son. They have to die so that new baby leaves can be born next spring.'

'That's sad,' the child answered.

'That's the way it is, lad. For everything on earth, that's the rule.'

He swallowed. 'Even us?'

Mavis nodded. 'Children are born, and their grandparents die. It's God's way.'

Billy pondered. 'Couldn't God think of a better plan?'

'If we didn't die, there wouldn't be enough food, so we'd all die anyway.'

'Oh!' He pointed. 'Look, a windmill!'

Mavis heaved a sigh of relief. Sometimes, she felt like

she needed a degree in how to distract her youngest child. His dog was much the same. She hoped Daniel the spaniel wasn't creating too much havoc in Elsie Gleason's house. Elsie was a dog lover, but Daniel would try the patience of a saint.

After two stops for refreshments, they finally crossed the hem of North London. So this was London? Why all the fuss? It could have been anywhere, just houses, some not well kept, others better cared for, a few corner shops, a bit of a park here and there. Finally, they crossed the invisible seam that divides outer from inner, and the London they'd seen on postcards and in magazines loomed large before them.

The city was stunning. They got the standard tour: the palace, the Mall, Piccadilly Circus, bridges, West End shops, Trafalgar Square, Westminster with its wonderful clock tower. Few Liverpudlians had visited before, and they were, for the most part, in awe of the impressive buildings.

When they passed St Paul's, Fred spoke up. 'See that there? London was burning and Winnie was probably somewhere underneath it in his little cell. And what did he say? "Save St Paul's." This church mattered to him. I suppose it mattered to a lot of folk.'

'I'm glad we came,' Mavis murmured. 'It's gorgeous, isn't it?'

Her husband nodded. 'It's gorgeous and it was built by the labour, blood, sweat and tears of the ordinary man. Credit went to Christopher Wren and all the rest who did nice drawings, but there's no mention of those who fell off roofs and died while this lot got put together.'

'Like Liverpool Proddy cathedral,' his wife replied.

'Yes, something like that,' he said.

They parked the vehicles on land owned by a London coach company. Coffin lids, wreaths and banners were distributed before Frank called the assembly to order. 'We walk from here to Whitehall, but we don't talk, even if people speak to us. When we get to Downing Street, the same rule applies. There's something menacing about a few hundred silent people standing in too little space. That's why the House of Commons is kept small, because packed government facing packed opposition is not a situation to be taken lightly. Small works, you see. They talk a load of cra— rubbish in the House, anyway, but we say nothing. Not a word. This has gone beyond the point where meaningful negotiation is useful. So, onward Christian soldiers.'

Billy stood at the front with his parents and Father Foley. Behind them, six nuns and several priests, all in their usual black, carried small cardboard coffin lids with the names of threatened schools and churches printed in red on the undersides. Shopkeepers bore wreaths stuck to cards with the titles of businesses printed in the centres. Others held the names of streets on plain sheets, and tall men supported banners bearing damning epithets like MURDERERS, DESTROYERS, THE STREETS BELONG TO US and HOMES, NOT ROADS.

Polly and Frank took lead position in front of the Blunts.

Polly turned to Billy. 'You shouldn't be here,' she whispered, 'but seeing as you are, you can take the petition to the door. A policeman will knock, then someone will open the door, and you give that person the petition. It's heavy.'

'Will it work?' the child mouthed.

Polly shook her head. 'It may make them think in future before they break up families and neighbours.'

'Stop talking,' Frank ordered.

They walked towards their target just as the Westminster chimes heralded the arrival of noon. Although this was a cold October day, the air was still.

Londoners stood back and watched while the procession of silent, black-clad invaders walked on. No one spoke. All eyes were fixed resolutely ahead until they reached Downing Street, where press photographers jumped and pushed and elbowed each other in search of a clearer view.

A Pathé news crew was in attendance, but no one would speak into a microphone. Shadows moved in the windows of numbers 10 and 11. Frank smiled grimly; the fools who were about to attack Egypt had been interrupted by ordinary working folk who were just dropping by for a quiet, peaceful visit.

And they stood in lines, packed so closely together that breathing became a privilege. Names of streets, schools, businesses and churches were held aloft, as were banners bearing accusations. Nuns prayed on their rosaries while little Billy carried the petition to the black door. When it opened, he broke the rule of silence. 'Why can't we have new houses where we live now, sir?' he asked, his voice shrill.

'Billy?' Frank called. 'Come here, son. They're deaf, blind and stupid.'

Billy returned to his parents.

Not another word was uttered when the Prime Minister came to the door. He stared impassively at the gathering, nodded, looked at his watch and backed into the lobby. Just before the door closed, his eyes locked with Frank's. It was just a moment in time, a time of great trouble in North Africa and in Hungary, but the man was distracted for a split second by the sight of loathing and contempt in the eyes of a citizen.

Frank squashed a grin. He would love to cross verbal swords with Eden one day, but it couldn't be yet. Today must be civilized, and the kind of debate that took place in the House of Commons was scarcely that.

The people of Scotland Road remained where they were for a further hour. When the clock struck one, they left coffins, wreaths and banners in the street and wandered off to find cafes and pubs where there would be longer than usual queues for bathroom facilities.

Frank, Polly, Chris, Hattie and Ida walked further along Whitehall and spoke to the news crew.

Only Christine and Richard Pearson remained at the end of Downing Street. Frozen and fearful, the former clung to the latter.

On the opposite pavement, a beautiful young woman stared at her mother. Elaine Lewis took a step forward and opened the purple purse.

Seventeen

For Father Chris Foley, everything slipped into slow motion. Riveted by shock to the pavement, he could only watch while Frank, his best friend, floated in the direction of Elaine Lewis. It was weird, because he knew that Frank was a fast runner, yet on this occasion everything moved at snail's pace. 'Dear God,' Chris mumbled after remembering to breathe. He watched aghast as the young woman raised her gun, pointing the weapon in the direction of her mother and stepfather. Would she fire? Would she really injure or kill her own mother?

Frank shouted, 'Elaine – no, don't do it!' He stopped moving.

Inch by inch, long second by long second, Elaine changed target. When she finally looked at Frank, she wore an absent, almost other-worldly expression on her face. Like an automaton, she froze, as if her power supply had suddenly failed or been switched off. But the hand that held the gun seemed to know what it was doing.

The Downing Street police also owned legs made of lead; they were running, but getting nowhere. Chris Foley heard the shot and watched horrified as Frank folded onto paving stones. There was blood. Elaine dropped the gun and fell to her knees, crawling until she reached her victim. She stroked the head of the man she had shot, her lips moving, until she was dragged away by police.

'I love him,' she screamed, hitting out at the men who held her. She was forced against a wall and cuffed. 'Why couldn't he love me?' she cried. 'Frank, Frank!'

The pace altered and life was suddenly in top gear. Polly flew past Chris and squatted at her husband's side. An ambulance, probably ordered by one of the policemen when Elaine produced the gun, ground to a halt near the fallen man. Chris moved at last. When Frank had been stretchered on board the vehicle, Chris climbed in with Polly. 'Will he die?' she asked. 'He's my husband.'

No one answered. 'Will he die?' she screamed. 'Answer me.'

'Not if we can help it, ma'am,' the attendant replied. 'Looks like the bullet's gone in and through, but I'm no doctor. Ah, he's with us. What's your name, son?'

'Frank. She bloody shot me.'

'Hello, Frank, I'm Harry. It seems you were in the wrong place at the wrong time. Don't worry, Tommy's will put you straight. Best hospital bar none, St Thomas's.'

'Polly?' Frank whispered. 'My Polly?'

'I'm here, love,' she wept.

'Don't cry, Pol,' he managed. 'The baby.'

She couldn't get near Frank, because ambulance staff were working on him to stop the steady flow of blood. Instead, she drew up her knees and leaned against Chris, her head resting on his shoulder. 'Pray,' she begged.

'I'm praying,' he answered.

'Hard,' Polly ordered.

'Any harder, and God would need a bullet-proof shield.' He planted a small, chaste kiss on the forehead of a woman who bore a close resemblance to the wife he'd never had. 'Are you praying?' he asked.

'Yes.'

'Good.'

The bell ceased its clanging as they turned left into the

436

forecourt of St Thomas's. A plethora of people awaited the arrival of this vehicle; an incident on or near Downing Street was always taken so seriously that the precision was almost military. Frank was whisked away within seconds, though he did manage to smile weakly at Polly and Chris before disappearing into the hospital.

Inside the building, Polly exploded, just as Chris had expected. She had to be with Frank. They shouldn't do anything to him unless she granted her permission. He wouldn't manage without her. She needed to know what the bullet had hit and should she tell his mother. He didn't like doctors. His blood was A positive and he was allergic to fabric plasters. She should be holding his hand, and no, she didn't want a bloody cup of bloody tea. If she couldn't be with him, she wanted to be nearer than she was. 'We're very close,' she ended stubbornly. 'We've never spent a night apart since we married. He sleeps better if he knows I'm near. He'll get better quicker if you put me with him.'

'Just leave him with us and trust us to do our best,' the harassed sister said. 'He'll probably be anaesthetized anyway.'

'He won't like that.'

'It's no fun for us, either,' the blue-clad woman snapped. 'This is a busy hospital, so sit down and shut up.'

Polly sat down and shut up.

Chris shook his head slowly. 'So that's the answer. You'll do as you're told by a woman, but not by a man.'

'You shut up,' Polly barked at the parish priest.

'He'll be all right; he's tough.'

Polly sighed heavily. 'Why did he call her name, Father Chris?'

'To save her mother's life.'

'Oh. He's a hero, then?'

'He is.'

437

'Well, he'd better be a live hero rather than a fallen one. Did you see how that terrible woman stroked his head? And did you hear her shouting that she loves him?'

'I did. What she feels for him is probably as near to love as she'll manage to experience. There's a lot wrong with Miss Lewis.'

'I know; I do read the papers. She's a prostitute.'

'She's ill, Polly.'

'Oh, so you're a doctor now, are you?'

He turned and took her hands in his. 'Polly, stop being mad at me. I told them that if he looked near to death, they should send for me to bless him. They haven't come and asked me, have they?'

'No.' Her tone was uncharacteristically soft. She bit her lip for a moment. 'I suppose she thought if she couldn't have him, nobody should. But she's seen Beth, Father Chris. She knows Frank's got a daughter.'

'Beth means nothing to her. She can't reach outside herself.'

'Why?'

'I don't know. All I'm sure of is that she's not right in the head. Polly, calm down, or you'll be needing a bed here yourself. Oh, Lord help us,' he mumbled. 'Here comes Armageddon on a first-class ticket.'

Ida and Hattie staggered in. 'She fainted,' Hattie declared.

'I fainted,' Ida agreed. 'How is he?'

'No idea,' Chris replied. 'Is Cal resting in a coach? It's been a tough day for him.'

The reply to his question was being pushed through the waiting area in a wheelchair. The wheelchair had been added to the Turnpike March in order to intensify the drama. In charge of the chair was Dusty Den Davenport, who seemed better at steering his horse. 'Sorry, sorry,' he

438

muttered after bumping into several chairs. Linda was there, as were Jimmy Nuttall, three nuns, the Blunt family and the Pearsons.

'I don't know what this world's coming to at all.' An angry Ida folded her arms and shook her head. 'Guns now. That's just what we need. Is he going to be all right?'

'Do us a favour,' Hattie begged. 'Faint again and leave the rest of us to try and cope. Polly has enough on without worrying about the state of the rest of the world.'

Christine bent down and hugged Polly. 'I'm sorry,' she wept. 'That bullet was meant for me, not your Frank. I managed to get a message to Norma, and I promised to let her know what's going on.' She turned to Chris. 'We've been interviewed quickly by the police, but we have to do proper statements. What's happened to her, Father? She was always a good girl.'

Polly stood up. 'Just you listen to me, Mrs Pearson. It's not your fault.' She swallowed a lump of fear. 'He's strong. He's going to be all right.' She clung to Ma's best friend. The ambulance men had said that Frank would be OK, hadn't they?

Matron arrived. A spherical figure in black and white, she bristled as she addressed the gathering. 'What's this?' she demanded to know. 'A prayer meeting?' She eyed the nuns and the priest. 'There's a church up the road.'

'We're from Liverpool,' Den answered with the air of a man who had just explained the law of thermodynamics.

'We're on a protest,' Linda added.

'Then why are you protesting in my hospital?'

'Because one of us got shot.' Chris rose to his feet. 'Everybody's leaving now except for me and the wife of the victim.'

'I want you to go, too, Father Chris.'

'But Polly—'

'Go. Do as you're told. There you are, Matron, you can

have your hospital back. This lot's supposed to be on its way back to Liverpool.'

Chris glowered before moving to stand with the rest of the crowd.

Mollified, the large, uniformed woman stepped back. 'We need this space,' she said. 'So, you're the wife?'

Polly nodded. 'He's Frank. Frank Charleson.'

Matron smiled. 'Ah, the Whitehall incident. He lost some blood, Mrs Charleson, so he's being topped up by transfusion. No major damage, just a chipped rib and a tear in one of his veins. There's some slight damage to the diaphragm, but he's as strong as a horse. We'll keep him for a day or two because the homeward journey's a long one. Oh, and the police want to talk to him as soon as he's a little better.'

The Liverpool contingent was making its way back from the large porch.

'He's going to be all right,' Polly told them. 'So go home.'

Christine dashed off to find a phone. Norma needed to know how her son was. Thank God, thank God Frank had survived; had Elaine killed him, that would have been . . . she closed her mind against the thought.

Ida was on her horse again. 'Me and Hat promised we'd look after you and Cal, Polly—'

'I'm fine, and Frank's not Cal. Go home, Ida. Make sure Ma and Beth are all right. In fact, you should all have left by now, so why did you come back? That includes you, Father Chris. They're going to let me sit with Frank, aren't you, Matron?'

Matron folded her arms – a difficult task, given so vast a bosom. 'If you can get rid of all these people, Mrs Charleson, we'll give you a cot to sleep on. I can't have my waiting area looking like a newly opened sardine can.' She glared at the interlopers, many of whom seemed to

440

quail beneath her flinty gaze. 'Well? Do I have to get you shifted forcibly?'

Polly fisted her hands and placed them on her hips. 'You heard the lady, so get gone. I've trouble enough without keeping an eye on a tribe.'

She was kissed and cuddled many times over before they left. As the last stragglers passed through the outer door, she spoke to Matron. 'Can I go to him now, please?'

'Not until you've eaten and he's out of theatre. Come with me, and I'll sort you out. We're breaking all my rules here, Mrs Charleson.'

Polly moved in for the kill. 'Erm . . . can I have a bath later on? And have you any spare underwear in the hospital? My name's Polly, by the way.'

Matron grinned. 'Cheeky Cockney sparrows? They don't hold a candle to you, Polly. Yes, we'll manage something. Step into my office, and I'll feed you.' She was fast growing fond of the little minx, just as Scotland Road had grown fond many years ago. If Matron had married and had a daughter, a girl like this would have filled the bill.

Someone knocked on the door. 'Come,' Matron called.

A nurse entered and announced that Mr Charleson was out of theatre.

Polly gulped down some tea before following Matron to the lift. Her Frank was alive.

They exited on the first floor. Matron, in an almost unprecedented show of empathy, held Polly's hand. 'He's going to be quite pale. Don't worry about it, because he'll pick up soon. We're intending to drug him against the pain once the anaesthetic wears off, but we don't want to interfere with his breathing, so he'll be awake for some of the time. Don't tire him. Try not to talk about what's happened. In you go. He has his own room. His mother phoned and she's paying for a private bed.'

Polly nodded. That was typical of Ma Charleson. 'Thanks, Matron.'

She opened the door and looked inside. Frank was a big man, tall and with good muscle tone; this fellow looked smaller, ashen and weak. In that moment, Polly wanted her fingers round Elaine Lewis's throat. But she swallowed her anger, sat, took his hand carefully and stroked it.

'Hello, love,' he rasped.

'Hiya, kiddo.'

'Have you missed me?' he asked.

'Only a bit. I had another boyfriend with me – Father Chris. Then the rest piled in – even a few of the coach drivers. They've all gone home now, because Matron was thinking of reading the Riot Act.'

He tried to sit up.

'Behave,' she chided quietly. 'You've blood going in at this side and some other stuff dripping into your right arm. And I've no clean knickers.'

He smiled weakly. Polly was great at non sequiturs. 'In my jacket pocket,' he told her. He noted the surprise in her eyes. 'So I'm a romantic fool – shoot me again. They're my good luck charm. I hope there's no bullet hole in them.'

She took his suit from a small wardrobe and found her underwear. 'You've carried them ever since then?'

'And slept with them under my pillow when we were apart.'

Polly blinked away a few tears. 'You big soft lad. I don't half love you, Frank Charleson. You never fail to make my day.' Because of the way they'd been folded, the knickers sported four bullet holes.

'See?' Frank said when she held them up. 'Talisman. They slowed the bullet down a bit. I told you. There's a lot to be said for a double gusset.' He sighed and fell asleep immediately.

She sat with her man for hours, leaving his side only when she needed the bathroom. He woke a few times, but she stroked his head until he slept once more. A young nurse popped in every twenty minutes. She brought pie and mash for Polly, iced water for the patient. Matron arrived on her way off duty. 'Two pairs of essentials and a nightdress. See you tomorrow, Polly.' She glanced at the man in the bed. 'Good,' she said. 'Bit of colour in his cheeks again.'

These were ordinary people like Scotty Roaders, except they talked funny. Frank's nurse was gentle when she monitored his blood pressure and encouraged him to swallow a bit of water. 'Don't worry, he'll wake up properly when he's ready. Don't feed him. And he's got a catheter, so he won't need the lav. I'll fetch your camp bed.'

Polly lay next to her husband, albeit at a much lower level. She tried not to worry about Beth, because her main priority was here recovering from a mad woman's attempt to kill him. Beth would be fine with Ma.

Frank woke. 'Polly?' He sounded confused and slightly panicked.

'I'm here.'

'She shot me, Pol.'

Polly leapt out of her makeshift bed. 'I know, love, but you're going to be fine.' She moved the chair across, sat in it, folded her arms on his bed and used them as a rest for her chin. 'Look, I'm right next to you. Go back to sleep. I'll still be here, I promise.' It wasn't like Frank to be scared, but then he'd never before been the victim of attempted murder, had he?

'She'll go to prison, won't she?' he asked.

'Thank God it won't be the gallows for murder. Rest now. I'm with you.'

'I don't believe in hanging.'

This was true, she mused. According to Frank, capital

punishment was murder by the state. 'Sleep now, babe. I may have a lie-down on this camp bed, but I won't leave you. OK?'

'Water,' he begged.

She gave him a few sips from the cup with a spout, then bent to donate a loud, sloppy kiss. 'We'll be all right, my angel. Soon be home.'

'Beth?'

'With your mam. Norma won't let anything happen to our daughter.'

'And our son?' he asked.

'Curled up and fast asleep where you left him. Just a blob in my belly, Frank. We'll all be fine.'

'Will we?'

Polly Charleson grinned. 'Course we will.' But she crossed her fingers just in case . . .

She'd been charged, searched, humiliated and stripped of all jewellery. The dolts had taken her belt, her handbag and even her scarf, and she was locked in a cell furnished with a lidded bucket, a small sink and a thin, dirty mattress on a solid base, no springs, no comfort. Why? Why was she here? Her head ached so badly that she wouldn't have been surprised if it had burst wide open.

A face appeared at the hole in the door. No chance of privacy here, was there? Suddenly, she swayed like a drunk. She felt as if she'd consumed the contents of a wine cellar. Control. She was losing control. The pain in her head intensified as she sank to the unforgiving floor. The last sound she heard came from Peeping Tom in the corridor. 'She's fitting, she's down—' Darkness enfolded her, and she embraced it gratefully.

*

Matron opened Frank's door and placed her head in the gap. 'All right, Frank?'

'Not too bad, thanks,' he replied. 'Transfusions are finished, and the catheter's disappeared, thank God, but I'm just dead tired.'

'Good morning, both of you. Polly? Come with me, please. Just a few forms to fill in. The police are on their way, too.'

Polly kissed the bump on her husband's nose. She called it his forgivable bit, because the rest of him was damned near perfect.

Out in the quiet corridor, Esme Burke, matron of St Thomas's Hospital, grabbed Polly's hands. 'There's been a development. We're besieged again, but not by Liverpool. Downstairs is crawling with press and police, and gossip's spreading like wildfire.'

Polly gulped. 'What's happened?'

'She's in this hospital under guard.'

'Elaine Lewis?' Polly whispered.

Matron nodded. 'Your husband's already front page news, as is Miss Lewis, so the papers are preparing for a few field days. She had a fit last night in her cell. According to her mother, she's never suffered from epilepsy. They're testing her for poisons just in order to eliminate possibilities, but they're also talking neurology or brain tumour.'

Polly swallowed hard. 'Hell's bells. So is there a chance that she didn't know what she was doing when she shot my Frank?'

Matron shrugged. 'I'm not sure, dear. I'm only in charge of running the nursing side; I'm not an expert in all areas of medicine. Her mother's giving as detailed a history as she can, but I can't discuss it, you see. All I want to say is that she's ill, she's here under guard, and you'd better stay where you are, with Frank. If the vampires downstairs hear your accent, there'll be chaos.'

Polly folded her arms. 'I'm not telling Frank she's here. Will you phone his mam and tell her he's doing OK? I left the number on your desk. And ask about Beth, our baby girl?'

'Of course I will. Now, Frank starts a light diet later on today, just broth and a milk pudding. I'll have your meals brought up, too. Let's hope no one takes a bribe in exchange for Frank's room number. And I'll try to find you something to read. Don't fret, and do your best to keep your husband from worrying. Nurse Barnes has removed his catheter, and we'll get you home as soon as we can.'

Matron was as good as her word. Within the hour, Frank was attended by two surgeons who had been involved in his treatment. If he continued to make such good progress, if he could eat and manage without the catheter, he could go home tomorrow afternoon.

'Just one more night, hopefully,' said the older man. 'With luck, we'll let you go after lunch. The buzzards have been cleared from downstairs, but they're gathered outside. If you can walk today, eat, get yourself to and from the bathroom, you will go home in a private ambulance courtesy of your mother, and you'll leave from the staff car park at the back of the hospital. Your wife, a doctor and a nurse will accompany you. It will be no mad dash, just a comfortable ride in a luxury vehicle. The internal bleeding has been stopped, but you must rest when you get home. You've suffered a trauma, a shock to the system, and that can affect organs that are nowhere near the injury site.'

'They'll follow us up in Liverpool,' Polly grumbled. 'Reporters, photographers. They're like a pack of hungry wolves when it comes to somebody being shot on Parliament Street.'

The two doctors exchanged glances. Instructed by Matron to say nothing about Elaine Lewis being in St

Thomas's, they offered no comment. 'We'll check on you later,' said the consultant before leaving with his paler, younger shadow.

'What's going on?' Frank demanded. 'Come on, Pol, you can't fool me. I wasn't fooled when you bossed me about in the cafe, when you pretended not to be bothered when I found you naked, when you blamed my mother because you wanted to look after Cal – you could have stood up to Norma any day of any week even blindfolded and hand-cuffed–'

'You're better,' she accused him. 'Get out of that bed and start walking, because we're going back to our daughter tomorrow. Bathroom's there, so clean your teeth.'

He raised his hand in the manner of a traffic policeman. 'Just go back a bit, girl, put your brain in reverse. What is going on?' He separated the four words as if speaking to a person with diminished powers of comprehension. Carefully, he got out of bed. His side hurt like hell, while his legs didn't know whether they were coming or going, but he stood as well as he could manage. 'Polly?'

'She's here. All right?'

'Who's here? My mother?'

'Elaine bloody Lewis. Sit before you fall.' She dashed round the bed and helped him into the armchair. 'I've two kids,' she snapped. 'You and Beth. Three if I count my passenger. Elaine was brought in after throwing a fit in her cell, apparently. And I don't mean she lost her temper; I mean a proper fit, like epilepsy. She's ill, love. They're looking for poison in her blood, but it may be something else.'

'Oh,' was all he achieved.

'So that's why all the lunatics are downstairs. It's a big, big story. Now, lean on me while we get you washed and tidy. Thank goodness that flaming catheter's gone. Oh, and we're being interviewed by the cops this morning.'

He stood up. 'Get a nurse; you're too little to deal with me.'

'Frank?'

'What?'

'The name of the road where my cafe is?'

'Scotland Road.'

'Exactly. Lean on me.'

'Born tough, eh?' He raised an eyebrow.

Polly nodded. 'And loving you makes me tougher still. Think about Ida and Hattie, and know that I'll go even worse as I age.'

'Is that a threat, babe?'

'It's a promise. Let's get you clean.'

Frank and Polly were home, thank God. Chris Foley's 'bezzie' mate was quieter these days, as if Elaine Lewis had kicked some of the joy out of him. The shop had been closed for weeks while its owner rested; all Chris wanted was to see Frank's wicked smile again, to have an argument, a game of poker and a drop of Irish. Polly. She had to manage this somehow. Pregnant and busy with Beth, she was also working hard to get her man back. The house was under guard by bruisers hired by Richard Pearson to keep the press at bay.

Elaine Lewis. Oh, what a sad, sad girl she was. It was thoroughly tragic. That talented and beautiful woman, whose behaviour had rocked foundations right across the establishment, had a brain tumour. According to her mother, it was huge, benign and very slow to grow. Although not malignant, although contained in a sac, it had pushed areas of Elaine's brain out of their rightful place. It had its own stem, rather like mistletoe clinging to and stifling a tree, a parasite feeding carelessly off its host.

He turned right, parked and studied the map. He was almost there, and he'd be glad of a cup of tea when he finally arrived.

They had removed the giant cyst, and were resting Elaine in a deliberately induced coma. Christine and Richard were staying in London with a priest who had trained alongside Chris. Day after day, the mother sat with her sleeping daughter, hoping against hope that Elaine's brain would sort itself out and reclaim ownership of her skull. 'Be gentle with her,' Chris said to his God. 'Mend her, please.'

The growth had been in her head for years, probably since her teenage. Her medical history, researched by doctors and relayed to her next of kin, seemed to confirm the diagnosis, as the poor girl's behaviour had deteriorated over a long period of time. No one could predict how she would be once woken from the long rest.

Ah, he had arrived. A new-looking sign adorned the gate; *Kingsmead Farm*, it announced, with the bracketed word *Drovers* underneath the main heading. A comical little man was dividing his time between feeding chickens and trying to escape from them. As he alighted from the car, Chris saw a pretty, plump and weathered face at a window. A hand rose up and waved at him, so he waved back. Gladys Acton was the woman who had seen the best and the worst of Eugene Brennan. She'd known and benefited from his farming skills, and she'd also seen the results of scourging, sackcloth, ashes and suicide.

She arrived at the door. 'Father Foley?' she asked.

'Indeed. But I'm in mufti, so I'm Chris. And you're Gladys.'

'I am.'

He looked over his shoulder. 'Who's the amateur with the hens?'

Gladys ushered her visitor into the kitchen. 'When Don

449

died, I went a bit funny for a few days, and Tom looked after me. Psychiatrist. Then he let me go to some neighbours, and I became a day patient once a week. Sit you down. And I baked cakes for him. Even when I was better, he made appointments for me just so that he'd get his cakes. Anyway, he retired a couple of weeks ago.'

Chris sat and grinned at her. 'So you wore him down, then?'

She managed an answering smile. 'Not at all. I made him cakes, pies and scones. He started placing an order with me, cheeky beggar.' She shrugged. 'I suppose I got fond of him, and he got fond of my baking. I'm selling the farm to the Croppers – they looked after me when I got out of hospital. Tom's sold his house, and we're opening a tea shop in a village not too far from here.' She blushed. 'It's not like Don and me; it's more like brother and sister. Tom makes me laugh, but he's hopeless with animals.'

'And Don didn't make you laugh?'

'Sometimes. He was a very good farmer, Chris.'

He took the proffered cup of tea. 'Well, I think I should have some cake, Gladys. It's a fair drive down here from Liverpool.'

'How about these scones with clotted cream and my home-made jam, then?'

'Oh, I think I'll manage to force one or two down, so.'

'You're Irish.'

'As was Father Brennan.'

A cloud seemed to pass across her face, and she sat down opposite her visitor. 'I didn't know he was a priest. We get a lot of itinerant workers, and he was just another of those. What was the matter with him, Chris?' She passed him a plate and a knife, a spoon, the jam and the cream.

'He followed a path that was wrong for him, drank too much, and suffered from bouts of temper.'

Gladys thought about that. 'He never lost his temper here.'

'That's because he loved farming. And he loved you, too. I'm here to make sure you know that you did nothing wrong.'

A tear trickled down her cheek. 'He did, though. How could I live with a murderer without knowing it?'

Chris swallowed a bit of scone. 'Delicious,' he said. 'Killers don't have their sins tattooed on their foreheads. When I spoke to you on the phone, you told me he'd almost stopped drinking. That was because he was living the wrong life until he found you. Yes, he should have left the priesthood, but he didn't, so he drank himself halfway to death instead. Just know this and remember it for the rest of your life – you did nothing wrong. I realize I've said that already but, as you noticed, I'm Irish, and we get a bit repetitive.'

'He was brilliant,' she murmured. 'Just a sniff at a handful of soil, and he knew what he called its constituents. He could balance a parcel of land to serve a crop, or he could choose the crop to suit the soil.' She shook her head. 'What a waste.'

'He was his mother's creature, I'm afraid. She wanted a priest, and she got one. He loved his mother. And the day he died, he posted a letter to me, begging me to make sure you were coping. You're coping. Which is more than can be said for your man with the chickens.'

'He's crackers,' she said, a wide grin on her face.

Chris chewed thoughtfully. 'Well, he'd need to be, so. Which normal person chooses to delve into human minds?'

The door opened slightly. 'May I come in?' Tom asked anxiously. 'I'm henpecked.'

'Oh, get inside,' Gladys ordered. 'My turn to henpeck you.'

'Are you the priest?' the newcomer asked.

'I am.'

Tom Evans stepped inside. 'You can do it, then.'

'I can do what?'

'Marry us.'

Gladys blushed to the roots of her hair. 'I've only known him for a few weeks.'

Chris fought his laughter. 'You're only interested in her cakes, but.'

'The cakes are a bonus,' Tom said haughtily. 'And she's divorced and I'm a widower.'

'He wore her out,' was Gladys's declared opinion.

'Register office,' Chris advised. 'Divorce remains forbidden in my faith. Unless you're loaded with money, in which case you might purchase an annulment.' He smiled when the other two stared hard at him. 'Yes, I question some of Rome's functions and decisions, just as Tom must doubt those who write about mental health. There is never a complete answer. We walk on blindly.'

'Intelligent priests. What next?' Tom held out his left hand. 'I can't give you my right hand, because it's bleeding.'

They shook awkwardly.

Gladys fussed about with first aid. Chris watched, listened to the banter and saw a couple who were perfect for each other. *I must change my name to Cupid,* he mused internally. *Polly and Frank, Gladys and Tom – perhaps I could charge for my services?*

'I'll look after her,' Tom said.

Chris rose to his feet. 'I'm sure you will. Now, I must be on my way, because my parishioners need me, strange as that may seem. God bless you both.' He walked to the door.

Gladys looked at Tom, who was almost as short as she was. 'Are you serious?'

452

He nodded gravely. 'Only if you make the wedding cake.'

She clouted him with a tea towel. 'I'm still in mourning,' she pretended to snap.

'I'll give you a month,' he warned, 'then I'll book the registrar.'

'All right, then.'

'And you can feed the chickens. I'm having nothing more to do with them, because they're nuts.'

'Oh, give them one of your pills, then.'

They watched their visitor as he drove away. 'Now, that's a good man,' Tom said. 'Few and far between, these days.'

She opened her eyes. Two people stood next to the high hospital bed. They were staring at her. The light was bright, too bright. To escape the glare and the pain in her head and neck, she went back to sleep.

Christine grabbed her husband's arm. 'She didn't know me.'

'She didn't stay awake long enough to see properly,' he replied.

'It's going to be Christmas soon. I want her home by then.'

'It's out of our hands, Christine.'

She nodded wearily. It was a waiting game, but who would win? Could anyone win against odds like these?

Father Chris Foley entered his presbytery. This was to be a big, ecumenical Christmas, the first so far in these parts. Mary was a Methodist, Joseph a Catholic, while the angel Gabriel attended a Church of England school. The dress rehearsal was tonight, and Chris had persuaded Frank to help him out. Something had to be done to make Frank snap out of his sad frame of mind.

Billy Blunt was up to no good; Chris felt it in his bones. It was connected to a couple of sheepskins acquired by the lad in exchange for helping in Bartletts' Butchers. Billy was head shepherd, and God alone knew what the child's plans were. Chris grinned as he ate the meal left by his housekeeper; Billy would drag Frank out of the doldrums.

The front door opened. 'Chris?'

'Hello, Frank.'

Frank entered the living area. 'Did you get to see Gladys?'

'I did, and she's grand. You're early.'

'For a reason,' Frank said before placing himself in a chair opposite his best friend. 'I want absolution. There's no point in the confessional box, because you know my voice as well as you know your own.'

'So you want to confess face to face?'

'Yes. And it has to be you, as long as you don't make me laugh.'

'Laugh? You haven't laughed since London. Though the committee they sent up to look at us was hysterical. No change of plan, of course. We're still to be demolished, and there are no short-term plans to rebuild on the site. I'll just go and get the essentials.' He fetched his stole and stood for a moment deep in thought. This, then, was probably the reason behind Frank's long silence. His decision to quit the faith had seemed so final, yet . . .

'Chris? You're standing there like a shop dummy.'

'Am I?'

'Yes. So, what's the matter?'

Chris smiled. 'Why, Frank?'

'Do I need a reason to ask for absolution?'

'No, but I'm curious.'

Frank nodded. 'All right. A quarter inch in any direction, and that bullet would have killed me.'

'Ah, so you've been thinking, is it?'

'And praying. And trying to come to terms with being alive and having a beautiful wife and a lovely daughter. Then there's Elaine Lewis and her poor mother. I mean, Elaine scarcely knew what she was doing, though she seemed so self-assured and proud. I'm grateful. So I'm back, put up with it.'

'I'll do my best.' Chris kissed the stole of advent, a beautiful item in purple and gold. He placed it across his shoulders and down his chest before laying a hand on the head of his closest friend.

'Bless me, Father, for I have sinned,' Frank began. 'It's been years since my last confession.'

'Kneel on a cushion, Francis. Welcome home.'

Ida and Hattie, in charge of wise men and shepherds, were flustered. The wise men were idiots, while the shepherds showed a marked lack of self-control; had they been in charge of a flock, there would have been many lost sheep.

'Billy Blunt?' Hattie yelled. 'Get your backside and your front side in here immediately, if not sooner.'

Billy's head insinuated itself round the door of the school hall. 'Did somebody shout me?' he asked innocently.

Ida went to break up a fight between Gold and Myrrh. Frankincense had disappeared with Mary. As Frankincense was Catholic and Mary was Methodist, their long-term relationship didn't look too promising.

'Billy, what are you up to?' Hattie asked.

'I'm not doing nothing.'

The greengrocer folded her arms. 'I know you're not doing nothing, because you are up to something.'

'Me?' he asked, wide-eyed.

'No, your shadow. Go and find Mary and Frankincense. They'll be holding hands in the Wendy house. Ida?'

'What?'

'Gold's gold's ripped.'

'You what?'

'The gold stuff covering his cornflakes box – it's torn.'

Frank and Chris walked in.

'Where've you been till now?' Ida demanded to know. 'Frank, have a go at mending this gold, will you? Father, Billy Blunt's looking for a courting couple – she's five, and he's eight. So now we need somebody to look for Billy Blunt while he's looking for . . .' She blew a strand of hair out of an eye. 'Just sort it out,' she snapped. 'And why are you late? This was all your idea, Father.'

'Guilty as charged,' he replied coolly, 'and I'm late because a soul wanted saving.'

Ida shook her head. 'Always the same story.'

'Sorry,' Chris mumbled. 'It's the truth this time.'

Frank tried to put Gold's gold together with glue and sticky tape while Ida adjusted crowns and cloaks, though she was still one wise man short, and Chris set off on a Billy-hunt. He found Mary and Frankincense, then Polly at the outer door. 'Go at once to the hall,' he ordered the children. They fled.

'Did he do it, Father Chris?' Polly asked.

'He did, so.'

'And is he OK?'

'He's great.'

'Who would have thought?' she said, almost to herself. 'Frank the unbeliever confessing–'

'No,' Chris said, interrupting her flow. 'Look at those who believe completely without doubt or question, Polly. Look at the eejits who bow and scrape and know the Latin Mass by heart. Then consider your husband and me. Yes, me. I fight for my faith and with my faith. Frank saw death, and it pulled him up sharp. Here we are, a few weeks later, and he reached his own conclusion, opened his own gateway to the future. There's value in that.'

She nodded. 'So quiet, he was.'

'That's because he had a long way to walk. Thomas was the greatest disciple in my book, since he doubted and had the guts to say so. And it was in St Thomas's hospital that Frank was saved. Now, we seem to have mislaid one Billy Blunt.'

'Oh no.'

'Oh yes.'

'Is he up to something?'

'I'd bet me best cassock on it. You cover the infants' side while I do the junior classrooms.'

Minutes later, the two met in the hall, each Billy-less. On the stage, the finishing tableau was being arranged. Shepherds (minus their leader) and wise men stood mute and motionless while Mary held the infant with Joseph posed behind her left shoulder.

A blur of activity broke the spell. Daniel the sheep, who was better used to being Daniel the spaniel, shot across the stage like a bolt of black-and-white lightning. He didn't like being hot, hated the sheepskin that was tied to him. He didn't like being on a lead while inside a building and he certainly didn't like being bossed about by Billy.

The manger was upended, while Mary's blue cotton veil got caught in the backdraught. Despite the chaos, the doll playing Jesus was heard calling 'Mama' before hitting the floor. Three wise men threw down their gifts and fled without seeking guidance from the star or from Gabriel, who fell off his perch during an uncontrollable bout of laughter, while Billy, refusing to let go of Daniel's lead, was dragged across the stage.

Methodists, Anglicans and Catholics in the body of the hall clung together in bunches of hysteria. Frank and Chris managed to capture dog and child. Frank sat on Billy while Chris calmed the dog.

'I just wanted it to look real,' Billy cried.

'Shut up,' Frank ordered. 'There's real, and there's frightening people out of their seats.'

Chris agreed. 'And putting Daniel in a sheepskin is cruel. It's too hot for him.' He sat on the floor next to Frank, a trapped Billy, a sheepskin and a panting spaniel. 'Why do you always have to do your own thing, Billy?'

'I don't know. I get ideas. I thought we should have a sheep.'

'He's not a sheep,' Frank snapped. 'He's a wolf in sheep's clothing.'

'A spaniel,' Billy insisted.

'All dogs are wolves,' Chris said.

'Are they?' The child's eyebrows shot skyward.

'Of course they are. Push them too far, and they run. Very brave creatures who came and sat by caveman's fire and helped him hunt for food. Respect Daniel, Billy. If you want a sheep, dress a human. Frank?'

'What?'

'You'll be Billy's sheep, won't you?'

Frank glared at his Father Confessor. 'Are you crackers, Chris?'

'That's a matter of opinion. Shall we take a vote?'

Polly arrived with a weeping Mary. 'It'll be all right on the night, folks,' she said. 'A bad dress rehearsal means a good performance.' She cuddled the star of the show. 'You'll be fine,' she added.

'Not if I'm being a sheep,' Frank groaned.

'Whose idea was that?' Polly asked.

Frank and Billy pointed forefingers at Chris, while the dog pointed his nose in the same direction.

'Father Chris, when will you learn? He's too big for a sheep. More like a woolly mammoth, my Frank. Were they extinct when Jesus was born?'

Frank released Billy and stood up. It was time for order to be restored, and he was the man to do it. He walked towards the chaos that had been a stage.

Chris and Polly watched. 'He's with us,' she said, sniffing back a tear. 'Thanks, Father Chris, for bringing the lost sheep home.'

'I thought you said he was a mammoth?'

'No. He's our boy, and we're lucky people.'

'We are so, Polly.'

'What do you mean, you haven't killed it yet? Where's poor young Father Cummings?' Frank paused and held the telephone receiver away from his face for a few seconds. He took a deep breath before re-entering the fray. 'Chris, for a priest, you don't half tell some porkies. Has his family arrived?' He paused for the reply. 'Right. Are you coming? Are you sleeping here? OK. Roger and out, you fool.' He replaced the receiver.

Polly was setting her Christmas table. 'What's he up to now?' she asked.

'Don't ask.'

'I've asked.'

Sighing, Frank sat on the sofa and picked up his daughter. 'He reckons to have a huge turkey running round the garden with Mr Cummings behind it waving an axe. That new priest is taking over for Christmas with his mam and dad so that Chris can come here. He can have the camp bed in my office. I despair of him, Pol. What do you think, Beth?'

The child delivered a perfect if rather damp raspberry.

'Good girl,' Polly chuckled.

'Out of the mouths of babes,' Frank sighed. 'So, that's Chris in the office on the camp bed, Cal, Linda and Cathy in the granny flat, Mother upstairs in Beth's room, Ida and Hattie in the spare room. As for . . .' His voice died.

'Christine and Richard?' Polly asked.

'They said they'd call in this afternoon.'

'We must be mad, Frank.'

'Absolutely. Have you had your head tested, love?'

'No. They're more interested in my nether regions while I'm expecting.' She sat down. 'Are you sure you're up to seeing Elaine?' she asked.

'Yes, I'm sure. She sounds pretty harmless, babe.'

Polly shivered. It had never occurred to her that she might sit and eat cake with the woman who'd tried to kill Frank.

Frank read his wife's thoughts. 'She was ill.'

'I know she was. It could have killed her even though it wasn't cancer. But I can't get what happened out of my brain, the way she turned and shot you. It runs through my head sometimes, like a trailer for a film. Christine says she's a bit like she was at fourteen, all horses and hairstyles.'

'And a bit weak all down her left side, Pol. We're Christians, aren't we? She's not been charged because of all the medical evidence. So, as Chris says, we have to open our hearts and our doors. Just knock back a Guinness and let it all happen.'

'OK. But stay away from her, lad. She loved you.'

'She was mentally ill.'

'Like I said, she loved you.'

He laughed.

'Well, I should know,' Polly insisted. 'I suffer from the same disorder. Have you peeled all the sprouts?'

'I have.'

'And put streaky bacon on the turkey and two spuds in its belly to keep it moist?'

He nodded gravely. 'And I've done pigs in blankets. Cal's bringing white sauce and brandy butter, Hattie's done the pudding and Ida's made a cake. Stop worrying.'

'I'm trying.'

'Yes, you are. Very trying.'

She stood up and returned to the kitchen. Everything would be all right; it had to be all right.

'I'm putting Beth in her playpen,' he called. 'There's not a lot of room in there; it's full of her Christmas presents. But I'm going for Hattie and Ida. Will you manage?'

'Yes.' Of course she would manage; she was a woman, wasn't she?

Christmas dinner was in full swing. Added to the usual condiments was a lecture from Ida on the subject of indigestion remedies. After making her way through Milk of Magnesia and bicarbonate of soda, she began on a list of ingredients that sounded as if they might have been put to better use on a building site.

Chris raised an eyebrow and interrupted. 'You left out eye of newt and toe of frog, Ida.'

She frowned. 'Are they any good?'

His answer was buried under gales of laughter.

Ida gazed at her fellow diners. 'What have I done now?' she asked.

'We're eating,' Polly said when the chuckles stopped. 'We're eating, and you're going on about stomach ache. Are you trying to say something about my cooking?'

Hattie saved the situation. 'You'd do better talking about my cooking, Ida. All the sixpences sank to the bottom of me pudding. I'm going back to plain flour next

461

year. I think all the fruit's sunk, too. So any indigestion will be my fault, not Polly's.'

Ida changed the subject by announcing that she was off upstairs to loosen her corsets. Hattie followed her; she intended to remove her restraining underwear altogether.

Cal asked the burning question. 'What time are they coming?'

'Four o'clock,' was Polly's tense reply.

Eating slowed down. Everybody present had been witness to the shooting of their host.

Chris laid down his cutlery. 'We're part of the process,' he announced, his tone as grave as Polly's had been. 'Her brain has to find its way home. What we must remember is that all her behaviour was created by the invader in her skull. Until her teens, she was an ordinary kid – spoilt, but normal. I spoke to Christine yesterday, and she said that Elaine suddenly recalled working in Liverpool. That's a huge stride. Remember also that this young woman had a mild stroke after surgery. She's now slightly disabled.'

Cal nodded; he knew about disability.

Norma spoke up. 'Christine's my friend. She's a good woman, and we don't want to lose her because of her daughter's illness. Let's have our pudding with the sunken sixpences and enjoy our day.'

Hattie and Ida returned, both corsetless. Ida was grinning. 'Nothing beats a good scratch when you rip off the whalebone. What? What have I done now? Have I missed something?'

Hattie nudged her companion. 'Ida?'

'What?'

'Shut up.'

'But—'

'Shut up,' Hattie repeated. 'And don't swallow any sixpences.'

*

462

A young woman arrived just after four with her mother and stepfather. Her beautiful blonde hair was short and curled, as the long tresses had been shaved prior to surgery. She had a slight limp and, in flat shoes, appeared to have shrunk in height by several inches. Smiling sweetly, she made a beeline for Beth and Cathy, placing wrapped gifts at their feet. 'Do they walk yet?' she asked Polly.

'No, but they crawl fast,' Frank answered for his wife.

Elaine sat on the floor with the babies and began to open their presents. 'My mother worked here,' she announced. 'We had a little house, and I'm a solicitor.'

Linda swallowed a sob. It was Christmas, and people shouldn't cry at such a joyful time. Hattie knelt on the floor and helped with the unwrapping, since Elaine seemed to be all fingers and thumbs. 'What did you get for Christmas?' Hattie asked.

'A horse,' Elaine replied immediately. 'I can ride it. And I got a riding hat, boots and jodhpurs.' She smiled benignly at the whole company. 'Mum says I'm good with horses. I go swimming, too.' She fixed her gaze on Frank. 'Are you the man I hurt?'

He nodded.

'I'm sorry,' she said. 'It was a . . . a thing in my head. Wasn't it, Dad?' Her attention focused on Richard.

'Yes, it was, love.'

Elaine smiled again, and an echo of her beauty shone briefly in her lovely eyes. 'New start,' she said. 'I'm all new.'

Polly fled to the kitchen. She stood at the window, silent sobs racking her body. Chris joined her. 'Come on, Polly. Let's not upset everyone. Will I make some tea?'

She nodded. Tea, Christmas cake and crackers were the plan. 'Where was God?' she asked when her breathing settled.

'I asked Him,' Chris replied. 'I'm not really expecting an answer.'

'Why not?'

'Because I already know that every malady, every mishap, every crisis, is man-made.'

'And the growth in her head?'

'Created by the way we live, what we eat, the effluent we produce. He made us perfect, and we deteriorated. We choose the way we live and, sometimes, the way we die.'

Polly thought about that. 'Are you sure?'

He shrugged.

'Are you really sure?' she repeated.

'No, I'm not. Because there is no pure truth on this planet. We have opinions and ideas, yet truth is elusive. There are facts, but truth is a whole different concept. Elaine's happier, isn't she?'

It was Polly's turn to shrug. 'I suppose. But will she get back to normal, back to her real age?'

'Does it matter as long as she's happy?'

Polly didn't answer, because he'd hit the nail on the head, as usual.

They carried tea through to the living room.

The woman who had hated babies held two in her lap. Softly, she hummed as the pair drifted off to sleep. Linda was swallowing emotion, Cal sat with his eyes closed, Richard, Christine and Norma smiled, while Hattie clung to Ida and Frank stared at the floor.

Chris looked at Polly. 'See?' he whispered. 'God sent an answer after all.'

Lament of a Twelve-Year-Old

I lived here till last Wednesday
With Mam and Dad and Auntie May
Cos Uncle Tommy died at sea
So she slept in my bed with me.

Nancy Byrne at number four's
Shut in, has bolted both her doors.
She's old and doesn't understand
That houses here have all been damned.
(That's a bad word. I don't care.)

Miles I walked to come back home.
And on my step I write this poem.
All Kennedys and Shaws are gone
And Mrs Byrne's the only one
Who shouted GO AWAY, I'M STOPPING
I've come to see if she needs shopping.

Far away is where we are
To get to work you'd need a car.
They're not too bothered about us
We haven't even got a bus.

From my bedroom I can see
The dockers coming home for tea.
Like ants they crawl until they grow
And I see faces that I know.

We have a garden, path and gate
But my dad always comes home late.
And we don't want to live out there
Cos Dad's too tired and sad to care
About three bedrooms, lovely house,
He's different, quiet as a mouse.

I want my dad back, want him here
Where town and docks are all so near.
I want my school and my best friend.
A new beginning? NO. An end.

Ruth Hamilton

extracts reading groups

competitions books new

discounts extracts

competitions

books new

reading groups extracts discounts

events

reading groups

events

books

extracts

new

titles

new reading groups

interviews

reading groups

books events extracts events

new

discounts

new books events

interviews new books extracts

events new

discounts extracts discounts

books

www.panmacmillan.com

extracts events reading groups

competitions books extracts new